Rip Van Dyke

Kate McLachlan

Quest Books

Port Arthur, Texas

ISBN 978-1-935053-29-3

First Printing 2010

9 8 7 6 5 4 3 2 1

Cover design by Donna Pawlowski

Published by:

Regal Crest Enterprises, LLC
4700 Hwy 365, Suite A, PMB 210
Port Arthur, Texas 77642

Find us on the World Wide Web at
http://www.regalcrest.biz

Printed in the United States of America

Acknowledgments

Several good friends read the raw and ragged early version of Rip and gave me unconditional praise anyway. "It's like reading a real book!" You kept me going. Patricia was there from the beginning. I miss our Friday nights. Lori Lake took that raw and ragged version and, with remarkable finesse and speed, helped me turn it into the book you're holding now, for which I am very grateful. Thanks to Cathy LeNoir for taking a chance on Rip. Thanks also to Liz and Anita and Tonie for doing all the driving and letting me work on Rip in the back seat during the most amazing road trip ever. Finally, thanks to Tonie for being my inspiration, my first reader, my biggest fan, and my wife. She is also my Patsy, my Bennie, and my Kendra, with maybe a little Van and Inez thrown in. But not a smidge of Jill.

For Tonie

"All stood amazed, until an old woman, tottering out from among the crowd, put her hand to her brow, and peering under it in his face for a moment, exclaimed, "Sure enough! it is Rip Van Winkle—it is himself. Welcome home again old neighbor.—Why, where have you been these twenty long years?"

~Washington Irving, Rip Van Winkle, A Posthumous Writing of Diedrich Knickerbocker, 1819

Chapter One

Van – 2008

VAN'S BUTT HIT the ground first, followed quickly by the palms of her hands, soft flesh crashing hard onto sharp rocks, the impact strong enough to jar every bone in her body and make her bite her tongue.

"Fuck!" She instinctively brought her fingers up to her mouth to check for blood before realizing she had much more pressing concerns than a nipped tongue. She dropped her hand and stared.

She had landed in the middle of a long driveway covered in crushed white rocks that shimmered in the sun like spring snow. The driveway was pristine, as if the gravel had recently been delivered and spread, and no car had yet dared to mar its perfection. The driveway meandered at a leisurely angle, seeming to boast that no one had needed to count the cost per square foot of graveling *this* driveway, down toward a three-car garage attached to an immaculate low rambler built into the hill above the banks of the river that glinted beyond. Red, white, and purple petunias erupted like fireworks from baskets hanging from each side of the garage, and larger grounded baskets of red geraniums lined the low steps leading up to a glass and brass front door. Decorative hedges bordered the house on both sides, and beyond them more pristine homes ranged along the river bank, a dock in front of each one, boats and jet-skis tethered to them.

"Fu-u-uck," Van said again, more slowly. She rose to her feet, brushing dust from her hands and the seat of her overalls. The sun beat harshly on the white rocks, and the air was still. Her chest clenched and her breathing grew thin. Almost afraid to move, Van spun in a slow circle. Something was terribly wrong. Only seconds earlier, hadn't she been sitting on a metal stool bolted to the floor of Jill's dingy camper? Which was parked in front of Van's house. In the woods. Under gray clouds. On a breezy day.

Van squinted against the glare and pivoted again in a slow semi-circle. Beyond the driveway was a road, covered in a layer of ordinary basalt gravel, and across the road were more houses similar to those on the river, but higher up on the hill.

There were no woods. There was no sign of Jill's camper. No sign of Jill. Or of Patsy or Inez or Kendra. Van's heart thudded hard and she broke out in a sudden sweat. Had Jill's machine actually *worked?* Where the hell was she?

Something about one of the houses across the road caught Van's attention. Though older than the other homes in the neighborhood, it was equally well maintained. The addition protruding from its right side was not familiar, nor were the new vinyl siding, windows, and roof, but she'd lived there for six years and she could not be mistaken. It was Van's house.

She grasped the left shoulder strap of her denim overalls, the one she had let hang fashionably unclasped down her back. She pulled it over her shoulder, and clamped it to the button on the bib front, as if girding herself for battle. Whatever was going on here, she preferred to face it fully clothed.

She stepped gingerly onto the graveled road, her sneakers popping on the rocks the only sound in the neighborhood. She crossed over to what had been a back deck when she'd last seen it, but it had apparently been converted to a front entrance. Where previously there had been a sliding glass door, she saw a wide slab of dark wood with an oval leaded glass design set into the center. Van climbed the steps, running her hand along the railing. It was smooth to the touch and sturdy, made of something that resembled wood, but wasn't. She'd always meant to put a railing up. When she reached the door, she wrapped her hand around the solid brass handle, pressed her thumb on the lever, and pushed. The door didn't budge.

She rang the bell and turned around to absorb the view, which was void of trees all the way down to the river. The last time she'd stood there, a few minutes ago, the view of the river was blocked by trees. In the winter, when the deciduous trees dropped all their leaves, she could see glints of the river between them, but in June the trees were too full to allow even a glimpse. The only way to see the river was to hike down the narrow trail that snaked through the trees. What the hell had happened to all the trees?

The door opened behind her, and she spun around. A chubby teenage boy stood there, two thin white wires dangling from his ears down to the pocket of baggy jeans that practically fell off his hips. Four inches of brightly colored boxer shorts showed above them.

"Help you?" he asked.

She ignored him for a moment and instead peered over his shoulder, taking in what she could see of the house. The living room walls were painted a dark brown, giving it the feel of a cave, and a giant television appeared to have been built into the wall so that the screen lay flat against it. The vibrant colors of a violent cartoon splashed on the screen. Another teenage boy lay sprawled on a leather couch in front of it, his thumbs busy with a controller.

"Help you?" the boy repeated.

Van was at a loss for words. "Is Patsy here?" she finally asked, her voice hoarse. He stared. She wondered if he was hard of hearing. Maybe the wires were some sort of hearing device. She raised her voice. "Is Patsy home?"

"You got the wrong place," he said, and started to close the door. Van put her hand out and stopped it.

"No," she said. "This is my house."

He grimaced and shook his head. "Lady, we've lived here for, like, ever." He started to close the door again, but a small girl, no older than six, popped out in front of him.

"That's the lady from the sign," she announced.

The boy made a grab for the girl, but she slithered out of his grasp and stopped in front of Van, her mouth gaping wide.

"Get back in here, Maddy."

Maddy ignored him. "No, that's the lady from the sign."

"What sign?" Van asked.

"I'll show you." Maddy squeezed past Van and ran down the stairs.

"Stay in the yard, then," the boy called after her, unconcerned, and slammed the door closed.

Maddy didn't go far. She stopped beside a small square of land that bordered the road, no more than three feet by two, fenced like a tiny garden. The fence was a low chain-link, bent and slightly rusted, out of place in the immaculate neighborhood. Inside the fenced square the ground was covered in old gravel and new weeds, contrasting starkly with the closely mown lawns around it. Inside the miniscule yard was a wooden sign.

MISSING PERSON – VANESSA (VAN) HOLLINGER
LAST SEEN JUNE 25, 1988
IF YOU HAVE ANY INFORMATION ABOUT HER
WHEREABOUTS CALL 509-555-1109
PRIVATE PROPERTY – DO NOT REMOVE THIS SIGN

"See?" Maddy pointed to a curling photograph beside the lettering. "That's *you*."

It was like looking into a faded mirror. Red hair curled to her shoulders and green eyes smiled back at her. She wore the same short sleeved white sweater, and one overall strap crossed it to hook on the bib at her chest. A gold heart pendant hung on a chain at her neck. Van raised her hand to touch the heart at her own neck with trembling fingers and half expected the woman in the photo to do the same.

"What year is it?" she asked.

Maddy shrugged. "I don't know. I'm only six."

Van tried to take a deep breath, but she couldn't get her lungs to expand. "May I use your phone?" she asked in a weak, high voice.

"Sure." Maddy took off running toward the house. Before Van even had a chance to follow her, Maddy was back, handing her a red metallic case, no bigger than a makeup compact.

"What's this?"

"It's our phone."

Van found where the top flipped open. Itty bitty numbers were arranged inside like a phone key-pad, along with other incomprehensible buttons. She searched for an 'on' switch, but couldn't find one. "How does it work?"

"You don't even know how to use a phone?" Maddy asked, her tone implying stupidity. "You push the number and then you talk."

Van pushed the miniature buttons and held the phone up to her ear, but nothing happened. Her eyes stung, and she blinked rapidly. "It doesn't work."

"You have to push the green button first," Maddy said. "Oh, and my brother said it's two thousand eight."

"What is?" Van asked, not finding a green button.

"What year it is. My brother said it's two thousand eight."

Van shook the phone. Damn toy, that's all it was. She handed it to Maddy and faced the sign. Two thousand eight? Her trembling grew worse.

"Joke's over," she called out to the air. She waited for someone to pop out and yell, "*Surprise!*" But no one did. "Jill? Patsy? Joke's over, you can come out now." Nothing happened. She raised her voice, tried to put more force behind it so it would reach farther, but like screaming in a nightmare, her voice came out thin and wobbly. She needed more air. "Jill, you stop this right now, you hear me? Patsy? Patsy!"

Maddy's eyes grew wide. She edged away.

Van reached over the low fence, grabbed hold of the sign, and shook it. "Jill!" Her voice grew shrill and frantic.

Maddy ran into the house.

"*Patsy!*"

A male voice called out from one of the neighboring houses. "Knock it off, lady, or I'll call the police."

A sob shook Van's voice as she screamed out. "*PATSY!!!*"

Chapter Two

Van—1988

VAN SLIPPED QUIETLY into the bathroom and stripped off her grubby clothes. She dropped them on top of the pile Patsy had left behind the door, eased back the vinyl shower curtain, and stepped into the opposite end of the tub from where Patsy stood with her eyes closed, her head tilted into the spray, arms raised to her head, lathering shampoo into her short brown hair. The angle of her arms caused her breasts to jut forward tautly, or at least as tautly as fifty-year-old breasts can jut. Van watched for a moment, enjoying the sight of the water dripping from the dark nipples, drops rolling down Patsy's belly which, while not flat precisely, was not bad at all for fifty. The wet triangle of hair at the top of Patsy's long, muscular legs also dripped with water, and Van contemplated getting down on her knees and licking the drips. But she didn't move quickly enough.

Patsy sensed her presence, opened her eyes, and saw Van standing, naked and shivering, at the edge of the spray from the shower. She wiped the water from her eyes with her hands, her face expressionless. "Well, well, this is a nice surprise."

But her eyes glinted and her nostrils flared, and Van smiled, recognizing the signs. She inched forward. "It's not every day a girl turns fifty." She tiptoed up to kiss Patsy on the lips, her breasts caressing Patsy's on the way up, and again on the way down. "Happy birthday, darling."

"Hot damn," Patsy said, smiling and gathering Van into her arms. "If I'd known about this, I'd have skipped the forties."

"You don't get to choose." Van slid the front of her wet body across the front of Patsy's. "Besides, we've showered together lots of times."

"Not for ages."

Patsy was right, but today was not the time to talk about that. Today would be a birthday to remember if Van had anything to say about it.

Patsy's eyes had already started to glaze, so Van pulled herself away a bit. "Not so fast. It's your birthday shower." She took the soap, worked up a lather, and rubbed the suds over every inch of Patsy's body, careful not to pay any more time or attention to one spot than another. First the front, from the hips on up, as Patsy watched her through narrowed eyes, nostrils flared again, in the familiar and beloved look of arousal. Van put her hands on Patsy's waist and rotated her so she could lather her neck and back and butt. She got down on her knees, letting the spray drench her, and soaped the back of Patsy's legs, then put her hands on Patsy's hips and spun her again so she could soap the front of her legs, beginning with the feet, the calves, the knees, the thighs. By the time she reached the patch of wet curls, Patsy was leaning against the shower wall, bracing herself up with her arms, eyes half closed, and her mouth open, gasping for breath.

"I don't think I want to waste any old soap on this part," Van said, setting the lathery bar into the soap dish. Still on her knees, Van leaned deliberately forward, her tongue stretched out, and lapped the water dripping from the longest curl. Patsy moaned. Van slipped her tongue past the curls to the soft mound of flesh within.

Patsy moaned again, and her knees quivered. "Oh, God."

Van placed her hands on Patsy's hips and pressed in harder with her tongue, working Patsy's swollen clit back and forth, gently at first, then harder and more quickly, occasionally sucking, occasionally letting her tongue probe farther, into the warm, slick folds before withdrawing and working at the clit again.

Patsy slid slowly down the wall as her legs gave out. "I can't–I can't–Oh, God!"

Van scooted back as Patsy slid down, but she didn't release her tongue from Patsy's hot swollen flesh, back and forth, faster and faster, until finally Patsy gave a convulsive jerk and clamped her thighs around Van's head. Patsy groaned long and loud. Quickly, Van pulled her head out of the grasp of Patsy's thighs and placed her hand where her mouth had been, thrusting with the pressure Patsy liked at the very end of an orgasm. Patsy heaved a great sigh, then another. She grabbed Van's shoulders and pulled her slippery body up over her own to capture Van's lips in a long, intense kiss. Finally, they lay panting together on the floor of the tub, the shower still spraying them with water.

"Oh my God," Patsy said breathlessly. "That was fucking unbelievable."

Though cramped in the tight quarters of the narrow tub, Van couldn't help wagging her butt a bit in self-congratulation. "Yeah," she said. "I still got it."

Patsy squeezed her arm around Van's shoulders. "Oh, baby, you still got it, believe me. Just let me catch my breath and you'll *get* it, too."

"I don't think we have time for that," Van said, reaching an arm up to turn off the cooling water. "Our guests will be here in an hour."

"We have time." Patsy sat up and brought Van with her. "And you know you want to. Unless you're cold?" She gently flicked Van's erect nipple with the tip of a finger.

Van caught her breath. "A little of both." She gasped as Patsy dipped her head, caught the nipple in her mouth, and sucked. Van felt the pull deeply below, as if silk ribbons connected directly from her nipple to the center of her crotch. She whimpered.

Patsy quickly kissed Van's nipple and stood, pulling Van with her. "I can warm you up," she boasted, "but not here. I need room to roam."

"Well, okay." Van grabbed a towel and let herself be led from the bathroom into the adjoining bedroom. "But it'll have to be a quickie."

"If I want to take time to make love to every inch of you, I get to." Patsy paused to plant kisses on Van's left shoulder. "It's my birthday. Our guests can go fuck themselves."

Even after six years together, Van still found Patsy unpredictable enough that she wasn't sure she wouldn't tell their guests to do exactly that. Just in case, Van thought it safest not to resist. If they got it over with quickly, they'd still have time to prepare and greet their guests on time. Besides, she really wasn't cold.

And when Patsy had her spread out on the sheets, sucking Van's nipple while her fingers worked magic at Van's crotch, Van forgot all about the upcoming party. And if any early guests had arrived when Patsy had her long, strong fingers all the way inside her, she'd have told them to go fuck themselves too.

It was less than an hour later that they stood at the front door together watching Sadie, their border collie, herd more guests toward the door. They'd had to shower again after they'd finished making love, and damp curls still lay heavily on Van's shoulders. Patsy's fine brown hair dried in minutes. She was overdue for a cut, and her long bangs fell into her eyes. Patsy pushed them away irritably, but they fell immediately back. Patsy looked very sexy in her button-up Levi's and blue denim shirt, but Van didn't tell her so. Compliments annoyed Patsy.

"What's Inez doing with Barbie?" Patsy asked, as Inez drew near with her date, who held a bunch of balloons bobbing on a long string.

"Hush." Van nudged Patsy with her elbow. "She'll hear you."

"So what? She has the nerve to bring Barbie to my party, she gets what's coming to her."

"I meant *Kendra* will hear you."

"Oh." Patsy was momentarily abashed, but then said, "You think she doesn't already *know* she looks like Barbie? I'm surprised she's not driving a pink plastic Barbie-Mobile."

Van decided it wasn't the time to tell Patsy that Kendra had a genuine shot at earning a pink Mary Kay Cadillac through her job. Kendra did bear an uncanny resemblance to Barbie, though, from her big blond hair and water-balloon boobs to her skinny hips and disproportionately long legs. She wore a nearly see-through white silk blouse and tight black stretch pants with shimmery pink leggings bunched artistically at her calves and ankles.

Next to Kendra, Inez looked like a librarian in her long denim skirt and red mock turtleneck sweater. Van hugged Inez tightly, stepped back, and examined her face. Still shell shocked, Van saw, even though six months had passed since her brutal breakup with Trudy. If Kendra could help erase that bruised look from Inez's face, she could dress like a Cabbage Patch doll for all Van cared. But so far, it didn't seem as if Kendra was having any success in that department.

"You must be Patsy," Kendra said, thrusting a bouquet of black balloons at her. "Happy birthday!"

"Look, Van," Patsy said with a deliberately fake smile. "Kendra brought balloons."

"Welcome to the fifties, darling," Inez told Patsy, kissing her on the cheek. "They're the best years of your life." Her words were unconvincing, given the misery still evident on her face. Patsy raised a skeptical brow.

Van hugged Kendra. "Thank you, thank you. You just won me a slave day."

"Huh? A what?" Kendra asked, blinking.

"I bet Patsy that someone would bring Over-the-Hill balloons. She didn't think anyone would."

"I didn't think anyone would be so damned insensitive," Patsy explained, glaring at Kendra.

"Oops." Kendra's lips made a Barbie-perfect moue.

"Don't pay any attention to her," Van advised. "She's crotchety in her old age."

Inez raised her eyebrows suggestively from Patsy to Van. "A slave day?"

"Pull your filthy mind up out of the gutter," Patsy groused. "We only get *that* kind of slave day when I win. When Van wins a slave day, I always end up washing windows or painting the garage or something."

"Not this time," Van said cheerfully. "I want a railing put on the deck." She gestured toward the door to usher everyone inside. "Besides, why would I waste a slave day on something I can get any time I ask?" She ran her finger lightly down the back of Patsy's neck as she passed through the door.

Patsy stopped and peered down at Van through narrowed eyes, her hair once again falling over her forehead. "Watch yourself, counselor," Patsy said softly, sliding her hand inside Van's overalls and running her finger along the top of her panties. "You may get *more* than you asked for."

Van laughed and kissed Patsy as she stepped into the house.

Inside, Inez was introducing Kendra to Jill, who had arrived several minutes earlier. Van could see Jill sizing Kendra up, trying to ascertain whether Kendra was someone who could be trusted around RIP. Jill was very private with her invention. She worked in a lab that conducted highly secure and carefully monitored experiments. If the lab learned about the experiments Jill was conducting on her own, she'd be fired, or worse.

"Inez told me about you," Kendra said as she lowered herself into the recliner on the other side of the cold stove. "You're the scientist, right?"

Jill nodded, her dark brown eyes deceptively placid, as she slid her gaze to Inez. "What exactly did Inez tell you?"

"I told her *all* about you," Inez said with a glint her eyes, causing a slight crease to appear between Jill's heavy brows. Inez sat in the rocking chair. "Like about the time you got arrested for breaking and entering."

Jill laughed a little, but seemed compelled to clarify. "I just needed to get in the lab to finish my chem experiment. I was only a freshman."

"And the time you ran outside without your shirt *or* bra on in broad daylight."

"Oh, that," Jill said. "It was raining. Parts of my...some of my parts were out on the lawn, and I couldn't let them get wet."

"Your parts got wet, all right," Patsy said, dropping down onto the couch and snatching the pack of cigarettes from the coffee table. "They were slick and shiny, and there were raindrops dripping off your—" She paused to light a cigarette. "Damn, I got *my* parts wet watching *your* parts get wet."

"I'm getting wet just hearing you talk about it." Van plopped herself down beside Patsy, plucked the cigarette from her fingers, and took a long drag. Everyone laughed, including Jill.

"And what about the time she dated that chick for six months before finding out she was a *boy*?" Patsy asked, shaking out another cigarette. "What kind of scientist is *that*?"

Jill's cheeks turned a darker red, and her smile lost some its luster. "Yeah, well."

"Hey, give her a break," Van said. "So she wasn't a biology major." Patsy and Inez had both known Jill far longer than Van had, but Van sometimes thought she was the only one who saw that their constant teasing sometimes hurt Jill's feelings. Jill was not handsome, like Patsy, or beautiful, like Inez. She was dusky and studious and serious. She reminded Van of that character from Scooby Doo, Velma, with her dark glasses and her scientific mind. Except Jill didn't wear a flippy short skirt, of course. She sometimes did try to dress fashionably, but she never seemed to get it quite right. Today she had played it safe in a gray sweatshirt and jeans.

Van looked from Patsy to Jill, who sat cross-legged on the floor with Sadie snuggled beside her, to Inez. "God, I wish I'd gone to school with you guys. You had so much *fun*."

Patsy, Inez, and Jill shared smug glances. "We were very lucky," Inez said. "Imagine it, 1956, and these three little dykes all end up on the same floor in the same dorm."

"Hey, I wasn't a dyke," Patsy said, offended. "Not 'til you corrupted me."

"Wait a minute." Jill sat up straight, eyes round. "You're dykes?"

Jokes from Jill were rare, so when she made one, they seemed especially funny. Everyone laughed hard. Kendra's eyes skipped from face to face in some bemusement, and Van suspected this might be her first all-woman party that wasn't a wedding shower or a baby shower or a party designed to sell Tupperware or cosmetics or educational toys. Van knew from Inez that Kendra had only recently decided she might be a lesbian and that, in fact, she was still married and had not yet sprung the news on her husband. Van had some understanding of where Kendra was coming from, being a late bloomer herself, but at least she had never gotten married.

Van leaned heavily against Patsy, still tingling from their pre-party love-making. Patsy responded by draping an arm around Van's shoulders and giving her a quick sideways glance, letting her know she was thinking of the same thing.

"Hello-oh!" The door opened and Ellen stood there in her long Mother Earth dress with a baby snuggled in a sling across her front. "Happy Birthday, P! Did you start the party without us?"

"You brought Michael." Patsy didn't sound pleased.

"Of course," Ellen said in mild reproof. "Did you think we'd leave a two-month-old baby at home?" She cradled the infant with one arm while she reached behind her to guide herself down into a soft easy chair, as if she were still pregnant. She unwrapped the baby. "Who wants to hold him?" she asked, with the self-absorbed belief of new mothers that every woman yearns to hold their babies.

Van had long since come to terms with the fact that she would not have children, and she had no desire to risk regret by cuddling an infant. Jill, she knew, had no affinity for babies, and the grimace of horror on Patsy's face should have tipped off even Ellen that maybe not everyone loves babies. Kendra may have loved babies, for all Van knew, but she made no move to take Ellen's from her.

The silence following Ellen's question grew awkward, and Van nearly caved in to the pressure when she saw her reprieve outside through the still open door. Terri was out there dodging Sadie and wrestling with a playpen, an immense diaper bag slung across her back. "I'd better go help Terri," Van said, rising.

Inez rescued the group. "Let me hold him, Ellen."

After Van and Terri got all the baby accoutrements into the house, a near crisis erupted over where to place the playpen. Ellen insisted that Michael not be exposed to cigarette smoke. Except for Ellen, everyone smoked.

"Put him in the bedroom," Van suggested.

"We sleep in there," Patsy objected. "I don't want any shitty diapers in my bedroom."

"His diapers don't smell bad," Ellen assured Patsy, "but that won't work anyway. We'd have to leave the door open to hear him, and he'd still be exposed to the smoke."

"Upstairs?" Inez suggested.

Ellen glanced up and assessed the ceiling. "We can't hear him from there. Can't you all go outside if you need to smoke?"

"Put *him* outside," Patsy suggested. "No, I'm serious. Put his playpen on the deck right there. It's not cold out. You can watch him through the glass, and he won't be exposed to our foul air."

"There are *woods* out there," Ellen said. "I'm not putting my baby out there in the woods while all the grown-ups sit inside *smoking* where it's safe and warm."

"We haven't had a grizzly bear attack up here in weeks," Patsy said her voice gritty with annoyance. "Besides, he's only a man cub."

Terri's calm, low voice cut through the outraged protests at Patsy's sexist remarks. "When I'm at home, I go outside when I want a cigarette."

"It's my fucking fiftieth birthday party!" Patsy hollered. "I'm not going to be kicked out of my own house."

But ten minutes later the party had moved outside to the wooden deck that ran across the back of the house. The playpen was set up in the living room, where Ellen could watch Michael sleep through the sliding glass doors. Sadie parked herself on the deck on the other side of the glass, so she could watch Michael as well. A slight breeze stirred, but the air was dry and warm enough that they could go without jackets, at least until the sun set.

"Watch out that your chairs don't tip off the deck," Van warned. "We keep meaning to put a railing up, but we haven't gotten around to it yet."

"Is the hot tub working?" Terri asked, seeming relaxed and happy for first time since her arrival.

"Yup," Van said. "I hope everyone brought their bathing suits."

"No suits in the hot tub!" Patsy called out from the other end of the deck where she, Inez, and Jill sat in deck chairs, fishing bottles of beer from a cooler. "It's bad for the filter."

Kendra's eyes widened.

"We wear suits when we have company," Van assured her. "Patsy just likes to scare people."

Kendra smiled with relief. "Is this all your land?" she asked, gazing at the woods in front of her.

Van contemplated the forest of trees that surrounded the house and allowed herself a smug pride-of-ownership moment. "Yes, everything you can see from here, anyway. There are neighbors about a half mile away." Van dropped down to sit on the edge of the deck with Terri and Kendra, six legs dangling.

"It's nice property, so close to town," Kendra said. "Have you ever thought of clearing those trees? Creating a view of the river?"

"God, no," Van said. "I love the trees. That's why I bought the place. The seclusion of it, the quiet. It comforts me, somehow. It's my hiding place, my base, you know? Like a womb." Van paused, a bit embarrassed at having opened up so much to a near stranger. "Besides, if I want to enjoy the river, I can go down that trail there to the water."

"Do you have a boat?" Kendra asked, but before Van could answer, Kendra's attention was diverted. "I hear someone coming."

Van, too, heard the sound of tires on gravel. She slid off the deck to the ground below. "It must be Waverly." She jogged over to the corner of the house and peered around at the gravel parking area behind it. "Yep. It's Waverly," she announced to the group. "And she's got her new girlfriend with her." She waved her arms. "Back here!"

Moments later, Waverly came around the corner of the cabin lugging one end of a heavy plastic cooler. She wore a stonewashed denim jacket with western fringe across the chest and shoulders and down the arms, matching jeans tucked into white cowboy boots that also bore a line of white leather fringe across the top. A white cowboy hat sat on top of her long wavy mane of brown hair.

Patsy whistled. "Where's your horse, Cow Patty?"

Waverly grinned. "Howdy, birthday girl." She set her end of the cooler down on the ground, and the woman carrying the other end followed suit. Waverly tipped her hat at the women lining the deck. "Howdy, ladies. Allow me to introduce my girlfriend, Grace. Grace, this obnoxious *old* woman is Patsy, whose half-century mark we've come here today to celebrate. And this is her girlfriend, Van, the lady lawyer."

"Thank you for including me in your invitation," Grace said softly. She was a slender woman of medium height, with short brown hair and pale eyes. She wore a plain yellow and white striped button up shirt and nondescript jeans, apparently as intent on avoiding attention as Waverly was on attracting it. She had the earmarks of a woman who worries too much, but she wore an eager smile that suggested she intended to enjoy herself, for the time being, at least.

"Of course," Van said. "We're glad to finally meet you."

"Yeah, any girlfriend of Waverly's is a girlfriend of ours," Patsy said, wagging her cigarette as if it were Groucho's cigar.

"Now remember what I said about Patsy?" Waverly cautioned

Grace. Grace blushed and shot a shy smile at Patsy. Waverly continued the introductions. "This is Jill." Jill nodded at Grace and looked somewhat despairingly from her to Kendra, and Van knew she was worried about exposing RIP to another stranger. "And this is Inez, who's here with...?"

"Kendra," Inez said, nodding to where Kendra sat on the edge of the deck. Kendra smiled and finger-waved at them both.

"Pleased to meet you," Waverly said to Kendra. "And this is Terri. Where's Ellen?"

"Inside with Michael. It's nice to meet you, Grace."

"Thank you. It's nice to meet all of you."

Waverly and Grace had only been dating a couple of weeks. But everyone knew the old joke about lesbians and second dates: What does a lesbian bring on a second date? A U-Haul. And the reason it was so funny is that it was so damned true. Van only hoped that Waverly and Grace could hold off the moving van until they realized how unsuited they were for each other. Knowing Waverly's track record, though, she doubted they would.

"Who wants beer?" Patsy asked, popping the caps off bottles of Rainier and passing them around.

"Who wouldn't want beer?" Waverly asked, grabbing a couple.

"None for me, thanks," Ellen said, finally coming through the slider to the deck. "I'm nursing."

"God, this is a beautiful place," Waverly said, settling with Grace into a glider Patsy had dragged onto the lawn. "You guys are so lucky to have a home like this."

"Yeah, we know." Van exchanged a smile with Patsy before turning again to view her domain.

"Whose camper is that?" Kendra asked, gesturing with her beer bottle toward the only jarring note in the view. An old yellow and brown camper perched on the bed of a Toyota pickup, nestled in a clearing a few hundred feet from the deck. A large antenna poked up through the center of the roof with at least a dozen prongs pointing like fingers toward the sky. Another pole laced with heavy wires and capped by a silver inverted bowl was mounted near the front. The door at the rear of the camper was not original to it. Made of steel, perhaps, or possibly lead, its frame was heavily reinforced with welding and bolts. The door itself was locked with two heavy padlocks.

There was a long, awkward moment of silence.

"That's Jill's," Van said, finally.

Kendra looked from the camper to Jill curiously. "Do you sleep in that?"

Jill shook her head slightly, assessing Kendra somberly with her heavy dark eyes. She shifted her gaze to Grace with the same, solemn attention. It wasn't the first time a newcomer had been introduced to one of Jill's experiments. Van herself had been a newcomer once, as had Waverly, and Jill had judged them in a similar fashion before ultimately deciding to share her secret with them.

"Kendra's all right," Inez said softly. "I wouldn't have brought her otherwise."

"Grace too," Waverly said, wrapping an arm around Grace's shoulders.

Jill hesitated a moment, exchanged meaningful glances with Patsy and Inez, the women she trusted the most, and she shrugged and answered Kendra.

"No, I don't sleep there. It's a machine. There's no room for a bed in there."

"What kind of machine?" Kendra asked.

"A Rapid Intertemporal Projector. It's an R.I.P. machine. I call it RIP."

"What does it do?"

"It's an instantaneous projection from the present to the future."

"Projection of what?"

There was a long silence, finally broken by Van, who said simply, "People. It's a time machine."

Chapter Three

Van—2008

"VAN?"

Van sat on a low rock wall that surrounded one of the new houses across the road from her home. She watched the sun's reflection fade into the river as evening fell. Sweat prickled underneath her arms and dripped down her sides, the sweater and overalls too heavy for the unexpected heat. Her mind was too numb to plan her next move. The sign with the faded picture grew long shadows that fell over her shoulder, reminding her of its presence, and she considered trying to find a phone she could use. And a bathroom. But damn it, that was her *own house* right there behind her. It wasn't fair that she should have to go somewhere else in order to make a phone call and pee.

After she'd finished screaming for Patsy and Jill, Van returned to her own front door, but it was locked and there was no sign of the teenage boy or the girl. She'd pounded and yelled some more, but her cries were ignored except by the neighbor, who'd warned her again that he was calling the police. She'd given up, finally, and ended up sitting on the rock wall. And that's where she had remained ever since. Just sitting.

"Van?" The voice was behind her, tentative and thin and a bit breathless.

Van raised her head and peered over her shoulder.

An old woman stood by the sign across the road, one hand on the fence and the other on her heart. "Oh my gosh, Van, it *is* you." The old woman raised her face to the sky, closed her eyes, and brought both hands to her chest. "Thank God, thank God." She opened her eyes and grinned at Van. "Don't you recognize me, Van? Have I changed so much?"

Van stared, mesmerized. Incredibly, she *did* recognize her. But not like this. The face was lined with fine wrinkles, her skin was dark and leathery, as if she'd spent a lifetime outdoors, something Van had never known her to do. She was thinner as well. A baggy pair of long army-green shorts sagged off her bony hips, and her hair had gone completely white, even her thick eyebrows. But her dark brown eyes were the same, behind wire-rimmed glasses.

Van rose. "Jill?"

Jill immediately crossed the road to Van, reaching out as if to hug her, but Van instinctively shrank back as if approached by a stranger, and Jill dropped her arms. "I knew you'd come back, eventually," Jill said, recovering quickly, and even her voice sounded the same. But different too. Deeper, huskier, and softer all at once. "I'm so glad I got to live to see it. I was so worried." Jill scanned Van from head to toe. "You look exactly the same. Even your clothes. How do you feel?" Her gaze focused intently on Van's face.

Van shared the only feeling she could identify with any clarity. "I have to pee."

"Oh." Jill became all business. "Let's go to my house. It's right over here." Van followed her toward the house that used to be hers. Van paused as she passed the sign, and Jill stopped with her.

"This sign," Van said. "Did you...?"

"I had it put up so you'd be able to find me. I knew you'd come back. That's my phone number. And it *worked*. Maddy called me and told me 'the lady' was here." Jill moved on, and Van continued following. She *really* had to pee.

"Is it really 2008?" Van asked.

Jill looked apologetic. "Yes, I'm afraid so." She led the way around the side of the cabin, past the new addition, and stopped at the small building behind it. "This is my house."

Van stopped abruptly. "This is my *garage.*"

"Yes, but it's not a garage any more. I had it converted." Jill opened the front door, which had once been an unused side door in Van's garage. The automatic garage door was gone, replaced by a wall and two wide windows. But there was no mistaking that it was a garage. "It's all I could afford around here. The prices have gone through the roof. And I couldn't leave the area. Not until you came back." She stepped aside and let Van precede her into her home.

It had been a two-car garage, no bigger than necessary to hold Van's Honda Accord, Patsy's Chevy pick-up, their ten-speeds, a lawnmower, and a few garden tools. Given its size, it made a remarkably comfortable house, but it was still cramped. The main room was a living room and a miniscule kitchen, separated only by a narrow counter that must serve as a dining area. Something steamed from a bowl on the counter, and a dropped spoon had left an orange skid mark beside it. The smell of burnt toast filled the room. Two open doors at the back revealed a tiny bedroom on the left and a bathroom on the right. Van veered toward the bathroom without a word.

As she peed, Van pondered her situation. Maybe she'd had too much to drink at the party, passed out, and this was nothing more than a fascinating dream. But she clearly remembered having only a couple of beers. She also clearly remembered entering RIP only—she glanced at her watch—was it really only forty-seven minutes ago? There'd been no period of unconsciousness, no blacking out, no lapse of time, no moment she could point to and say, "There, that's when I must have passed out." Simply, one second she was in RIP, sheltered

by the trees in front of her house in 1988, and the next second —
maybe even nanosecond — she was bouncing on her butt on gravel,
apparently in the exact same spot she'd been a moment before. And
twenty years had passed.

She studied her reflection in the mirror as she washed her
hands. Jill was right, she hadn't changed. Her hair was as red as ever,
her skin just starting to show middle age lines around her mouth, the
same smile lines around her green eyes. She grimaced at her
reflection and studied her teeth. Good God, why didn't someone tell
her? Stuck between her two front teeth was a large speck of freshly
ground pepper from the blackened chicken she'd cooked for Patsy's
birthday dinner.

Jill had clearly aged, though. She was a month older than Patsy,
so if this was 2008, she'd have recently celebrated her seventieth
birthday. And forty-seven minutes ago she'd been a mere fifty.

Van shook her head in a feeble attempt at denial. Bad beer, that's
all it was. She picked the pepper from between her teeth and dried
her hands.

When she stepped out of the bathroom, Jill was perched on a
stool at the counter talking into what looked like a Star Trek
communicator.

"Hurry, okay?" She saw Van. "Here she is. I gotta go." She
clapped the communicator shut, shoved it into the front pocket of
her baggy shorts, and stared at Van expectantly.

"Is that a phone?" Van asked.

Jill's brows rose. Apparently that wasn't what she had expected
Van to ask. She took it out of her pocket and handed it over.

Van opened it up and saw what looked like a mini color
television screen. The time, 8:17 pm, was displayed across the top,
and underneath, there it was, the date, June 25, 2008. Various
symbols on the screen moved as she watched, the words "Menu" and
"Contacts" lit up on the screen. On the bottom side of the flip-open
phone were the tiny buttons she'd seen on Maddy's phone, the one
she'd thought was a toy.

The phone vibrated in her hand. "Aaah!" She threw it from her
like it was a spider.

"No, no, it's okay. It's okay," Jill said soothingly, stooping to pick
up the phone where it had skidded near her foot. "It's on vibration
mode. It means I have a call." She glanced at the screen, pushed a
button that stopped its buzzing, and slipped it into her pocket. "It's
not important. Sit down, Van. Sit. Isn't there anything you'd like to
ask me about besides phones? Do you have any questions?"

Van perched on the edge of a love seat that served as a couch in
the poky house. She said nothing, but gazed at Jill trying to make
sense of what she was experiencing.

"Would you like a drink or something?" Jill asked. "Are you

hungry? I just made some tomato soup and a grilled cheese sandwich."

"I just ate, thank you," Van said, a bit of sarcasm creeping into her voice. "Blackened chicken, remember? Steamed asparagus, sautéed mushrooms, pineapple upside down cake?" Jill looked slightly abashed, but Van was feeling too unnerved to care. "What I'd really like is a cigarette."

Jill was dismayed. "I'm sorry. I don't smoke."

"What do you mean, you don't smoke?" Van stood and prowled around the small area, absently scouring for a pack that Jill might have mislaid. "You've smoked ever since I met you. You've smoked for years. You must have one somewhere."

"I quit," Jill said apologetically. "But hold on." She pulled the phone out of her pocket, opened it up, pushed a single button, and held it to her ear. "It's me again. Can you stop and pick up a pack of cigarettes?"

"Vantage Ultra Lightss," Van said.

Jill repeated it into the phone. "Well, do your best. And hurry." Jill closed the phone and dropped it back in her pocket. Van avoided Jill's steady gaze and continued to prowl the room.

A column of three photographs hung on the sliver of wall between the bedroom and bathroom, and Van stopped to examine them. The top photo showed Jill, Patsy, and Inez in their college days, three girls in 1959 with their arms slung around each other's shoulders. Van knew the photo by heart, as a copy of it sat on the dresser she shared with Patsy. In the photo, Jill stood on the left, slender and tall, in a pair of pedal pushers, sneakers with white socks rolled down to her ankles, and a white button-up shirt hanging untucked and loose. She was the serious one, her dark frizzy hair growing untamed and unstyled in a mane around her face. She stared straight ahead, unsmiling, black cat-eye glasses hiding the remainder of her face.

Next to Jill, in the center, was Inez, the beauty of the three. Although the photo was in black and white, Van could tell she wore dark red lipstick. The Inez of 1959 wore her blond hair in loose curls around her face, a soft light sweater that emphasized gravity-defying cone-shaped breasts, sheer hose, pumps, and a full skirt that needed only a poodle on a leash to fit the classic Fiftie's stereotype. She was laughing in the photo, glancing flirtatiously up at Patsy.

Standing on the right, in loose-fitting dungarees, a plaid jacket over a plain sweater, and boots, Patsy was clearly the "butch" to Inez's "femme." As always, when she examined the photo, Van felt gratitude that time had eased the pressure on lesbians to assume one gender identity or the other. In reality, Inez didn't enjoy makeup, preferred short hair to long, and abhorred wearing nylons, while Patsy, Van knew, had an affinity for pretty pastels and silk lingerie, not only for Van but for herself as well. In 1959, though, when being a lesbian could still land you in jail, if not a mental institution, the labels of butch and femme actually simplified the mating dance between women. Lesbians had enough to worry about, without adding the anxiety of defining themselves within a relationship. By assuming roles already created by the straight world, they managed to save themselves a lot of time and confusion.

Van was struck, as always when she saw the photograph, by the adoration in Patsy's face as she gazed down at Inez. Every lesbian she knew was still good friends with an old lover. Van and Waverly, for example. Patsy and Inez were no exception, and Van knew their friendship was nothing more than that. She wasn't jealous that Patsy had loved Inez, but she was jealous of their carefree puppy love, jealous that they knew they were lesbians when they were still so young and had no qualms about throwing their hearts out, loving without fear.

Van slid her eyes down to the second photo in the column. She recognized this one also, since she was the one who had taken it at their twenty-five year college reunion. Van and Patsy had been lovers for barely a year, and she hardly knew Jill and Inez. Patsy had attended most of the reunion functions—the beer night, the banquet—without Van, but she'd brought Van along with her to the barbecue. By then, Van was already familiar with the 1959 photo, and she'd suggested the three women strike the same pose for a new photo.

Jill had changed the least. She was still slender, hair dark brown and frizzy, her expression solemn, and her eyes still hidden behind glasses, only this time the frames were plastic blue tortoiseshell. She'd made an unfortunate wardrobe decision to pair a tube top with a billowing pair of parachute pants, which had prompted Patsy to refer to her as Harem Girl for the entire day.

Inez again was the only one wearing a skirt, but not with nylons this time. Her skirt was a wide, indigo-dyed, sari that she wrapped around her waist and allowed to drape unevenly on the ground, creating a long, wide slit through which her leg could be seen. Leather sandals wrapped around her ankles. She wore a loose halter top that allowed her breasts to drop naturally into a soft fabric pouch, forcing the conclusion that they'd escaped their bondage of 1959 and had no intention of returning. Her hair was cut into a Princess Diana wedge, and she gazed at the camera with Diana-like bemusement, though Van knew she was simply stoned.

On the right, Patsy wore the short cut-off Levi's Van loved best, having a weakness for legs. Patsy's legs had been at their best that summer. Patsy and Van had still been in their honeymoon phase, and Patsy had spared no effort at trying to win Van's approval, primarily by showing off for her in those things at which she excelled: softball, waterskiing, biking, hiking—anything she could do well, Patsy did for Van, and the result was in the photo. Her legs were long and tanned, all muscle and no fat, from the Levi fringe at the top of her thighs to the rubber thongs at her feet. Van had run her hands, and other things, all over those legs, and treasured the memories. Patsy hadn't had such a good leg year since, and likely never would again. In addition to the cut-offs, Patsy wore a plain white tank top with gaping armholes and a sports bra underneath, once more showing off her tanned muscles. Her hair was cut into an athletic shag, and her tanned face made her eyes and teeth appear whiter than ever, the picture of health and strength.

As in the first photo, Patsy wore a look of adoration, but this time it was directed not at Inez, but at the camera, behind which stood Van. For the first time, Van noticed the bottle of beer Patsy held. When had a beer bottle in Patsy's hand become such a common sight it was hardly even noticeable? Van frowned and focused her attention on the third photo in the column.

She'd never seen this photo before, and with a tightening in her chest she realized that she'd never seen it because it hadn't been shot yet. Not in 1988. Van tried to fathom where she had been when the photo was taken, but she found the thought too troubling, and instead examined the photo itself.

Jill, Inez, and Patsy were in this photo as well, sitting in a boat this time, flapping hair and clothing testifying to the fact that the boat was moving. Jill was again on the left, her eyes inscrutable behind dark sunglasses. Her frizzy hair was streaked with white and gray; it was not the pure white hair of the Jill who sat still and silent behind her now. The Jill in the photo wore a long-sleeved button-up shirt, open in the front, over a loose-fitting navy tank top. Unlike the Jill in the other photos, this Jill smiled, but it was an awkward stiff smile, and Van thought she would have looked happier had she simply stared ahead expressionlessly as she had in the previous photos.

Inez sat on the right. She wore a wide-brimmed straw hat tied beneath her chin with a huge bow. Over a one piece bathing suit with a flamboyant flower design, she wore a loose, white filmy jacket apparently designed to protect from sun and nothing else. This time it was Inez who gazed at the camera with adoring eyes, and Van wondered who had snapped the picture. The last time she'd seen Inez, she'd still worn tragedy in her eyes, but by the time this photo was taken, the tragedy had been swept away by love. Inez's face was more lined than Van remembered, her jowls sagged, and she had developed what in 1988 they called chicken neck. But she was happier than Van had seen her in years.

In the center this time sat Patsy, and Van's heart lurched. She wore a sleeveless white shirt, button front, but open at the collar. Her arms and neck were red from the sun, as was her face. She wore a baseball cap, but it was backward, and Van could clearly see her face. Patsy laughed at something or someone behind the cameraperson, her mouth open in a harsh smile and her eyes sharp and hard. Her arms were flung around the shoulders of Jill and Inez. In her left hand, resting on Inez's shoulder, she held a short squat glass filled with a dark amber liquid, and Van wondered when she had switched from beer to hard liquor. In her right hand she held a slim cigar, the smoke wafting disregarded into Jill's clenched face. Patsy looked mean.

Van glanced over her shoulder and saw Jill watching her anxiously. "When was this taken?"

"1998."

Ten years in the future. Ten years in the past. "Where was I?"

Jill appeared stricken, and Van wanted to take the question back, afraid of the answer.

"You weren't there," Jill answered, and Van felt a rush of grief that she and Patsy had not survived another ten years together. Then she noticed Jill's normally stoic face had taken on an expression of misery so profound it chilled Van's heart.

"What? What happened?" Van had an awful guess. "Did I die?"

Jill shook her head. "You disappeared, Van," she said, despair in her voice. "You disappeared in 1988. Nobody ever saw you again. Until today."

Van felt the blood drain from her face. "No. That's not possible."

"It's what happened," Jill said gently.

"No," Van repeated. "I didn't go anywhere. I had to be somewhere. I'm here now, and I didn't go anywhere else." Her voice rose in desperation. "I had to be somewhere!"

Jill opened her mouth to speak, but at that moment a rapping hit the door. Jill jumped up with agility remarkable in a seventy-year-old woman and opened the door.

The woman in the doorway appeared to be in her fifties with ash blond hair knotted in a loose bun, apparently in great haste, as messy bits of hair stuck out at angles from the back of her head. She still had a bombshell figure, and her smile was all confidence. "Don't worry," she said firmly, splitting her reassurance equally between Jill and Van. "Everything will be okay."

Van squinted in confusion. "Barbie?"

Kendra moved into the room and stared at Van. "My God, it really is you."

Van noticed the pack of cigarettes Kendra held in her hands.

"Are those for me?"

Kendra handed them over. "No Ultra Lights, I'm afraid. I don't think they make them any more. I hope those will do."

Van ripped into the pack of cigarettes, shook one out, and

snatched the matches Jill held out to her. Her hand trembled as she held the flame to the tip of the cigarette, but she finally got it lit. She inhaled the unfamiliar tobacco and closed her eyes as her body accepted the hit and began to relax. She blew out the smoke and perched on the stool.

"So, does somebody want to explain what the hell is going on?"

Chapter Four

Patsy — 1988

"IT'S NOT REALLY time travel," Jill said as she passed the steamed asparagus to Kendra, who sat on her left. "At least not the way we've been taught to think of it in TV shows and the movies. It's a time *projector*."

"What's the difference?" Kendra placed six long stalks of the tender vegetable next to her blackened chicken. "This is great, Van. You're a fabulous cook."

Van gave a modest shrug. "It's the only thing I can cook. But it's Patsy's birthday. She only gets it once a year, so I give it a little extra effort."

Waverly's eyes grew round. "You only get it once a year? My God, no wonder you're such a cranky old bitch."

Patsy had just shoved a large bite of tender blackened chicken into her mouth. Too polite to speak with her mouth full, she contented herself with picking up a sautéed mushroom and threw it at Waverly. For good measure, she threw one at Van as well, at the far end of the table. Waverly's hit its mark, and she screamed in outrage as she plucked it out of her hair. Van, though, had warning, or maybe a sixth sense, and was able to dodge it. The mushroom landed on the floor.

"I just had these carpets cleaned," Van scolded.

"You shouldn't have ducked," Patsy managed around her mouthful of chicken.

"Lesbian bed death strikes again," Inez commented mournfully. "I never thought it would happen to you, Patsy."

Patsy threw an olive at Inez and swallowed. "There is no goddamn lesbian bed death in *this* relationship. If you'd been here a couple of hours ago you sure wouldn't say that."

Inez smiled and nodded knowingly. "Once a year, on your birthday."

"First in the shower, then in the bed—"

"Patsy," Van warned. "Shut up."

Patsy grinned at her. She loved making Van blush. It was so easy, and she was so damned cute when she did it. "Then in the bed again and then..."

Van resorted to throwing a mushroom back at Patsy, but she threw high. The mushroom landed with a greasy thud on the wall over Patsy's head and left a slime trail, like a slug, as it slid down the wall. Patsy howled at Van's dismay.

"Time travel transports a person into the future," Jill continued, ignoring the food flying around her. "Or the past, theoretically, though that's not relevant to my current research. It takes the person into a future time period and drops him or her there."

"Like in *Back to the Future*?" Grace asked.

"I love that movie," Waverly squealed, delighted by Grace's comment. "Especially that part where she thinks his name is Calvin Klein. I laughed so hard."

Patsy rolled her eyes. Waverly was at the stage with Grace where she found every shared feeling to be a significant indicator that they were meant to be together, never mind that *everyone* loved that movie.

Patsy met Van's eyes and Van sent her a little frown and a tiny shake of her head as if to say *I agree with you, but not here, dear.* Patsy grinned, an immense feeling of well-being spreading through her body. Could anything be better than this moment? Her dearest friends were gathered around to celebrate with her, the most beautiful and loving woman in the world was sitting across from her trying to control her with wifely scowls, only hours ago they had made fabulous love not once but twice, and her favorite meal had been lovingly prepared and placed before her. She picked up her beer and took a long swallow. Heaven.

"*If* we were talking about traveling into the past, it might be like that," Jill said sternly. "But we're not. In my current experiments, time projection is only to the future. And the idea is that the person projected into the future doesn't actually interact with the future, the way Michael J. Fox did. It's more like a sneak peek. A person is projected in the future to see what's happening, and they return to report on what they saw."

"It's the Ghost of Christmas Future," Patsy said in sepulchral tones.

"Huh?" Kendra asked. "I don't get it."

"Remember in the story of Scrooge?" Van asked. "How the Ghost of Christmas Future takes him into the future to see what happens? And he sees that Tiny Tim dies and everyone's sad, and he sees that when *he* dies nobody cares?"

Ellen picked up the story from where she sat, pushed away from the table, nursing Michael. "But then he asks the Ghost, 'Is this what *is* going to happen, or just what *might* happen?" And the Ghost doesn't answer, but Scrooge figures out that the future he was shown was how it would turn out *if* he didn't change his ways. So, of course, he did."

"That's right," Jill said. "That's what RIP does. It's like the Ghost of Christmas Future."

"So how long are they there?" Kendra asked, hiding any skepticism she might have felt.

"It can be programmed for different lengths of time," Jill said. "I plan to start with just a couple of minutes, while we're still in the experimental stage. Then we can expand it to a couple of hours, or a few days or even weeks, however long we want. The purpose will be defeated if the person doesn't have time to observe and gather the necessary information to report back."

"What necessary information?" Kendra asked.

"I want her to check out gay parenting rights," Ellen said, switching Michael to her other breast. "Everyone's so afraid of how Michael's going to grow up, with two lesbian moms, like we're going to make him queer or something. I want Jill to send someone into the future to find out how Michael grows up, as proof that kids of gay parents will be just fine. Maybe then they'll let us get married."

"Hah! That'll never happen in our lifetime," Patsy said. "Besides, most of the kids of gay parents *are* totally screwed up."

"That's because most of the kids you know are totally screwed up anyway," Ellen said. "I just want proof that the kids of gay parents aren't screwed up any *worse*."

"Catherine's all right," Van pointed out.

"Who's Catherine?" Kendra asked.

"Patsy's step-daughter," Van said.

"Ex," Patsy clarified. She glanced at the clock. Six-thirty, and Catherine still hadn't called to wish her a happy birthday. "And the jury's still out on whether she's screwed up or not. Look who she's hanging around with. She doesn't even know if she's straight or not."

"She's straight," Van said. "She's only playing with lesbians for now. She's not afraid of them, thank God."

"The potential for RIP is immense," Jill said, not distracted from her topic. "You could peek into the future and see what would happen if a particular person is elected president. Or you can check out the results if the country chooses to go into war, or chooses not to, or whether a particular law is passed."

"You could make a killing on the stock market," Patsy said. She stood and struck a Hamlet-like pose, raising her beer bottle as if it were a chalice. "To buy, or not to buy? That is the question."

Inez popped up in imitation. "To marry, or not to marry?"

"To come out," Kendra asked, "or not to come out?"

"To abort, or not to abort?" Waverly asked, and instantly flushed bright red.

"Like *It's a Wonderful Life*," Grace exclaimed, her eyes alight with wonder. "Can you send someone back to see how the world would have been different if they had never been born? I've always wanted to do that."

"Theoretically it could be done, but it's beyond our current capabilities to go backward."

Patsy couldn't stand it any more. "It's beyond your current

capabilities to go *forward*, Jill. Jesus Christ, you're all talking about this as if it was *real*." She leaned forward on her elbow toward Kendra and Grace. "This is all just pretend, you know. She's never *done* anything with this RIP machine."

"I'm getting very close, though," Jill said defensively. "I've made some significant adjustments that I think will be very effective."

"Whose turn is it today?" Waverly asked.

"The birthday girl's," Van said.

"But it's my birthday. I shouldn't have to do it on my birthday."

"Why don't you want to?" Kendra asked. "What do you have to do?"

"You have to sit on this hard little stool in that cramped tin can, with nothing to do, sometimes for *hours*. And there's no air conditioning."

"I parked in the shade this time," Jill said. "And it only takes a few minutes. Unless there are technical difficulties."

"Which there always are," Patsy said. She pushed her plate away and reached for the cigarettes on the side table, encountered a glare from Ellen, and said, "Fuck." There was something wrong with the world when a woman couldn't even smoke in her own home on her own goddamned birthday. She had just pushed her chair away from the table to head outside when the phone rang.

"That must be Catherine," Van said, smiling. "You get the phone. I'll get the cake ready."

Patsy took the phone out to the deck.

"Hello."

"*Happy birthday to you, happy birthday to you. You look like a monkey, and you smell like one too!*"

Patsy grinned and lit a cigarette. When the song was finished, she said, "You know that was a little bit funny when you were eight."

"It's tradition now," Catherine said. "You'd miss it if I sang it the regular way, and you know it."

That was true, but Patsy only said, "Mmm."

"We lost two games. We're out of the tournament," Catherine announced, as if sharing good news.

"How'd you do?"

"Oh, you know," Catherine said vaguely. "But now we get to come out for your birthday party. Have you had cake yet?"

"No, we'll wait for you," Patsy said, thrilled that Catherine could celebrate her birthday with her. "What do you mean 'we'?"

"The lesbians on the team. They love hanging out with you guys, seeing how real grown up lesbians live. Wendy and Donna and April. And Bennie."

After a moment's pause, Catherine said, "Come on, I know you don't like Bennie, but I don't know why. She's great."

Patsy wasn't about to tell Catherine that she didn't like Bennie because of the way she ogled Van. Or the way Patsy sometimes caught Van sneaking peeks back.

"Would you rather I didn't come?" Catherine asked.

"God, no," Patsy said. "Get your asses out here, all of you, and wish me a happy birthday."

"Great. We're right by Joe Albi. We'll be there in a half hour, maybe less. Bye."

Patsy hung up. The ebullient feeling she had felt moments before was gone. She hated the way Bennie made her feel so insecure and jealous, but she couldn't help it. Bennie made her feel threatened.

But, damn it, she wasn't going to let Bennie ruin her birthday. Patsy stubbed out her cigarette, grabbed another beer from the cooler, and went inside.

"Hold the cake for a while," she said, seeing Van had brought in the pineapple upside down cake, decorated simply with five tall candles, one for each decade. "Catherine's coming. They're out of the tournament, so she's coming for birthday cake."

"By herself?" Van asked. Patsy met her eyes and felt a tug of tension deep in her gut. She knew what Van was really asking. And Van knew she knew, which is why Van averted her eyes, as if she regretted asking.

"No," Patsy said carefully. "Some of the lesbians on the team are coming too."

"Yeah!" Waverly shouted, "Baby dykes!" She met Grace's eyes and added hastily. "Not that *I* like baby dykes. It's just kind of fun to have them around sometimes. You know, 'cause they're so cute. Not that all baby dykes are cute, or that you have to be a baby dyke to be cute. In fact, *you're* cute. I mean—"

Grace looked dazed.

"Waverly," Patsy said sternly, and waited until she had Waverly's attention. "Shut up."

Everyone laughed. Waverly nodded and took a deep breath to calm herself.

"Why do you call them baby dykes?" Kendra asked.

"Because they're so young," Inez said. "We were all baby dykes once, too."

"Not all of us," Van clarified. "I was never a baby dyke. You have to be a lesbian early on to be a baby dyke."

"That's true," Inez agreed. "Patsy and Jill and I were baby dykes, though. Patsy, where's that picture?"

"I'll get it." Van hopped up and went into the bedroom and returned with the photograph from Patsy's side of the dresser. She handed it to Kendra.

"Weren't we cute?" Inez asked, peering over Kendra's shoulder at the photo. Kendra nodded and passed it along to the rest of the table.

"How old were you here?" Grace asked.

"That's when we were seniors in college," Inez said. "Twenty-one or twenty-two."

When the photo reached Patsy, she examined it briefly, although it was as familiar to her as her own face. She tried to remember what it felt like to be so young.

"They were unique," Ellen said. "I think most of us weren't even out to ourselves at that age. It wasn't like it is now. When we were kids, most of us didn't even know lesbians existed."

"It helped that we found each other early on," Inez agreed.

"How old are the baby dykes?" Kendra asked, using the lingo like an expert.

"Catherine's twenty-two," Patsy said, passing the photo to Grace. "Most of the team's about that age."

"Except Bennie," Van said. "She's twenty-eight."

Patsy took another drink of beer and tried not to care that Van knew exactly how old Bennie was.

Kendra sighed. "I wish I'd been a baby dyke. I'm thirty-nine. I suppose that's too old?"

Inez laughed. "You're just a baby to me, sweetie, but you're too old to be a baby dyke."

"You can be a Barbie dyke, though," Patsy said, and everyone laughed.

Chapter Five

Jill — 2008

"I MADE A mistake," Jill said, lowering herself onto the love seat.

"A *mistake*?" Van asked. "I disappear for twenty years and you call it a *mistake*?"

Jill squared her shoulders and met Van's ire head on. "I'm sorry."

Kendra sat next to Jill, almost but not quite touching. "She's paid a heavy price."

"She has, has she?" Van said, harshly sarcastic. "It seems she's not the only one." She rose and paced the room, while Kendra and Jill watched.

Although she'd always believed Van would reappear one day, Jill still could not get over the *realness* of Van, right here in her tiny house, exactly as she'd been twenty years before. Even her clothes were the same. The guilt Jill had lived with for the last twenty years reasserted itself as Van paced miserably in front of her. But at the same time, she felt a small guilt-laden spurt of pride at what she had done. She sent Van into the future, and here she was, apparently none the worse for it. She was upset, of course, but the vigor, the health, the energy of Van was obvious as she prowled the room, touching and picking up random objects.

"My God, Jill, it wasn't supposed to really *work*. I thought you were just testing measurements, weights, densities, that kind of thing. I thought you were getting ready so that someday — *someday* — you could try it for real. What happened?"

"I knew I was getting close," Jill said. "But I didn't think it was capable of working yet. When we opened the door to RIP and you weren't there, I thought — I couldn't believe it. I knew there wasn't anywhere to hide, no other way out of RIP, but I hoped you were playing a joke on us or something. I couldn't believe it actually worked."

"And, of course, it didn't," Van said pointedly, glancing over her shoulder from where she'd been randomly punching buttons on Jill's dead laptop. "Since I didn't come back."

"She always believed you'd show up someday," Kendra said. "That's why she bought this house and had that sign put up out by the road. She didn't know *when* you'd show up, but when you did, she wanted to be here to help you."

Van came over and sat in the chair opposite them. "Where's Patsy?"

Unsure how to answer, Jill glanced at Kendra, who shrugged uncertainly in reply.

Their momentary silence made Van wary. "What is it?" she asked, as if bracing herself for bad news. "Is she dead?"

"No, no," Kendra said quickly. "She's not dead."

Van looked from one to the other. "Then what is it? She has a girlfriend? Is she married? Crippled? Demented? *What?*"

"No," Jill said. "Nothing like that."

"I want to see her," Van said firmly. "Where does she live?"

"Deer Park," Jill said, naming a town no more than twenty minutes away.

"I want to see her," Van said, stubbing out her cigarette and standing again.

"It's getting late," Kendra said. "Tomorrow would be better. After we've all had a good night's sleep."

Van glanced at the clock. "It's 8:35." She gestured toward the window that showed the June sun still shining in the western sky. "It's too early to sleep. I want to see her. Don't worry, I can take it."

"It's not you I'm worried about," Kendra said. "Do you want to give the woman a heart attack? She doesn't even know you're alive. You can't just go waltzing in out of the blue. You could kill her."

Van crossed her arms in front of her chest, unsympathetic. "Call her."

"That's not phone news," Kendra argued, but she stood and plucked her keys from where she had dropped them on the counter. "At least let me go over first and warn her. Give me a half hour. Jill? Wait a half hour, then bring Van over to Patsy's, okay?"

"Okay," Jill said, relieved to have Kendra make the decision for her.

"It's her birthday," Van said as Kendra reached the door.

"What?" Kendra asked.

"Patsy. It's June 25th, right? Today's her birthday. Her seventieth. Just so you'll know."

Kendra nodded and left. Van shook out another cigarette as Jill watched. Jill noticed Van's fingers shook as she lit the match. She tried to imagine what Van must be feeling, but it was impossible. How did one cope when transported without warning twenty years in the future? Van seemed to be holding up very well, so far, though Jill didn't think she truly understood her situation. And, of course, she hadn't seen Patsy yet.

"Who took that picture?" Van asked, pointing to the 1998 photograph of the three women on the boat.

Jill was relieved. She'd been afraid Van would want to talk about Patsy, and Jill wasn't sure what she would say. "Grace."

"Grace? The same Grace who came to Patsy's party?"

Jill was momentarily surprised before she remembered that, of course, Van couldn't know. "Yes. She and Inez fell in love. They were together for fifteen years."

"Wow. That's a long time. Did they break up?"

"No. Grace died. Breast cancer."

After a moment, Van said, "Poor Inez."

"Not really," Jill said. "They were happy together for a long time. I think Inez would say she was lucky."

Van fixed her gaze on Jill, as if truly seeing her for the first time since her arrival in 2008. "What about you? Do you have someone?"

Jill laughed and shook her head. "No, not me. You know I'm not a relationship person. And I'm old enough now not to have to try anymore."

"You're not that old," Van said, but the words sounded hollow and foolish in the face of the sudden twenty-five year difference in their ages.

"I've been blessed with good friends instead," Jill said. "Inez and Patsy and Kendra."

"Yeah, what's up with Kendra? Last I knew, she was dating Inez."

"*Inez?* Oh, that. No, they didn't last beyond that one night. There was never really anything there. But Kendra was amazing, the night you disappeared. She was like a rock. Everyone was so upset and worried, no one could even think straight. She's the one who talked to the police, organized search teams, made sure we ate and slept. We all knew you weren't lost out in the woods, but it made us feel better to be doing something to try to find you. So we searched."

"Why didn't you try to bring me back," Van asked peevishly. "If you were so sure I was in the future, why didn't you search *there?*"

"I tried," Jill said, "for a while, anyway. But then the police confiscated RIP. And it didn't matter anyway, because I didn't know how to do it. It was never supposed to work the way it did."

"Yeah." Van smoked silently a moment. "Did Kendra ever figure out if she was gay?"

Jill had to smile. "Kendra's dated a lot of people. Men and women. She used to say she was bisexual. Now she just calls herself sexual."

Van smiled. It was the first time Jill had seen her smile in twenty years. It was a weak smile, but Jill was heartened by it.

"What about Waverly?" Van asked. "She was dating Grace."

"I think I heard she moved to Seattle or Portland, somewhere over there. A job or something took her there."

"Probably a woman, if I know Waverly. What about Ellen and Terri? And Michael? Did he get all screwed up from having two lesbian moms?"

"They're still together. They're a legend in the community. Twenty-seven years. And Ellen's a whatdoyoucallit, a state representative."

"No kidding?"

"Yeah. She's trying to get same-sex marriage passed."

"Still?"

"And Terri's stone cold deaf."

"Did Michael grow up queer?"

"I don't think so, but who can tell these days? Kids go around in groups, boys and girls together, and you can't even tell who likes the girls and who likes the boys. He likes math, though."

"Math?"

"Yeah. He wants to be an accountant, I think. It's a big disappointment to Ellen. She thought he'd change the world, I guess."

"Interesting." Van sat playing with her cigarette box nervously, and Jill suspected she was thinking about the one person they hadn't caught up on yet, but she didn't ask. Finally, thirty minutes had passed, and it was time to go.

Jill's car was a shrimpy white Ford Festiva. Van strapped herself in. "I think I recognize this car. Isn't this Inez's car?"

"It was," Jill agreed. "She sold it to me years ago. It's old, but it runs, and it gets great gas mileage."

"Shouldn't cars be running without gas by now? Or flying, like on *The Jetsons*?"

"Some do," Jill said.

"Cars *fly?*"

"No, I mean they can run without gas. Some use electricity. I don't know of any cars that fly."

Jill pulled out of the driveway, onto the short gravel road, then onto a paved street that hadn't existed twenty years ago. Van sat silently inspecting the landscape passing by.

Though already dusk, it was the best of the warm early summer weather. People were out walking, jogging, or biking along the sides of the road. Two boys raced by on motorized scooters, and Jill saw Van turn her head to watch. Many people wore iPods strapped to their arms, or spoke into headsets wrapped around their ears. Jill wondered what Van made of it all, if she even noticed, or if she was lost in thoughts of 1988, or of Patsy.

At a sudden vibration in her pocket, Jill grabbed her earpiece from the dash and tucked it into her left ear. She pushed the button. "Hello?"

"It's me," Kendra said. "Are you on your way?"

"Yes, we're a couple of minutes out."

"Okay. I did the best I could here. There's really not a whole lot we can do. How's Van?"

"Fine. Real quiet, though."

"She's got a lot to think about."

"Yeah."

"We're as ready as we're going to be. See you in a few."

"Okay. Bye."

Jill glanced at Van to find her staring at her open-mouthed.

"Who are you talking to?" Van demanded.

"Kendra. On my cell." She quickly pulled the earpiece from her ear and handed it Van. "It's an earpiece. For talking on the phone."

Van examined the tiny device for a moment, turning it in her hands, and passed it back to Jill, her jaw clenched.

Moments later, Jill pulled into a trailer park on the outskirts of Deer Park and guided the Festiva to a bare spot of dirt in front of a shabby single-wide. The strip of grass alongside the trailer was full of weeds and needed mowing. Jill climbed out of the car, and Van followed, pale and quiet. Jill led the way to the rickety steps that led to Patsy's door and knocked. An overflowing cat box was shoved to the wall beside the door, and they both stared at it silently while they waited.

Finally, the door opened and Kendra stood there, more frazzled than when she'd left Jill's house. Her face was red and damp, and her blond hair stuck out at all angles from her face, a few tendrils stuck to her cheek and the back of her neck. But she smiled a welcome. "Come in," she said. "Patsy's expecting you."

They entered. Patsy sat on the couch. Steel gray hair, still wet, was slicked back, and she wore a crumpled terrycloth robe. The smell of shampoo and soap hung in the air and confirmed that Patsy had just emerged from the shower. She saw Van and her eyes widened. She tried to rise, but halfway up she lost her momentum and fell back on the couch. Her eyes were red and watery, her skin pasty white. She stared at Van with a look of hope, fear, despair, and love. Her chin quivered, and the jowls on both sides of her face wobbled. Tears sprang to her eyes. She tried to rise again, still off balance, but Kendra helped her this time, and she made it to her feet.

"My baby," Patsy whispered. "Oh my Van, you came back!" Tears coursed down the wrinkles in her face as she reached for Van.

Van stepped forward and let Patsy fall into her arms. She staggered a moment under Patsy's weight, got her footing, and held her firmly. Over Patsy's shaking shoulder, Van's eyes, wide and dark with shock, flitted rapidly from Jill to Kendra and back again.

Along with the fresh smells of shampoo and soap and toothpaste and coffee were older, more firmly entrenched odors. Spoiled food, dirty clothes, cat urine, and, overriding it all, the strong and sour smell of stale alcohol. There was no point in trying to hide the truth from Van. Even after Kendra's hurricane attempt, it was still obvious.

Patsy was stinking drunk.

Chapter Six

Van—1988

INEZ AND GRACE sat in the hot tub, holding a subdued conversation that couldn't be heard over the jets. Waverly wandered back and forth between the hot tub and the women on the deck, reluctant to get into the hot tub, but equally reluctant to allow Grace's attention to be diverted from her to Inez for even a moment.

"For God's sake, Waverly, land somewhere, will you?" Patsy asked. "I give you my word, if Inez jumps Grace's bones right there in that hot tub, I personally will leap in there with all my clothes on and drown her."

Waverly smiled and reluctantly sat in the deck chair Patsy held out for her.

"You don't see Kendra all worried that her date's sitting in the hot tub with another woman do you?" Patsy asked, nodding toward Jill's camper, where Kendra was helping Jill prepare for the evening's experiment. "And Van wouldn't even let them get in naked."

"I know," Waverly said. "I'm not worried, exactly. It's just, I don't know, all I can think about is Grace, like that's all there is in my mind. Yet she's perfectly happy talking to Inez and not even thinking about me. It's not fair."

"Maybe they're talking about you," Van suggested, and Waverly raised her brows in interest.

"But probably not," Patsy said, squelching Waverly's hopes. "Come on, Waverly, do you really want a woman who can't think of anything but you? No offense, but you're not that interesting. You keep dating these highly intelligent women, women like Van here, women who've spent their whole lives thinking deep and interesting thoughts, and you want them to stop thinking them because they're dating *you*? It's not going to happen."

Van smiled, enjoying Patsy's mood. Her delivery might be brusque, but there was no arguing with the wisdom of her words.

"Besides," Patsy said, "it's not true that you can't think of anything else. You're thinking about your beautiful hair right now more than anything else. Otherwise you'd be in that water with Grace instead of sitting here whining to us."

"But we're going line dancing later," Waverly wailed, running her fingers through her luxurious curls. "Do you know how long it took me to get it like this?"

"She's right, though," Ellen said. "Van, when you dated Waverly, did you think about her all the time?"

Van laughed. "All I could think was, 'Oh my God, I'm dating a woman.'"

Waverly shook her head mournfully. "Never be anyone's first. *Never*. They use you for sex, figure out that they really do like women, then dump you and go find a 'relationship.'"

Ellen laughed. "That's quite a compliment. One taste of Waverly, and they never go back to men."

"Besides, someone's gotta break 'em in," Patsy said. She grasped Van's hand and kissed it. "And I, for one, am very grateful to you."

"Glad I could oblige," Waverly said sourly, then pointed her nose into the air like a hound that caught a scent. "The baby dykes are here!"

They listened and heard the roar of a motorcycle approaching. Van felt Patsy's grasp on her hand tighten and let go. They stood.

Kendra ran up from the tree line where the camper was parked. "Jill says remember not to talk about RIP around the baby dykes. It's a secret." She darted to the hot tub, where Inez and Grace were climbing out, and repeated her warning.

In addition to the motorcycle, now they could hear car tires popping on gravel.

"Catherine better not be on that bike," Patsy growled. They all moved off the deck and around the hot tub to the side of the house to where they could see the new arrivals.

Van watched Bennie pull up on the motorcycle, turn off the motor, and tap the kickstand down with her toe. A young woman in tight denim cutoffs rode on the back of the bike, arms wrapped tightly around Bennie's middle, though the bike had stopped. Bennie removed her helmet, ran her fingers through her short black hair, grasped the woman's hands, and loosened them from her midriff. The woman on the back, who was not Catherine, slipped off. Bennie swung her long denim-clad leg over the bike and stood for a moment. She squinted at the women coming around the house, then bent to pet Sadie, who danced around her legs.

A rusty, beat-up Toyota rattled to a stop behind the bike. Catherine leaped out of the passenger side. She was tiny, no more than five feet tall and a hundred pounds. The smallest softball shirt was still big on Catherine, and the cuffs of her shorts barely showed beneath its hem. She spied Patsy coming around the house and ran toward her, a fat brown braid flapping against her back like a tail. "Happy Birthday, Mama P!" She threw herself at Patsy, flung her arms around Patsy's neck and wrapped her legs around her waist, like a little kid. She planted a loud smacking kiss on Patsy's cheek.

Patsy's face lit up in laughter, but she said, "Goddamn you, Catherine, I'm fifty fucking years old now. You can't keep jumping on me like I'm a jungle gym."

"As soon as you stop catching me, I'll stop jumping," Catherine said, sliding to the ground. "Hi Van." She gave her a hug too, then Inez, Jill, Waverly, Ellen, and Terri, and finally, when only the strangers remained unhugged, she introduced her friends. "Most of you have met Bennie and April and Donna, and this is Wendy."

Van tried hard not to notice Bennie's gaze on her. It wasn't easy. Bennie was very attractive. She called up a picture of what Patsy must have been like at that age. At five ten, she was two inches taller than Patsy, but they were both slim, athletic, arrogant, and the center of attention in any gathering of women, including straight ones. Bennie had the black eyes and dark skin of her Mexican heritage, though, and thick black hair cut short. Her features were stronger than Patsy's, her jaw more angular, her nose more sharply defined, even her forehead more chiseled, reminding the onlooker that a skull lurked beneath her skin.

Van had met April and Donna before, but Wendy, the woman who'd ridden behind Bennie, was new to her. Unlike the other women, she didn't wear the red and white uniform t-shirt.

"Wendy's our groupie," Catherine announced unapologetically. "She comes to all our games. Came, I mean. There won't be any more, because we lost the tournament. Yeah!"

"Congratulations," Van said.

"Thank God you weren't on my team," Patsy said. "We used to play to *win*."

"Didn't they play softball half court when you were young?" Catherine asked, eyes wide.

"That was basketball, not soft—" She broke off when she saw Catherine's face. "You little bitch. I ought to put you over my knee. You're not too big for a whipping, you know."

"But it's *your* birthday. I promised everyone they could spank *you* today." Catherine lunged for Patsy's back side, and a wrestling match began, members from both generations joining in.

Van took the opportunity to slip into the house to retrieve the cake from the kitchen. She gathered additional plates and forks for the softball players and tried to juggle them with the cake balanced on top. She turned toward the dining room and stopped abruptly. Bennie had followed her in.

"Let me help you with that," Bennie said, taking the cake from Van's arms.

"Thank you." Van moved toward the door, but Bennie stood in the way and she didn't move. Van raised her eyes to Bennie's and was jolted.

Bennie stared at Van, her dark eyes gleaming. Her eyes traveled over Van's face, resting on her eyes, then her lips, which Van ordered herself not to lick. But she forgot to order herself not to sink her teeth into her bottom lip, which she did as Bennie watched. Bennie smiled. Her eyes moved down to Van's neck and chest. Van swallowed nervously and glanced down. The loose bib of her overalls did nothing to hide the cleavage created by her snug, low cut sweater.

"You are so hot," Bennie said softly,

Van caught her breath. "Don't."

"I haven't done anything," Bennie said. "Yet."

Van closed her eyes briefly, but when she sensed Bennie leaning toward her, she opened them and took a step back. "Don't," she said again, more firmly. "You know I'm with Patsy. We're partners. We're committed to each other. Like if we were married."

Bennie leaned one shoulder against the door jam, still balancing the cake, and assumed a challenging expression. "How many women were you with before Patsy?"

Van frowned. "That doesn't matter."

"Of course it matters. How many?"

"It's none of your business." Van grabbed a handful of paper napkins and added them to the stack of plates. "And it doesn't change anything. I'm committed to Patsy." She met Bennie's eyes and said sternly, "Bennie, you're just a kid. I'm forty-five years old. I'm old enough to be your mother."

It was Bennie's turn to frown. "Barely. And age doesn't matter, Van. You know that. Men date younger women all the time." With a little smile, she added, "And my mother is fifty-eight."

"I love Patsy."

"But you want me," Bennie said, so softly Van only knew she said it because she read it in her lips.

A burst of noise erupted from the living room as the birthday spanking wrestlers stormed in. Van moved forward, grabbed Bennie's arm and spun her around, put her hand in the middle of her back, and shoved her forward into the living room with the cake. Van followed and pretended she didn't notice Patsy trying to catch her eye.

The women shuffled chairs, thrust Patsy into the seat at the head of the dining table, and prepared to sing. Van stood next to Patsy and lit the five candles. As she blew out the match, Patsy grabbed her around the waist and pulled her onto her lap. Van normally resisted sitting on Patsy's lap, especially in company, but she sensed Bennie's presence was driving Patsy's need to assert some sort of macho possession, and since it was her birthday, after all, Van laughed self-consciously and let her. Someone's camera flashed. "Happy Birthday" rang out, with Catherine loudly singing that Patsy looked and acted like a monkey. Patsy leaned over and blew out the five candles. Everyone clapped and laughed. Van put her arms around Patsy's neck and kissed her soundly while everyone clapped and hooted again.

"Gift time," Catherine called out, pulling a wrapped package from behind her back.

Van got up from Patsy's lap and let her reach for the present. Patsy ripped the paper and revealed three compact disks. "Hey, did Van tell you?"

Catherine nodded, grinning.

"Van got me a CD player for my truck," Patsy announced. "It'll hold three CDs at once, and changes them automatically. Or it'll skip around from song to song if you want it to."

"Nice gift," Waverly said. "Those things are expensive."

Van peeked over Patsy's shoulder. "What CDs did you get?"

Patsy held them out at arm's length and reared her head back, squinting. "They make the print so goddamned small on these things."

"Here, old lady." Inez handed her a pair of reading glasses. "You'd better lay in a stock of these."

"Shut up," Patsy said mildly, taking the glasses and putting them on. "Let's see, Linda Ronstadt, oh I love her. Whitney Houston. What's this one?"

"That's a brand new one." Catherine bounced on her toes in her excitement. "Melissa Etheridge. She's a little different than what you're used to, but I think you'll like her. They say she's a lesbian."

"She is," Bennie said. "I saw her perform in a lesbian bar when I was in LA. She's hot."

"Really. Hm. Well, let's go hear it." Patsy stood and moved toward the door.

"But we haven't had cake," Van said. "And we have a CD player right here."

"It'll only play one CD," Patsy said. "Besides, I can smoke in my truck, just not in my *house*." She shot a scowl at Ellen. "Cake can wait." She blew a kiss at Van and stepped out, followed by the rest of the party.

Van started to follow too, but Bennie moved to block her path. Van raised a hand and shot her an unyielding look. "Don't," she mouthed, barely shaking her head. Bennie hesitated, pressed her lips tightly together, and stepped back to let Van pass.

Chapter Seven

Van — 2008

VAN WANDERED THROUGH the dark, silent trailer, occasionally picking up an object, examining it, and putting it down again. She was intrigued by some of the modern objects, like the music player that was the size of a credit card and a camera that let her take a picture and instantly showed her how it turned out on the back. But she was more fascinated by some of the older objects, especially those she recognized.

She stroked the porcelain cat with the pouting face that she and Patsy had bought in Portland one spring. Patsy said it looked like Van when she didn't get her way. A stained-glass tulip hung in a window. Van had started making it in a class she'd taken three weeks earlier. She hadn't quite finished it, but someone had. Van's rough soldering around the pink petals was childlike compared to the much more competent job someone had done completing it. The bookshelf where Patsy kept her CDs was familiar, though more battered than when Van had last seen it. Van skimmed the titles on the CDs. Many names were unfamiliar, of course, but several she recognized. The Melissa Etheridge CD Patsy had received for her birthday twenty years ago, or three hours ago, depending on how you counted, was there, but had been joined by several others by the same artist. Apparently being a lesbian, if she really was one, hadn't stood in the way of Melissa Etheridge's success.

But the one thing in the trailer Van kept coming back to again and again was Patsy, asleep in the bedroom. She was drawn repeatedly to the bedroom doorway to watch Patsy sleep. She was so much like *her* Patsy, and yet she was so different.

Not long after Van and Jill had arrived, the effects of Patsy's hasty shower and quickly consumed coffee had worn off, and Van had helped Jill and Kendra get her to bed. Patsy wept as Van pulled the covers up to her chin, and she grabbed Van's hand.

"Don't leave me again, Van. Please don't leave me."

"Hush," Van said. "Go to sleep, Patsy. I won't leave. I promise."

And she hadn't, despite Jill's and Kendra's urgings that Van spend the night at Jill's.

"She won't remember that you promised to stay," Kendra said.

"She might not even remember you were here," Jill pointed out prosaically.

"You need to be thinking of yourself right now, Van," Kendra said. "You need to be with someone who understands what you're going through. Patsy's too, uh, distracted right now to think about your feelings. Besides," her eyes skimmed the room, "look at this place."

Van did look. The quick brush-up Kendra had given the rooms before their arrival had merely masked the filth at first glance. When Van assisted Patsy to the bedroom, she'd seen piles of clothes, both clean and dirty, some stained with cat urine, on every surface and the floor, and the sour sheets clearly hadn't been washed in months. In the kitchen, dirty dishes were piled everywhere, many of them with rotting food on them, and the garbage overflowed into a mound on the floor. Van was repulsed.

But this *was* Patsy. Only two years ago they'd made private vows, the closest they could get to marriage, to love and cherish, for richer or poorer, in sickness and health, 'til death would they part. There wasn't anything in there about twenty-year time leaps, but still. She *loved* Patsy. She'd insisted that very thing to Bennie earlier in the day — twenty years ago — and she'd meant it. Twenty years may have passed for Jill and Kendra and Patsy, but not for Van. How could she go away to stay the night with Jill and leave Patsy all alone? She couldn't do it.

Reluctantly, Jill and Kendra left. Van found some rubber gloves and began to clean. There was no dishwasher, so she filled the sink with suds and washed the dishes by hand. When she went to put the dishes in the cupboard, Van found three bottles of rum, one half empty. Beside the back door three more empty bottles lined the wall. She gathered the garbage and the empty bottles and stepped though a covered back porch and out of the trailer to locate the dumpster. She hadn't seen the cat yet, and she scanned the area for it as she dumped the trash.

The trailer park was located on the edge of Deer Park, off a busy highway and down the street from a grocery store with a neon sign that flashed "Lotto." Across from the trailer park was a vacant strip mall with an immense parking lot and a string of blank windows. After the beautiful solitude of their house in the woods, the trees, the river, how could Patsy stand to live here? Van took a deep breath and longed for home, but instead she re-entered the trailer.

She went to the bedroom door again. Patsy lay on her back, her mouth open in a snore in a way that was very familiar to Van. The slackness of her neck and chin were new, as were the dark pouches beneath her eyes and the deep wrinkles that fanned out from them. Although she'd fallen asleep instantly from the stupor of alcohol, Patsy slept fitfully, tossing and turning and mumbling in her sleep. But the perpetual frown wrinkles in her forehead had smoothed out a bit, and she seemed more at peace than when she was awake.

Van fought fatigue. It had been a very long day, starting with clearing the brush beside the house that morning so that people would have a place to park, cleaning the house, cooking Patsy's favorite dinner, baking the pineapple upside down cake, making love—twice, of course the party, the scene with Patsy and Bennie, and finally leaping over twenty years in time. It was no wonder she was exhausted. But she could not go to sleep.

The trailer was narrow and cramped. The rooms were laid out in a row, first the living room, then the kitchen and eating area, a laundry niche in the narrow hall, and finally the bathroom and the only bedroom. The back door off the kitchen led to an enclosed porch that had clearly been added on to the trailer after it was installed in the park. Patsy had it packed with boxes, broken furniture, bags of clothing, and a bicycle.

Although Van had slept by Patsy's side nearly every night for the last six years, she simply could not make herself climb into bed with Patsy tonight, and it wasn't because of the sheets, since Van and Kendra had changed them before they tucked Patsy in. No, it wasn't the sheets that kept her out of the bed, it was the stranger who slept between them.

Van stepped further into the bedroom, intending to confiscate a pillow and a blanket to take to the couch. A bevy of photographs on Patsy's bedside table caught her eye. The first one, and the largest, was instantly familiar to her, though she had never seen it before. In fact, it had been taken earlier that day, right after Van had lit the five birthday candles, and Patsy had pulled her onto her lap. Van was wearing the same overalls and sweater she had on now. She squinted and held the photo closer to her eyes. There it was, a speck of black pepper between her two front teeth. Van wasn't facing Patsy in the photo, and when the picture was snapped, she hadn't seen the tender look on Patsy's face as she smiled at Van. Glancing from that Patsy to the Patsy sleeping in the bed, Van wanted to weep.

Next to the photo of Patsy and Van were three heart shaped frames hinged together, and within each heart was the face of a child. A teenaged boy deigned to give the camera a tight, close-mouthed smile that didn't reach his eyes, a preteen girl flashed a smile filled with braces but her eyes were half closed, and a little guy about five years old looked like he just got out of bed, with a dazed expression and his hair sticking out at all angles. Van smiled. School pictures hadn't changed. Behind the school grouping was a larger family photo showing the three children arranged around Catherine and a serious paunchy man. So Catherine had finally figured out she was straight.

Van picked up the third photo, one that had to have been taken a few years after 1988. Patsy was older, but not as old as she was now. But what the *hell* was she doing with her arm around Waverly?

Van dropped the photo and left the bedroom. A better question was, what the hell was she doing in Patsy's home in the middle of the night? Patsy was a stranger. She'd spent the last twenty years of her life without Van, dating other women, getting older, becoming a grandma, becoming a *drunk*. Van was not a part of this life.

She wanted out. She was so tired, and she felt cheated. She should be home in her own bed, sleeping beside her own Patsy, in their own bedroom, in their own sweet house. Instead, here she was, virtually homeless, no place to lay her head except beside this stranger, no money, no car, *nothing*.

Jill and Kendra were right. She should not have stayed. Van stormed into the back porch and grabbed the bicycle she had seen there. Checking it quickly, she was surprised to find that the tires were fully inflated and the gears and brakes were in good repair. She wheeled it out of the porch, locked the door behind her, and threw a leg over the bar.

An hour later she braked the bike in front of Jill's house. She stood a moment on slightly wobbly legs and regarded the former garage. Lights from neighboring homes lit it up in a way that was unfamiliar. She was used to seeing the place in the shadows of surrounding trees, no light but that from the moon and the bit cast from her own back porch light. She turned to examine her house. A light was on in the addition that hadn't existed twenty years ago, and she heard the faint thrum of a bass coming from it. The rest of the house was shadowy and still. Van turned back to the garage, took a shaky breath, and knocked on Jill's door. After a long moment, the door opened and Jill stood there, clad in boxer shorts and a t-shirt. From the force of a pillow, one red cheek pushed upward as if she were smiling.

"You have to send me back, Jill."

Jill blinked and rubbed her eyes. "What?"

"You have to send me back," Van repeated. "This is ridiculous. I can't stay here. I've lost twenty *years*. I won't do it. You have to send me back."

Jill frowned with concern, but shook her head. "Let's talk about it in the morning. You need some sleep." She ushered her in.

Van was too tired to argue. She wanted answers, but even more, she wanted sleep.

"You take my bed," Jill said. "I'll sleep on the couch."

Van glanced at Jill's four-foot-long 'couch'. "No, you keep your bed. Give me some blankets and a pillow, and I'll bunk on the floor."

"No, take the bed. You're a guest."

"A guest who's twenty-five years younger than you are," Van reminded her. "I'll take the floor."

Jill couldn't seem to find fault with Van's logic, so she went to get blankets.

Several hours later, Van opened her eyes and saw feet. The two on the right were clad in bright orange rubber clogs, and the legs rising up out of them were tanned and ropy with long dark hairs erupting sporadically, as if they hadn't been shaved in years. The two feet on the left wore white leather sandals with sparkling rhinestones embedded in the straps, and the toenails were neatly trimmed, polished with an opalescent lime green sheen. The nails on the biggest toes were painted with miniscule palm trees. A colorful tattoo of a hummingbird was etched above the right ankle.

Van closed her eyes. She ran her tongue over her teeth, immediately aware that she hadn't brushed them the night before. How could she have? She didn't even have a toothbrush. Still without opening her eyes, she rolled over to her back, stifling a groan at her stiff muscles. She didn't know if it was from riding the bike from Patsy's, sleeping on the floor, or simply leaping through time, but she was *sore*. Her arms and legs felt shackled. She'd crawled in between the blankets fully clothed, and her overalls and sweater now uncomfortably constricted her limbs. And she didn't even have a clean pair of underwear.

She opened her eyes again and sat up. Jill and Kendra sat facing her, side by side on the loveseat, watching her anxiously, like parents of a newborn. Van expressed her most immediate concern. "Coffee," she croaked.

At her one word request, Kendra popped up and hurried to the kitchen. She wore a form fitting white t-shirt with green piping and a bug-eyed frog on the front, and matching lime green trousers cropped midway up her calves. While her breasts appeared more securely harnessed than they had in 1988, her body still called Barbie to mind. Her ash blond hair today was pulled into a very loose pony tail at the top of her head, with fat strands escaping and falling on her shoulders. Based on how meticulously coordinated Kendra was in all other respects, Van assumed the messy style was deliberate.

"Cream?" Kendra asked.

"No, black." In contrast to Kendra, there was nothing deliberate about Jill's appearance. She wore the same baggy, olive shorts she'd worn the day before, but now they were wrinkled as if they'd sat in a wad on the floor all night. Today she had paired them with a seersucker plaid blouse in shades of mauve and blue, which clashed garishly with both the shorts and the orange clogs. Her gray hair variously stuck out at odd angles or lay flat on her scalp, and Van could tell instantly it wasn't a deliberate effect. She suspected Jill had simply not given her appearance a thought that morning.

"How do you feel?" Jill asked, scrutinizing her with a clinician's eye.

"I have to pee," Van said, in what was becoming her stock answer to that question. She pushed herself up off the floor and went to the bathroom, peed, then foraged in the medicine cabinet for a tube of toothpaste. She squeezed a bit on her finger and rubbed it vigorously over her teeth. She ran her fingers through her hair and grimaced at herself in the mirror. She was scarcely better groomed than Jill, but it would have to do. She returned to the living room, took up the cup of coffee Kendra handed her, and sat in the rocking chair that faced the two women.

Van lit a cigarette, dismayed to see how few remained in the pack. She took a sip of coffee, then another, and let the caffeine and nicotine seep into her system before she spoke. Finally, she said, "Where's all my stuff?"

Jill raised an eyebrow and peeked at Kendra, who patted Jill's knee reassuringly. It was not the question they'd prepared for. "Your stuff?" Jill asked. "You mean, like..." She trailed off, as if unable to think what Van might mean.

"I mean my *stuff*. Where are my clothes, my books, my *things*. Where's my bike? Where's my *car*? What happened to all that stuff? It didn't disappear when I did, did it?"

"No," Jill said, her voice troubled. "It didn't disappear."

"So where is it?"

Jill looked blank.

"For a long time, your stuff all stayed right where it was," Kendra said, stepping in to rescue Jill. "It took a while for us to believe you'd really vanished. It was so hard to believe. We called the police and organized search parties. People came from all over, and we searched the woods for days. But when the police figured out they were dealing with a bunch of lesbians who were talking about time travel, they decided we were loonie toons. For a while, they even thought one of us must have killed you and created the whole RIP story as a cover up."

"Mostly they suspected me," Jill said, "since it was my machine, and the last time anyone saw you, I was closing the door on you and pushing a button. I think they thought I'd disintegrated you or something. But they couldn't find any evidence of it. Without a scrap of a body part, and no explanation for how I could have made you disappear, they eventually let me go."

"Let you go?" Van asked, surprised. "You were actually arrested?"

"Not arrested. Just 'questioned.'" But the distress on Jill's face, even twenty years later, confirmed Van's hunch that the 'questioning' had not been a pleasant experience for her.

Kendra patted Jill's knee. "They kept her for two days. They questioned Patsy too."

Jill said, "They thought, if I didn't kill you, maybe Patsy did. They learned about the fight that night, between Patsy and Bennie. About you."

Van winced. "It wasn't a fight," she said, but without conviction. That scene was still very fresh in Van's mind, and she wasn't comfortable with her own part in it. "How did they find out about it?"

"It came out in one of their interrogations," Jill said vaguely. Kendra looked self-conscious. "They took Bennie in for a while too. Their theory was that either Bennie killed you so Patsy couldn't have you, or Patsy killed you so Bennie couldn't have you."

"Finally they decided that you'd probably run off," Kendra said, "most likely with a man, which meant that you were the sanest one of all of us, as far as they were concerned."

Jill leaned forward, her elbows on her knees. "Patsy took it so hard. For a while she tried to believe you *had* run off, and she blamed Bennie for it."

Van wasn't ready to talk about Patsy. "So, what happened to my stuff?" But it seemed there was no leaving Patsy out of the telling.

"Patsy kept as much as she could," Jill said. "For at least a few years. But then she lost her job. She'd been drinking a lot, and—"

"But what about my money? I had a savings account, investments, a retirement account. What happened to all that?"

There was a long silence. Van looked from Jill to Kendra, but they avoided her eyes. Kendra's gaze darted about the room, lighting on nothing, while Jill stared at her lap. Finally, Jill spoke. "They declared you dead, Van. After seven years had passed."

Van felt a chill ripple through her. "So, Patsy? Did she—Did she get...?" But she already knew the answer.

"Patsy didn't get anything," Kendra said. "You didn't have a will, Van. Your mother and your brothers, they got everything."

Van shook her head in silent protest. Not her mother, not her brothers, not the people who'd tossed her out of their lives when they'd learned she was a lesbian. She'd rebuilt her life without them, she'd built her life with Patsy, and Patsy was the one who should have inherited, if anyone did. It was the ultimate irony, the lawyer without a will. Like the deck railing, she'd always meant to get to it. But it was especially bitter that her family inherited everything she owned, when she wasn't even dead.

"I need a toothbrush," she said abruptly. She rose and marched to the sink with her empty cup. "Do you realize I haven't brushed my teeth since 1988?" Her voice wobbled. "And I need something to wear. I need some clean underwear!" She was only beginning to understand the magnitude of her destitution. Not only had she lost her toothbrush, her clothes, and her car, but she'd also lost her home, her money, her job, even her life partner, the woman she'd expected to spend the next twenty years and more growing old with.

Van felt a sudden onrush of tears. She bolted for the bathroom, slammed the door, turned the shower on full blast, stripped, and stepped into the compact stall. She lifted her face and let her tears merge with the hot spray.

When she finally emerged to towel off, she had calmed somewhat. She saw that someone had placed clothing on the toilet seat. They had to be Jill's. Denim pants that were either very long shorts or very brief trousers, designed to hit just below the knee, a mint green t-shirt with a footrace logo on it, a blue sports bra, and a pair of white cotton briefs. Second-hand underwear. Yum. But she was a beggar, and she couldn't afford to be choosy. Jill was thin, but she'd always preferred loose clothing, which was a good thing for Van. The pants were snug through the hips and the sports bra barely stretched over Van's breasts, but the t-shirt was loose enough to cover any bulges that resulted from the too tight fit.

She ran a comb through her tangled wet hair. Somewhere between the shampoo and the rinse she'd decided there were two options before her. She could either remain in 2008 and try to build her life over from scratch, or she could insist that Jill send her back to 1988. Somehow. She set the comb down on the side of the sink and opened the door to confront Jill.

The day was warming up, and there was no air conditioning in the former garage. Jill had propped open the front door with a box fan on a chair to move air in, and she'd put an oscillating fan on a stand in front of the side door to move air out and create a cross breeze.

At the sink, mixing batter, Kendra glanced up and smiled.

"Feel better?" she asked brightly.

"Yes, thanks."

Jill came out of the bedroom with a duffel bag. "I'm gathering laundry. I don't have a washer or dryer here, but I can go to the laundromat and wash your clothes."

"Wait on that," Van suggested. "There's something else I'd like you to do."

Jill raised her brows in inquiry.

"I want you to send me back, Jill."

Jill shook her head slowly, dismay on her face. "Van, I can't."

"Why not? You sent me here. Why can't you send me back?"

"I tried, Van. I did everything I could think of, but nothing worked."

"No," Kendra said from the kitchen, "you haven't tried."

Jill gaped at Kendra in astonished betrayal. "Kendra, you *know* how hard I tried."

"I know how hard you tried to *bring* her back, but she wasn't here then. You've never tried to *send* her back."

A flash of anguish crossed Jill's face, and she shook her head again. "You don't understand. I don't *do* that any more." She swung toward Van. "After you disappeared, and I couldn't bring you back, I quit doing experiments altogether. They took all my equipment. They took RIP. I mow lawns for a living. I pet sit. I wash windows. I water people's plants. I haven't done a scientific experiment in twenty years."

"But honey," Kendra said softly, "you could try."

Jill's jaw dropped in surprise, but before she could respond, car doors slamming nearby caught their attention and they all watched the front door.

A slightly plump elderly woman stepped into the room. She had immaculately coifed silver hair and wore a crisp white polo shirt and tennis shorts. She gaped at Van with astonishment first, then pleasure.

"Oh, my God, it's true, you're really here!" She rushed over and threw her arms around Van. Van allowed the hug to last only a moment, then pulled away to examine the woman's face.

"Inez? Is that you?"

Inez laughed and wiped sudden tears from her eyes. "Yes, it's me. Oh, Van, it's a miracle. You look fabulous. And so young. Look at you!"

But Van stared beyond Inez to where Patsy hovered in the doorway, hands clasped and wringing. Her eyes met Van's, and she gave a tiny smile. A smile at once nervous, hopeful, and afraid. And sober.

Chapter Eight

Bennie — 1988

BENNIE FOLLOWED VAN into the garage. Patsy was already in the driver's seat, sliding the CD into the new player. Inez sat in the passenger seat, and Catherine perched between them with the gear stick protruding between her legs.

"I'm riding bitch," Catherine crowed.

"Looks like you're riding something else," Waverly said from the far side of the truck.

"Hey," Patsy said. "Don't talk that way around my...truck."

Wendy, April, and Donna climbed into the bed of the truck and leaned over the top so they could listen to music from the open windows. Bennie joined them and used her hip to shove Wendy to the side so that Bennie was on the left, behind Patsy. Wendy slipped her hand possessively into the back pocket of Bennie's Levi's. Bennie ignored her.

Van stood beside Patsy's open door, her hand resting on the edge of Patsy's seat. Bennie could tell, from the way Van stood so resolutely *away* from her, that Van was fully aware of Bennie standing over and behind her, only inches away. Normally Bennie had to sneak peeks at Van, pretending to make nothing more than friendly eye contact, and taking care not to let Patsy see how she felt about Van. Not that Bennie cared about Patsy's feelings. Patsy didn't deserve that much consideration, and she sure as hell didn't deserve Van. But because she cared about Van, Bennie was careful.

But now, from where she stood, no one but Wendy could see Bennie's face, and Wendy didn't matter. Bennie took full advantage of the opportunity afforded her, and let her gaze feast on Van. How could anyone be so sexy in overalls? The baggy denim hid more of her figure than it revealed, but it was snug enough at the butt cheeks to suggest their firm, round contours. The denim gapped loosely at the waist, and from her perch above, Bennie thought she could see inside where the white of Van's sweater ended and her flesh began. Bennie longed to jump down from the cab, slip behind Van, and slide her hands inside that gap for a feel around. Van's white sweater was tight, but because of the loose bib of the overalls, she could only catch glimpses of the shape of Van's breasts as she moved. The bib was hooked only on one side, with a strap hanging foolishly down Van's back. Bennie had always thought it was a silly style, but on Van it was adorable. She felt an impulse to reach down and give it a tug, like a schoolboy pulling a little girl's pigtail. Overalls, Bennie decided, were a damned flirtatious piece of clothing. Exactly like Van, come to think of it.

The clear and perfect sound of guitar strums came from the cab of the truck, followed by the low and slightly husky voice of Melissa Etheridge resonating throughout the garage. The women stilled as they listened, the voice from the CD player so clear, so close and intimate, it was as if each woman were being personally serenaded. Bennie had heard the song before, but she watched the faces of the other women as they heard it for the first time, expressions somber or woeful or puzzled, depending on whatever experience they brought to the music. The focus of Bennie's attention rested finally, as always, on Van. She couldn't see Van's face, only the top of her head, and the strawberry red hair that curled down to her shoulders. Bennie propped her foot up on to the edge of the truck, so that the toe of her shoe was no more than two inches from Van's shoulder. Why didn't Van look up? Surely she could sense Bennie there.

The second song sent the women rocking, and Patsy was so immersed in it she didn't even object to the bouncing of her truck. Then the third song came on, and Melissa Etheridge's voice crooned the words directly from Bennie's heart. When Melissa asked again if *she* could love you like *I* do, Bennie could stand it no longer. She inched her grass-stained Reebok forward and nudged Van gently on the shoulder, out of the range of Patsy's vision. Van raised her eyes steadily and deliberately, as if she had been waiting, and Bennie was more certain than ever that Van had been aware of Bennie's scrutiny all along.

"Does she?" Bennie mouthed silently.

Van's green eyes were wide, her moist red lips parted slightly, and her chest rose and fell as her breath quickened. More than anything, Bennie wanted to leap from the bed of the truck, grab Van into her arms, and spirit her away. Claim her, own her, take her like a caveman.

But Van was spared having to answer, and Bennie was spared from doing something foolhardy, when Inez erupted from the passenger side of the truck, tears streaming down her face, sobbing harshly. With a hand to her mouth, she pushed past Waverly, nearly knocking her down, before running out of the garage to get away from the hurtful song. Inez's date, Kendra, stared after Inez in dismay and slowly followed her from the garage.

Bennie peeked back at Van and saw that she had taken advantage of Bennie's temporary distraction to sneak out of the garage as well. Damn. The rest of the women appeared settled in to listen to the CD. Bennie reached behind her, pulled Wendy's hand out of her pocket, and placed it on top of the truck's cab. She quietly hopped down and slipped out of the garage.

Van was only a few yards ahead of her, heading toward the deck. Bennie quickened her pace to catch up, and when she was within reaching distance, she said softly, "That's going to be our song, you know."

Van spun around and looked past Bennie at the garage.

"Don't worry," Bennie reassured her. "She's still listening to the music. She didn't even notice I left."

Van glanced toward Jill's camper. Aside from Ellen, who was laying down with Michael, Jill was the only woman at the party who had not joined the group in the garage, preferring instead to tinker with her rig. Presumably she was inside the camper at the moment, as she was nowhere to be seen, and Kendra, who had not followed Inez after all, was half inside as well, with only her shapely pink-and-black-clad bottom protruding out the back door.

Bennie smiled. "They won't come to your rescue either, Van."

Van wheeled around and climbed the stairs to the deck. Bennie followed closely behind, and when they reached the top, Van turned to face her.

"Bennie," she said firmly, "you have to stop acting this — "

"Don't." Bennie cut her off sharply, then said, more softly, "Don't tell me what to do." She stepped closer, and Van took an involuntary step back. She was already at the edge of the deck, though, and had nowhere to go. The deck was only about four feet off the ground, but a tumble straight back from it could be nasty. She wobbled slightly at the edge, and Bennie grabbed Van's arms to keep her from toppling off. Van instinctively clutched Bennie's shoulders. Van met Bennie's gaze, and what she saw there made her gasp and lean farther back. Unfortunately for Van, the only way she could lean back and still maintain her balance on the edge of the deck was to change her center of gravity, which forced her to thrust her hips forward. Her pelvis pressed against Bennie's, and Bennie felt an electric jolt in her groin.

"I'm a grown woman," Bennie said softly, holding her firmly in place, not letting Van budge from her precarious and provocative position. "I'm not a kid. I've been on my own for a long, long time, and I've known a lot of women. I know when it's real, and what we feel is real." As she spoke, Bennie stroked her thumbs along the soft underflesh of Van's arms and felt her shiver.

"Look," Van said, slightly breathless. "I know we flirted. It was fun, and I enjoyed it. But I shouldn't have done it. I didn't mean anything by it, I swear."

Bennie gave a slight but deliberate thrust with her pelvis. Van gasped and clutched harder at Bennie's shoulders. Her pupils were huge, her green eyes nearly black. "I know you feel it too, Van. You feel me every time I come into a room. Why won't you admit it?"

Van said nothing, and Bennie gave another thrust, a thrust so slight it was barely more than a shared pulse. "Admit it," Bennie whispered.

Van sucked in a quick breath and stared into Bennie's eyes, mesmerized like a trapped rabbit, and said nothing. Bennie stroked her thumbs in circles, edging them underneath the short sleeves of Van's sweater, inching toward more sensitive skin. She gave one more tiny thrust with her groin.

"I—I admit it," Van gasped. "I admit there's...s...something."

"Something real."

Van closed her eyes, but nodded slightly. "Something real."

Satisfied, Bennie stepped back, mourning the loss of the groin-on-groin pressure, but consoling herself with the thought that it was only a matter of time. Van straightened and took a sideways step, rotating Bennie with her, so that she no longer stood on the edge of the deck.

Opening her eyes, Van said, "But just because we feel something doesn't mean we have to act on it."

"Something real," Bennie corrected her, keeping her hold on Van's arms even though she was no longer in danger of falling.

"Even for something real. We don't have to do anything about it. People could get hurt."

"You mean Patsy."

"Of course I mean Patsy. But not only her. It could hurt us too."

Bennie laughed, soft in sound, but hard in emotion. "No, Van, it'll hurt us if we *don't* act on it."

"It would be fun for a while. But there's no future for us together. We're too different. You're too young. I'm too old."

"It's only seventeen years. People do it all the time."

"*I* don't. I can't. I love Patsy, and I'm committed to her. This would be a—a fling. I'm not going to hurt her or throw away what I have with her just so you and I can have some fun for a while. I won't do it."

Bennie ground her teeth in frustration. What she felt for Van was more than a fling, more than just fun, but how could she convince Van of that? "You're not being fair. You admit there's something between us, something real. You felt it now, same as me. But you're going to deny me the right to love you because Patsy's *older?* That's not fair."

"It's not fair, but it's the way it is. It has to be."

"No, it doesn't. If you'll give me a chance to show you—"

"Well, happy fucking birthday to me."

They jumped apart. Van's face paled as she wheeled toward the bottom of the stairs. Bennie took her time, almost glad the moment had finally arrived. This wasn't how she would have chosen to do it, but at least something would happen now. It had to.

Because there, at the bottom of the stairs, with her face full of rage, stood Patsy.

Chapter Nine

Van — 2008

AS THEIR EYES held across Jill's living room, Van saw what she hadn't seen the night before when Patsy was drunk. It was truly Patsy gazing at Van from deep within her heart and soul. With instant recognition Van automatically smiled and advanced toward her.

Patsy visibly relaxed and her own smile became less nervous and more genuine. Van stopped in front of her, and Patsy raised a hand to softly stroke Van's cheek with the pad of her thumb. Van tilted her cheek into the palm of Patsy's hand. Patsy's gaze flitted from Van's eyes to her lips, her hair, her chin, her nose, as if she couldn't take it all in, that Van was truly standing there in front of her.

"My baby." Patsy's voice barely more than a whisper. "It's really you. You came back. You're alive!" She gently wrapped her arms around Van, held her in a tight hug, and rocked back and forth. "You're here."

Unlike the hug of the night before, which had felt more like the gropings of a drunken stranger, this hug felt like Patsy. Despite the fact that her body was different, that she was bigger around and softer, that her belly protruded and pressed against Van's, that her arms lacked the vigor they'd exhibited in hugs of the past, despite all that, it was Patsy, and Van melted into her as she always had. She closed her eyes and absorbed the feeling. They stood like that for a long moment, oblivious to their silent audience. When they finally broke apart, Patsy smiled and leaned toward Van to kiss her. Van pulled back.

A pained expression quickly crossed Patsy's face, but she recovered and smiled again. "Of course, you need some time to get used to me," she said, patting her hand on Van's shoulder. "It's been twenty years, after all."

"No, it's only been a day."

Patsy appeared taken aback, but said vaguely, "Of course."

"Have you eaten?" Kendra asked. She stood at the counter with a hot griddle in front of her. "I'm making pancakes. Wheat germ pancakes, with only raw honey for syrup, but it's the best I could do in this health nut's kitchen."

"No, we didn't eat," Inez said, perching on a stool at the counter, across from Kendra. "Patsy called me first thing this morning and told me I had to come get her, because Van was back. I thought she was crazy, of course, or—" Inez cut off her sentence, and Van suspected she was going to say, *or drunk.* But Inez recovered quickly and said, "Or had sudden-onset Alzheimers or something, but she insisted, so we didn't have time to eat. I barely had a chance to have a cup of coffee."

"There's coffee here," Kendra said. "Organic, but it tastes okay."

"Organic tastes *better*," Jill corrected. "And it's better for you."

"When did you become a health nut?" Van asked, grateful for the feeling of normalcy the easy banter created. Patsy sat on the left side of the love seat, and Van sat stiffly next to her, their shoulders and hips brushing. It felt both very familiar and foreign at the same time.

"I'm not a health nut," Jill said, bringing two cups of coffee from the kitchenette. She handed one to Inez and the other to Patsy. "But after you disappeared, I knew I had to take better care of myself. I knew you'd show up someday, and I wanted to be here when it happened. So I decided I'd better try to live as long as I could."

"And look at you now," Inez said. "You have the body of a sixty year old."

"And sixty *is* the new fifty," Kendra said.

Jill assumed the pose of a body builder, and everyone laughed.

Van lit a cigarette, and noticed no one else lit up. "Doesn't anyone smoke anymore?"

Heads shook. Inez said, "It's illegal now nearly everywhere except your home. You can't even smoke in bars anymore. And it's too expensive for people on fixed incomes, like us."

"Nearly five dollars for a single pack," Kendra said.

"You're kidding." Van held her cigarette out from her and stared at the smoke, dismayed. She only had a couple of cigarettes left and had been about to ask if someone could get her another pack.

Kendra brought over a tray table that she unfolded and set between the rocking chair and the love seat. "Of course, everything's gone up in the last twenty years."

"Houses, cars, food." Jill put a jar of honey and a dish of butter on the tray table. There was no room for five people to properly eat a meal in Jill's house, so they would have to make do with balancing plates on their laps.

"Everything's gone up except my pension," Inez said ruefully.

Patsy did not join in the conversation. Glancing sideways, Van saw Patsy's hand shake as she raised her coffee cup to her lips. Was she nervous? Hung over? As odd as it felt to be sitting next to a seventy-year-old Patsy, Van was relieved she was not sitting across from her, where she'd be forced to meet her eyes. Instead, she could watch everyone else.

The conversation curled around her. She knew they were trying to tell her how much things had changed in twenty years, something about a Hillary, an Obama, an Osama, nine-eleven, and Iraq. But Van was too preoccupied by Patsy's strange presence to listen. She watched Patsy's hands. She'd placed the coffee cup on the arm of the love seat and was running her hands up and down the front of her legs, as if wiping away sweat. Van noticed the nails were bitten and the cuticles were ragged and torn, evidence that Patsy had resumed her nail-biting habit, something she'd quit shortly after moving in with Van. Fragile long bones and prominent tendons on the backs of Patsy's hands created little tents of slack skin along the ridges, and age spots dotted the wrinkled skin. They resembled Patsy's mom's hands. Was Patsy's mom still alive, she wondered? She'd be ninety-nine years old, Van calculated quickly, and she'd already been frail at seventy-nine.

Van impulsively placed her hand over Patsy's nearest restless one. Patsy stilled and turned her hand over so that she could grasp Van's. Van lifted her eyes and was startled anew at how old Patsy was. She appeared to have aged more than twenty years and looked considerably older than either Jill or Inez.

"Is your mother still alive?" Van asked. The abrupt silence in the room suggested the women had merely been filling the space with words, waiting for Van to speak.

"No. She died in her sleep, the year after you left."

"I'm sorry." She wanted to add that she hadn't *left*, exactly. It's not like she *went* anywhere, time had simply shifted underneath her. Time is what had moved, not Van. It certainly hadn't been of her volition, and she resented the slight implication that perhaps it was

Kendra brought a plate of steaming pancakes over, and Jill followed with a stack of plates and a fistful of forks. Van took a plate and forked two pancakes onto it. She was starving. She shoveled pancakes, butter, and honey into her mouth. They weren't bad, for wheat germ. "Do you still have any of my stuff?" she asked, after she'd assuaged the worst of the hunger.

Patsy frowned, puzzled. "Stuff?"

"Yeah, my stuff. Like my clothes," Van said, thinking of her borrowed underwear. "What happened to my clothes?"

Patsy blinked. "I don't know. Jesus, it's been twenty years. I didn't think—"

Van regarded the group of women, who stared at her, perplexed.

"We didn't think you'd be coming back," Inez finally said. "Except for Jill, that is. She always insisted that you would."

"So you got rid of everything?"

Patsy said, "After you left—"

"I didn't *leave*," Van interrupted. "I didn't *go* anywhere. Stop saying I left."

Patsy's brow furrowed. "But what happened, Van?" she asked, truly puzzled. "Where have you been?"

"I haven't *been* anywhere." Van stood abruptly and stalked to the counter where she slid the plate with her half-eaten breakfast into the sink. She faced the four women, all but Jill seeming to expect an explanation. "All I know is, yesterday it was 1988 and Patsy's fiftieth birthday party. Yesterday you were all fifty years old, except for you," she pointed to Kendra, "you were in your thirties! Now you're all talking about pensions and fixed incomes and it's illegal to smoke, and I'm legally dead, and my entire life has disappeared over night. I don't have a home, I don't have a car, I don't have a job or any clothes or money. I don't even have a damn toothbrush."

"You can live with me, Van," Patsy said eagerly. "I can take care of you. I'll buy you a toothbrush. And I'll buy you some clothes. At least—" She broke off, her face reddening, "after I get my check, I mean. After the first of the month."

Inez said, "We'll all take care of you, Van. Patsy doesn't drive any more, but you can borrow my car whenever you need to."

"And my clothes fit you okay," Jill said. "I don't have anything fancy, but you can wear them until you can get some new ones of your own."

Van examined one aged face after another, each so eager to help her. But she couldn't be the indefinite guest and charity case for a group of senior citizens, which is exactly what they were. Except Kendra, but even she was nearly sixty. They were her friends, her peers, her lover, her partner, but they were old and she was not. Their offers to help only emphasized how little they had to offer.

"I gotta pee," she announced and ducked into the bathroom. She gazed at herself in the mirror, pondering what to do. She compared her appearance, surprisingly youthful all of a sudden, with those of her friends and lover in the other room. Chin still relatively firm, no creases around her lips, barely even any wrinkles around her eyes, skin smooth and unlined. To think, only a couple of days ago she'd examined herself in the mirror and thought she looked old. Of course, she'd been comparing herself to twenty-eight-year-old Bennie at the time. She grimaced, wrinkled her nose, and watched lines form in her face and disappear as she let her muscles relax.

Well, if Jill truly couldn't send her back to 1988, Van was going to have to find a way to live in 2008. She supposed she could take them up on their offers of help, at least until she could find a way to resurrect herself in the eyes of the law, reclaim the property that had devolved to her family, perhaps renew her membership with the bar and practice law again. But as for living with Patsy...

Van loved Patsy, of course she did. But that didn't mean they could pick things up where they'd left off. Even if Patsy weren't twenty years older, she'd still experienced twenty years without Van, twenty years that had to have changed her in ways unknown to Van. Patsy was a stranger. Van wondered if Inez or Kendra had an extra bedroom.

She pulled down her pants and sat on the toilet to find blood on her borrowed underwear.

"Fuck!"

She fought back tears. What were the odds she'd find a tampon under Jill's sink? Zero, it turned out, and zero in the medicine cabinet as well. She wadded up some toilet paper and shoved it in her underwear, flushed, and stormed out of the bathroom.

"Does anyone happen to have a tampon?"

Four blank faces met her question. Even Kendra, her last hope, merely shook her head apologetically. "Not for years, sweetie."

"Fuck, fuck, fuck!" Van stomped into the living room, pumping her arms in fury. "I can't live like this," she raged, tears spurting from her eyes. "I want my life back, I want some money, I want new underwear, I want some cigarettes! And I want a fucking tampon!"

"I have one."

Van wheeled around. A woman stood in the open doorway. Tall, in her mid-forties, with dark hair, dark skin, and black eyes that, meeting Van's, crinkled in a smile.

Van gasped.

"Bennie?"

Chapter Ten

Van — 1988

PATSY SLOWLY ASCENDED the stairs of the deck, her eyes fixed on Bennie. Van felt the blood drain from her face. Not like this, not this way, this was not how Patsy was supposed to find out about — well, there was nothing to find out, really. But if ever there were, this was not the way. Van would choose the time, the place, and it would *not* have been Patsy's birthday party.

"It's not what you think." Van stepped quickly in front of Bennie and spread her arms wide, like a defensive basketball player.

"Get out of the way, Van," Patsy said, never taking her eyes from Bennie.

"Yeah." Bennie put her hands on Van's shoulders and moved her aside. "Stay out of the way."

Van whipped around, but Bennie elbowed her off to the side. The two women faced each other, so similar and yet so different. Patsy's face was red with fury, Bennie's dark and defiant. They stood no more than five feet apart, their hands ready at their sides as if they were about to draw weapons.

"Oh, knock it off, both of you." Exasperated, Van stepped between the two women, one arm stretched out toward each of them. "What is this, showdown at the OK Corral?"

"Stay out of this, Van," Patsy warned. She swept Van aside with her arm, as if Van were nothing more than an annoying puppy.

"Don't you shove her like that!" Bennie yelled.

"Mind your own fucking business!" Patsy exploded, and as she did so, she charged at Bennie and shoved, hard. Bennie wasn't expecting it. She flew off the deck and landed on her back.

"Bennie!" Van ran to the edge of the deck and saw Bennie bounce up onto her feet, apparently unhurt. From the corner of her eye, she saw the rest of the party-goers emerge from the garage. Van wheeled on Patsy. "What the hell do you think you're doing?"

Patsy ignored her and instead roared down at Bennie. "Get the fuck off my property."

"*Your* property?" Bennie sneered. "Don't you mean Van's property? I'm not leaving unless *she* tells me to."

"You leave Van out of this."

Bennie's face showed outraged disbelief. "Are you crazy? Van *is* this. There's no way to leave her out of it. Tell her, Van."

For the first time, Patsy looked directly at Van. Van glanced from one angry face to the other, each equally expectant and demanding. For a moment, Van said nothing, but that brief moment was long enough for a flicker of doubt to cross Patsy's face. "Van?"

"Tell her," Bennie demanded again.

"You," Van said, pointing at Bennie, "get on your bike and go home. And you." She pointed at Patsy. "Stop overreacting. I told you, this is not what it looks like."

Patsy ignored Van's directive and simply glared at Bennie. "She told you to leave. Now get the hell out of here. Or do I need to help you?"

"Patsy!" Van said. "Stop it. You're drunk." She blinked back tears at the brutal words she'd thought many times, but refrained from saying aloud. "You're drunk. You don't even know what's going on."

"Don't worry, Van," Bennie said. "I'm leaving." She moved toward her bike, but stopped, whipped around, and pointed her finger at Van. "But you need to think about what you really want. Either piss or get off the pot." She stomped toward her bike.

Wendy emerged from the group of onlookers and caught up with Bennie just in time to throw her helmet on her head and her leg over the bike before Bennie kicked it into life and roared down the driveway.

As the sound of the bike faded, the silence it left behind became overwhelming. The women by the garage huddled in an awkward group, Kendra and Jill stood beside the camper, and Inez fidgeted on the path leading up from the river. They all stared uneasily at Van and Patsy, who stood silently on the deck not looking at each other.

Finally, Waverly spoke. "Did she say piss or get off the pot?" And the group around the garage erupted into nervous laughter.

Chapter Eleven

Van — 2008

VAN FELT FOOLISH, caught screaming and stomping her bare feet in the middle of Jill's living room.

Bennie didn't seem to mind, though. Her smile widened. "Welcome back, Van."

Patsy's face reddened. She struggled to rise from the love seat, gripping the arm of it to push herself up. "What the hell are you doing here? Get out."

Bennie glanced at her briefly, dismissively, then back at Van. She made a motion with her head for Van to join her and backed out the door. Van gently pressed her hand on Patsy's shoulder, pushing her back into her seat. "Don't get up, Patsy." She followed Bennie.

"Van!" Patsy's cry was an anguished plea, but Van was unmoved.

"I need a tampon," she said over her shoulder.

Outside, Bennie leaned against a low, sleek, dark green sports car. Van was struck by the change in Bennie. While the other women were inevitably the worse for wear after the passage of twenty years, Bennie had simply grown up, and it suited her. She was not the slender athlete of 1988, but she still moved with an athlete's grace and strength. She wore pressed khaki slacks and a white silky blouse, with a turned down collar and short sleeves. Her collar was open at the neck, where a silver and black pendant hung. Her black hair was cut close to her head in a style that emphasized and enhanced the shape of her face and head. Her jaw had firmed, and her strong, prominent cheeks had lost their youthful softness. She wore no makeup and was all the more striking because of the forthright simplicity. Her dark eyes gleamed as she watched Van approach.

The sharp gravel of the driveway bit into Van's bare feet, and she felt frumpy as she limped toward Bennie in her borrowed shorts and baggie t-shirt.

Bennie reached out and gripped Van's elbow to help her.

"You're barefoot. Here, sit down." She opened the car door and guided Van to the passenger seat.

Van sank down onto soft luxurious creamy leather. Except for the dashboard, which was highly polished dark walnut, practically the entire car was lined with leather, even the steering wheel and the gear shift knob. Tiny pieces of gravel fell from Van's feet onto plush cream carpet and she tried to hide them with her toes. "Nice car."

Bennie stood with one arm resting on the open passenger door, the other propped onto the roof of the car, and stared down at Van with bemusement. "Thank you."

"Does it use gas?" Van had sat automatically to relieve the pressure of her feet on the gravel, but now that she was sitting, with Bennie looming so closely above her, she felt a vulnerability that unnerved her.

Bennie laughed. "Of course it does."

"Oh. Jill said some cars don't any more."

Bennie shook her head, her gaze wandering from Van's face to her hair to her bare feet and back again to her face. "I can't get over you," she said softly. "I can't believe you're really here."

"How did you find out?"

"Kendra called me." Lines fanned out from Bennie's eyes as she smiled, reminding Van that Bennie had aged twenty years over night just like everyone else. She would be forty-eight years old now, three years older than Van. "She thought I deserved to know, since I was one of the suspects in your disappearance."

"I heard about that. I'm sorry. That must have been horrible, being questioned by the police."

Bennie's smile vanished. "It *was* horrible. But the police questioning was the least of it."

Van looked down at the polished dashboard, a bit overwhelmed, as always, by the intensity of Bennie's attention. "You...you said you have a tampon?"

Bennie leaned down to open the glove box in front of Van, her arm brushing against Van's breast as she did so. Bennie stilled, her hand frozen on the glove box. Her head swiveled and she met Van's eyes, no more than four inches away. Van caught her breath and froze, pinned against the luxurious leather with the force of Bennie's gaze. After a long moment, Bennie finally closed her eyes, took a deep breath, held it, and let it out again with a whoosh. Only then did she open her eyes. She smiled at Van, a normal friendly smile, the intensity gone.

"Yes, here you go." She straightened up and handed Van a small blue box she had retrieved from the glove box. "There are only a few there, but they should hold you for a while, 'til you can get to a store."

Van took the box. "Thank you."

Bennie shifted her feet but didn't step back to let Van out. "Where are you staying?"

Directly in front of her, through the windshield, Van eyed her beloved house. She glanced from it to Jill's garage house, and tried to quash the desolate feeling that came over her. "I...I'm not sure. I think, one of them — "

"I have a place you can stay," Bennie said, then added quickly at

Van's expression, "I have lots of room. You'd have plenty of privacy."

"I don't think I can —" Van broke off and peered anxiously at Jill's house, thinking of Patsy sitting inside. "I think I need to —"

"Hey, it's all right, Van," Bennie said soothingly. "Whatever you need to do. I just want you to know that I have a place you can stay, if you need one."

Van smiled at Bennie for the first time. "Thank you."

Bennie smiled back. "I learned two important lessons when you disappeared." She gently tugged a lock of Van's hair, still slightly damp from her shower. "The first was, never pressure a woman into making a decision she's not ready to make. That day, at your party, right here, in fact, though it's hard to believe it's the same place, I tried to pressure you into making a decision. I had no right." Bennie rubbed Van's curl between her finger and thumb, watching it somberly. "I was young, but that's no excuse. And then you vanished, and I didn't know what had happened to you. I thought you'd either run away or that Patsy had..." Bennie trailed off, shrugged, and dropped Van's curl. "I thought that if I hadn't pressured you so much, you'd never have disappeared like that."

"But that's not true. It was a fluke that Jill's machine sent me off to the future. It didn't have anything to do with you."

"I know that now, but I didn't know it then. So anyway, I don't pressure women anymore, for *anything*." She smiled. "I'm telling you that so you'll know you would be safe with me, I guarantee it. But it's entirely up to you. In fact..."

Bennie leaned down and opened the console between the two front seats. Van pressed herself back into the soft leather as Bennie brushed past her. She smelled faintly of citrus and flowers and sweat, intimate and stirring smells, and Van was relieved when Bennie pulled back and stood again in the open door.

"Here, take this. It's all the cash I have on me." She handed Van a fold of bills. Van hesitated, but recalled that she was truly impoverished and, judging from the opulence of her car, Bennie could well afford it. She took the money. "And here," Bennie said, writing on the back of a white business card, "here's my personal cell number." She handed to it Van. "If you need to get away from here, if you need a place to stay, or some money, a friend. Anything at all, Van, you call me. Any time of the day or night. Okay?"

Van nodded, tears of relief stinging her eyes. For the first time since arriving in 2008, she felt as if she was not completely bereft. Bennie was someone she felt she could depend on, someone who understood. It wasn't that the other women weren't willing to help. It was simply that they had so little to offer.

"Thank you." Van tried to smile.

Bennie brushed the back of her fingers along Van's cheek, then rubbed the start of a tear from the corner of Van's eye with her thumb. "Any time, Van. I mean it. Any time." She stepped back so Van could climb out of the car.

Van braced her feet on the gravel and stood. She started toward the house, but stopped and peered back at Bennie. "What was the second lesson you learned, Bennie?"

Bennie smiled ruefully. "I've learned to be careful with my words. Do you remember the last thing I said to you?"

Van smiled with genuine amusement. "Of course I remember. It was only yesterday, after all."

Bennie rolled her eyes. "Well, I've had to live with those words for twenty years. 'Piss or get off the pot.' Angry, manipulative, stupid words. They've haunted me. You never know when the words you say may be the last words a person hears from you, so I've learned to be careful with them."

"It turns out they weren't the last words, though, because I'm here now."

Bennie grinned. "Yes, you're here now, and I'm very, very grateful for that."

Van started again toward the house, shoving the cash and the card into the pocket of her shorts as she did so. She heard the car door close behind her and the smooth purr of the engine as Bennie drove off. Van didn't watch, but where the card nestled at her hip, she felt a warm patch of security that radiated out to comfort her. She opened the door to her former garage and went in.

When Van entered Jill's house, Patsy's face was a picture of tragic betrayal, but it soon transformed into one of relief and triumph when Van told her she intended to stay with her, for the time being anyway. She had to give Patsy a chance, and she had to give *herself* a chance, to see if their love could survive the twenty-year leap in time. What better way to find out than to stay with Patsy? Besides, her choices were practically non-existent. Jill clearly didn't have room for a guest of indefinite duration. Inez lived in a retirement community that did not allow guests, and Kendra's apartment was already crowded with her son, wife and toddler in tow, newly arrived home from military duty in Iraq. Van hadn't asked what the war was about. There was always a war.

Bennie, of course, was out of the question, even though she did say she had extra room. If Van chose to stay with Bennie, it would break Patsy's heart.

But the relief everyone expressed when Van announced her decision to stay with Patsy gave Van a sudden trapped feeling, as it emphasized that she truly had so few options. Bennie's card, snug against her hip, was all that kept her from lashing out in another tantrum. That's what she'd been indulging in, she admitted, right before Bennie's arrival, an all out, foot-stomping, arm-waving tantrum, like a two year old who didn't get her way.

She refused Inez's offer of a ride back to Patsy's. Van had to get Patsy's bike home somehow, and she welcomed the time alone. The bike ride from Patsy's to Jill's the night before hadn't been bad, so the ride back shouldn't be any more difficult.

She'd forgotten, though, that it's the day *after* an unconditioned bike ride that the effects are felt, particularly when sitting again on the bike seat. Patsy's legs were longer than Van's, too, and the seat was a good two inches too high. Van had been too agitated during her midnight ride to notice, but now the same pressure points hit her bruised pelvis, and she ended up riding nearly the entire twelve miles standing up on the pedals. The gentle rolling hills on the Deer Park Milan Road seemed to climb straight up as though she were riding to the top of Mount Spokane. Her legs quivered and her lungs burned, and every time she tried to rest on the seat, her sore butt prompted her to stand up on the pedals again. It was with profound relief that she finally saw a sign announcing Yokes Fresh Foods ahead on her right. She had nearly reached the Deer Park Trailer Court.

Van coasted through the busy parking lot of Yokes and found the bike rack practically hidden along the far edge of the building. She swung her leg over the bar and ordered it to stand straight, when all it wanted to do was collapse her to the pavement. She'd borrowed a spiral cord bike lock from Jill, and she used that to lock up Patsy's bike. Then, for first time since Bennie had handed it to her, Van took the wad of money from her pocket and counted it. Forty-eight dollars. She had no idea what forty-eight dollars would buy in 2008. If a pack of cigarettes cost five bucks, how much might everything else be? Van crossed her fingers and went into the store.

Inside the door, buckets of fresh flowers competed with giant bins of colorful fruit for her attention. The store was brightly lit and spacious and clean. Van was overwhelmed at first by the size and the bustle and the noise of the store. A constant pinging sound made her wonder if an alarm was going off, but no one else seemed disturbed by it. Finally she realized it was caused by the dozen or so cashiers sweeping products across a screen, each sweep setting off a ping. A young boy, perhaps ten years old, glided smoothly toward her as if he floated on air. How did he do that? She craned her neck down to peek at his shoes after he passed and saw a tiny wheel in the heel of the sneaker. She straightened and tried to squelch a spurt of envy. They'd never had anything so cool when she was a kid.

She located the bathroom first thing and peed. She nearly peed again when the toilet automatically flushed as soon as she stood. At the sink, there were no handles for the faucet. Van pushed and prodded at every spot she could find and had almost given up, when a little kid came in and thrust her hands underneath the spigot and water immediately flowed. The girl waved her hand at a wall dispenser and paper towels shot out. Van mimicked her movements and finally managed to wash and dry her hands.

Aside from the size and the noise and the bathroom, grocery stores hadn't changed a great deal in twenty years. There were certainly sights she found strange enough, like the large number of people talking as if to themselves, wearing tiny earpieces like Jill's, and the fact that there was an entire vending machine devoted to selling bottles of ordinary water for a dollar and a half each. Van had drunk water straight from the tap at Jill's, and she wondered now if she should have done that. Was tap water unsafe? Girls still wore tight clothing, toddlers still cried when they didn't get candy, the wheels on the grocery carts still wobbled, and the store intercom system still boomed out, "Clean up on aisle 12."

Van scanned the shoppers, searching for a familiar face, then realized she wouldn't be likely to recognize anyone even if she did run into someone she knew. Everyone had aged twenty years. She felt vulnerable at the thought that others might recognize her even though she probably wouldn't know them. Creepy.

Twenty minutes later Van emerged from the store triumphant, with a box of tampons, a six-pack of cotton underwear, toothbrush, toothpaste, deodorant, a plain white tank top, a plastic bottle of Diet Coke, and a Snickers bar. And she still had over twenty dollars left. She'd been tempted by a backpack that she could fill with all her worldly possessions, but the $17.99 price tag resigned her to a plastic shopping bag instead.

Before unlocking the bike, she took her purchases to a patch of grass beside the store, sat down, opened her soda and took a long drink, then unwrapped the candy bar and took a healthy bite. The sunny June day insisted that spring was indeed over and summer had arrived. Van stretched her legs out in front of her, leaned back on her elbows, tilted her face to the sun, and wrestled with herself.

She hadn't bought any cigarettes. At first, she couldn't find any, and she wondered if stores even sold them anymore. But they had to be available somewhere if Kendra had been able to bring her a pack. Finally, she'd found a puny rack behind a locked counter, and the only way to access them was to ask the woman at the register. Van peeked over the counter at the meager selection. They hadn't been kidding about the price. The cheapest pack she saw was $4.89, an outrageous price for what was clearly an off brand. Who knew when she'd get money again? Her last pack had lasted her less than twenty-four hours. She didn't normally smoke that much, but she'd been under an unusual amount of stress.

She was still under a lot of stress, she reminded herself, and it's never a good idea to quit smoking under those conditions. So she should go back in and buy a pack. Then again, if she spent too much of her remaining bit of cash on cigarettes, she'd only be adding to her stress, wouldn't she? She wouldn't have money for other things, and in the end she'd have to quit anyway, because eventually she'd run out of money and cigarettes and be under even worse stress than before. Of course, you never know what's going to happen in the future. Van had carefully saved money all her life, she'd worked hard and invested wisely, she'd purchased the house and all the acreage surrounding it so that it would remain untouched and pristine forever. And see what happened to it all? Her money was gone, her home belonged to strangers, her pristine wilderness destroyed, her investments dispersed among whatever remnants of family she had. What was the point?

Van popped the last bite of candy bar into her mouth, washed it down with Diet Coke, stood, brushed at the grass on her butt, and went inside. Moments later she emerged victorious with a pack of cigarettes. It would be difficult enough to get through the next few days with this strange Patsy, without craving nicotine at the same time. She opened the pack and smoked a cigarette before even unlocking the bike.

To carry her purchases, she rigged a makeshift backpack by stretching the handles on the plastic shopping bag and looping them around her shoulders. It wasn't optimal, but it worked. Van's legs had regained some strength from her rest and the infusion of sugar and caffeine, which was good, since her crotch was still too raw to allow her to sit on the bike seat for more than a few seconds at a time. She pedaled standing the remaining mile to the Deer Park Trailer Court.

Patsy was watching for her. She opened the door as Van wheeled up on the bike. "I was starting to get worried," she said, smiling and holding the door open for Van to push the bike through. She saw the bag on Van's back and her smile faltered. "You went shopping? I thought you didn't have any money."

There was no hiding it. "Bennie gave me some." She pushed the bike through the living room into the back porch and shrugged her shoulders out of the plastic bag backpack. "I needed some tampons." She emptied her purchases from the bag. "And some other things." She held up the toothbrush.

Thoughts warred on Patsy's face. Van had no doubt Patsy was resentful that Bennie was able to provide some necessities when Patsy herself could not, but there was simply no arguing with the fact that Van needed tampons, and Patsy could not get them for her. In the end, fairness won out over feelings, and Patsy smiled. "I do have toothpaste," she said, nodding at the pile of purchases. "You could have saved a couple bucks."

Van shrugged. "I didn't think about that."

Patsy moved to the stove, where a pot simmered. "Are you hungry? I made a tuna noodle casserole. I remember that you always liked it."

Van did like tuna noodle casserole very much, with homemade buttery cream sauce, chopped celery and onion, baked in the oven with seasoned bread crumbs sprinkled and toasted to a crisp shell on top. Van's mouth watered. She followed Patsy into the kitchen and peered into the pot Patsy stirred on the stove. It looked like boxed macaroni and cheese with a can of tuna fish mixed in. Van's mouth dried up.

"What I'd really like is to take a shower. But you can go ahead and eat, if you're hungry."

"No, no, I'll wait for you. You go right ahead. Lunch will wait."

Van grabbed her new treasures and retired to the bathroom. The shower felt marvelous, as did the clean underwear and tank top. Van stuffed Jill's stained underwear in the garbage, and repacked all her possessions into the plastic bag. She wasn't ready to lay them out on the bathroom sink. That would be too much like she lived there.

When Van emerged from the bathroom, the table was set. In appearance and smell, the trailer was in much better shape than it had been even when she'd left it the night before. Patsy had clearly been trying to clean it up. Van wondered if she'd been mistaken about Patsy having a drinking problem. Maybe she'd been drunk the night before because it was her birthday, or because it was the twentieth anniversary of Van's disappearance. Now that Van was back, perhaps Patsy would return to her old self. Then, as Patsy pulled the pot from the stove, Van noticed the glass of dark liquid in the glass at Patsy's elbow.

"You ready to eat now?" Patsy asked, grinning at Van over her shoulder.

Van nodded and pulled a chair up to the table. Patsy spooned a mound of the bright orange goo onto each plate and replaced the pot on the stove. "Do you want something to drink? I know you like milk, but I don't have any. I have some Coke. If you want something stronger, I can add some rum to it."

"I'll just have water. It's a little early for something stronger, isn't it?"

Patsy laughed. "Not today, it isn't. I'm celebrating. You came back!" She lifted her drink to Van as if toasting her and took a large swallow. "Ah, that's good." She filled a glass of water from the tap and carried it to the table along with her own glass.

Van accepted the water, took a sip, and said, "I didn't go anywhere."

"What?" Patsy asked, fork halfway to her mouth.

"You keep saying I came back, but I didn't go anywhere. So how could I come back?"

Patsy waved her hand in the air. "You know what I mean. You're here now, and if that's not a reason to celebrate, I don't know what is."

Van took a bite of macaroni and cheese. It was no tuna casserole, but it tasted better than she thought it would. "It's not really a cause for celebration for me, though." She felt a need to tame Patsy's mood. Patsy tilted her head inquiringly and Van went on. "Think of it from my point of view." She glanced at the clock on the microwave. 2:00 pm. "Yesterday at this time we were getting ready for your fiftieth birthday party, remember that? This time yesterday, I was making your pineapple upside down cake, and you were outside hacking down the weeds in the parking area. We had the music blaring because no one would be bothered by it. You came in to get cleaned up, and I joined you in the shower, because it was your birthday, after all, and we fell onto the bed soaking wet and made fantastic love, and then we had to shower all over again because we smelled like sex and our friends would all know what we'd been doing. Do you remember that?" Van could see from the wistful smile on Patsy's face that she did. "That was literally yesterday for me. Just yesterday."

Patsy put her fork down and laid her hand over Van's on the table. "I know, baby. This isn't easy for you."

"Not *easy*?" Van pulled her hand away, astounded by the gross understatement. "Patsy, I've lost everything. In one day. *Everything*. The house is gone. Have you seen what they did to our land? My job is gone, I have no money, and my beautiful fifty-year-old lover is an old woman who drinks hard liquor in the middle of the day. You expect me to celebrate *that*?"

Patsy had been nodding sympathetically at Van's outburst, but at that she stopped, stared in dismay at Van, and glanced at the nearly empty glass at her elbow. "This was just a little something..." She pushed the glass away from her with a finger, frowned, and looked up. "I've regretted so many times these past twenty years that I let you get into RIP that day instead of me. It was my turn. I was just being a big baby about not wanting to get in on my birthday. It should have been me who got sent away for twenty years, not you." She reached automatically for her glass, then quickly diverted her hand to pick up her fork instead, but she didn't eat. "I'd trade places with you if I could. In a minute, I would."

"It's not your fault I got into RIP. I wanted to do it. That whole thing with Bennie—" A tremor of Patsy's fork warned Van to go no further with that subject. "Besides, how would it be any better if you'd gone instead of me? I'd be the old one and you'd be the one in shock."

Patsy smiled. "You wouldn't be old. You'd only be sixty-five. That's just a baby." Van gave a little laugh that caused Patsy's smile to grow. "And I'd be fifty, so there'd only be fifteen years between us. That's not so much, not like now, when there's twenty-five." Patsy expression turned grave. "Twenty-five years. Is it too much Van?"

Van shook her head. "I don't know, Patsy. Honest to God, I don't know. I...I guess that's something we need to find out." She took a deep breath, determined to be honest. "I think we need to get to know each other again. You've lived the last twenty years without me. Who knows if we'll even like each other now?"

"Always so cautious," Patsy said, smiling. She laid her hand over Van's on the table, her eyes filled with loving wonder. "God, kid, you don't know how much I've missed you."

Van felt some of the hard tension in her chest ease. Patsy had always had the ability, at random moments, to make Van feel as if she were the most profoundly loved and cherished person in the world, and she hadn't lost that gift. Van was so frightened of being alone and adrift in this new century. She didn't know if she would remain with Patsy, she didn't know where she would ultimately land, but she did know now that she was not alone. She was loved.

Chapter Twelve

Kendra — 2008

AFTER SEEING VAN off on Patsy's bike, Kendra expertly gathered three cups in one hand and balanced four dishes, forks, and knives in the other, drawing on her many experiences as a waitress.

"You don't have to do that," Jill said, picking up the butter dish and honey. "It's my mess."

"It was my bright idea to feed the masses with such messy food." Kendra placed the dirty dishes in the sink and ran water until it turned hot. "Besides, Leslie works today and Kevin's home alone with Bridgette. If I go home, he'll saddle me with her and take the day off. He needs to get used to taking care of her himself, now that he's back."

"All right, then," Jill said.

As water filled the sink, Kendra wiped the counter and silently watched Jill maneuver chairs and tray tables across the floor, a furrow between her heavy brows. Kendra didn't think the furrow was caused by the exertion of moving furniture, and she wasn't surprised when Jill abruptly spoke.

"Did you mean that? About me sending Van back?"

"I did." Kendra turned off the water and dipped her hands in the hot suds.

Jill squeezed around Kendra to grab the broom from behind the refrigerator. She swept up dirt and crumbs from the kitchen, moved into the living room, and swept there as well before she finally spoke, standing in the middle of the living room with a dustpan full of crumbs. "What if I mess it up again?"

"If you manage to send her back, maybe you won't have messed up at all."

Jill's frown deepened.

Kendra continued rinsing plates and stacking them in the drying rack. "If you can send her back," she said smoothly, "Van won't have vanished."

Jill raised her eyes hopefully, but the furrow remained. "What if I make it worse than it already is?"

Kendra swiveled and leaned her elbows on the counter, hands dripping. "Jill." She waited until Jill met her eyes. "You owe it to Van to try. You have to at least try, honey."

Jill blinked with surprise. Kendra swung back to the sink, dunking measuring cups and spoons into the water. "How hard would it be to make another RIP? Are the parts hard to get?"

"I have RIP."

The heavy mixing bowl slipped from Kendra's hands into the sink, splashing water all over her legs and sandals. She hopped away from the sink and stared at Jill. "What did you say?"

"I said I have RIP." Jill carried the dustpan to the kitchen and reached around Kendra to dump the contents into the trash underneath the sink. She turned and faced Kendra, who stood dripping and open-mouthed.

"I thought you said they confiscated it."

"They did. They kept it for years. But eventually they called me and told me to come get my 'jalopy.' I guess it was taking up too much space."

"Where is it?"

"At a friend's place."

"Then let's go get it!" Kendra wiped her hands on a towel. "How far?"

"He's about three hours from here, but it doesn't matter." Jill followed Kendra out of the kitchen. "I can't send Van back in RIP anyway. It's not designed to send people *back* in time."

"That's not true," Kendra said, wheeling around. "At Patsy's fiftieth you said it could be done. You said you were only researching forward travel, but that traveling back was possible. All you have to do is research it."

Jill gaped at Kendra helplessly, her expression half hopeful, half scared. "It's not that simple. I haven't kept up. I haven't done any research in years."

"Then we'd better get started." Kendra pulled her keys out of her lime green purse. "Let's go get RIP. Do you want to drive, or shall I?"

Moments later, in Kendra's black Jetta, Jill said, "I need to make a phone call first to give him some warning, so he doesn't shoot us."

Kendra looked to see if she was kidding, but Jill was intent on scrolling through her contact list, and Kendra remembered that Jill didn't kid.

Kendra pulled out into the road and headed toward the highway. She tried to glean some information from Jill's side of the phone conversation, but it was typically short and to the point.

"It's me, Grover. I need to come up and get RIP. Don't shoot us, okay? Three hours... Huh? All right, but they'll be cold by the time we get there. Okay, will do." Jill hung up. "We have to stop at Zips in Chewelah and pick up a bacon cheeseburger and a tub of fries, with lots of tartar sauce."

"Who is this guy? Where are we going?"

"Grover used to work with me at the lab. He got fired too, after they found out he'd been slipping me materials for RIP."

Kendra had never learned the details of Jill's termination, which occurred shortly after Van's disappearance. "You smuggled materials out of the lab?"

"Well, I couldn't exactly pick them up at the hardware store. A lot of the materials were not legal for civilian use. How else was I going to get them?"

"I see. Of course you had to smuggle them," Kendra said, with an irony that was lost on Jill. "So where are we going?"

"He's got a place in the mountains up past Northport, right on the edge of the Canadian border. Secluded. Hidden. He's a little paranoid, but that doesn't mean they're not out to get him."

"Who?"

Jill regarded Kendra solemnly. "Everyone, according to him. That's the paranoid part. But they really were out to get him and me too, after they found out what we were doing."

"*Who?*"

"The Lab Rats. That's what Grover and I started calling them, after we got fired. 'Cause they're rats. Get it?"

"I get it. But how were they out to get you?"

"The police always thought that one of us killed Van, or that she ran away, but the Lab Rats always suspected more. When they learned about my part in Van's disappearance, and about RIP, they came after me."

"What did they do?"

"Interrogated me. Did you never wonder why I was questioned for two days, but Patsy and Bennie were only questioned for a couple of hours?"

"I guess I just thought it was because RIP was yours."

"That's true. But most of those two days weren't spent with the police. I was being interrogated by the Lab Rats. The Feds."

"The Feds!"

"The lab is supported by federal funds. We were never told exactly how it worked, where the money came from, but we knew it was federal. The lab was doing a lot of study with time travel, but it was all theory. The powers that be wouldn't let us do any experiments. They said we weren't ready. So finally Grover and I decided to try it on our own. He had access to a lot of the materials I didn't have, so he sneaked them out to me. We did that for years before I even built RIP. It seemed pretty harmless."

"Like that Johnny Cash song, about the Cadillac."

"Huh?"

"Where he took the pieces out in his lunchbox, and built that Cadillac from parts from every year." Kendra started singing "One Piece at a Time," but stopped when Jill stared at her blankly. "Never mind. Go on."

"We never knew if it was the FBI or the CIA or some other secret agency, but they flashed their badges, and the police let them take me."

"What did they do to you?" Kendra asked, visions of waterboarding and rubber hoses making her shudder.

"Nothing much," Jill said vaguely. "Mostly because I told them everything they wanted to know. At that time, all I wanted was to find a way to get Van back. I thought by telling them what I knew, they'd be able to help."

"They didn't?"

"No. I thought they were helping, at first. Except at the very beginning when they were angry because I'd been conducting experiments on the side, outside of work. That's when they fired me. They called me a rogue scientist. But after they found out that RIP worked, they wanted to examine it, take it apart to see how it worked, and the police wouldn't release it. It was one thing to the let the Feds question a suspect, I guess, but something else altogether when it came to turning over evidence. The police flat out refused to do it. The Feds probably could have forced the issue, but I think they were afraid of blowing their cover. So instead, they rehired me at the lab so I could teach them how I did it. They wanted to re-create RIP. I agreed to go back on the condition that they help me bring Van back. They said they would, but after a while I figured out they never had any intention of doing it. All they wanted to do was pick my brain to learn how I made RIP in the first place. They wouldn't let me work on any projects to bring Van back. So I quit." Jill grew silent and stared out the window.

"But the police did release RIP," Kendra prompted, after a few miles.

"Yes, but only about four years ago. If you ask me, the police never really believed it had anything to do with Van's disappearance. They still think one of us killed her or she ran off. So they called me, and I called Grover, and we took it up to his place before the Lab Rats found out they'd released it. They did finally find out and come asking, but I told them I'd had it scrapped. I don't think they believed me." She paused, glanced at Kendra, and said hesitantly, "I know I'm watched sometimes."

Kendra raised an eyebrow.

"Don't look at me like that. I'm not paranoid. I don't think we're being followed today, though. I've been keeping an eye out."

Kendra checked the rear view mirror. This close to the city the highway was well-traveled, and there were numerous cars behind them, some right on their bumper, some trailing hundreds of yards behind. How could Jill know they weren't being followed?

"They have someone keeping an eye on Grover, too," Jill said. "I think they suspect RIP is at his place, but they can't get in to know for sure. When we first hid RIP on his property, I went up pretty often, and I know I was followed at least once. So we stopped working on it, and I stopped going up there. There wasn't much point to it anyway, since I couldn't figure out how to bring Van back."

They drove on, mostly in silence. They stopped once in Chewelah to pick up the Zips burger and fries, and Kendra used the restroom. As she returned to the car, she scoped out the other vehicles parked nearby. Were any of them familiar? Had she seen them on the road? Was someone ducked down in the front seat so she couldn't see him? The thought that they might be watched, for whatever reason, made Kendra uneasy. Before she climbed into the driver's seat, she raised her hands in both directions.

"What did you do that for?" Jill asked as they got under way.

"I just flipped off anyone who might be following us," Kendra said, grinning.

"You just flipped off the whole town of Chewelah."

Kendra laughed and gave Jill's hand a quick squeeze before returning her own to the steering wheel.

More than an hour later they passed through the quasi-ghost town of Northport, a town so decrepit, if Van had been transported there from 1988, she would have thought she'd gone back in time, rather than forward. Outside town, they snaked up the mountain, past farms, past homes tucked away behind trees, finally to heavy woods with no homes in sight. The pavement stopped and the road became rough and narrow. Occasionally a lane veered off deeper into the woods, usually marked with nothing but a No Trespassing sign, and Kendra assumed there were homes hidden in there.

Finally, Jill told Kendra to turn right into one of the lanes. Nailed to a tree was a sign that said, "Insured by Smith and Wesson," and beyond that *two* No Trespassing signs. Grover took his privacy seriously.

"Maybe we should have borrowed Kevin's truck," Kendra said as they rocked forward on the road. "My shocks will never the same."

"Oh no! We should have taken my car. Its shocks are already shot."

Kendra chuckled and patted Jill's hand. "Relax, honey. I'm just teasing you. It's not that bad."

They arrived at a padlocked iron gate barring the road. Kendra stopped the car. "Now what?"

"He's coming," Jill said, cocking her head.

Kendra listened and heard a motor approaching. Through the bars of the iron gate Kendra saw a shiny black four-wheeler careen down the road toward them, two sizable dogs loping alongside. The four-wheeler stopped, and a gaunt man, about eighty years old, climbed off and ambled toward the gate. He wore a holster at his hip, a gun nestled inside, as much a part of his outfit as his stained khakis and thin white t-shirt.

Jill got out of the car, smiling. "Hi Grover."

The smaller of the dogs, a young pit bull terrier mix, rushed toward Jill, barking, stopped only by the gate from attacking her. The mastiff was older, slower, wiser. He watched his master and kept an eye on Jill and the car.

Grover kept his hand at the ready by his gun and squinted at the car. "Who's that?"

Reassured only slightly by the locked gate, Kendra stepped out of the car so he could see her.

"She's my friend, Kendra," Jill said. "She's helping me. You can trust her."

He grunted and shuffled forward to unlock the gate. "Haven't had company in a long time. Wesson, sit. Smith, knock it off, you damn dog. Did you bring my burger and fries?"

"Sure did." Jill leaned back into the car to retrieve them. "Though I don't know how you can eat cold fries."

"I got a microwave," he said, still examining Kendra. He seemed particularly struck by her rhinestone-studded sandals, or her toe ring, or perhaps her lime green toenails. He opened the gate and took his bag of food. "So what's up?"

Jill spoke softly. "Van came back."

Grover aimed piercing gray eyes at Jill. "*What?*"

"She came back. She—" Jill broke off when Grover held up a hand and shot a leery squint into the surrounding woods.

"Wait," he said. He swung the gate open wide, motioned for Kendra to bring the car through, and he shut it behind her and locked it again. Jill climbed into the car, and they followed Grover as he led them down the lane, the dogs running alongside his four-wheeler.

"I forgot to warn you about Grover," Jill said.

"You did warn me. He shoots people."

"No, I mean about your feet."

"My feet?"

"Grover likes feet. Women's feet. Fancy feet, I mean. Feet like yours."

Kendra had known men with foot fetishes before. She wasn't troubled if Grover had one. What she said was, "You think I have fancy feet?" and was intrigued when she saw Jill blush.

They pulled up in front of an old, single-wide manufactured home set into a clearing in the thick trees. Grover drove the four-wheeler into a massive barn on the left of the clearing. To the right was a two-story shed at least three times the size of the manufactured home. Grover shambled from the barn to the house, tossing cold fries over his shoulder for the dogs, and ushered the women inside.

The place was built in the days when manufactured homes didn't even try to resemble a regular house. The front door opened straight into the narrow living room, which abutted a kitchen, where the back door was. Beyond the kitchen were a bathroom and bedroom. It was the same layout as Patsy's, but smaller, everything condensed.

Kendra thought she detected a familiar odor and was only a bit shocked when Grover sat in a worn rocking chair, took up a pipe and lighter, lit the contents of the bowl, and inhaled deeply. He closed his eyes and held his breath for a long moment, before allowing smoke to trickle from his mouth. He offered the pipe to Jill, who shook her head absently while gazing out the window, then held it out toward Kendra. She met the steel gray eyes and thought she detected a challenge in them. Was this a test? Was he trying to determine whether she was trustworthy? Kendra took the pipe and the lighter, determined to gain his trust. Or maybe she just wanted a smoke. It had been a very long time. She lit the contents of the bowl, inhaled deeply, and allowed the pot to permeate her body. She let it seep out her mouth and handed the pipe to Grover.

He smiled. "So that ring you have on your fourth toe, does that mean you're married or engaged or something?"

Kendra wiggled her toes and grinned. "No, that's not what it means. And I'm not married. But I am something." She peeked at Jill, who still stared out the window.

Grover followed the direction of her gaze and grimaced. "Figures." He took another toke from the pipe. A few moments later he exhaled. "So tell me about this. She came back?"

Jill perched on the edge of the couch. Kendra scooted next to her. "Yes," Jill said. "Yesterday."

Grover passed the pipe to Kendra, who met Jill's surprised look, grinned, and lit the pipe again.

Jill said, "She's exactly the same as when she left. Same age, same clothes, same everything. To her, yesterday was 1988."

Grover sank back in his chair with a sigh, his eyes gleaming at the idea. "So it really did work."

Jill tried not to smile, but a glint in her eyes revealed her genuine satisfaction. "Yeah. But now she wants to go back. And I have to try to send her. I need RIP."

Grover sat upright. "By God, don't let 'em find out." He leaned over and grabbed Jill's knee. "Jill! Do you know what they'll do if they find out about her? They'll tear this place, your place, any place apart to find RIP. Hell, they'll tear that poor girl apart to figure out how it worked." He shook Jill's leg. "Don't let 'em find out about her, you hear me?"

Jill pried Grover's fingers from her leg. "I won't. I promise," but she shot a worried glance at Kendra.

Grover might be paranoid, but Kendra felt a shiver of fear. They had sent Van off to Patsy's without any word of warning about keeping her existence quiet. Only a few people knew Van had reappeared, but what was to stop any one of them, or Van herself, from announcing it to the public? And if these Lab Rats Jill talked about found out...

"I won't let them find out about Van," Jill said again, and Kendra hoped she was as confident as she sounded. "But now I need to get RIP and take it back to town. I have to figure out how to reverse the process."

Grover pursed his lips. "Where will you work on her? Not here. They watch me all the time. Do you have a secure place? A garage, a shed, something like that? Everyone would see her at your place."

"We can rent a garage at my condo," Kendra said. "No one would think to look there." She leaned heavily into Jill, prompting Jill to sag into the back of the couch, and into Kendra. Kendra wondered if Jill was as aware of Kendra's breast pressing against Jill's arm as Kendra was.

"All right," Grover said with a sigh. He pushed himself up from the chair and moved to a gun safe in the corner, punched in the combination, and removed a key ring from inside. "Let's go have a look-see. I haven't touched anything since the last time you were here, except to run the engine now and then, make sure it works, especially in the winter. It's in pretty good shape."

Kendra watched Jill rise from the couch, carefully keeping her left arm still, not using it to push herself up, and Kendra smiled. She had noticed.

Kendra followed them out the back door. She expected to go to the barn or the shed, but instead they veered off into the woods behind the house. When they reached the edge of the trees, Kendra saw a narrow lane, barely discernable until they got to the entrance, so cleverly were the trees at the opening cut. It was darker and cooler on the lane, the trees on both sides towering and dense, and the lane itself was overgrown. Kendra jogged a couple of steps to catch up with Jill. "Wait for me." She tucked her hand in Jill's arm.

A few yards down the lane they came to another shed, locked with a huge padlock, and painted forest camouflage to blend in with the dark green pines. Grover unlocked the door and swung it open, and Jill and Kendra stepped inside.

Kendra gasped. RIP was instantly recognizable and yet unfamiliar at the same time. She let go of Jill's arm to circle it, examining it as if it were a rare artifact in a museum. The yellow and brown camper on the Toyota pickup sported a heavy padlock on the camper door. All that was missing were the antennas and the bowl that should have been sticking out the top, but Kendra could see where they would emerge when RIP was set up to function.

Kendra watched Jill reorient herself, although the thing had to be nearly as familiar to her as her own bedroom. Jill took the keys from Grover, unlocked the camper's padlock, and climbed inside. Kendra was reminded of the day she'd first met Jill and of how she'd been drawn to helping her with RIP, neglecting her own date who, she recalled, had been busy falling in love with Grace. Everything had started that day. How different would their lives have been if Van had simply never vanished? If they'd opened the camper door, and there she'd been. She'd climb out, and Patsy would still be angry with her for that scene with Bennie. Inez would give Kendra a ride home. Would Inez try to kiss her? Would Kendra let her? Maybe Inez and Grace never would have fallen in love. Jill wouldn't have lost her job and, come to think of it, neither would Grover.

Kendra studied the paranoid old man. He lived alone up in the middle of nowhere, just him and his dogs, smoking pot and craving fast food. How would his life have been different if Van had never vanished? And how would it be different if Van were to return?

"Jill!" she called out, suddenly frightened.

Jill poked her head out of the camper. "What is it?"

"If you send Van back, then what?"

"What do you mean?" She climbed down to stand next to Kendra.

"What happens to all this? What happens to the present? It won't exist any more, will it?"

She looked from Grover to Jill, saw them exchange somber looks, and realized they had all along understood the ramifications of sending Van back in time. Kendra thought she had, but now she could see that she hadn't truly understood until this moment that sending Van back to the past would simply erase them from the Now. It was as if they were signing their own death warrants. Who knew how the events of the last twenty years would unfold if Van had never disappeared?

"I need some air." She pushed past Grover and stepped outside, gulping in lungs full of fresh, pine-scented air, air so fresh it almost made her dizzy to breathe it. The mastiff, Wesson, lay on the ground watching her. Smith wagged his tail and tucked his nose into the palm of her hand, seeking a petting. Kendra knelt down and wrapped her arms around Smith, grateful for something to hold on to as her view of reality shifted and spun.

Then Jill was beside her, lifting her to her feet, and Kendra transferred her hug from Smith to Jill, holding on as if Jill was the only thing that kept her world from spinning out of control. After only a slight hesitation, Jill held her tight. Softly, gingerly, Jill raised her fingers to thread them through tendrils of Kendra's hair that had escaped her pony tail. She stroked a finger along Kendra's neck below the hairline. Kendra shivered, raised her head, and had to smile. Jill's eyes were wide and uncertain. Undaunted Kendra leaned in, her eyes on Jill's lips.

Grover's voice spurred them apart. "Take your time, ladies. You can't sneak it out of here until after dark anyhow, and it won't get dark this time of year 'til 9:30 or so. Come on Smith, Wesson." Grover whistled at the dogs and headed toward the house.

Jill averted her eyes. She put her fingers to her lips as if trying to block the kiss and hurried after Grover.

Aggravated, Kendra followed. "Chicken," she whispered loudly. But if Jill heard her, there was no sign of it.

Chapter Thirteen

Jill — 2008

JILL DROVE RIP and followed Kendra down the mountain into Northport. She kept her headlights off, keeping close on Kendra's tail to make sure she didn't veer from the road. She'd tried calling Kendra to let her know she was still behind her, but there was no reception, so every now and then she flashed her lights, in order to reassure Kendra that she was still there.

Grover had fed them venison chili for dinner while he ate his reheated Zips burger. They waited for dark, and Grover and Kendra smoked some more pot. Jill had rarely smoked pot even in the Sixties, when everyone was experimenting with mind-altering drugs. As far as Jill was concerned, she *was* her mind, and her mind was her. If her mind were altered, then who would she be? *What* would she be? Something different, that's all she knew. From a scientific point of view, it might have been an interesting experiment, but if her mind were altered, would she even care about that? The whole purpose of the experiment would be thwarted. It didn't make sense to try.

Besides, in those days Jill hadn't needed any drug to have mind-bending thoughts. Any time she wanted to, she could escape into the world of her mind, where anything and everything was possible. All she had to do was figure out how. People assumed that because she was a scientist, Jill lacked imagination, thinking her nothing but a clinical realist, but that was far from the truth. Her mind was filled with a host of what-ifs, and any one of them could engage her imagination for untold hours, days, or weeks. Or, like time travel, it could become an obsession that lasted for decades.

After Van disappeared, though, and all Jill's attempts to bring her back had failed, she deliberately put the world of imagination behind her. It was fine for pretend, but real life was different. She had only been playing around with a what-if, and it had turned out to be a simultaneous success and failure, bringing a great deal of misery into the lives of her dearest friends. She could not forgive herself for that, and she couldn't risk it ever happening again. From then on, whenever Jill imagined a what-if, she forced it from her mind.

But now, thanks to Kendra, she *was* playing with what-ifs again. What if she could send Van back? What if she could make all the misery she'd brought into her friends' lives vanish, as if it had never happened? Because it *would* never have happened. That was as

exciting as any of the ideas Jill had ever had when she was young.
And this time she didn't have to force it from her mind. In fact,
Kendra had convinced her that it would be wrong of her *not* to try.
The excitement of working with RIP again made Jill feel like a kid.

And so did Kendra. Jill didn't have a great track record with
women, but she knew a come-on when it hit her over the head, and
Kendra was definitely coming on to her. First, she'd leaned into Jill
on Grover's couch, rubbing her breasts against Jill's arm, although
that could have only been because Kendra was stoned. But no, before
that even, Kendra had *three times* today called her honey, something
she'd never done before in their twenty years of friendship. Jill
initially put it down as a new speech affectation of Kendra's, but
combined with the breast rub and that near kiss out behind Grover's
house, it assumed greater significance.

What was she playing at? Jill had always been very aware that
Kendra was beautiful and desirable, ever since the first day they'd
met at Patsy's party. But Kendra had been Inez's date, and Jill had
carefully *not* placed Kendra into the compartment of her brain that
contained potential girlfriends. Jill had put her into the "friends"
category, and Kendra had never before strayed from it. After Van
disappeared, Kendra's friendship was invaluable and, until now, she
had never given Jill any reason to think she'd placed her in the
wrong compartment. On the contrary, over the years Kendra had had
scores of lovers, male and female. She'd freely shared tales of her
conquests with Jill, cried on her shoulder when one of them hurt her,
and occasionally tried to set Jill up with one of them. Never had
there been any indication that Kendra saw Jill as girlfriend material.
Until now.

They had almost reached Northport when her Bluetooth beeped
in her ear. She pushed the button. "Jill here."

"It's me," Kendra said. "I've been trying and trying to call, but
there wasn't any reception. Don't you think you can turn your lights
on now? I can't see if you're behind me."

"I'm right on your tail." There was a moment of silence as they
both absorbed the import of those words. "Er, I mean, yeah, I'll turn
my lights on as soon as we get past Northport."

"Is that what you meant?" Kendra sounded disappointed. "You
don't really think someone's watching Grover's place, do you?"

"I can't be sure. But I do know I was followed on my way home
from there once. And I wasn't even in RIP that time. RIP's what
they're after."

"And Van. We need to call her, let her know to keep hidden."

"Yeah." Jill pulled onto Northport's main street. The town was
too small to have a police force, so she wasn't concerned about
driving through town with no headlights. "But it's after ten already.
I'll call her tomorrow."

"How do you suppose she's getting along at Patsy's?"

Jill grimaced in the darkness. "I can't imagine it's going well. Not unless Patsy stops drinking all of sudden."

"Maybe she will. People do stop sometimes, and Patsy's got a very good reason to try right now. She worships Van."

"Yeah. It's possible, I suppose, but I doubt it'll happen overnight. And even if it did, there's still the time gap to consider. And the age gap. Patsy's seventy years old, and Van's only forty-five."

"Age doesn't matter. Not if two people truly love each other."

Jill wasn't so sure. "Not so much, maybe, when you're as old as Patsy and me. But to Van, it's got to be a pretty big deal."

"True love transcends time." Kendra's voice was high and lilting.

Jill laughed. "Where'd you hear that, a fortune cookie?"

"I think it's in the Bible or Shakespeare or something. Okay, we're through Northport. *Now* will you turn on your lights? You chasing my tail is something I want to *see*."

"I didn't say I was chasing it," Jill said, switching on her headlights. They were on a state highway now, but it was little traveled in the remote area, especially at night. "I just said I was *on* it."

"Either one's fine with me."

There she went again. This was not the sort of conversation one had with a *friend*. What was she trying to accomplish? It was almost like she was trying to...

"Hello?" Kendra's voice interrupted her thoughts. "Jill? C'mon, say something. It's okay. This is something people do. It's called flirting."

"Yeah, like you did with Grover?"

"Grover? I didn't flirt with him."

"Kendra, you had your feet in his lap, rubbing them all over his, his, his *lap*."

Kendra laughed. "Did that bother you? I know you like my 'fancy' feet."

Jill opened her mouth to protest, but closed it when she couldn't think of anything to say. She *did* find Kendra's feet to be very attractive, with their pretty pedicure and that little toe ring and all.

"Besides," Kendra said, "he's eighty years old. He doesn't have much '*lap*' to be worried about. And I had an ulterior purpose."

"What's that?"

"He has some really good weed."

"*Kendra.* You rubbed your feet all over his crotch in order to get marijuana?"

"Why not? It made him happy, and it didn't hurt anything."

There was a pause as Jill contemplated that. No, watching

Grover give Kendra a foot rub hadn't hurt anything, but she'd caught herself wishing Kendra's feet had landed in *her* lap rather than Grover's.

"Jill?" Kendra's voice was small. "It didn't hurt anything, did it? I wouldn't have done it if I thought it would hurt you."

"No, of course not. They're your feet. You can rub them all over anything you want."

"Really? Is that a promise?"

"Uh..."

Kendra laughed. "I'll take that as a yes. But don't worry, honey, I'll be gentle."

"Um, Kendra," Jill said uneasily, "I don't know..."

"Come on. I'm just teasing you. *Flirt-ting.* Remember?"

"But *why?*" Jill burst out in sheer frustration. "Why are you flirting with me? For heaven's sake, we've been friends for twenty years, and *now* all of a sudden you've decided to flirt? Why?"

Kendra sighed heavily. "I like you, okay? I thought you liked me."

"I do. You're my best friend. But this is different."

"Good different or bad different?" When Jill didn't immediately answer, Kendra pressed. "You liked feeling my breast rubbing against your arm today, didn't you? And you *did* almost kiss me back there. And you're the one who caressed my neck and sent shivers down my spine."

Jill couldn't deny she'd enjoyed the feel of Kendra's breast, nor could she deny that she'd almost kissed her, but at the last she said, "I didn't do that!"

"Yes, you did, you big liar. Right outside RIP's shed, when you were holding me, you ran your fingers through my hair and you stroked my neck. My legs nearly gave out on me."

And then Jill did remember. She'd done it without conscious thought, her hands moving of their own volition. She'd needed to touch Kendra and comfort her in her distress. The almost-kiss had driven what preceded it completely out of her mind. How could she have forgotten? "Oh my gosh."

"Yeah, so tell me. Good different, or bad different?"

"Um, good different, I guess, except—"

"You *guess?* Wow. Thanks."

"Well, Kendra, things like this have been known to ruin friendships. You're the best friend I've ever had. If I lost that because I want to touch you and, and, and..."

"Ye-es? And what?"

"I'd regret our lost friendship for the rest of my life."

"But darling," Kendra said softly, "if you succeed in sending Van back, the rest of your life—*this* life, anyway—might be very, very short."

The light bulb went off over Jill's head, and it finally made sense that Kendra was making these unnerving advances *now*, of all times. She was astonished it had taken her so long to see it. It was a classic what-if scenario. What if you knew the world was going to end in a matter of months or weeks or days? What would you do? Wouldn't most people want to spend that time loving, and being loved? What else was there, really? And if you had a best friend who possibly could be more than a friend, isn't that the time to take a chance, to risk your pride or your ego or your friendship and throw your heart out there, just in case?

But even as Jill pondered Kendra's insight, and before she could appreciate the fact that Kendra had apparently chosen *her* to be the person she would turn to in the last days of her possibly foreshortened life, Jill was jarred out of her thoughts by a dark shape hurtling toward her in the rear view mirror.

"Kendra!" she shouted, accelerating quickly. "Someone's after me!" The dark shape, camouflaged by its lack of headlights, had no difficulty keeping up with RIP's ancient engine, finely tuned though it was. It loomed again, rose up immediately behind her, and gently bumped RIP's back bumper. Jill fought the steering wheel to keep RIP on the road. She pressed the gas pedal to the floor. "They're after RIP!"

Chapter Fourteen

Kendra — 2008

IN HER REARVIEW mirror Kendra saw Jill careen back and forth on the highway, nearly losing control of RIP. Jill straightened it up momentarily, then shuddered again from side to side again as if she'd struck something. Or been struck by something.

"Kendra!" Jill yelled from her phone. "They're hitting me from behind. Keep going. Don't let them know you're with me."

"Fuck that," Kendra said, angrier than she had been since the day Kevin came home from eighth grade all beaten up and bloody. She'd surprised herself at what a Mama Bear she'd become that day, unafraid of anything in her furious defense of her son. She'd grabbed the fire extinguisher from the kitchen wall, ran to her car, tracked down the high school boy who'd attacked Kevin, and sprayed him in front of all his friends. It hadn't stopped the kid from picking on Kevin, but at least he'd never beat him up again.

With this new threat, Kendra surprised herself again at how angry and unafraid she was. After finally getting up the courage to let Jill know how she felt—or at least the tip of her feelings—Kendra was damned if she was going to let anyone hurt her now. "You keep driving. I'll distract them."

"What? No, Kendra, your car's too little, too— Oh!" RIP veered as Jill was struck once more from behind.

"It's little, but it's tough!"

Kendra quickly sped up and pulled over to the side of road. She killed her own lights, kept her foot on the clutch, and revved her engine.

"They're dropping back a little," Jill said.

A moment later, the old truck hurtled past and, Kendra blew it a kiss. She turned on her lights, lifted her foot off the clutch, and hit the gas. With a squeal, the Jetta sandwiched in right behind Jill and in front of the dark shape following her. The driver of the dark truck wasn't expecting Kendra. The sudden appearance of the Jetta between him and RIP threw him off guard. He hit his brakes hard and fishtailed on the asphalt. Jill and Kendra pulled ahead.

"I'm chasing your tail now, darling," Kendra sang into her headset. "Turn off your lights, and take the very next cutoff you see. Here he comes. He's turned his lights on."

"Kendra, *no*," Jill yelled, but RIP's lights flicked off. "They only want RIP. Get out of the way."

Now Kendra could see the truck was a giant Dodge Ram, and Jill was right, Kendra's Jetta was a small car, but it had a turbo engine.

"Stealth Jetta," Kendra whispered. She zipped forward and again pulled over to the side of the road, revved her engine, and watched the Ram come closer. She timed it as tightly as she could, pulling out in front of the Ram at the last second, hoping to make him slam on his brakes again. But the Ram was moving faster this time and didn't slow down a whit. Blinding headlights came right into the Jetta, they were so close.

"Ooohhhh fuuuuuck!" she hollered, pressing even harder on the gas. The turbo kicked in. She zoomed ahead. "Whooowhooo!" Turbo was *fast*.

Jill's voice caught her attention, screaming at her from the phone. "What's going on? Kendra, talk to me."

Kendra hit her brakes as she realized she was barreling through the dark toward Jill, who was driving without lights. Wouldn't that be a joke if she managed to get the Ram off Jill's tail only to crash into it herself?

"Where are you?" Kendra asked, trying to keep her attention on the road ahead, so she wouldn't hit Jill, and the rearview mirror, where the Ram was gaining on her. "Have you pulled off yet?"

"Not yet, but I just passed a sign for Onion Creek Road in a couple miles. On the left. Where are you?"

"Right behind you, sweetheart. Right on your tail." Kendra's heart thumped hard in her chest. She was afraid she was about to be sandwiched between the Ram, closing in fast, and RIP, an unknown distance in front of her. But seconds later she passed the Onion Creek Road sign and saw she had two miles to go. Jill had passed the sign at least twenty seconds ago, maybe longer, giving Kendra a gauge of how far ahead she was. She had enough time.

She turned off her lights and turboed ahead again, counting the seconds as she put distance between herself and the Ram. At seventeen, she slammed on the brakes, turned the wheel, and spun around in the opposite direction. Heading straight toward the oncoming Ram, she counted silently, then flipped on her highbeams.

The reaction was all she could have wished for. The Ram veered off into the lane for oncoming traffic, which fortunately was still empty of cars, but the driver was going too fast and lost control. The truck fishtailed, slid off the road toward an embankment, and with an ear-piercing screech flipped and skidded on its side.

Kendra switched off her lights, wheeled around, and sped back. The driver's door, now facing the sky, shoved open and Kendra saw a figure trying to wriggle out. She didn't waste time watching, but accelerated away, intent on finding Jill. When she was certain she was far enough away to escape notice, she turned on her headlights, just in time to make the cutoff.

Only then did she become aware of Jill's voice in her ear.

"Kendra, if you don't answer me, I'm pulling this truck around."

"I'm on the Onion Creek Road. Where are you?"

"I'm ahead of you by a couple of minutes. Are you all right? What was all that noise?"

"Truck went bye bye," Kendra said, but her voice, so strong only moments before, was high and wobbly. "Oooh, Jill."

"What? What is it?"

"I wet my pants." Kendra burst into tears.

"I'm pulling over, I'll wait for you. Hang on."

Kendra nodded, as if Jill could see her, sniffed, and wiped her eyes. She crept forward, extra cautiously now that it didn't matter. "I chased him off the road."

"You're sure he's not following you?"

"His truck's on its side."

"Holy moley."

"Yeah, h-h-holy m-moley." Kendra's voice shook uncontrollably. It seemed to take forever before she saw RIP's running lights in the road ahead. She pulled up behind RIP and shut down the engine, crossed her arms on the steering wheel and dropped her forehead onto them, exhausted and weak. Then the door opened, and Jill was there, drawing her out.

"C'mere." Jill pulled Kendra to her feet and wrapped her arms around her. Kendra let herself go. She stood on wobbly legs, sobbed into Jill's shoulder, and shook, knowing she wouldn't shake apart, because Jill held her tight.

"Shhh, don't cry. It's all right now."

"I w-was very b-b-brave," Kendra wailed.

"Yes, dear, you were." Jill patted Kendra's head and stroked her neck, as she had done earlier that day.

"I could have died," Kendra said into Jill's shoulder. She had the satisfaction of feeling Jill's arms tighten around her.

"No, don't say that." Jill's fingers stroked like mad on Kendra's neck.

After a moment, Kendra pulled back slightly so she could see Jill's face in the shadows cast by the Jetta's lights. "I risked my life to save you," Kendra pointed out, smiling damply. "Remember that episode of *Gilligan's Island*? Or maybe it was *I Dream of Jeannie*? Since I risked my life to save you, that means you belong to me now."

In the dark, all she could see of Jill's eyes were tiny glints picked up from the car lights, but Kendra thought she detected a change in them. Suddenly Jill leaned forward and captured Kendra's lips in a kiss that made Kendra shake all over—just when she was beginning to settle down too. Kendra opened her mouth and let Jill's tongue sweep in with an expertise surprising for someone who had dated so rarely, despite her seventy years. It was a wet kiss, in part because of Kendra's tears, still dripping down her cheeks, but after a moment

Kendra noticed her tears weren't the only ones moistening their kiss. She pulled her head back and touched Jill's cheek. Jill was crying too.

But she was smiling as well. "Yes, dear," Jill said. "I belong to you now."

Kendra felt a moment of pure triumph, and then they were kissing again, long satisfactory kisses, until finally common sense returned. They leaned against the Jetta catching their breaths. Kendra sagged against Jill who wrapped an arm around her shoulder.

"Was he hurt?" Jill asked. "The guy in the truck?"

"I don't think so. I don't give a flying fuck, either. He was trying to run you off the road."

Jill's arm tightened. "Did you see what kind of truck it was?"

"Dodge Ram pickup. A big one."

"He's probably all right. We have to assume he is. We can't go to your place now. They'll be able to track you down, from your car."

"They never saw my car. I had my lights off the whole time. You should have seen me, Jill. I buzzed them like a mosquito. They never saw me coming."

Jill squeezed Kendra's shoulder. "I'm glad I didn't see you. I would have had a heart attack. I was scared enough as it was, not knowing where you were or what you were doing." She gave Kendra a little shake. "Why didn't you answer me?"

"I didn't hear you. I was in the moment, you know? But I'm sure they didn't see my car, so they can't trace me."

"We have to assume they were watching us, Kendra. How else could they have come out of nowhere like that? They must have seen your car leaving Grover's."

"Oh." Kendra shivered. "I'm kind of wet."

Jill put a hand to Kendra's cheek. "Me too, but we don't have time to do anything about it right now. We have to find somewhere to hide first."

Kendra giggled. "I mean, I'm wet because I wet my pants. Not that you don't make me wet too."

Jill put her hands on Kendra's shoulders and held her away from her, into the light from the headlamps, which illuminated a dark patch on the front of Kendra's green pants. Jill whistled. "You really did wet yourself, didn't you?"

Kendra tugged at her crotch, which was beginning to itch. "I know a place we can hide."

"You do?"

"My ex and I used to have a hunting cabin up near Ione on the other side of the mountains. We can be there in a couple of hours."

"Used to have?"

"It's all his now. He bagged it in the divorce, but his wife made him get a place on the lake. So he never uses the old cabin anymore.

It's kind of primitive. Just one room." And one bed. Kendra smiled. "And I know where the key is."

Chapter Fifteen

Van — 2008

VAN AWOKE TO a quiet rustling in the darkness. Her heart hammered in her chest for a moment, before she recalled where she was. This was Patsy's couch, and the rustling sound was Patsy padding from her bedroom into the kitchen. Van heard the almost silent *snick* of the cupboard door closing and knew Patsy had removed a bottle of rum. Patsy didn't risk the clink of a glass or the chink of ice. Like the night before, she would drink straight from the bottle.

Van hadn't said anything last night, had cowardly kept her eyes closed and pretended to be asleep as she heard Patsy's bare feet whisper on the kitchen floor. Just as she cowardly hadn't said anything that first day, when she'd returned from the grocery store, only to find that Patsy had taken advantage of her brief absence to have a drink, or two, or more. No, Patsy hadn't taken advantage of Van's absence; she'd *engineered* it, deliberately maneuvering Van out of the trailer so she could have some private time with her liquor.

Van was still embarrassed by how easily she'd been manipulated by Patsy. They'd finished their macaroni and cheese with tuna. Patsy had carefully placed her unfinished drink on the counter beside the sink, as if preparing to wash it, but she didn't dump it out. Then they'd sat in the living room, becoming reacquainted.

In the odd one-sided conversation, Patsy told Van all about Catherine's marriage to Ron and the birth of their three children, about her early retirement, about a shoulder operation she'd undergone a year before, from which she'd recovered nicely. Van learned it was Kendra who had completed the stained glass tulip after Van disappeared, that Patsy was on medication to control her cholesterol, and that Melissa Etheridge had become a superstar.

Van said very little. She recalled other times she and Patsy had been apart, usually as a result of Van's job taking her out of town for a few days at a time. Their long-distance telephone conversations were all too brief, with never enough time to share all they needed to before one or the other would say, "This must be costing a fortune." And they would reluctantly hang up. When they finally did see each other, their words stumbled over each other as they tried to share everything they had experienced, thought, and felt during their time apart, whether it was that the toilet had stopped up or that the boss was a jerk, a suggestion for their next vacation or an observation about reducing crime in the city. It didn't matter what it was. There was never an awkward silence or thoughts best left unsaid or uncomfortable feelings.

Not this time. Van found she had nothing to share. Aside from leaping twenty years ahead in time, not much had happened to Van since the last time she'd seen Patsy. On the other hand, Patsy had twenty years worth of experiences to catch Van up on. But many of Patsy's experiences were so fraught with ominous emotions that neither of them had the nerve to venture near them. As a result, the conversation was stilted, awkward, full of uncomfortable pauses. Van's leg jiggled up and down with nervous energy, and she chain-smoked.

Finally, Van asked about the photograph of Patsy with Waverly. "I saw it on your bedside table. Did you date her?"

Patsy looked momentarily guilty. "I wouldn't call it 'dating,' exactly. We were both lonely and didn't have anyone else." She broke off and grinned, sheepish but unapologetic, very much the Patsy of old. "Hell, you'd been gone for four years. Yes, we dated. I'm sorry if that hurts you, but I didn't know you were coming back. Nobody can be alone forever."

Van wasn't sure how she felt. A bit jealous, certainly, but part of her was relieved as well, as if Patsy had given her a get-out-of-jail-free card, one she could stick into her back pocket and pull out if needed. She tucked it carefully away. "But, *Waverly?*"

"I know, I know, I always made fun of her. But she's a good kid when you get to know her. And," Patsy leaned forward, her elbows on her knees, "she was there that day, the day you disappeared. Well, she wasn't there when it happened, she was out dancing, but she knew about it, she understood about RIP. That's not the sort of thing you can explain to people. Sure, if I was lonely, I could always go pick up a woman in a bar, take her home, but when it came to trying to share who I was, where I was coming from, I couldn't do it. I couldn't explain to people that the love of my life had disappeared in a time machine. With Waverly, I didn't have to. She already understood what happened. At least as well as any of us did."

"How long were you together?"

"Just over a year."

"Did you live together?"

Patsy hesitated slightly. "Yes."

"At our house?" Van didn't know why that mattered, but it did.

"No, the house was gone by then."

Van felt oddly relieved at that. "So why did you break up?"

"We didn't love each other, Van. We were only together because we both loved you. It was enough to *bring* us together, but it wasn't enough to *keep* us together. We helped each other get through a hard stage. Until then, I don't think either one of us had really accepted that you were gone."

As Patsy spoke, Van could see behind the gray hair, the wrinkles, and the sagging skin, and she saw Patsy as she was, before. It was like looking at a Cracker Jack ring that showed a different picture when you tilted it a certain way. And when her own Patsy showed through, Van was surprised to feel lickings of desire flare up. The Patsy of old, not the old Patsy, was who Van wanted. But how much of that Patsy was still there, inside the body and mind of this other, seventy-year-old Patsy? There was a way to find out, she suspected. And no time like the present. Hesitantly, Van rose from her chair and moved to sit next to Patsy on the couch. She angled herself toward Patsy, put a hand to her cheek, and tilted Patsy's face toward her.

There was fear in Patsy's eyes, and Van knew Patsy was very aware of the struggle Van was having trying to reconcile the two Patsy's. Everything rode on this moment. What if they kissed, and the feelings they'd had for each other simply weren't there any more? Or, worse, what if they kissed, and Van was repulsed at kissing an old woman? Patsy's breathing was fast and shallow, and her hands trembled as she placed them on Van's shoulders. Van leaned in, closing her eyes as she did so, and pressed her lips to Patsy's.

Patsy's lips trembled at first, moving tentatively against Van's. She caressed the back of Van's neck, and Van leaned in. Patsy's lips opened and the familiar tongue probe gently at Van's lips. She opened her own lips to allow Patsy to get closer, to caress the inside of her with her mouth. Her breathing quickened, and she pressed closer still, bringing her hand up to stroke Patsy's breast. Only then did she hesitate, the unfamiliar feel of the drooping breast reminding her that this woman was not the same Patsy she had made love to the day before. As if aware of Van's thoughts, Patsy took Van's hand and held it out away from her body. She broke off the kiss, still trembling and breathing hard, and stared deeply into Van's eyes.

"Oh, kid," she said raggedly. "You're going to give me a heart attack."

Van smiled, rather pleased with how quickly Patsy had responded to her, and even more pleased with how quickly she had responded to Patsy. She sat up and moved to the end of the couch. "I don't want you to have a heart attack. But, I had to make sure you were really you."

"I'm still me. I know I'm old and wrinkled and gray, and I'm fatter and my boobs hang low. But I'm still me." With an odd, shy smile, she added, "Maybe later you'll let me show you how little I have changed."

"Maybe," Van said, a bit uncertainly, and Patsy smiled to let Van know she understood.

Patsy took a sudden deep breath. "Now," she said briskly, slapping her hands on her legs, "exactly how much money did that bitch give you?"

Van leaned away from Patsy, taken aback. "You mean Bennie?"

"Did another bitch give you money too? Of course, I mean Bennie. And don't look so shocked. You know I don't like her."

"I know."

"I just wondered if you have enough money to buy some milk and eggs and stuff. The food I have around here isn't much to your taste." Van already knew that the food Patsy had around was practically non-existent.

"I have a little money left." Van was not eager to part with her tiny stash of cash, but she had no choice if they were to eat. "Enough to buy a few groceries."

Patsy reached for a pen and paper and talked as she wrote. "Shall we make you a list? We'll need milk, eggs, bread, butter. Maybe a little hamburger and some potatoes. An onion, and a can of mushroom soup. That should do it. Here you go."

"Okay." Van took the list, feeling a bit rushed out the door.

It wasn't until she returned from Yokes, with hardly any cash left at all, that she understood why she'd been hurried out of the trailer that way. The half-full glass that had been sitting on the kitchen counter was nowhere to be seen, but it was evident from Patsy's slightly glazed eyes and slurred words that she had swallowed its contents, and probably a refill or two as well.

The desire Van had carefully cultivated on her stroll back from the store, deliberately nurtured, to convince herself that she had to make love to Patsy with all her heart, body, and soul, to really give Patsy a *chance*, evaporated when she saw Patsy slouching against the door jamb with a lazy smile on her face, clearly the worse for drink.

Van hadn't said anything then, not about the drinking. She'd only told Patsy that she intended to sleep on the couch that night. Patsy had seemed relieved more than anything else and went to find clean sheets and a pillow.

The next day, after a sleep disturbed by Patsy rummaging for rum, Van had started the task of clearing out a space on the back porch to fit in a bed. If Patsy was going to drink every night, at least Van was entitled to have a door between them. The nights were growing warmer and the porch would make a fine summer bedroom. But clearing the space proved difficult. Dozens of boxes, plastic and paper bags, all filled with odd assortments of old bills and receipts cluttered the space along with shoes, books, photograph albums, Christmas decorations, all the things that normally find a place in an attic or a basement or a garage. Van couldn't tell how indispensable any of it was without going through it item by item.

The job was made more difficult because Van kept getting

distracted by such mundane items as yellowed gas bills from 1999 with exorbitant rates, receipts from a debit account for something called a Cricket phone, and Patsy's retirement papers. From the latter, Van learned that Patsy's retirement from her prison job had not been voluntary, but was a deal brokered by her union after she had shown up at work drunk, apparently more than once. Only Patsy's long and glowing work history prior to Van's disappearance had prevented her from simply being fired.

Patsy's cat had finally shown himself, a lean and scruffy tabby. He leaped to the top of a stack of boxes and watched Van with unblinking yellow eyes. Van petted him and he hissed at her. She stuck her tongue out and ignored him.

Van had been returning from dumping a sack of obvious trash in the dumpster when she heard Patsy's little fold-up phone chirp. Patsy was not yet awake, so Van picked it up. Hesitantly, Van opened the phone and put it to her ear. "Hello?"

"Van?"

"Yes. Is this Jill?"

"Yes. Listen, we're in an area with low reception, I could get cut off any second, so I have to be quick. This is important. Don't let anyone know you're back, okay? I mean, like the newspapers or TV."

"I'll hold off on calling the press," Van said, forgetting for a moment that sarcasm was wasted on Jill.

"Okay, good. And don't do anything about trying to get your money back, or your job or your driver's license or anything like that, okay? Not yet."

"Why not?" Van hadn't yet formed a plan, but if she was stuck here in 2008 for good, those were obvious future steps.

"Kendra and I are working on RIP. I'm going to try to send you back to '88. But there are some people I used to work with, if they find out about it, they could try to take RIP from us. They already suspect something, so we're hiding. If they find out about you, they'll come after you too."

At the first part of Jill's speech, a knot of tension Van didn't know she had eased somewhat. If Jill could fix RIP to send her back, she wouldn't have to worry about creating a nest for herself on the edge of Patsy's grim life. Then Van heard the second part of Jill's speech. "Come after me? Why?"

"To help them figure out how it all worked. You're a major key to figuring out how time travel works, and its effects on people. They'll want to know whether it had any effect on your cells or your DNA, things like that. How are you feeling, anyway?"

"I'm fine, as far as I know. But if someone's after you, why don't you call the police?"

"No, we can't let them know either. They'd tell the Feds, and we'd lose our chance."

"Feds?"

"Yes. If you have ... know ... give ...me?"

"What? I can't hear you."

"—ing up." And the phone went dead. Van examined the phone's screen to see if the connection had truly been lost. She closed the phone and opened it again. "Hello?" There was no answer.

Patsy didn't rise until 11:30, much later than Van had ever known her to rise in the past. Though pale and shaky, she insisted she felt great and willingly entered into Van's porch project. She helped Van sort and carry the discards to the dumpster. But sorting alone was not enough to clear the room. By the end of the day, with a break midway during which Van went for a long, solitary ramble through Deer Park and Patsy rejuvenated herself with a few quick drinks, they had cleared a space on the porch. It was nowhere near ready for a bed, though, so Van slept again on the couch.

And now, for the second night in a row, Van's sleep was disturbed by the sound of Patsy supplying herself with liquor during the night. Van kept her eyes closed, vowing to get the porch ready the next day for sure. At least instead of lying with her eyes closed pretending everything was all right, she could lie with her eyes open—and pretend the same thing.

It was an impossible situation. The classic elephant in the room. It was the biggest problem facing them, greater even than the twenty-year time leap that they kept pretending was their only difficulty, and yet they tiptoed around it, pretending it didn't exist. Hiding herself on the porch was not a solution.

"Patsy."

Patsy stopped, a shadow in the darkness, her hands behind her back. "Did I wake you?" she whispered. "I'm sorry, I'll be quieter. Go to sleep, baby." She backed toward the bedroom.

"No, wait. I know what you're hiding behind you."

Patsy hesitated, then brought the bottle out in front of her. The faint light from the bathroom nightlight glinted off it. "This? I wasn't hiding it. I couldn't sleep and thought a little nightcap might help. I tried to be quiet, but since you're awake anyhow, care to join me?" She moved into the kitchen.

"No." Van swung her feet to the floor, sat up, and pulled the blanket around her shoulders. "Did you have a nightcap last night too?"

Patsy stopped. She came into the living room and lowered herself rigidly to the chair across from Van. "As a matter of fact, I did. Is there a law against that?"

"I don't know." Van switched on the lamp beside the couch. Patsy squinted in the light and held her hand up to shield her eyes. "All of a sudden it's illegal to smoke in bars and to not wear a seatbelt. How do I know if it's legal to get sloshed every night?"

There was a taut moment of silence before Patsy spoke. "I don't *get sloshed* every night."

"You did last night and you did the night before that." Van's voice was brusque. "And that's a new bottle you have there. So that means you already finished what was left in the other one."

Patsy slumped back in her chair and shook her head, her bravado gone. "You don't know what it's been like since you left," Patsy said, her voice trembling. "I'm lucky to be *alive* still. The fact that I drink a little is nothing."

"I didn't *leave*."

"Okay, fine," Patsy said, a bit of exasperation in her voice mingling with her tears, "you didn't *leave*. But you *evaporated* from my life. Is that better? You weren't there. Can you imagine it, Van? You were the best thing that ever happened in my life. You *were* my life. And then you were gone, and I didn't know where you were, or if you were all right. I wanted you to come back so badly, but sometimes I found myself hoping you were dead, because I was so scared about what might be happening to you. I worried that you were hurt or scared or sad. I couldn't take it. Can you blame me for taking a drink now and then, to ease that pain and the fear, just for a little while?"

Van watched Patsy as she spoke, mesmerized by the illusion created by the shadows cast from the lamp. One side of Patsy's face was in the light, every sag and wrinkle and gray hair clearly visible, a tiny pool of tears collecting in the crease between her right eye and the gray pouch that sagged beneath it, before finding a path to trickle down the side of her face to drop off her chin. The other side was cast in shadow, only the general contours of Patsy's face visible, the moving lips, and tears glinting in her eye before making a shiny trail down her cheek, and Van could imagine the cheek smooth and clear, like it used to be.

Her heart did ache for Patsy. Van's disappearance must have been brutal for her. Van tried to imagine what it would have been like if Patsy had vanished that day, leaving Van to wonder for twenty years where she was.

As if reading her mind, Patsy said, "Remember what I said yesterday, that I'd trade places with you if I could? That wasn't true, baby. I would never let you go through what I've gone through in the last twenty years. I'd die before I'd let you live through that."

Van felt tears burn her own eyes, and she brought the edge of the blanket up to dab them away. Then Patsy was beside her, arms around her, her face close. "Don't cry, baby. You know I never could stand to see you cry."

The smell of rum was overpowering. Van turned away, but Patsy put her hand to Van's cheek and pulled her face back toward her. "Don't cry," Patsy said again, and kissed Van's cheek.

Van jerked away. "Don't, Patsy."

Patsy didn't seem to hear. She pressed her lips hard against Van's eye, as if trying to kiss her tears away. Van moved, and Patsy shifted to kiss the other eye, but instead, her jaw hit Van's cheek in a blow hard enough to cause Van to rear back. Patsy persisted, this time pressing her lips hard against Van's.

Van wrenched away. "Patsy, stop it. I don't want to."

"Don't worry, baby." Patsy did not release her hold on Van. "I won't pressure you. I'm comforting you, that's all." Again she closed in on Van. Van put her hands on Patsy's shoulders and shoved as hard as she could, jumping up at the same time.

"No!" Van grabbed the blanket and wrapped it around her, stepping out of Patsy's reach. "I don't want your comfort. You're drunk, Patsy. You've been drunk practically every minute since I got here."

Patsy stood as well, her cheeks red with embarrassment or rage. "I told you, I only drink to deal with the pain. After you left—"

"I didn't leave!" Van shouted. "It's not my fault. Don't blame me because you drink or because I don't want to kiss a drunk."

"Goddamn it." Patsy grabbed the unopened bottle of rum by the neck and pulled her arm back, barely missing Van's head with the bottle. "You don't want me to drink this? Fine, I won't fucking drink it." She threw the bottle with all her might toward the wall behind the couch. The bottle shattered, glass and rum spattering the wall, the couch, and the floor.

Van dropped the blanket, snatched her clothes, and ran to the bathroom, locking the door behind her. Sobbing, she hastily dressed, gathered her meager belongings with shaking hands, and threw them into the worn plastic bag she'd brought them in. Toothbrush, deodorant, tampons, shampoo. She paused to look at herself in the mirror.

Her eyes were huge and dark, face pale, hair wild. In all the time she'd lived with Patsy, they'd never had a fight like that. Disagreements sometimes, of course, now and then a full-blown argument, but never the sort of violence Patsy had just displayed. Except, she recalled with a chill, when she'd shoved Bennie off the deck.

A soft knock on the bathroom door made her start. "Van?" Patsy's voice was weak and wavering, no longer violent. "Are you okay in there? I'm sorry, baby. I'm sorry for what happened out here. Come on out and let's get some sleep. I won't try to kiss you any more, I promise."

Patsy still didn't get that it was the *drinking* that was the problem, not the kissing. Van grabbed both handles of the plastic bag and twisted them into a knot. After checking her pocket to make sure she still had her meager cash and Bennie's card, she unlocked the bathroom door and opened it.

Patsy stepped back, an ingratiating smile on her face that vanished when she saw Van dressed and holding the sack. "You're not...you're not leaving."

Van pushed past Patsy and headed for the door, eyes burning from the liquor fumes permeating the living room.

"Van, no." Patsy grabbed for Van's arm, but Van shook her off.

At the door, she stopped and turned back to Patsy. "I need some time," she said simply, and left, closing the door behind her.

Chapter Sixteen

Patsy — 1988

PATSY SLAMMED THE door to the garage, climbed into her truck, banged that door closed too, and cranked up her new CD as high as it would go. Quickly, she turned it down again, as the high on her new CD player was even louder than Patsy's fury could handle.

"God damn it to hell!" She slammed her hands on the steering wheel. "That fucking punk ass cunt." How dare that bitch put her hands on Van that way, on Patsy's fucking birthday too? And Van *let* her.

Patsy had watched the two of them for several moments as she strode from the garage to the deck, shocked as shit. First Bennie held Van precariously at the edge of the deck, and Patsy had actually started to run, thinking Bennie meant to drop Van off the deck. They'd straightened up, though, and Van moved so she wasn't tipped over the edge any more. But she hadn't moved away, she hadn't pushed at Bennie, she hadn't removed Bennie's hands. By the time Patsy reached the deck, she'd been close enough to see Bennie's thumbs stroking the soft flesh of Van's arms, and Van didn't do a damn thing to stop her.

"God damned fucking, fucking bitch." She didn't know whether she meant Bennie or Van. There was guilt in Van's eyes when she'd seen Patsy standing there. Why would she feel guilt if she was innocent? And it was Patsy's goddamned birthday, for Christ's sake. God, she wanted a beer. That's what she'd headed to the porch for in the first place, but her rage at seeing Bennie and Van like that made her forget to grab one. She'd stormed off the porch and back to the garage, ignoring their mesmerized friends. She hoped to God none of them came in to talk to her. She needed some fucking time alone.

Patsy dropped her forehead to the steering wheel and closed her eyes. Despite what Van had said, Patsy was not drunk. It took a helluva lot more beer than what she'd had so far to make Patsy drunk. Not that she wasn't *planning* to get drunk. It was her birthday. Of *course* she planned to get drunk. She just hadn't even come close yet. Patsy clasped her hands on the top of the steering wheel and bounced her head on them a couple of times, trying to calm down.

She couldn't fuck this up. She wasn't a kid anymore, she was fifty years old, for God's sake, she had to be smart. Whatever she did, she couldn't risk losing Van because she was too angry to think before doing something stupid. Never had she loved anyone the way she loved Van, never had she felt so complete and happy and secure with anyone. Maybe there was nothing in what she'd seen on the porch. Probably there was nothing. She couldn't be that wrong about Van. Patsy had had many lovers, and she'd had her heart broken on more than one occasion, but her feelings in those cases were minor league compared with her feelings for Van. She couldn't be that wrong.

She thought she'd found true love with Linda, Catherine's mother. They'd lived together for six years, from the time Catherine was seven until she was thirteen. Patsy had bought into the whole family idea. She was tickled to be Catherine's "Mama P," had taught her to throw and hit and catch a ball, took care of her when she was sick, and convinced her she could still go swimming when she started her period. Patsy would have sworn she'd loved Linda with her whole heart. But when Linda finally dumped her for another woman, it was Catherine Patsy missed, not Linda. Not until she'd met Van did Patsy understand what it meant to truly love another woman with her whole heart.

If she lost Van, the bottom would drop out of her world.

The words on the CD caught her attention as Melissa Etheridge begged someone to bring her some water, she was burning alive 'cause her baby'd found another lover. How did that woman know exactly how Patsy felt? Except Van didn't have another lover yet, please God.

And, Patsy acknowledged, she wanted something stronger than water. She drank too much. She knew it. Van had been hinting about it for some time, but Patsy had suspected it herself for even longer. She'd been trying to cut back, but today was her birthday. She'd been looking forward to it for days—no, weeks—in part because it was an excuse to drink as much as she wanted to. If she couldn't drink on her fiftieth birthday, when the fuck could she?

A chilling thought edged into her mind. Could it have been the drinking that made Van turn to Bennie? Patsy reeled away from the uneasy thought. No, she didn't drink *that* much. It wasn't like she ever passed out or got falling down drunk or anything, and she would *never* do anything to hurt Van. Still, it had crossed her mind now and then to talk to Van about it. Not until after her birthday, of course.

But her birthday was almost over.

The thought of telling Van, of saying the words to her, "Van, I think I have a drinking problem," was terrifying, but the thought of losing Van was even more so.

Patsy considered saying the words out loud now, for practice. "Van," she said. "Van—" But her voice wobbled and she couldn't say the rest. Why was it so damn hard? Somewhat desperately, she grabbed the CD cover and studied the photograph. Melissa Etheridge stood with fists clenched tight, her head thrown back in despair or rage or heartbreak. Melissa would understand.

"Melissa," Patsy said, her voice unusually shaky and nearly drowned out by the song, "I think I have a drinking problem." Patsy was surprised at the effect her own spoken words had on her. Suddenly it was clear to her. She didn't *think* she had a drinking problem. She *knew* she did. She'd known it for a long time, but had refused to admit it, even to herself. But now she had said it out loud, and she couldn't deny it any longer. "I have a drinking problem, Melissa," she said again, her voice stronger.

She turned her head in the direction of the house and, nearly shouting, said, "Van, I have a drinking problem." Immediately, she felt relief. She would be able to talk to Van about it, first thing tomorrow, maybe even tonight after everyone left. Van would help her. Van wouldn't make her fight this thing alone.

She pushed eject and replaced the CD in its case, got out of the truck, and shut the door with no excess force. The scene with Bennie suddenly took on a new perspective. What had happened, after all? It's not like they were making out or making love or anything. Van had said it wasn't what it looked like, and she did order Bennie to leave. Van was right, Patsy *was* overreacting. She could hardly wait to talk to Van, let her know she wasn't upset about Bennie any longer.

Patsy headed toward the house and saw that Jill already had her RIP machine fired up, the antennae rotating smoothly in the air above it. Jill sat in the cab of the truck, headphones over her ears, and Kendra stood next to the cab, her boobs practically falling out of her shirt as she tiptoed to watch Jill through the window.

Inez sat in the rocking deck chair with Michael nestled under her chin. She glanced up when Patsy reached the steps and smiled, obviously recognizing that Patsy's anger had run its course.

"You're all right," Inez said softly.

"I'm fine." Patsy sat in the deck chair next to Inez. "Where is everyone?"

"The girls left. Catherine said to tell you good bye. Waverly and Grace went line dancing. They took Ellen and Terri with them. I'm babysitting."

Patsy raised her brows. "Earth mother left her newborn cub to go dancing?"

"She jumped at the chance."

"What a hypocrite," Patsy said without vigor. "Where's Van?"

"In RIP."

"But it's my turn."

"She said she'd take your turn for you, since it's your birthday."

"That little brat. She's using all her sweetness and charm to disarm me. She knows how much I hate sitting in that thing."

"She's too good for you," Inez said, with the certainty of many years' friendship.

"I know," Patsy said solemnly. "Believe me, I know it." She flipped up the lid of the cooler behind her. Nestled in with the bottles of beer were a couple of cans of 7-Up. What the hell. She pulled one out, popped the top, and took a long drink. Pretending she didn't notice Inez's curiosity at her choice of beverage, Patsy relaxed back into her chair, watched RIP, and waited for Van to come out.

Chapter Seventeen

Van — 2008

VAN'S ANGER KEPT her warm, at first. What the hell had Patsy been thinking? Practically forcing herself on Van, throwing the bottle of rum that way, blaming Van for her drinking. Was it the alcohol or the twenty years that had changed Patsy so much? Van didn't know, but she was certain of one thing. That was not her Patsy back there. The loyalty and love she'd felt toward Patsy, that had prompted Van to try to stay with Patsy and give her a chance, that loyalty and love was not for this Patsy. This was a different person, a self-centered, cowardly person, an alcoholic, a stranger. Van had no loyalty to her.

Of course she loved Patsy. Van had no doubts on that score. At that very moment she longed for Patsy more than anything. Patsy would understand how desolate Van felt right now, how frightened she was, how angry and confused and alone she was, how much she needed her. Patsy wouldn't let Van be alone in the middle of the night like this, in a strange century. She would stay with her, hold her, love her, protect her, and comfort her. But that woman back there was *not* Patsy.

Van shivered. The unseasonably warm weather was as fickle as June weather typically was. It was now cold, windy, and damp, more like March than June, and Van was not dressed for it. She pulled Jill's t-shirt out of her plastic bag and put it on over her tank top. Her overalls were still at Jill's. Van hadn't missed the warmer clothes yesterday. She had kept herself comfortable by moving the furniture and boxes on Patsy's porch. But she missed them now. Jill's shorts and t-shirt were not enough to keep her warm in the plummeting temperatures.

Van's anger at Patsy faded as she grew increasingly concerned about her situation. She had no idea what time it was, except it was the middle of the night. The entire town of Deer Park was closed and dark, even Yokes. Van had given no thought to direction when she left Patsy's, and now she had no clue where she was headed. She wished she'd thought to grab Patsy's bike, but she would not go back to retrieve it.

The street had once been a thriving core of the town, but now was relegated to second hand shops, pawn shops, and the like. There was no traffic. Van kept her eyes open for a pay phone. She hadn't decided yet who to call. Jill and Kendra were apparently hiding out somewhere working on RIP. Inez? But she lived in a retirement home. And anyway, Van remembered the relief that had been evident on Inez's face—on everyone's faces—when Van had announced she would be staying with Patsy. Inez wouldn't know what to do with Van, any more than Van knew what to do with herself.

Van grew increasingly frustrated by her helplessness. She had always been self-reliant. From a very young age she had taken responsibility for herself and let her parents focus their attentions on her two younger brothers, who were more demanding and needy. Van hadn't tried to compete with her brothers for her parents' attention, she'd simply removed herself from that arena and took care of her own needs. She did her homework, got good grades, earned scholarships, and put herself through college and law school. She'd never asked for help. When problems arose, as they inevitably did, when her car broke down or when her she didn't have the rent money or when she got sick, she muddled through it, and she always managed to come out on the other side stronger and more resilient than ever before. Not until Patsy entered her life did Van learn the comfort of leaning on another person. But even then, it was a choice. Van didn't *need* Patsy, she *wanted* her. She chose her and she loved her and she leaned on her, when she wanted to, but she didn't need her. Van didn't need anybody.

Now, for the first time in her life, Van needed help. She had no clue how to muddle through being thrust into the twenty-first century. How could she? As far as Van knew, she was the only person who'd ever leaped twenty years in time to find herself impoverished, homeless, unemployed, and legally dead. And friendless, she added to herself, blinking away tears even as she castigated herself for deliberately courting self pity. She was *not* friendless. Jill would not abandon her, nor would Kendra or Inez. Even Patsy would do what she could for Van, if Van would only let her. And, of course, there was Bennie.

Van had trudged nearly three miles when she finally found an all-night mini-market. The warmth that struck her when she entered the building made her realize how cold she was. The Asian woman behind the counter glanced up from the want ads and with a heavy accent said, "Can I help you?"

"Do you have a phone I could use?"

The woman pointed out the door. "Pay phone down block." She returned her attention to the paper.

"How far is it?"

The woman kept her head down but raised her hand and made a shooing gesture at Van. "Jus' down block. Not far."

"How much does a pay phone cost?" Van fingered the cash in her pocket. She didn't need to count it. She knew to the penny how much money she had left. Two dollars and eighteen cents.

The woman did look up at that. She took in Van's disheveled

appearance and her plastic bag. "You no get money here. You go use pay phone down block. Go. Go."

"I don't want money. But I might need change. Can I get change for a dollar?"

The woman relaxed slightly when Van pulled a crumpled bill out of her pocket. "You buy something, you get change."

Van sighed. She grabbed the smallest pack of gum she could find on the rack and slapped it on the counter, pocketed the two quarters she received in change, and pushed out the door into the night, heading the direction the woman had indicated.

She found the pay phone a couple of blocks further on, mounted on a wall outside a closed laundry mat. Van was relieved to see that a call was only fifty cents, but when she dropped in the two quarters, she heard no dial tone. She pushed the coin return, but nothing happened. "Damn it." She slapped her hand against the box several times, punched some numbers on the face of the phone, and hit the side of the phone box itself with the palm of her hand, but nothing happened. "Fuck, fuck, fuck!" The label on the front of the phone said that calls to 911 were free. She wondered if the phone would work if she dialed 911. If she did, what would she say? "Hi, this is an emergency. I've been transported from 1988. Will you help me get back there?" That would be a pretty picture. They'd find her, if they even bothered to try, wandering the streets with all her worldly possessions in her sack, a typical bag lady obsessed with her delusions of living in the wrong century. They'd take her straight to the loony bin. Besides, Jill had said no police.

Van pushed herself away from the phone and continued walking. She was tired, but it was too cold to remain still for long. The wind whipped at her brutally, and she snaked her arms inside Jill's roomy t-shirt to keep them warm, the plastic bag nestled against her belly like the pregnancy simulator Terri had worn when Ellen was pregnant with Michael.

A mile farther on, she came to another all-night gas station and mini-market. Van pulled her arms out of her t-shirt, tried to finger comb her wind-tangled hair, and pushed inside. The thin young man at the counter was very fair, with a shock of straight white hair and pale blue eyes. He didn't seem old enough to sell the beer and wine that stocked half the store's shelves. He examined Van with interest.

"Is there a pay phone around here?"

He shook his head. "Not that I know of. Nobody uses those things any more."

Van turned to go, but the young man's voice stopped her. "Why don't you use my cell?"

He held out a shiny black phone. Smiling thanks, she took it, flipped it open, and hesitated. Sheepishly, recalling Maddy's ridicule, she said, "I've never actually called anyone on one of these before."

"Huh? You've never used a cell phone?"

"If I give you the number, will you dial it for me?"

"Sure," he said, staring at Van as if she'd dropped in from another planet. Or century.

Van read aloud from Bennie's card. He punched the numbers and handed the phone to her. Van turned away and stared blindly at the selection of sodas and beer in the coolers. She listened to the ringing. A glance at the wall told her the time. What was she doing calling Bennie at two o'clock in the morning? She was about to hang up when she heard Bennie's voice.

"You've reached Benita Sanchez. Please leave me a message." *Beep.*

"Hi Bennie," her voice sounded unnaturally loud in the empty market, and she lowered it so the young man couldn't hear. "This is Van. I'm sorry for bothering you this time of night. Although, since you didn't answer, I guess I didn't really. Um, anyway. You said if I needed anything, to give you a call, so... I'm at a mini-market, in Deer Park. I've been staying with Patsy, but I left..." Van heard her voice waver, and she took a deep steadying breath before continuing. "I left there. And, you said if I needed anything to give you a call. So, I need, I need..." Van couldn't control it any longer. Her voice cracked and rose, as tears started from her eyes. "I need some help, Bennie. I...I don't know wh-what to do or wh-where to go. I've been walking and walking. I...I—" Van pulled the neck of the t-shirt up to wipe her eyes and took two more deep steadying breaths. "I've been walking and I'm at mini-mart so... Well, anyway, you...you're not there, so I...I guess I'll call you tomorrow. G'night."

Van closed the phone and wiped her eyes again on her shirt, and handed the phone back to the young man, who watched her somberly. "Thank you." She turned to go.

As she reached the door, he spoke. "You take care of yourself." She gave him a weak smile over her shoulder and left.

Van still didn't have a destination, so she continued slogging aimlessly. She felt foolish for breaking down while talking to Bennie's answering machine. Why had she even called? She should have waited until morning. Although it was cold, it would start getting light in a couple more hours. If she could make it through the rest of the night, the morning wouldn't be so bad. She'd find a restaurant, sit down and have some coffee, find another phone. She only had to manage a little while longer, and she'd be fine.

Then she felt the first cold stinging pricks of rain. "Fuck!" She darted for the doorway of a check cashing business and huddled into it, her plastic bag held over her head to ward of the worst of the rain. A moment later she reeled out of the doorway, driven away by the overpowering odor of urine. After darting from smelly doorway to smelly doorway trying to keep dry, Van accepted defeat and simply trudged along the sidewalk and let the cold rain beat down on her.

Chapter Eighteen

Bennie — 2008

IT HAD BEEN a long time since Bennie had closed down a bar. Her shirt clung to her back and under her arms from the sweat she'd worked up dancing. She hadn't sat out more than a couple of dances. Not bad for forty-eight years old, especially since, more often than not, she'd been the one asked to dance, and usually by girls in their twenties and thirties. It was either the ego thrill of being chased or it was that last Jello shot, but her blood was still singing in her veins. Jello shots! What goes around comes around, she guessed. Who'd have thought they'd be serving Jello shots in a lesbian bar in 2008?

She wasn't sure what had gotten into her tonight. A sense of freedom, she guessed. She'd put Arlene on a plane that afternoon for an indefinite stay with her mother. Arlene was thrilled with the plane ticket, and Bennie was thrilled to have her out of the picture for a while. Arlene was acting way too comfortable in Bennie's house. The price of the plane ticket was a cheap way to start letting her down easily. She'd been thinking of ways to cut Arlene loose for some time, but it took on a greater urgency now that Van was back.

Thinking of Van made Bennie feel like a kid. She guessed it was normal, in a way. She'd fallen for Van hard, her first love, even though she'd been twenty-eight years old at the time. Bennie was a player in those days. The game was to get the girls to love *her*, not the other way around. Van was the first to make Bennie fall. And don't people always carry a torch for their first love?

Even though Van hadn't loved her back. Yet. Bennie handled that whole situation badly. She'd been a jackass, in fact, trying so hard to convince Van to give her a chance. Van *had* felt something for her, Bennie was sure of that, at least. But she understood now, as she hadn't then, that feeling something for someone wasn't an excuse to act upon it. She also understood now that Van could have felt stirrings of something for Bennie and still truly loved Patsy, as much as it galled her to admit it.

Bennie was certain that if Van hadn't disappeared, Bennie would have destroyed, with her arrogant clumsiness, any nascent feelings Van may have had for her. She would have pushed too hard and too fast, and she would likely have made Van hate her, rather than love her. Which is what she had wanted more than anything.

But now Van had reappeared, the very same Van, and Bennie hadn't ruined anything. She hadn't had a chance to because Van disappeared before Bennie had a chance to truly screw things up. It was like a miracle, or fate. Bennie had another chance, and this time, she hoped, she had the maturity and wisdom to handle it right, with the care it deserved.

If Van would let her. If Bennie had learned anything in the last twenty years, she'd learned that. Van got to call the shots, Van got to give the cues, Van had to be the one who let Bennie know when she was ready. Bennie smiled. It wasn't as if Van was hard to read. Every thought and feeling showed so clearly on her face.

Her smile faded, though, as she recalled Van's face the day before. As soon as she got Kendra's call, she'd raced up to Jill's house, her heart in her throat, wanting so hard to believe Kendra. Bennie had known about the time machine—not at first, but Kendra spilled the beans eventually. Bennie just had a hard time believing it. She hadn't been there when Van disappeared. She hadn't seen it, as they all professed to have. Part of her never stopped suspecting Patsy of getting rid of Van somehow, though she knew the police hadn't been able to find any evidence of foul play. It was just...time travel? Incredible.

Then to find out it was true! She could still see Van standing there, screaming for a tampon, surrounded by her old friends, her old lover, who were—let's face it—*old*. She'd been so forlorn, so frightened, so confused. How could she not be? Bennie's heart had melted for her. She'd wanted to take Van into her arms, put her in the car, carry her away, and take care of her forever. And she got her as far as the car.

Bennie smiled again, briefly, as she recalled those few moments. Van had been so beautiful, so vibrant and alive and real. Bennie was tempted to kiss her then and there. But Van had also been vulnerable and afraid. It would have been indecent to take advantage of her at that moment.

Now as Bennie got into her Jag, her phone chimed. She took it out of her jacket pocket and was surprised to see she had a message. An unknown number. She put the phone in its hands-free cradle, pulled the Jag out of the parking lot, and hit the button. At the sound of Van's voice, she braked. An old Ford pickup, packed with at least four women in the cab, lurched to a stop behind her, then pulled around, the occupants all flipping her off, but Bennie didn't respond. Van's plaintive voice filled the Jag. "I need some help, Bennie. I...I don't know wh-what to do...." As the message played, Bennie stared outside at the black night, the wind whipping the trees, and, as she watched, raindrops started pelting the windshield, and the wipers began their automatic sweep to keep the glass clear. The call had come in only minutes before.

"Sweet Jesus." With trembling hands, Bennie grabbed the phone from its cradle and hit last call return.

"Curt here." It was a young man's voice.

"I got a call from this number, a few minutes ago, a woman?"

"Yeah, I let her use my phone."

"Is she there?"

"No, sorry, man, she left right after."

"Do you know where she was going?"

"I don't think she was going anywhere in particular, you know? She looked, like, sort of lost, you know?"

Bennie closed her eyes, as if trying to block out the vision of Van wandering in this storm, alone and lost.

"It would be good if you could find her, you know?" the man said. "She looked pretty cold."

"I'll find her. Where are you?" She jotted down the address and hung up the phone. "I'll find her," she repeated firmly. She put the car in gear and headed for the highway.

The dealer had expounded at great length about the magnificent speed and handling of the Jag, regardless of weather, but Bennie hadn't expected to ever have an opportunity to see what the Jag could really do. That night, she did. Still, the twenty minutes it took her to reach Deer Park felt like eons. Why was Van calling her for help in the middle of the night? What was it she had said? "I've been staying with Patsy, but I left." In the middle of the night? *Why?* Bennie knew — hell, everyone knew — that Patsy was a drunk. Why had they let Van stay with her? Where the hell were Jill and Kendra? Where was Inez? When Bennie had left Van with the three older women — four, if you counted Patsy — it hadn't occurred to her that Van would simply be abandoned, like an unwanted child, on Patsy's doorstep, and left there to fend for herself. She'd never have left her at Jill's that day if she'd known that. Van *needed* their help right now.

The storm gained in intensity with every mile. And with every blast of wind, Bennie imagined Van being buffeted by it. With every slap of rain on the windshield, she saw Van drenched with it. She watched the outside temperature gauge drop as she drove north, and by the time she reached Deer Park, it had plummeted to thirty-nine degrees. And she could feel Van shivering in it.

Bennie forced herself to slow down when she got to the outskirts of town, peering through the driving rain, in case she saw her. Would Van have stayed on the main streets, or would she have ventured into side streets? With no idea where to begin searching, Bennie programmed the mini mart into the GPS and drove straight there.

"Are you Curt?" she asked abruptly upon entering the store.

The pale young man glanced up. "Yeah." His eyes assessed Bennie rapidly. "You're looking for that woman?"

"Yes. Have you seen her again?"

"No." Curt tilted his head and examined at Bennie curiously. "She asked to use a payphone. When I gave her my cell, she didn't even know how to use it."

Bennie's heart clenched at the thought of Van wandering around in the wrong century, not even knowing how to make a phone call.

"Did she, like, escape from a mental hospital or something?"

"God, no."

"Hey, it's okay with me if she did." Curt assured her. "I won't turn her in or nothing. There's too many fucking people trying to make us all think the same way, if you ask me. Crazy's good."

"She's not crazy. She's lost. Did you see which way she went?"

"Yeah, she took off down that way." He pointed west. "But I don't think she knew where she was going."

"What was she wearing?"

"Man, just this green t-shirt and shorts. Tennis shoes, I think. No coat or nothing."

The same clothes she'd been wearing when Bennie had seen her two days ago, when it was hot. Jesus, couldn't they have even given her something decent to wear?

She pulled a card from her wallet, scrawled her cell number on the back, and handed it to Curt. "If you see her, will you give me a call?"

"Sure."

The rain pelted Bennie's head on her dash to the car. Each drop was an icy bludgeon, and Bennie didn't see how Van could possibly survive it in her thin t-shirt and shorts. She had to have taken shelter somewhere, but Bennie's only hope in finding her was if she hadn't, if she was out in the open. She steered the Jag west.

An hour later, Bennie still cruised the westerly streets of Deer Park, no nearer to finding Van. Her eyes were gritty with the strain of peering through the dark rain to discern shadows moving on sidewalks and streets, indistinct shapes in doorways and under awnings and bridges. She saw few people. A trio of young men hunched in a doorway smoking something they hid as soon as they saw her car. They hadn't seen any woman wearing a t-shirt and shorts. Neither had the elderly woman wearing crepe-soled shoes who stepped purposefully down the street with her sturdy umbrella, nor the tearful young couple having an earnest conversation in a parked car. No one had seen Van.

Finally at the edge of town Bennie reached a bridge that spanned a deep ditch and noticed a faint, flickering glow coming from beneath it. Someone had a fire going under there. Bennie pulled over to the side of the road, got out of the car, and was instantly slapped in the face with a sheet of rain. She pulled the collar of her leather coat up and moved forward to investigate. The ground sloped underneath the bridge and was slick with mud. Bennie held onto the bridge pilings to prevent herself from sliding downward and ducked to see the fire.

A primitive camp clung to the slope beneath the bridge. A large tarp was draped to form a makeshift tent, and shapes underneath it huddled in blankets and sleeping bags. Bennie smelled coffee. Two figures tended the fire and sipped from steaming mugs.

She stepped forward. "Excuse me, I'm looking for—"

The figures at the fire jumped instantly to their feet. "Fuck off, man!" The voice was loud and harsh and young. The figures underneath the tarp stirred. "Get the fuck away from us."

"No, wait. I'm looking for a woman. She's lost—"

"I said fuck off!" The fire tender bent to the ground, picked something up, and threw it toward Bennie. The other figures scrambled up as well, grabbed things, and threw them.

She was pelted with rocks and sticks, nothing large enough to hurt her, but she got the message. She turned and pulled herself back up to the road, and the frightened voices behind her subsided. But when she got to her car, she heard a childish voice call after her.

"Hey, lady! She was here. That woman. She went across the bridge."

Bennie's heart leapt. "How long ago?"

"I don't know. I fell asleep."

The harsh voice chimed in. "About a half hour ago. Now fuck off."

Bennie smiled. "Thank you." She jumped into the car and drove across the bridge.

As soon as she got to the other side, a shape careened toward the car. Bennie hit the brakes and the figure ran smack into the driver's side of the car. Palms slapped flat against the window right beside Bennie's head. Her first thought was that one of the teenagers had somehow followed her and was trying to get her attention. Then she realized the drenched figure was calling her name as she again slapped her hands against Bennie's window.

"Bennie. *Bennie!*"

"Jesus, Van!" Bennie quickly opened the door and got out. Van took a short stumbling step back. "Van, my God, look at you."

Her hair was plastered to her head, her t-shirt hung dripping and heavy nearly to her knees, and she shivered uncontrollably. Bennie grabbed her arms before she fell backward. "Get in the car." She wrapped an arm around Van, guided her quickly around the car, and bundled her into the passenger seat. She hurried back into the driver's side, pulled the car over to the side of the road, cranked up the heat, and shifted in her seat to examine her sodden companion.

Van's hair hung in dark dripping strings around her face, her eyes were red from crying, and her lips were blue and trembling. Purple gooseflesh covered her legs. The wet t-shirt was stretched beyond recognition, and Bennie suspected that at one point Van must have wrapped the t-shirt around her whole body. She carried a soggy plastic Yokes bag clenched in one hand. She stared at Bennie with huge eyes, as if she didn't trust her to be real.

"You poor little drowned rat." Bennie touched Van's dripping hair, then pushed the seat-warmer button. She struggled out of her jacket. "Here, put this over you."

Bennie watched as Van, shivering uncontrollably, closed her eyes and snuggled into the jacket's warmth. "Oh, it's s-so w-warm. Th-thank you." She opened her eyes and smiled wanly up at Bennie. "You f-f-found m-me." she said, as if Bennie had done something very clever.

As Van nestled into the jacket, Bennie felt the anxiety in her chest unclench. "It wasn't easy. Didn't anyone ever tell you, if you're lost, to stay in one place?"

"I w-wasn't lost. I j-j-just didn't know wh-wh-where to go. I was under the b-b-bridge. I saw you t-talking to those kids on the other s-s-side. I thought it was y-y-you. You got my m-message?"

"I did. I'm glad you called me."

"Were you s-s-sleeping?"

"No, I was out. I didn't hear the ring."

Van's hands hugged the collar of Bennie's jacket under her chin. "Out? What d-day of the w-week is it?"

"It's Saturday morning."

Van shook her head, momentarily puzzled. "It should b-be T-Tuesday, no, W-w-Wednesday..." Her voice trailed off. "Were you on a d-date?"

"Not a date. Just out, you know, dancing."

"Dancing b-by yourself?" Her eyes grew wide. "Is my s-seat heated?"

Bennie laughed softly "It is."

Van closed her eyes and snuggled further down into the seat. "It f-feels so good."

Bennie watched for a moment, wishing there was something more she could do to warm Van up. She recalled her old high school phys ed teacher once telling her that the remedy for hypothermia was to get naked with the suffering person and rub your body all over theirs. At sixteen, she'd nearly had an orgasm right there in class just thinking about it. But the sporty Jag was not set up for naked body rubbings, and in any case, Van didn't seem to be suffering from hypothermia after all. Her shivering had eased, and she gradually relaxed in the warmth. Bennie again pushed the hair back from Van's face, took a handful of it, and squeezed out the excess water.

Van's eyes fluttered. "Your poor seat. I'm getting it all wet."

"It'll dry out." Bennie leaned over and pulled Van's shoulder belt to buckle her in. Van blinked at her, eyes heavy with fatigue. Her lips were no longer blue, but full and red and smiling with sleepy gratitude. Bennie was overwhelmed by the desire to kiss her and leaned forward to do it but Van's eyelids fluttered again, as if they were too heavy to keep open. Van was falling asleep before her eyes. Bennie contented herself with pressing her lips to the side of Van's head and saying a brief prayer of gratitude, before she pushed the button to lower Van's seat to a reclining position. Van eased back gently and didn't stir.

"Sleep, Van." Bennie pulled the Jag into the street and made a U-turn. The sky was slightly brighter in the east. Dawn was near. "Sleep. We're going home."

Chapter Nineteen

Jill — 2008

JILL LAY WITH her left arm behind her head and her right arm around Kendra, who rested her head on Jill's shoulder. Kendra ran a finger around Jill's left breast, then the right, bringing it up to circle the aureole. As the nipple swelled, Kendra leaned over and let her tongue follow her fingertip, pulling the nipple into her mouth and sucking gently. Jill gasped.

"I love your breasts," Kendra breathed softly, giving the erect nipple a kiss. She kissed the left as well before settling back into the curve of Jill's shoulders.

"What, these old things?" Jill asked. "They're seventy years old, you know."

"Yeah, but you have the body of a sixty year old, and sixty is the new fifty. Your breasts definitely look younger than mine. I wish I had small breasts like yours."

She was blatantly fishing, but it worked. Jill was horrified. "Don't even say such a thing. Your breasts are magnificent." She sat up in the bed, gently moved Kendra's head onto the pillow, and gave Kendra's breasts a thorough scrutiny that was not entirely scientific. They were definitely large, and as Kendra lay on her back, they drooped off the sides of her body. Jill gently cradled them in her hands and lifted them to the front of Kendra's body and held them there, plump and erect.

Kendra averted her eyes, surprisingly bashful at Jill's candid appreciation. "Come on, I've nursed two children with these breasts. And they were large even before that. If it weren't for that harness they call a full-figured bra, they'd hang to my belly button. And look at the stretch marks."

Puzzled, Jill asked, "Why would you think that's bad?" Still holding Kendra's breasts full and lush on her chest, Jill buried her face between them and kissed the smooth breastbone between. She gazed up at Kendra and said simply, "They're the most beautiful things I've ever seen."

Kendra smiled, tremulously at first, then with increasing delight. She cupped Jill's face in her hands and tugged gently, making Jill crawl up for a kiss. They settled into each other's arms, bare legs entwined. "How could we have wasted the last twenty years apart?"

"We weren't exactly apart," Jill said. "We've been friends all along. That wasn't wasted time."

"I know, but that's not the same. *This* is what I wanted."

"No, it's not. You've had lots of girlfriends *and* boyfriends in the last twenty years. You weren't wasting away lusting after me."

"Wrong," said Kendra. "I've had lots of girlfriends and boyfriends, but I always lusted after you. From the first time we met at Patsy's fiftieth."

Jill raised herself up on an elbow and stared down at Kendra, astonished and skeptical. "Nuh uh, you did not." But when she saw the eloquent expression in Kendra's eyes, she faltered. "Did you?"

"Think about it, honey." Kendra drew Jill's head down and pressed it on her chest. "There I was, Inez's date, and all I did was hang around you and RIP. And you know I don't have a scientific mind. Why did you think I did that?"

"I didn't think about it." Jill skimmed the palm of her hand across Kendra's large dark nipple. "I thought you were interested. In RIP, I mean. What about all your girlfriends? What about Megan? You lived with her for three years."

"So I wasn't celibate. That doesn't mean I didn't have my eye on you the whole time."

"But you never said anything. Why didn't you ever say anything?"

"At first I was too intimidated by you."

"By me?" Jill raised herself up on her elbow again to goggle at Kendra, more astonished than ever. "*You* were intimidated by *me*?"

Kendra laughed. "Don't let it go to your head, honey, I know you a lot better now. But back then you seemed so smart and confident and self-contained. You'd been out for absolutely forever, and you were so confident in your sexuality." It was Jill's turn to laugh, but Kendra ignored her. "And there I was, at my first lesbian party, still married to Paul. I sold Mary Kay cosmetics, for Heaven's sake. How could you possibly be interested in *me*?"

Jill pondered that for a moment. "I certainly noticed you. How could I not? You were a knockout. I still remember what you wore. Tight black pants and that thin white blouse. And a black bra." She smiled at Kendra's look of surprise. "But you were Inez's date, so I couldn't think of you that way. And then Van disappeared, and I couldn't think of anything else for—"

"Years." Kendra sat up and linked hands with Jill, fingers intertwined. "I know. You were in bad shape for a long time after that. You needed me as a friend, so I just made sure I was there for you. But meanwhile," Kendra shrugged, "well, I'm not a nun."

Jill watched with a smile as Kendra's breasts swayed as a result of her shrug. "No, you're not a nun, thank God."

"Heretic," Kendra accused, deliberately giving her breasts another thrust for Jill's amusement. "And as the years passed and we became such *good* friends, I got too scared to say anything. I love our friendship, and I wasn't about to risk losing it because I wanted to jump your bones half the time. Sex is easy to come by, but a good friend is a miracle. Oh, not what we just had here," she said quickly, seeing Jill's wounded look. "*That* kind of sex isn't easy to come by. That wasn't sex, honey, *that* was making love. And making love with your best friend is the very best miracle of all."

For a moment they simply stared into each other's eyes, too overwhelmed by emotion to speak, saying it all without words. Jill took a deep shuddering breath, threaded her fingers through Kendra's hair, and pulled her in for a long, deep kiss.

"And now? After being my best friend for all these years, why did you decide to say something now?" Jill asked, though she was pretty sure she knew.

"Van showed up. Everything's changed now. If you can send her back, we might only have a little bit of time left here. In the present. And everything will be different."

Jill looked solemnly at the rumpled sheets of their borrowed bed, where they'd spent most of the last twenty-four hours, the clothes strewn on the cabin floor, the fire in the wood stove needing replenishment again, their naked bodies making contact at every opportunity as if magnetized. She released Kendra and slipped out of bed. She threw Kendra's ex's old jacket over her naked shoulders, went into the lean-to, and grabbed some more wood. After she stoked the fire, she stood at the window to take stock of the storm. It had raged all night, but it was finally wearing itself out with the dawn.

"A lot of things will change," Jill said, staring at the dripping trees. "We're living in the future that exists only if Van vanishes in 1988. If I send Van back, the future's bound to be different. I know *my* life would have turned out very differently if she hadn't vanished. And Patsy's, of course."

"It would change everyone's life. If Van didn't vanish that night, I would have gone home with Inez. And we wouldn't have had a second date, I know we wouldn't, and I might never have even seen you again. Would you and I have even become friends if Van hadn't disappeared that night? *Will* we become friends, if you send her back?"

Jill regarded Kendra, lying naked and tousled on the narrow bed, her bleached blond hair a frothy mess, her lips red and full, all the makeup worn off her face, her breasts swaying as she leaned forward. Jill felt anew the wonder of discovering that this extraordinary and beautiful woman, who happened also to be her best friend, loved her. For the first time in her seventy years, Jill felt truly loved by another woman. Kendra meant more to her than anyone ever had in her entire life, and the thought of not having her in it for the last twenty years, and especially now, was wrenchingly painful.

Could she give Kendra up? Just to send Van back to 1988? It wasn't fair. Van already knew what it was like to be truly loved. She'd had it with Patsy in 1988. They'd had six years together before Van disappeared, and she was still only forty-five years old. If Van didn't go back to 1988, she'd be fine. She'd fall in love again. But Jill, at seventy, had found love for the first time. Was it fair for her to have to give it up now? But was it fair *not* to send Van back, just because Jill had finally found love?

She sighed. "The weather's clearing up. Good day to work on RIP."

"You're a lot sexier in that old jacket than Paul ever was."

Jill peered down and laughed. "Did Paul ever wear it with his bare buns hanging out?"

"Not that I ever saw. It's a good look for you. C'mere and let me show you how much I like it."

Her voice was teasing, but as Jill returned to the bed, she saw tears in Kendra's eyes and knew she was genuinely frightened. Jill was too.

"Don't worry about it," she said softly, gathering Kendra into her arms. "Maybe I won't be able to fix RIP." But she knew she had to try.

Chapter Twenty

Van — 2008

VAN WOKE UP in a soft, warm bed and felt a flood of relief. The whole 2008 nightmare was just that—a nightmare. She reached for Patsy, but found the bed empty. And these didn't feel like their sheets.

She opened her eyes. She was alone in a strange bed in a strange room. Jill's borrowed t-shirt and shorts lay in a damp wad on a nearby chair, where she must have shed them, her sordid plastic bag plopped on top, like a cherry. Reality dropped, like a stone, into the pit of her stomach.

She remembered now, vaguely, being led up some stairs to this room. Tentatively, Van lifted the covers and peeked at herself. She was wearing a blue t-shirt. She couldn't recall whether she'd put it on herself or had help. She touched herself—no panties—and blushed. What a mess she'd been last night. She'd never been so cold in her life, nor so frightened. She wiggled her toes and was relieved when they all cheerfully responded. Frostbite probably wasn't possible when the temperature was above freezing, but you never know.

Van swung her legs out of bed, surprised at how she ached all over. Was it from shivering for so long? Her feet sank into a luxurious carpet, and she stood and stretched long and hard. Wood blinds covered two windows on one side of the spacious room, but a faint light showed around them. Van crossed to them, her feet leaving carpet for smooth, gleaming hard wood. She opened the blinds and took in the view. The rain had stopped, and weak sunlight shone through broken clouds. She was on the second story of a house overlooking Spokane. The city was immediately recognizable, though Van hadn't seen it in twenty years. There were taller buildings downtown, and more of them, but she could see the unmistakable clock tower and pavilion in Riverfront Park and an edge of the low building where her office had been twenty years before. She was on the South Hill, in an area that was considered upscale in 1988.

Based on the plushness of her surroundings, the neighborhood was still upscale. She swung around and inspected the room. It was clearly for guests, with no personal touches to indicate anyone lived there, but it was very comfortable. The bed was king size with a dark cherry wood headboard and matching dresser, chest-of-drawers, and two bedside tables. The walls were painted cream, and the comforter, pillows, and area rug were all tones of cream and tan, creating a subdued and elegant effect. Van wandered to an open door and found a bathroom the size of Jill's living room, with two sinks, a walk-in shower, and a toilet separated from the rest of the bathroom by another door. The bathroom was fully stocked with soap, shampoo, toothbrushes, razors, even tampons. Van quickly stripped and took a long hot shower, relishing the feel of being pampered. Was this all Bennie's?

After her shower, she dried her hair, brushed her teeth, and found a thick yellow robe hanging in the closet. There were no slippers to be found so, barefoot and with the robe brushing the floor, she opened the bedroom door to explore her surroundings.

She stepped out to a long landing about four feet wide. On the left, floor-to-ceiling bookshelves ran from wall to wall, separated occasionally by a closed cabinet door. The shelves were filled with books, art objects, and photos all tastefully displayed. On the right of the landing was a railing, rib high, that allowed her to peer out over the spacious entryway into Bennie's house. Below, in the center of the entryway, she saw large double doors made of dark wood with leaded glass windows on the top. Hardwood floors gleamed. The foyer was sparsely furnished, but the pieces spaced around the entryway appeared to be antiques in immaculate shape.

She was about to let out a low whistle of appreciation when she saw a movement from below. Bennie stepped out into the entryway from a wide doorway on the left and looked up. She wore a short, light tank top and an old pair of sweatpants that hung low and loose on her hips. An inch of smooth skin between the top of the pants and the bottom of the shirt showed off a hint of flat stomach. Bennie's short hair stuck out in all directions as if she'd just woken up, and she carried a steaming mug. She smiled when she saw Van.

"I thought I heard something." She held up the mug. "Would you like some coffee?"

"I'd love some." Bennie met her at the bottom of the stairs.

"The kitchen's right here." Bennie lead her into a massive room gleaming with chrome and granite. Van perched on a stool beside the breakfast bar, and Bennie poured her a cup of coffee. "Cream?"

"Black."

Bennie brought the coffee to her and sat on the stool next to her. "This is a nice place."

Bennie nodded. "I was lucky to find it. How are you feeling?"

"Fine. Well, kind of tired, and a bit achy. Thank you for rescuing me."

"My pleasure." Bennie smiled crookedly. "Hell, how many women get to ride to the rescue of their first love? It was a fantasy come true."

Van smiled and felt herself blushing. A sleek gray cat hopped up onto the counter and nudged Van's hand with her nose. Van petted it. "Who's this?"

"That's Pearl. There's another around here somewhere, Minnie, but she's shy."

"Minnie?" Van raised her eyebrows at Bennie. "Minnie and Pearl? You a *Hee Haw* fan?"

Bennie laughed. "My grandma was. I inherited the girls from her. I hope cats on the counter don't bother you. I can't train it out of them. Well, I haven't really tried."

"No, it doesn't bother me. I'm sorry about your grandma."

"Oh, she's not dead. She moved into a retirement home, and they don't allow cats. So I took them. We get along all right, the three of us."

Van inspected the spacious kitchen. "You live here alone?"

"Most of the time."

Van sipped her coffee and stroked Pearl until the cat grew bored and leaped down. She traced patterns in the granite with her finger and silently absorbed the feelings of calm, quiet, peace, warmth, and safety that fell over her. She couldn't help but compare her present surroundings with the last two nights spent on Patsy's couch, and before that a night spent on Jill's floor.

As if reading her mind, Bennie asked softly, "What happened last night?"

Van met Bennie's dark eyes, full of gentle warmth and understanding. It felt safe to tell her. "She's a stranger to me," Van said. "But, she doesn't understand that. She says she does, but she doesn't. She seems to think I should just, you know, be the way I always was with her, love her like I did before, but I can't! That's not the Patsy I know." Van spoke urgently, as if trying to convince Bennie of the truth of her words, but Bennie needed no convincing.

"Twenty years have passed. We've all changed, except for you. I know I have." Bennie covered Van's tracing finger with her hand, quieting it. "I'm sorry she doesn't understand that."

"And she's drinking." Van squelched the sense of betrayal she felt in saying it out loud. "A lot." Bennie nodded sympathetically, as if she'd already known.

Impulsively, Van gripped Bennie's hand hard. "Bennie, can I stay here? Just for a while? I don't want to go back there."

"Of course you can," Bennie said quickly. "You can stay as long as you like. I have lots of room."

"Thank you." Van bit her lip, feeling tremendously relieved and also embarrassed. She clutched the neck of her robe. "But Bennie, I don't have anything. I mean, I really don't have a thing. No clothes, no money, nothing."

Bennie smiled. "That's easily remedied. We'll go shopping. But have you thought about having yourself resurrected, legally I mean?

Can't you get declared *un*-dead, retrieve some of your money and property? You're a lawyer, isn't there a way?"

"I don't know, maybe. But I can't try yet. Jill says I need to keep myself under wraps for a while. Apparently there are some people from her old lab who want to get their hands on RIP. If they find out I'm here, they'll track it down."

"RIP?"

"Jill's time machine. She's trying to get it working again to send me back."

Bennie's smile faded. "Back?"

"Yes, back to 1988. She doesn't know if she can, but she's going to give it a try. *Ouch*, Bennie, my hand."

Bennie let go. "God, Van, I'm sorry."

Van stretched her fingers and smiled. "Hey, don't worry about it. Anyway, for now Jill wants me to lay low and not call attention to myself. So I can't try to resurrect myself yet."

Bennie tilted her head slightly and stared thoughtfully at Van for a moment, then seemed to make up her mind about something. She smiled slowly. "Okay, then, let me get you something to wear for now. We have some shopping to do. Fetching as that robe is on you, it won't do at Nordstrom."

Chapter Twenty-one

Inez — 2008

INEZ FELT SOME trepidation as she approached Patsy's door. She loved Patsy dearly, always had and always would. But it had grown harder in the last few years to *like* her. The natural give and take of an easy friendship had given way to awkwardness and dysfunction as Patsy's drinking spun out of control. Inez had played many roles in Patsy's life, but ever since Van disappeared, none of those roles were particularly pleasant. She gave Patsy emotional support when her heart broke and financial support when she lost her job. She'd offered tough love and interventions and advice, and when those didn't work, when Patsy hit rock bottom anyway, she had simply offered unconditional love.

But loving an alcoholic is a one way street, and even that waned eventually. In truth, Inez got nothing out of their friendship anymore. She was there for Patsy because of the first thirty years, not because of the last twenty. And if it hadn't been for Grace's loving and generous voice still ringing through her head and her heart, Inez doubted she'd be there still.

Where Inez couldn't help but take it personally every time she was slighted or embarrassed or ignored by Patsy in her drunkenness, Grace had seen Patsy's alcoholism as a sickness, something to be pitied, not something to cause anger. Maybe it was because Grace hadn't known Patsy before Van left. She never knew the Patsy who'd taken two scared little freshman lesbians under her wings — even though she'd been a scared little freshman lesbian herself — and made them a family. She never knew the Patsy who'd watched her friends like a hawk and, gruff as she was, knew before anyone else who was hurting, who was in love, who needed a helping hand, and she never knew the Patsy who would have cut off her right arm to give that helping hand if it was needed. Grace hadn't known what it was like to watch their beloved Patsy vanish into the abyss of alcoholism after Van disappeared. So maybe that explained why Grace didn't feel the dismay and the disappointment and the anger Inez felt watching it happen, when nothing she did could stop it.

Or maybe Grace just had a bigger and more forgiving heart than Inez had. Grace *definitely* had a bigger and more forgiving heart. Even when she was lying in her hospital bed, days away from death, and they'd been planning her funeral, Grace spared thoughts for Patsy.

"Don't get mad at her if she gets drunk at my funeral," Grace had warned.

"God, she *will* get drunk. I don't want her there. I won't tell her about it."

"It's not your funeral, love, it's mine. And I want her there." Grace had smiled at Inez's frustration, and even with her gaunt, pale face and ghastly sunken dark eyes, she managed to look serene and wise and full of love. "And you'll want her there too. You'll regret it forever if you let anger at Patsy mar my funeral. I won't let it happen."

"But if she gets drunk and makes a scene, that'll mar your funeral too. And *I* won't let *that* happen."

"Maybe you should make a plan. Get Jill in on it. Have her take care of Patsy, so that you can take care of yourself." Rocking her rainbow turbaned head back on forth on the pillow in a rare show of frustration, Grace had said, "I wish I could be there to take care of you. That's the worst part about all this — that I can't be there for you." She reached her hand out to Inez, who took it and cradled it gently in both of hers. "My love, you have to take care of yourself for me, okay? And that includes taking care of Patsy. Someday, if you're lying in a bed weeks, or maybe days, away from death, I don't want you to have any regrets about how you treated Patsy. Will you promise me that?"

Of course she had. She had kissed the dry lips and stroked the pale brow and promised to take care of Patsy, no matter how angry she made her. And at Grace's funeral, which had indeed occurred only two weeks later, Patsy had been there, not too drunk yet, and Inez had fallen into her arms, grateful at that moment for comfort from her dear friend who had known her for most of her life. Later, Jill and Kendra had carted Patsy off for something "a little stronger" than the wine being served, and Inez was spared worrying about a scene from Patsy after all.

So Grace was right, and Inez had kept her word. She had not abandoned Patsy. But she couldn't help the anger that licked up in her now and again as she thought of her darling Grace, lying on her death bed, worrying about Patsy's behavior after her death. In more recent years, since Patsy's pension and Social Security had kicked in and Inez knew Patsy had a roof over her head and a meager but steady income, she had excused herself from worrying about Patsy's life. Patsy would drink herself to death eventually, Inez speculated, which was tragic and stupid, but there was nothing she could do to prevent it. Inez had resigned herself to the role of occasional chauffeur when Patsy needed to go someplace outside of biking distance or bus routes.

Patsy's call the day before yesterday, though, was far from ordinary. She'd been nearly incoherent, babbling about Van coming back, showing up at her trailer the night before, and disappearing again. It had made no sense, but Patsy had been adamant that they go to Jill's house and see Van. Inez was skeptical, but hopeful enough that she'd agreed to drive her to Jill's to check it out.

Inez could hardly believe her eyes when she saw Van at Jill's that morning, looking the same as she had the day she'd disappeared. It was a miracle, nothing less. Inez had never doubted that Jill's RIP machine caused Van to disappear. She'd been there, after all, sitting on the deck rocking Michael, and she'd seen Van go into RIP and never come out. Where else could she have gone? She'd simply vanished, but Inez had always thought it likely that Jill's machine had caused Van to disintegrate or evaporate, not that she was transported to another time. She'd certainly never expected Van to miraculously reappear seemingly none the worse for a trip through twenty years.

It would have been nice if Patsy were so affected by the miracle that she stopped drinking, but that hadn't happened. Patsy was almost sober the morning Inez took her to Jill's, but it hadn't lasted. When Inez called Patsy later that night to see how Van was doing, she could tell Patsy had been drinking. Though she should have known better than to expect anything else, Inez was disappointed once again.

And now Patsy had called for a second time in three days, nearly incoherent once more, saying something about Van disappearing again, and this time it was Patsy's fault. Inez felt guilty about not checking in the day before. She'd told herself Van needed a day or two to get oriented before being bothered with visitors, but secretly she'd been hoping Van's presence would somehow make everything all right, the way it used to be. Maybe Patsy would become Van's responsibility now, instead of Inez's. She knew better than that, really, and she was ashamed that she had tried to convince herself otherwise. She could hear Grace's voice as clearly as if she were standing right next to her, scolding her for leaving Van alone with Patsy. The rest of them had had twenty years to grow used to Patsy in her alcoholic state, but it couldn't have been anything but shocking to Van.

Bracing herself for bad news, Inez rang the bell, and the door was immediately opened.

Patsy said, "Thank God." She grabbed Inez's arm to draw her into the trailer. In her other hand she held a dripping cloth. The smell of rum and disinfectant was overpowering, and Inez's eyes watered. The couch was moved out into the middle of the living room, a large damp splotch marred the wall beyond the couch, and a pan of sudsy water sat on the floor in front of it.

"What happened?" Inez asked. "Where's Van?"

Tears spurted from Patsy's eyes, which were already red and swollen from crying. "She's gone. I ruined everything, Inez. You have to help me. Help me, please!"

Inez was unmoved by Patsy's tears. She'd often seen Patsy in worse shape, too many times to count. But she was concerned about Van. "What happened? What's that smell?"

"I threw a bottle of rum at the wall." Patsy sniffed, wiped her nose on the back of her hand and held up the dripping cloth. "I'm trying to clean it up. Van and I had a fight. We never fought like that, not once in six years. I s-scared her, I think." Patsy sniffed again, and looked directly into Inez's eyes, something she had avoided doing for years. "Inez, I need help." Her voice wobbled, but she held Inez's eyes with her own. "It's my drinking, and I need help." She sank onto the couch, dropped her head into her hands, and sobbed.

Inez stared down at Patsy, feelings of hope and dismay warring in her. Patsy had never before admitted she had a drinking problem. This could be a breakthrough. Acknowledging that she needed help could be the first step toward recovery. But, selfishly, Inez almost wished Patsy hadn't said anything to her. It would be so much easier for Inez if Patsy just continued her path toward self-destruction. She'd tried for years to save Patsy, but she'd eventually given up, and now she was used to the way things were. It would be wonderful if Patsy stopped drinking, of course, but Inez couldn't help feeling a bit resentful that Patsy was telling *her*, making it *her* problem all of a sudden.

But it was her problem now. Patsy had asked for help.

"Do you mean that?" Inez asked, feeling hard, but needing to be sure. "Do you really want me to help you stop drinking?"

"I do. Please help me. I'm a monster. Van doesn't even recognize me any more. How could she? I'm a monster."

Inez sneaked a glance at the kitchen, where she knew Patsy kept her liquor, and raised her eyebrows in surprise. Three empty bottles perched upside down in the sink. "You poured out your rum?"

"I had to. I have to stop drinking, Inez. But look at me." She held out a shaking hand. "It's been less than twelve hours, and I'm already a mess. I can't stop shaking and I can't stop crying. I can't do this by myself."

"I'll help you," Inez said automatically, the habits of fifty years allowing nothing less. "But I can't do it by myself either. You need to see a doctor, Patsy. Let's go down to Group Health."

"No!" Patsy shook her head vehemently. "I can't leave here. What if Van comes back? She left in the middle of the night. She doesn't have any money. Where could she go?"

Inez lowered herself to the couch, more ashamed of herself than ever. She could have sneaked Van into her retirement community for a day or two. Or she could have insisted Van stay at Jill's. They should never have let her stay with Patsy. "She probably went to Jill's. I'm sure she's all right."

Patsy shook her head again. "No, no, she didn't. Jill called yesterday and said she and Kendra were taking RIP off somewhere to work on it, somewhere in the hills. Van couldn't have gone there."

"Why not? All the more reason to go stay at Jill's. She'd have a place to stay for a while, by herself."

Patsy sniffed and blinked, momentarily hopeful. "You think she did? But how would she get there? And how would she get in?"

"Maybe Jill told her where the key was. And she'd figure out a way to get there. She did it before, remember?"

"I'll call her," Patsy said with determination, searching for her phone. But when she snatched it up and pushed the buttons with trembling fingers, she faltered. "No, I can't. Jill doesn't have a phone at her house, only a cell, and she has it with her." She gaped up at Inez, frantic. "What should I do?"

"Calm down, Patsy." Inez was getting worried, not only about Van, but also about Patsy. She was pale and agitated and sweating profusely, and Inez didn't think it was worry about Van that caused it. Twelve hours was probably longer than Patsy had gone without alcohol for years. Inez didn't know a lot about it, but she'd heard of delirium tremens. She knew enough to realize it could be very dangerous for someone who drank as heavily as Patsy did to quit suddenly without any medical help. "You know Van's a smart woman. She can take care of herself. Right now we need to take care of you."

Patsy crossed her arms stubbornly. "I'm not leaving here. Not until I know Van's safe. If she comes back and I'm not here—"

"How about if we leave a note on the door for her? You can leave a key with the manager. If Van comes back, she'll be able to get in."

Patsy wept, her hand to her mouth. "I'm so sorry. I'm sorry I'm such a mess. I'm sorry I'm a monster!"

Inez took Patsy's wrist and checked her pulse. It was extremely rapid. "Patsy." She gave her arm a firm shake. "We're going to leave a note for Van on the door. Where's your wallet? Your insurance card?"

"She was scared of me," Patsy wailed. "*Van.*"

Inez sighed deeply. She was on her own. She got up and rummaged through Patsy's things until she found the necessary documents and put them into a backpack along with a change of clothing, toothbrush, deodorant, and a comb. She didn't know how long Patsy would be gone, but Inez could always come back for anything else that was needed. She made a mental note to have someone feed the mangy cat and returned to Patsy, who wept into her hands. She sat next to her and pulled her hands away from her face.

"Patsy," she said gently, holding the shaking hands tight, "you're not a monster. You're sick. Now let's go get you well, okay?"

Patsy made a moaning sound.

"You want to be well for Van, don't you?"
"I do. I want to be well for Van."
"All right, let's go."

Chapter Twenty-two

Van — 2008

VAN FLIPPED DOWN the vanity mirror in the passenger side of the Jaguar and crinkled her nose at her reflection. It only hurt a little bit.

"I can't believe you talked me into this."

"Hey, I don't remember twisting your arm," Bennie said, pulling out of the parking lot of Pierce Tatty and into the stream of traffic.

"It was your idea."

"Only because you were too chicken to get a tattoo."

Van tilted her head to the side, admiring how the sun glinted off the diamond chip on the side of her nose, still marveling that her nose was pierced. In 1988, nose piercing had still conjured up the image of an iron ring in the nose of bull.

"A tattoo is permanent," Van said. "But if I change my mind about this, I can pull it out."

"Permanent is the point. When you get a tattoo, you're making a statement about who you are."

"What kind of statement? Look at me, I'm a biker babe? An ex-con? A sailor?"

Bennie laughed. "My dear, you have so much to learn. Everybody has tattoos now."

"They don't in 1988. I can't go back there with a tattoo."

Bennie's smile faltered, and Van wished she hadn't brought up the subject of returning to 1988. In the five days she'd spent at Bennie's house, there had only been one — well, it wasn't an argument, more of a disagreeable discussion — and it was about that. Bennie didn't believe Jill could send Van back and thought Van was setting herself up for grave disappointment if she expected that to happen. Instead, Bennie had urged her to get acclimated to 2008. But for Van, the possibility of going back to 1988 was what kept her sane in the bewildering new world she found herself in. She clung to the thought in the middle of the night when panic set in and she feared she'd be stuck in 2008 forever.

Not that she was having a bad time in the twenty-first century. Bennie had gone out of her way to make Van comfortable and happy. She'd taken her shopping, bought her a whole summer wardrobe, and convinced her that snug, low-riding jeans were fashionable.

"Everybody wears them."

"You don't," Van said.

"I don't have the ass for it. You do. The kids call them apple-bottom jeans." Bennie held out cupped hands and jiggled them up and down as if comparing the weights of two apples.

"Hm. Watermelons, more like," Van said.

Bennie gave her a playful swat on her rear and said, "Cantaloupes, maybe."

Van had giggled, and jiggled her bottom, liked how it felt, and bought the jeans.

Bennie gave her a cell phone and showed her to use it, bought her an iPod, and taught her how to download songs from the Internet, though the concept of the Internet itself was still too mindboggling to tackle. They'd spent an entire day playing Bennie's Wii game, bowling and cow racing and playing pretend guitar, laughing so hard Van's abs were sore the next day. They'd gone to a party one night and Bennie introduced Van as an old friend, which raised a few eyebrows among Bennie's closest acquaintances. Although Van couldn't help noticing the smoldering looks Bennie shot her now and then, they were never followed up with actions or words, for which Van was grateful. Not that she wasn't attracted to Bennie. She'd been attracted in 1988, after all, when Bennie was a cute, cocky twenty-eight. At forty-eight, she was stunning. All the same, Van was relieved Bennie hadn't tried to talk her into anything other than the casual, slightly flirtatious, camaraderie they had developed in the last few days. She didn't want to risk losing her safe haven by taking a wrong step with Bennie. After all, where else could she go?

She needn't have worried. No matter what her eyes said, Bennie was a perfect gentleman and did nothing to make Van uncomfortable. The opposite, in fact, as if Bennie knew exactly what Van needed and did whatever she could to provide it for her without being asked, whether it was comfort, distraction, or security.

Only in her quiet moments alone, like when Bennie disappeared into her den for an hour or so to work and left Van to her own devices did the fear flood in. Van would be hit with a sudden wave of terror that shook her so hard, she thought she might shatter. When the terror hit, she'd lace up her old sneakers, put on some of her new workout clothes, and go for a jog in the hot sunshine, chasing the fear. Or running away from it. She would take off running with her insides all wound up tight, but after a while she'd loosen up inside, relax, and she didn't fall apart after all. She returned sweaty and tired, but calm again, in one piece.

But at night, when she was alone in bed, there was nowhere to hide, nowhere to run, nothing to do to ease the tightness inside. Those were the moments she dreaded the most. She developed strategies for avoiding it as long as possible. She borrowed Bennie's GameBoy toy and played a game called Sims that kept her up until the wee hours of the morning. One night she and Bennie stayed up late watching recorded episodes of a television series Bennie called *The L Word*, with love scenes between women so erotic that Van couldn't bear to meet Bennie's eyes as she said good night, and she sought relief that night with her hand. Bennie loaned her a DVD player and she sat up in bed watching movies, classics, apparently, though they didn't exist yet in 1988, comedies like *When Harry Met Sally*, and lesbian movies, such as *Better than Chocolate*. Pearl would visit with her, keep her company until the middle of the night, when she'd yowl to be let out of the room, and Van was alone.

Eventually, the time would come when Van would have to lie down and close her eyes, and she could escape it no longer. It was then that she missed Patsy with an agonizing, gut-wrenching pain that tore through her and made her weak. She missed the way Patsy loved her, the way Patsy liked her, the way she'd catch Patsy watching her at unexpected moments, her eyes crinkled up at the corners, the tiniest of satisfied smiles on her lips. Van might be brushing her teeth or reading the newspaper or sipping coffee, and she'd glance up and catch Patsy watching her with eyes so full of love it made Van squish inside. Even after six years of it, Van still blushed, which made Patsy laugh. She missed the way Patsy touched her every time she passed her in a room, sometimes no more than a finger touch, often without even realizing she had done it, as if she couldn't help it. She missed Patsy's relentless caustic humor and her strength. She missed the way it felt entering a room on Patsy's arm, how Patsy captured everyone's attention and kept it. How everyone liked Patsy and tried to catch *her* attention, but Van knew she was the one, the *only* one, who really truly had it, all of it, all the time. No one would ever love her like Patsy did. God, how much she missed her. Then Van simply buried her face in her pillow and wailed and flailed and cried until she finally fell asleep.

Van peeked at herself in the vanity mirror again, this time noticing the dark circles under her eyes. She crinkled her nose. The nose jewel was cute, but the dark circles would have to go.

Van flipped the mirror up. "When did you get your tattoo?"

"Which one?"

Van raised her eyebrows. "You have more than one?" She touched the thorny vine that circled Bennie's right bicep.

Bennie flinched at the unexpected touch, then smiled, raised her right arm like Popeye, and flexed the muscle. "You like?"

Van laughed and obligingly squeezed Bennie's arm. "Oooh, nice. How many tattoos do you have?"

"Three." Bennie returned her hand to the wheel. "This is my newest." She waved her right elbow indicating her bicep again. "I got it four years ago."

"What does it mean?" Van ran her fingertip around the vine to the underside of Bennie's arm.

Bennie sucked in her breath. "Van, if you don't stop touching me like that, this Jag's going straight into a tree."

Van pulled her hand back to her lap as if she'd burned it. "Sorry."

Bennie shot her an exasperated look. "A girl told me I was too thorny." She gave a quick smile that reminded Van of the young Bennie she'd known in 1988. "Not horny, *thorny*. And I liked it. So, thorns."

Van laughed. "And if she'd said you were too cocky, you'd have tattooed a ring of cocks?"

"Ick." Bennie laughed. After a moment, she asked, "Do you think I'm cocky?"

"No. At least not now. But you were kind of cocky when you were twenty-eight."

"I know. But I've tried to outgrow it. You think I have?"

"Definitely."

Bennie seemed pleased. "Good. I don't want to be cocky. But being thorny, well, I have a reputation for holding women at arm's length, not letting them get too close, and I've kind of cultivated that reputation, so when she called me thorny, I liked it. And it makes a great tattoo, don't you think?"

"Yes, very nice. Why don't you let women get close?"

"Don't you want to know about my other tattoos?"

"Later. Stop weaseling. Why don't you let women get close?"

"I don't know." Bennie drove in silence for a minute. "They expect more from me than I can give them. And when they don't get it, they get hurt. Sometimes badly." She shrugged helplessly. "I don't like hurting women. I love women. But I've never loved *one* woman enough to give up all the others. And sometimes that's all it takes to hurt someone."

"Never?"

A self-conscious expression crossed Bennie's face so quickly that if Van hadn't been watching closely she would have missed it. "Once, a long time ago," Bennie said softly, as if reciting a bedtime story, "there was a woman. But it didn't work out. It couldn't work out."

They drove in silence for a moment, and Van was left to wonder. Finally, Bennie spoke again. "Lips."

"What?"

"My second tattoo. Women's lips. Right here." Bennie rubbed her hand in the crease between her right leg and her torso, near her crotch. "It's my favorite place to kiss a woman. So I got some lips tattooed there. Hurt like hell."

Van watched Bennie's stroking hand and felt a surprising tingle in her own crotch. "Any others?"

"The traditional butterfly on my breast. I got that one on my twenty-fifth birthday."

"You had it when I knew you before?"

"Quite a lot of us were getting tattoos back then." Bennie pulled into her driveway. "Only you conservative old fogies still thought it was radical."

Van laughed. "Careful, you're the old fogey now."

But Bennie was squinting in the rear view mirror and didn't answer. "Who's here?"

Van spun around. A car was parked on the street in front of Bennie's house. As they watched, a woman got out and walked toward them. "It's Inez." Van scrambled out of the car and hurried to meet Inez in the driveway.

"Inez!"

"Hi, Van." Inez smiled and gave Van a quick hug. She stepped back and immediately noticed the glint in Van's nose. "That's new."

Van laughed a bit self-consciously. "Yeah." She was unexpectedly delighted to see Inez. Wearing lemon yellow capris, sandals, and a t-shirt, Inez seemed much younger and healthier than she had previously, or maybe Van was getting used to her friends being older. She no longer saw their age first.

"What brings you here? How did you find me?"

"Jill told me. I left her a message a couple of days ago, and she just got back to me today. Apparently she's hiding in the mountains somewhere with Kendra."

"Yeah, working on RIP. She calls me every day or so." Van noticed Bennie, still standing next to the open door of the Jag, keys dangling from her fingers, as if poised to leave. "You remember Bennie?"

"Of course." Inez strode over and held out her hand. Bennie juggled her keys and shook hands with Inez. "I'm so grateful, we all are, that you're taking such good care of Van."

Bennie smiled quizzically. "*All* of you?"

"Those of us who know about it," Inez clarified. "Jill and Kendra and me."

Bennie seemed to read something in Inez's eyes. "Hey, listen, I have a couple of errands I need to run. Van, why don't you take Inez in, give her some coffee? I'll be back in a couple of hours."

Van glanced at Inez and nodded at Bennie. It was clear Inez had come to talk. Bennie gave Van a reassuring wink, slid into the Jag, and backed it out to the street.

"I'm glad I finally get a chance to see the inside of this place," Inez said, as Van led her in the front door. "It was a wreck when she bought it. People were outraged because the house was going to be torn down, and the historical preservation people were up in arms. When Bennie rescued it from the wrecking ball, she was the heroine of the week."

"Really?" Van scrutinized the beautiful entryway with new

appreciation. "I didn't know."

"Yeah. Apparently it was built by some big mining baron. They say it cost a fortune to restore it, and I believe it. Look at this place."

"Bennie's pretty well off, I guess."

"Well off?" Inez raised her eyebrows. "She's like our own Bill Gates over here."

"Who?"

"He's about the richest man in the world. Okay, Bennie's not quite in that category, but she's got money, for sure."

As they talked, Van led Inez into the kitchen, where she fiddled with the coffee machine. Inez stroked the shiny surface of the granite countertop, then sat at the breakfast nook that overlooked the street.

Inez said, "I was so relieved when I heard you were staying here. I should never have left you with Patsy."

"What could you have done about it?"

"You could have come to my place for a night or two. They have rules about no overnight guests, but how would they even have known?"

"Don't they come in and check up on you?"

Inez laughed. "No, I'd leave in a minute if they did that. It's not a retirement home like you're imagining. It's a retirement community. I started investigating them a couple of years ago for my mom."

"Your mom's still alive?"

"Yes. Ninety-four years old and still sharp as a tack. But physically, she couldn't live on her own any more, and she *does* need someone to check up on her every day, make sure she hasn't fallen down and can't get up, that sort of thing. I found out that a lot of the places are great communities for *young* old people, like me. So after I got Mom settled into her retirement home, I found one for me."

"Do you like it?"

"I love it. It's like being in a dorm again, only a lot better. No homework for one thing, and no roommate. We play all day long, golf or poker or swimming or shopping. They take us out to the casino a couple times a week, and they prepare all our meals for us."

"The casino?"

"Yes, casinos are legal on Indian reservations. They're all electronic now, with fun little games. No more boring seven-seven-seven. You'll have to come out with me some time. You'd enjoy it."

Van smiled. She'd always enjoyed her yearly visit to Reno with Patsy, Jill, and Inez. "I'd like that." She paused to grind the coffee beans, surprised again at how much trouble people went to for a cup of coffee in the future. You'd think progress would have simplified the process, but instead it took several minutes to make a pot. She started the coffee and sat across from Inez. Her fingers were restless. She itched for a cigarette, but she hadn't smoked since she'd arrived at Bennie's, when she'd found her last three cigarettes at the bottom of her plastic Yokes bag, shredded and damp. Rather than ask Bennie to buy her more cigarettes, Van had decided she might as well quit, like everyone else. Except Bennie, of course, who had never smoked in the first place.

"Are the meals good there?"

"Yes, they are," Inez said. "And they serve us, like we're in a restaurant, for every meal. Don't fear getting old, Van. Embrace it. It's got some great perks. The only sad and lonely farts are the ones who get all depressed because they're not young any more. If they'd see the positive side of aging, they'd have a much better time. The down side is that it's not a gay and lesbian retirement home. I heard they have those down in Florida and Arizona, but there aren't any around here yet."

"Are you 'out' there?"

"Yes. I've been out since my first day. If they don't like it, too bad. What are they going to do, kick me out? I'd sue them for discrimination. It's illegal to discriminate because of sexual orientation in this state, you know."

"It is?"

"Yes, has been for a few years now. And most of them at the community are tickled to know a lesbian. It makes them feel all hip and liberal. I've caught a couple of the old nuns who live there giving me the eye—and not in a bad way, if you know what I mean. One of them's kind of cute."

Van laughed, and Inez clasped her hand in a strong grip. "See, it's not all bad here in 2008, is it? We have casinos *and* equal rights."

"Marriage?"

Inez scowled. "No, not that yet. And that's a sore spot, for sure. It would have made a hell of a difference when Grace died if I'd been married to her."

"I'm sorry about that. I barely knew her, but Jill said you were together for fifteen years."

"Yeah. They were the best years of my life, no doubt about it." Inez let go of Van's hand and unconsciously played with a gold band that circled her left ring finger. "I'll never be that loved again. Not that I'm unhappy. I am happy. And if I can convince Sister Alice into giving up her vow of celibacy in her ripe old age, things will look up even more."

Van laughed and touched the side of her nose as her laughter made her aware of her recent piercing.

"I like what you did with your nose, by the way."

"You do?"

"Yeah. It kind of blends in with your freckles, but when the light hits it just right, it sparkles."

"Thanks. It was this or a tattoo."

"Why didn't you get a tattoo? I'd get one if I were your age."

Van smiled, enjoying this conversation with Inez very much. The Inez she knew in 1988 was a conservative middle school teacher who was terrified her students would find out she was a lesbian. This Inez was feisty. "I can take a nose stud out when I go back to 1988. A tattoo is forever."

"Van, I know it's hard for you here right now, but I don't think you should hold out too much hope for getting back to 1988."

Van's smile faded. "But Jill's working on RIP. She's been working on it all week."

"Jill worked on RIP for years before Patsy's party, when she accidentally shipped you off into the future. She didn't know what she was doing then, and she hasn't worked on it at all in the last twenty years. What makes you think she can figure it out now, in a week, or a month, or even years? She could die before she figures out how to send you back."

Van slumped against the back of her chair. "But how can I stay here, Inez? It's not my century."

Inez squeezed Van's hand. "Embrace it, Van. There are a lot of good things about this century. Don't waste your life wishing you were back in 1988. You're here now."

Van bit her lip, only half listening to Inez's words. How could she stay in 2008? What would she do? Where would she live? She couldn't stay with Bennie forever. And what about Patsy?

The coffee was done. Inez got up to fill two cups, letting Van absorb her words. She put a cup in front of Van and pressed her hand gently on Van's shoulder. "Get yourself a tattoo, Van. Live in the twenty-first century."

Van took a sip of very strong brew, the only way Bennie's coffee machine knew to make coffee. Inez sat across from her, took a sip as well, and said, "Now, I have to tell you about Patsy."

Chapter Twenty-three

Kendra — 2008

"I NEED TO go down to Ione to see if Grover's package is here yet," Jill said.

Kendra stirred beside her. "Um. Good morning, darling." She draped an arm over Jill's stomach. "I love you too."

Kendra could practically hear the wheels spinning in Jill's head as she processed the message. "Oh, yeah. Sorry. I love you too. And good morning." Jill leaned over to give Kendra an obligatory good morning kiss.

Kendra wrapped her arms around Jill's neck and opened her mouth, prolonging the kiss, but she wasn't surprised to feel Jill become restless, slipping her legs out from under the covers, even as the kiss continued. Reluctantly, she released her. After spending the last seven nights together, Kendra had learned she could expect nothing else in the morning. Jill fell asleep the instant her head hit the pillow, and she slept like the dead. When she woke up, her batteries were fully charged, and she hit the ground running. Except for their first morning together, there were no languorous sensual morning lovemaking sessions. Sometimes, like today, there wouldn't even have been a good morning kiss if Kendra hadn't reminded her. They still made love, but Kendra had already learned she needed to warn Jill ahead of time, so she could adjust her approach to the day and schedule Kendra in. It was maddening, but that was Jill.

Jill's mind still fascinated Kendra, though, as it had when she first met her. She'd heard of people who solved problems in their sleep, but she'd never seen it in action the way she did with Jill. She'd hit a dead end working on RIP, nearly tear her hair out in frustration, sleep on it, and wake up in the morning spouting the solution. "I need some mercury, and copper wire," she'd said one morning. Another morning her first words were, "It needs to be porous."

Only a couple of mornings earlier, her first announcement had been that she needed to call Grover and have him send her some chemicals. Apparently they were substances that were not available in Ione, or perhaps anywhere else—legally. They'd already ditched their cell phones, in case the Feds tracked them, so they'd had to sneak back over the mountain to Colville to buy a couple pay-as-you-go phones that couldn't be traced back to them. Jill had put in her call to Grover, and another call to Van, when they'd finally located her at Bennie's. They'd rented a post office box in Ione, and Kendra took the opportunity to buy some food and toiletries and to call Kevin, give him her number, and let him know she'd be gone a few more days.

Now Kendra threw back the covers and grabbed her shirt. "Shall we get breakfast in town?"

A moment of silence passed before Jill said, "I'm only going to the post office. You don't need to go."

Kendra looked at Jill in surprise. "Are you nuts? Of course I'm coming along." Jill's face had grown impassive, and she avoided Kendra's eyes while she slipped on her Crocs. "I've been cooped up here for days too, you know," Kendra said. "I want to check my messages and call Kevin."

Jill grunted, and Kendra rolled her eyes. Sometimes Jill was as bad as a man.

"You drive," Kendra said, when they got out to the Jetta. "That way I can check for phone reception on the way down."

Jill grunted again and took the keys.

"I'm sorry I'll miss Bridgette's first Fourth of July." Kendra switched on her phone to check for a signal. "She's eight months old. That's big enough to appreciate sparklers and things. Kevin said his first real word when he saw a sparkler on the Fourth of July. He said, 'Pretty.' And he was only seven months old."

"You could go home," Jill said, keeping her eyes straight ahead as she snaked the Jetta through the narrow bumpy driveway to the single lane dirt road that led down the mountain. "Spend the Fourth with your family."

Kendra eyed Jill. "Are you trying to get rid of me?"

Jill shrugged, but didn't take her eyes of the road. "I can work on RIP by myself. There's no need for you to stay up here too."

Kendra turned sideways in her seat and gave Jill her full attention. "You *are* trying to get rid of me."

Jill shot a quick, uneasy glance at Kendra. "No, I'm not."

"No?" Kendra waited. Something was up.

"It's just that..."

"Yes?" Kendra prompted, false sweetness oozing from her voice. "What is it, Jill?"

"It's just—" Jill looked uneasily at Kendra, then burst out, "Kendra, I've lived alone for seventy years!"

"Ooh, seventy years. What a prodigy you were, to take care of yourself when you were only an infant."

"No, what I mean is, I've been single all my life. And I've lived alone for over fifty years, ever since I went away to college."

"You had a dorm room all to yourself?" Kendra asked, deliberately ignoring Jill's point.

"No. Okay, not fifty years, but what I mean is—" Jill stopped and took a deep breath. "I've never lived with a woman, Kendra. You and

I have been cooped up in that cabin together for *a week*. I've never spent that much time alone with a woman in my life."

"Poor baby."

Jill made an exasperated grimace. "What I'm trying to say is, I need a little time alone."

"You need a little time to yourself, do you?" Kendra said, with furious sarcasm. "Isn't that sweet? I'm so glad I bothered to save your life and lead you to a safe refuge so you can putter with RIP to your heart's content. Never mind that I'd have to go back to my crowded apartment with my son and his wife and their baby, where the living room is a fucking nursery. Never mind that the Lab Rats are after you and probably me too, by now. Never mind all that. Jill wants to be alo-o-one."

"Kendra, I'm sorry." Jill reached for Kendra's hand, but Kendra pulled away, and Jill sighed heavily. "I'm sorry. Of course you don't have to leave. I don't want you to leave. But maybe you could be a little less...intrusive."

"Intrusive?" Kendra asked, bewildered.

"Yes. Like when I was working on RIP and you asked me if I wanted a sandwich, and when you brought me that jacket, and when you held the flashlight for me that time."

"Were you hungry?"

"Well, yeah, but—"

"Were you cold?"

"Yes, but that's not—"

"Was it getting too dark to see?"

"Yes, but that's not the point." Jill hit the steering wheel in frustration. "The point is, how did you *know* I was hungry? How did you know I was cold, or that it was getting hard for me to see? You know when I'm tired and you know when I'm scared and you know when I'm worried. It's like you're inside me somehow. How else could you know what I'm feeling? It's...it's...it's an invasion of privacy."

Kendra shook her head in baffled amusement. "Jill. Honey. That's not an invasion of privacy. That's love."

"Love?" Tragic dismay crossed Jill's face.

"Yes," Kendra said solemnly. "Love. And you'd better get used to it. But don't worry, it won't always be this bad."

"It won't?" Jill asked, pathetic hope in her voice.

"No. For one thing, I don't know anybody who could enjoy someone else's company for every minute of every day for seven days straight. Everybody needs a break now and then. Do you think you've been a ray of pure delight this whole time?"

"I haven't?"

"Nope. You know how you've teased me about going to the bathroom all the time?"

"Yeah."

"Sometimes I don't have to go to the bathroom at all."

"Huh?"

"Sometimes," Kendra said, with the air of sharing a great secret, "I *say* I have to go to the bathroom when I don't. Sometimes, I just want to be alone."

Kendra laughed at the relief on Jill's face and shook her head in wonder at how Jill had survived all these years without her. She returned to examining her phone for a signal. After several minutes, Jill touched her hand. Kendra looked up.

"Thank you," Jill said softly, not taking her eyes off the road.

A few moments later, Kendra's cell phone showed a signal. "Here it is. I have three messages." She dialed her voice mail and was shocked to hear her ex-husband's voice. After the first few words, she grabbed Jill's arm.

"What is it?"

"It's Paul. Someone's been — oh wait, this one's from Kevin."

"What's going on?"

"Shh. Oh my God."

"What?"

"Someone's been talking to Kevin and to Paul. About me, and you."

"Me? Who?

"I don't know. Men with badges, Paul said. He wants to know what sort of trouble I'm in. Wait." Kendra held up a hand as she listened to her third message. "It's Kevin again. They asked about the cabin. Kevin thinks they're on their way up here. It must be the Lab Rats!"

Jill scanned both sides of the narrow road. There was nowhere to turn around. "What time did Kevin call?"

Kendra scrolled through her messages. "The last call was sent at 9:01 this morning."

They both glanced at the clock on the dash. It was 10:30. If the Lab Rats had left right when Kevin called, they'd be almost to Ione by now. But if they had left earlier... At that moment, there was a break in the trees, and the view opened up to show the winding road below them. A dark car, appearing no larger than a Matchbox car, was winding its way up. It could have been any car, but somehow Kendra didn't think it was. It was too sleek, too clean, too...federal. It drove with a purposefulness that suggested they should find a place to turn the Jetta around immediately.

Jill must have had the same idea. She slowed down. "Hold on." She nosed the car into an impression in the foliage no larger than a deer bed and jockeyed the Jetta toward the edge of the road where it dropped steeply.

Kendra put her hands over her eyes. They were on a blind curve.

They had several minutes before the black car would be upon them, but if any other car were to come around that curve, they were toast. "I love you, Jill!" she yelled, in case she never got to say it again.

Jill edged the car forward and backward, then hit the gas and they were zipping forward, up the mountain toward RIP.

Kendra took her hands from her eyes and peeped at Jill. She was grinning.

"What you smiling at?"

"Your last words. They were good ones. I love you too, Kendra."

Kendra laughed too. "What are we going to do?"

"We're going to get RIP and head down the other side of the mountain."

Kendra was skeptical. "That's a very primitive road."

"I don't think we have any choice."

"What about Grover's package? It's back in Ione."

"I know, and I need it. We'll have to get it another way."

Chapter Twenty-four

Bennie — 2008

BENNIE GAZED STEADILY into Van's green eyes. "Are you sure about this?"

"I am."

Bennie watched, mesmerized, as Van unbuttoned the top of her tight new jeans, slid the zipper, and tugged them down, inching them over one hip, then the other, until a thin strip of yellow silk showed the top of her bikini underpants. A few stray strawberry hairs curled over the elastic band, as if trying to crawl up and peek out over the edge.

"That's far enough," Tonya said, wheeling her cart over to the padded table. "You want it at the top of your butt, right?"

Bennie sighed, resolving to one day see the rest of those curls.

"Yes, right here." Van touched the top of her left buttock.

"Okay, why don't you hop up here and lay face down? Is this what you have in mind?"

Tonya handed Van a computer print-out, and Van studied it closely. Bennie stood behind Van and examined the drawing as well. It was a sketch of a tombstone, with "R.I.P. 1988" written on its face. A single climbing rose hung over the stone, providing a splash of red. Tonya was too inured to the many different tattoos chosen by her customers to show any curiosity about Van's, but Bennie was intrigued. What was Van trying to bury?

Van hadn't given her any warning about the tattoo. She'd been quiet the day before, after Inez left. She'd claimed a headache and gone to her room early. This morning, she'd woken up heavy eyed, but strangely buoyant. After she'd asked Bennie if she had time to give her a ride, she'd directed Bennie back to Tonya's, where Van had her nose pierced the day before. It was a good thing Tonya worked above the shop, or Van might have been out of luck. It was the Fourth of July, after all, and most businesses were closed. But Tonya was awake, answered their knock, and was willing to earn a few extra bucks for the holiday.

"Yes, that's what I want," Van said. She handed the drawing to Tonya, climbed up onto the table, and lay down, her jeans barely hanging on. She crossed her arms and rested her head sideways on top of them. She met Bennie's eyes and gave her an impish smile, diamond stud glinting among the freckles. The smile reminded Bennie of the flirtatious Van she'd known in the past, the Van who had made Bennie fall in love with her in the first place.

Bennie remembered vividly that day in the country western bar when Van sang Shelly West's "Jose Cuervo" right at her. Van had smiled at her like that, impish and sexy and flirtatious. Patsy was drinking at the bar and hadn't even paid any attention to what Van was doing. Van danced up to Bennie and moved her hips practically in her face, taunting her. And Bennie had fallen, hard. She'd had a lot of women already, but there was something about Van that struck her in a different spot, and she'd never been the same since.

Now Van was smiling at Bennie the same way, this time with her pants halfway off her ass, butt dimples flashing, the top inch and a half of crack showing, and Bennie fell all over again. Her heart pounded so hard she thought the thumping must show through her white t-shirt, like it did on cartoons. Her ears roared with it, and her face burned.

Van saw her reaction—how could she not?—and her eyes widened in surprise and, a moment later, trepidation. Bennie was tempted to back away, hide herself, pretend to examine the dozens of sample tattoos on Tonya's wall, anything to stop Van from looking at her like that, but something made her stop. She clenched her jaw instead and stood resolute, breath coming heavily through her nose, her eyes fixed on Van's. She was rewarded. The fear on Van's face disappeared and was replaced, in quick succession, with interest, speculation, and finally pleasure. Van smiled again, slow and sultry. She *liked* the effect she had on Bennie. Bennie felt a glimmer of hope.

Van gasped as Tonya rubbed cold alcohol on Van's butt cheek, and it was Bennie's turn to smile. Van's look changed to one of pure fear-of-needle-pain, and she opened her mouth in a wide grimace as the first needle pierced her skin.

"Hold my hand," Bennie said, and Van grasped it and held on tight. She buried her face in her arms, and Bennie took advantage of the opportunity to examine more closely what she could see of Van's bare ass than she'd been able to while Van was watching. Beautiful. Tonya caught her eye and gave her a quick wink before sinking the needle again into Van's porcelain flesh.

An hour later, Bennie pulled the Jag into the driveway, hopped out, and ran around to help Van out of her seat, careful not to jostle her sore butt cheek. "Okay?"

"It's not like I had a baby or anything. It's a tattoo."

"Yeah, well, I know how much a new tattoo can hurt, if you're not careful. You should probably get out of those jeans. If I'd known what you were going to do, I'd have told you to wear something looser."

"I wanted to surprise you." Van headed toward the stairs that led to her room.

"You did that all right. Beer on the veranda?"

"Sure. Be down in a sec."

The day was perfect, sunny and hot. They were invited to a Fourth of July party that evening at the lake cabin of Bennie's friends, Stacy and Sue, but that was hours away yet. Bennie pulled four bottles of Stella Artois from the fridge, stuck them in a bucket of ice, and pulled two frosty beer mugs from the freezer. She opened the sliding glass door from the dining room to the veranda and set the bucket and glasses on the low glass-topped table. The veranda led out into a surprisingly spacious and private yard, considering how near the house was to the center of the city. There were neighbors on both sides of her, but their presence was blocked by giant spruce trees on one side, and an overgrown trellis and stone potting shed on the other. Behind the house the hill rose steeply, providing privacy for Bennie and purchase for a few hardy rock-clinging plants. She hadn't yet refurbished the gardens and yard, but they still provided a pleasant aspect on beautiful days like this.

She pulled two white wicker chairs over to the table, reconsidered, and pushed them aside to put a two-person glider there instead. She shook her head and moved the two wicker chairs back once more.

She felt a bubble of excitement that she tried to restrain. Something was different about Van today. She was no longer wandering around the house like the walking wounded, weighted with grief. She seemed stronger, happier, more vivacious, and definitely flirtatious. It had to have been her conversation the day before with Inez. Bennie couldn't help but hope it might signal a change in their relationship. She was glad she'd been able to provide Van with the safety and comfort of her home when she needed it, but she longed to be more than Van's protector and provider. Much more.

She shooed Pearl off the glass table top and was giving it a swipe with a paper towel when Van stepped out onto the veranda. She wore a simple cotton sundress with giant yellow sunflowers splashed on the fabric. Van had resisted purchasing the dress, arguing that she'd never have occasion to wear it, but Bennie had liked the look of her in it and had insisted on buying it. Was she reading too much into it that Van had decided to wear it today? Or was it simply the most comfortable thing she could find to wear against her tattoo?

"Great dress." Bennie opened a bottle of beer and poured it into one of the glasses. Sheets of frost slid down the sides.

"Thanks." Van sank into one of the wicker chairs and accepted the glass.

Bennie sat in the other chair and was thankful she had decided against the glider. She could watch Van better this way. She held out her own glass. "To your tattoo."

Van smiled and clinked her glass against Bennie's. "To my tattoo."

They each took a drink. "So," Bennie said, "what prompted your change of heart?"

"Well, you know Inez and I had a long talk yesterday."

"Yes."

"She doesn't think Jill will be able to send me back."

Bennie kept her face impassive. "I'm sorry, Van."

"She thinks I should live in the present, stop thinking about going back to 1988. I know you've been telling me the same thing for days. But it was different hearing it from Inez. Forgive me if I'm wrong, but," Van raised a questioning brow, "I get the idea you would prefer it if I stay in 2008?"

Bennie smiled slightly in acknowledgement. "You're not wrong."

"I thought so. So, considering that you might be a bit, ah, biased about it, I guess I needed to hear it from someone else before I could accept it." Van ran her finger up the side of her glass and watched the condensation drip from it. "It's a hard thing to accept."

"I wish there was something I could do to make it easier for you."

"But you've been great, Bennie," Van said earnestly. "You gave me a safe place to figure things out, and I am so grateful to you for that." She reached her hand across the table and Bennie took it. Gratitude was something.

Van gazed into her beer. "Patsy's in the hospital." She took a deep shaky breath, blew it out hard, and glanced up at Bennie with a haunted look. "Drying out, Inez said. Everybody tells me Patsy started drinking—really drinking, I mean, heavily—when I disappeared. And I feel so guilty about it. I feel so guilty, but it wasn't my fault. What could I have done? I couldn't help it. I didn't mean to disappear."

Bennie leaned forward and gripped Van's hand tightly in both of hers. "No, it wasn't your fault. Don't blame yourself."

"In my head, I know it wasn't my fault, but in my heart, I feel so bad." Sudden tears flooded Van's eyes and spilled down her cheeks. "I miss Patsy. I love her. But that woman who's in the hospital, that's not Patsy."

Bennie didn't know what to do. It tore her apart to see Van so unhappy, and crying over another woman, of all things. She released Van's hand, moved around to kneel in front of her, and wiped Van's tears away with her thumb. "Don't cry, please. You'll get snot on your pretty little nose stud."

Van gave a wet chuckle and sniffed. Bennie tore a paper towel off the roll she had stuffed behind the barbecue grill. Van took it, wiped her face, and gingerly blew her nose. Seeing she had composed herself somewhat, Bennie returned to her chair.

"Sorry, I didn't mean to cry. I've thought a lot about this, and I thought I was over the worst of it, but I never said it out loud before."

"Cry all you need to."

"Thanks." Van wiped her eyes one more time and took a long drink of beer. "Anyway, I was telling you about my tattoo. Inez said that even if Patsy goes through rehab and stops drinking, I shouldn't expect her to be the same. She'll still be seventy years old, and she's still gone through the last twenty years, pretty brutal years they tell me, without me. Inez thinks I need to move on, rebuild my life here in the present. Without Patsy."

If Inez had been in front of her, Bennie would have given her a giant kiss. She was careful not to let her feeling of triumph show.

"Inez is right," Van said. "She'll never be my Patsy again, but it's not like she *died*. She's very much alive, and I can't wipe out my feelings for her just like that." She made a snap with her fingers. "So, last night I was lying in bed, trying to figure out how I can stop thinking and feeling like the Van of the past, and start thinking and feeling like the Van of the present. And I finally got it."

"And?" Bennie asked, with some trepidation. There was a strange, forced jerkiness in Van's demeanor that caused Bennie some concern.

"Patsy didn't die. But Van did." Her smile didn't reach her eyes. "The Van of 1988 is dead, and may she Rest in Peace. That's what the tattoo is about, RIP 1988. It's Independence Day. Today is the day the new Van is born. Van of 2008." She ran her hands through her long curls, shook them out, and raised her face to the sun. She stood, spread her arms wide, twirled in a circle, and stopped in front of Bennie's chair. "Bennie, meet the new Van."

Bennie stood slowly, not sure how she felt. "Welcome, Van of 2008." She smiled gently down into Van's grinning face. "I'm glad that you're here. But I'm sad, too."

"Why?"

"I liked the Van of 1988."

Van's smile grew shaky. "Me too," she said. "But I don't think I have any choice."

Chapter Twenty-five

Jill — 2008

"I CANNOT BELIEVE I slept on the ground." Kendra rolled over onto her hands to push herself up from the hard dirt. "At my age."

"I can't believe you reached the ripe old age of fifty-nine without ever sleeping beneath the stars," Jill said, sitting up as well. The sound of so many joints cracking filled the air that she couldn't tell which came from her and which from Kendra. "It's an experience everyone should have before they die. And if you think it was hard on you, what about me? I'm seventy."

"Yeah, but you have the body of a sixty-year-old, and sixty is the new fifty. Oh, I'm sore."

Jill was too. Her back ached, her neck ached, her knees ached, and her head ached. But it was a beautiful morning. Once Jill finally made it to her feet, she stretched and spread her arms wide and took in a deep breath. "Smell that air, Kendra. It's glorious."

"Great. I'd rather smell fresh coffee."

"Yeah, that sounds good too." Jill shook out the blanket, rolled it up, and put it in the back of the Jetta. "And bacon."

"Bacon! You're a vegetarian."

"I don't want to *eat* bacon, but sleeping in the fresh air makes me want to smell it. It reminds me of camping when I was a kid."

"This isn't exactly camping. It's more like squatting."

Jill had to agree. They had spent the night illegally in the park. On Fourth of July weekend there were no campsites available anywhere for latecomers like Kendra and Jill. They'd entered with a day pass and simply hadn't left.

When they'd retrieved RIP from the cabin, they'd grabbed what they could quickly: clothing, blankets, some food. But it wasn't until they were driving away from the cabin in their separate vehicles that they'd discussed over their new cell phones where to go. The best place to hide RIP, they'd decided, was in a campground. Like the purloined letter, the camper would be hidden in plain sight. But they were totally unprepared for camping. They had no tent, no sleeping bags, no camp stove. RIP had the shell of a camper, but inside there was no room to do anything but sit upright on a cold hard stool, surrounded by equipment. They couldn't even build a fire without risking being caught. So they'd spent the night on the cold hard ground, wrapped up in blankets and each other's arms, which sounded romantic, but in actuality it was just plain uncomfortable.

Kendra staggered over to a tree, pulled her pants down, and, bracing herself awkwardly against the tree, squatted down to pee. "Yuck." She pulled her pants up and kicked pine needles over her puddle. "Why didn't we grab toilet paper? I can't spend another night like this."

Jill used a tree to pull herself up from her own squat and had to admit that primitive peeing was a lot more difficult than it used to be. "We can pick some up when we go pick up Grover's package."

"*We* can't go pick up Grover's package. *I'll* go get it. You have to stay here with RIP. We're here illegally, remember? If the park rangers show up and no one's here, they could haul RIP away."

"What if someone's watching the post office?"

"Do you need the package?"

"Yes."

"Then we have to take that chance. Don't worry, I'll be sneaky. Maybe I'll wear a disguise. And I'm going to call Kevin to meet me. He has a bunch of camping equipment stored at his dad's, and he can bring it to me."

"No, he can't know where we are."

"He's not going to tell anyone. He didn't tell them anything last time they talked to him."

"How do we know that? Maybe that's how they zeroed in on the cabin."

Kendra glared. "We *know* that because he's my son."

"So? The prisons are full of people who are somebody's son." Jill knew as soon as she said it that it was the wrong thing to say, and the flash in Kendra's eyes confirmed it.

"Kevin is not a felon."

"I know, I know. That's not what I meant. All I meant was, mothers are not very objective when it comes to their children. Of course *you* trust him, but that doesn't necessarily mean he's trustworthy."

She hadn't made it better.

"I think I know my *own son*," Kendra's tone was biting, "well enough to be sure he would never turn me over to the Lab Rats." She marched over to Jill and thrust her face inches away from Jill's, her blue eyes glinting. "Do you trust *me*?"

"Of course I do," Jill said. "I love you." How could she not trust Kendra? Kendra was the instigator of the whole venture to try to send Van back, and she'd been with Jill and supported her every step of the way since they'd started. And besides that, she *loved* Kendra. She brought her hand up to stroke Kendra's cheek, but Kendra brushed it aside.

"Good." Kendra kissed her briskly on the lips and scooted over to the driver's door of the Jetta. "I'll be back later today with the package *and* camping gear *and* toilet paper *and*, if you're nice, maybe I'll even bring you some coffee." Kendra slipped into the driver's seat.

"Wait!" Jill opened the passenger door. "I'm going with you."

Kendra sighed. "You *can't* come with me. Someone has to stay here with RIP."

Kendra was right, of course. It only made sense for Kendra to go and for Jill to stay. But she was terrified to let Kendra out of her sight. She leaned through the open door, reluctant to let her go. "What if they see you? What if they follow you? What if—"

Kendra rolled her eyes.

"I don't want you playing another game of chicken on the highway. What if you get hurt? Maybe you could call Kevin and have him pick up the package and bring it here."

"He doesn't have the key. He can't pick it up. Are you worried about me, honey?"

"Yes. What if something happens to you?"

Kendra brought Jill's hand up to her mouth for a soft kiss. "Yeah, love bites sometimes, doesn't it? You have to worry about me now."

Kendra released Jill's hand and made a shooing motion with her own. Reluctantly, Jill stood straight and closed the Jetta door. Kendra started the engine and guided it down the primitive road away from the camping spot. Jill smiled when Kendra's turn signal flashed prior to pulling onto the road, as though they weren't the only vehicle they'd seen since the night before. She watched until the Jetta disappeared. She sighed and turned back to RIP.

Love bites.

Fueled by granola bars, peanut butter, and water, Jill worked on RIP until noon, but eventually she stopped in frustration. There was nothing more she could do until she got Grover's supplies. It was too soon to expect Kendra. She would have to drive to Ione and back, with a stop somewhere along the way to meet up with Kevin and collect the camping equipment, and who knew how long that could take? If Kevin brought Bridgette along, Kendra would have to spend some time gurgling and cooing over her, and it could be hours more before she arrived back in camp.

Jill didn't understand the almost manic bond between Kendra and Bridgette, but she'd seen it in other acquaintances of hers who were grandparents. She supposed she'd have to get used to it. At least, she would have to if she wasn't able to send Van back. If she did manage to send Van back, Bridgette might not even exist. Had Kendra thought of that?

Jill took her cell phone, wandered out to the road, and headed uphill, watching for a signal. She hadn't talked to Van for a couple of days. She tried to imagine what Van must be feeling, stuck for more than a week now in the wrong century. She was relieved Van was staying at Bennie's. The Lab Rats wouldn't expect Van to be there. She was safely hidden.

Her phone registered two bars, so Jill pushed in the numbers and greeted Van when she picked up.

"Hi Jill. How are you?"

"I'm fine. A little stiff from sleeping on the ground, but other than that."

"Sleeping on the ground? Why?"

"It's a long story. We've moved RIP again. I won't tell you where, but it's hidden and it's safe."

"That's good." Van's voice was flat, as if she didn't really care whether RIP was safe.

"How are things at Bennie's? Are you all right there?"

"Everything's great." But Van didn't sound great.

"Good, good." From where she stood on the low hill, Jill could see a corner of RIP through the trees, and she could watch the road as well. No park ranger or Lab Rat could sneak up on her from this vantage point, and she could watch for Kendra as well.

"Jill, how much longer do you think—"

"It won't take too long, not once I get all the supplies I need. If all goes smoothly, it should be ready in two or three weeks. Maybe a month."

"A *month*?"

"But maybe less. Probably less. It could be ready much sooner."

Van sighed. "It's just, well, this would all be a lot easier to deal with if I could be *alive*, you know? Legally, I mean. I don't have a driver's license or a credit card. I can't even get a job without a Social Security number."

"But Van, you can't let them know you're back. If you apply for any of those cards, they'll find out. And once they find you, there's no telling what they'll do to you. You have to hang on a little while longer."

"Do you really think you'll be able to make it work?"

"Yes," Jill said, with more confidence than she felt. "At least, I know I'll be able to get RIP up and running again. And I *think* I know how to invert it. You have to be patient. Please, Van, don't do anything to tip them off to where you are, or where I am. If I can't make RIP function properly, then we'll figure out the next step. Maybe we can create a new identity for you. But don't do anything, yet. Please?"

There was a long silence before Van said, "How long do you want me to wait?"

Jill hesitated. "Give me a month. If I can't get RIP up and running by then, we'll find a way to make you legally alive again. Okay? Will you give me a month?"

Another long silence had Jill bracing herself, but finally Van said, "Okay. A month. I'll wait a month, but after that—I need to be alive, Jill."

Chapter Twenty-six

Van — 2008

"C'MERE, VAN, LET me put some of this sunscreen on you."

Van plopped herself on the sand in front of Bennie and scooted herself back between Bennie's legs. They both wore bathing suits, Bennie's a navy blue one-piece Speedo over which she'd pulled a loose pair of khaki shorts, and Van's a green-and-purple-striped tankini, a style she'd never heard of in 1988, but wished she had. It had normal bikini bottoms, but the top came down nearly to the upper edge of the bikini bottoms. It gave the impression of being a one-piece, but was not.

"I swear the sun is hotter than it used to be," Van said. "It used to take me an hour or more to burn."

"It is stronger." Bennie rubbed a puddle of lotion between her hands to warm it. "Less ozone, stronger UV rays, global warming, and all that." She gently smeared the lotion on Van's already hot shoulders.

"Really?" Van looked around at Bennie. "It's hotter than it used to be?"

"It's getting hotter every minute," Bennie said seriously, hugging Van briefly with her thighs.

Van laughed and twisted around to squint at the lake. They were at the summer cabin of Bennie's friends, Stacy and Sue. Though "cabin" was a misnomer. The house was a massive four stories built into a hill rising up from the edge of Lake Coeur d'Alene. Five bedrooms, five bathrooms, and a loft that crossed the entire top floor and held a dozen beds in a row, dormitory style. The house was built from the type of logs that came from old growth trees, which even in 1988 were harvested only amidst controversy about spotted owls. A gigantic log and slate fireplace dominated one wall of the main floor living room, and the other wall was all windows overlooking the lake. Two decks, upper and lower, allowed guests to sit on deck chairs and watch the water skiers, wake boarders, and jet skiers play in the water, but Van and Bennie had chosen instead to lounge on the small private beach, created by specially imported white tropical sand, that nestled below the lower deck.

"Look at me again."

Van obligingly swiveled her head around and met Bennie's eyes. Bennie carefully scrutinized Van's nose and cheeks and smiled at her. "Your freckles are getting darker."

Van crinkled her nose. "Already?" She rubbed her finger on her nose, as if trying to rub them off.

"I like them, but we should put some of this on your face too, or you'll fry like a lobster."

"Do lobsters fry?" Van obediently sat still while Bennie smeared lotion on her face. Then she swung around again and let Bennie resume putting lotion on her shoulders and back. "You're lucky to have such nice dark skin." Van rubbed her hand along Bennie's bare muscular thigh, down to her knee, and back up again. "You don't have to worry about burning."

"Oh, I'm burning," Bennie said carefully. "Just not from the sun."

Van's hand halted its motion on Bennie's leg but, after a thoughtful moment, she resumed stroking.

Bennie was as gentlemanly as ever. Flirtatious at times, but she never crossed the line to make Van feel uncomfortable or pressured. Van knew Bennie wanted her. It wasn't something she could hide. But Bennie had gone out of her way to make sure Van knew she was safe with her. Bennie would not go where Van did not invite her.

Van was considering issuing an invitation. She meant what she'd told Jill earlier that day on the phone. She needed to be alive. She'd buried the Van of 1988 that morning when she got her tattoo. She was having a harder time making the Van of 2008 feel alive. She couldn't get a job, she couldn't get a drivers license, she couldn't get her own money or her own home. What did that leave her?

Bennie's cool fingers kneaded the lotion into the hot skin on Van's arms, reminding her of what was left. Bennie was all she had. But Bennie might be all she needed to make herself feel alive. And, Van resolved, she *was* going to feel alive. So she continued stroking Bennie's leg as Bennie rubbed lotion into her back, saying nothing, both very aware that something had shifted between them.

A couple of women brought their jet skis to a stop at the dock in front of them and climbed off laughing. "You guys ready for a turn?" one of the women called to them. Bennie nudged Van from behind.

"Get up. Let's do this. Have you ever jet skied before?"

"No." Van rose and brushed fine white sand from her butt. Jet skis had existed in 1988, but they were not common, and she'd never ridden on one. The lake today was crowded with them. Visions of out of control drivers and head-on collisions flitted through her head. "Isn't it like riding a motorcycle?"

"Easier than that, and you don't have to wear a helmet. Do you want to ride with me first?"

"Yes." What was the point in worrying about accidents now? Technically, she was already dead. And what could make her feel more alive than riding on the back of a jet ski with Bennie on the Fourth of July? Well, she could think of one thing, but it was still too early for that. "Yes, I want to ride with you."

Bennie grinned, her teeth flashing bright in the sun. "Great.

Here, we need to find a life vest to fit you."

Moments later she was stepping onto wobbly footrests while Bennie stood in the water holding the craft steady. "I got you. Now put your leg over." Van sat. "Okay, great." Bennie hopped up onto the dock and pulled the jet ski over to her. "Now scoot back a little and let me in." Bennie climbed in front of Van. "Put your arms around me and hold on tight." Van did, and seconds later she let out a whoop as they shot toward the center of the lake. At first Bennie was careful to avoid the wake of other watercraft and kept the ride smooth, but after Van got her bearings, Bennie deliberately crashed into the wakes of other vehicles and cast them bouncing and flying through the air. Van screamed and laughed and held Bennie as tightly as she could, momentarily regretting that they were both wearing life vests that prevented Van from pressing more intimately against her back.

While riding, Van forgot she was legally dead, forgot she was in the wrong century, completely forgot about Jill and RIP and Patsy. For the duration of the ride she was happy and carefree and fully alive. When Bennie pulled up to the dock, the memories flooded back briefly, but Van blocked them, refusing to let them in. She *liked* feeling happy and carefree and alive. When Bennie asked her if she wanted to try it on her own, Van said yes. Bennie gave her a brief lesson, and soon they were both darting through the water, laughing and playing like dolphins on bikes. Van rejoiced in the feel of her hair flapping behind her, the fine spray of water that flew up, and the drenching she got when Bennie taunted her by zipping near enough to douse her. Finally, they had to come in. The afternoon was growing late, and other women wanted to play on the jet skis before it got too dark.

"We better change," Bennie said, after they'd removed their life vests. "How'd you get so wet?"

"Like you don't know."

Their clothes were in a duffel bag on the floor of one of the spare bedrooms. When Van bent over it to rummage for her dry underwear, Bennie asked, "How's your tattoo doing?"

Van knew Bennie was ogling her butt. Without standing up, Van leaned over a bit farther and peeked at her from between her legs. Bennie sat on the edge of the bed, no more than four feet away, and she was indeed gawking at Van's ass.

"I don't know," Van said, causing Bennie's gaze to drop quickly from Van's butt to her eyes. "Do you want to check it?"

Bennie's eyes smoldered. "I'm not sure you want me to do that."

Van straightened and sidled over to Bennie. "But I *am* sure." She turned so her butt was only inches from Bennie's face. "Will you check my tattoo, please?"

Bennie didn't move for a moment. Then, gingerly, she brought the index fingers of both hands up to the top of Van's bikini bottoms. Bennie drew the spandex material away from Van's skin and lowered it, releasing it with a snap right below the full curve of Van's butt cheeks. Van felt the cool air on her exposed bottom. With a touch as light as a whisper, she felt the tip of Bennie's finger trace the skin around the tattoo. Van's crotch clenched.

"It looks pretty good," Bennie said with a thin, controlled voice. "You need to keep it moisturized."

Without pulling her bikini bottoms up, Van stepped over to the duffel bag and bent over. She knew she was giving Bennie a show, and the thought excited her. She felt very alive. She stood and circled back with a bottle of Curel in her hand, aware that the drape of her bikini bottom below her butt drew the front of the bikinis exceedingly low as well. She handed the bottle to Bennie, who still sat on the bed, watching Van with dark gleaming eyes.

"Will you moisturize me, Bennie?" Van asked softly.

The muscles in Bennie's jaw clenched. She took the bottle of Curel from Van and set it beside her on the bed. She placed both hands on Van's bare hips, her thumbs moving ever so slightly up and down barely above Van's hairline. "Don't toy with me, Van."

At the feel of Bennie's thumbs, Van felt a gush of moisture surge into her bikini. "I'm not toying with you," she whispered, longing to feel Bennie's thumbs move lower.

Bennie stared up into Van's eyes for a moment, then rotated Van's hips so that Van's butt was in front of her. After rubbing the Curel between her hands to warm it, as she had the suntan lotion earlier, Bennie gently smoothed the lotion into the soft, smooth flesh of Van's butt cheek. It hurt a bit where the needles had sunk in earlier in the day, but Van barely noticed. As Bennie's left hand caressed the lotion onto Van's butt cheek, her right hand moved around Van's hips toward the front, matching the left hand stroke for stroke. Bennie's hand slid underneath the narrow strip of spandex that covered the lower juncture of Van's thigh and torso, the spot Bennie had said was her favorite part of a woman's body. Van felt hot fingers slide further, back and forth, threading through her pubic hair and over the top of her mound, closer and closer to where she throbbed. Van's legs gave out on her, and she dropped back onto Bennie's lap, straddling one leg and arching her crotch upward to assist Bennie in reaching the center of her. Bennie's left arm, abandoning the tattoo, wrapped around Van's waist and held her tightly against her, as her right hand stroked back and forth across Van's mound before finally reaching in to—

The door opened. "Jesus Christ, Bennie, can't you keep it in your pants until you get home?" The door snapped closed.

Van jumped up, pulling her bikini bottoms back up as she did so. Her face flamed.

"Fuck!" Bennie dropped backward on the bed and brought her hands up to press them on her eyes.

"Who was that?" Van asked, though it hardly mattered who it was. They were all strangers to her.

"Dionne." Bennie sat up and heaved a great sigh. "Don't mind her. She's so jealous, she pees green. C'mere, let me finish your tattoo. *Just* the tattoo. It needs the moisturizer."

So Van stood before Bennie again, this time holding the bikini bottoms down herself just far enough to give Bennie access to the tattoo. But even as she recovered some of her more customary modesty, she wondered why. Like with the jet ski ride, she'd felt so *alive*. Isn't that what she wanted? What did she care what Bennie's friends thought of her? They didn't even know her.

When Bennie finished rubbing in the moisturizer, she gave Van a friendly pat on the butt, tugged her bikini up, and turned her around to face her. "Don't worry about what almost happened here. It won't happen again, I promise. Not unless you want it to."

"But I do." Van took Bennie's hand in hers and placed it between her legs, smiling as Bennie's eyes grew wide. "I do want it to. After we get home. Please."

She dropped Bennie's hand and moved back to the duffel bag. She quickly stripped off the wet bikini and drew on her dry panties, pulled the tankini off over her head and was hooking her bra behind her back when Bennie said plaintively from the bed, "Do we have to stay for dinner?"

Van laughed, threw her sundress over her head, and spun toward Bennie. "I'm hungry." She came over to stand between Bennie's legs. "Besides," she pushed Bennie so she lay back on the bed. Van followed and landed on top her, "I want to see the fireworks."

Bennie grinned and wrapped her arms around Van. "I can show you fireworks." She rolled Van over and kissed her.

At the pressure from Bennie's lips, Van opened her own, and Bennie's tongue swept in, stroking Van's tongue with her own, gently at first, then more urgently. Finally, Bennie raised her head to gaze into Van's eyes. They both breathed heavily. Van licked her lips and watched Bennie watch her do it. She put her finger up to Bennie's lips. "Tonight."

Bennie captured Van's finger with her lips on sucked on it briefly. "Tonight." She sat up, rose from the bed, reached back, and pulled Van up. "Now get the hell out of here and let me get dressed."

Van grinned and blew her a kiss.

Chapter Twenty-seven

Kendra — 2008

KENDRA FOUND AN old spiral notebook in the back seat of her car and ripped out three sheets of paper. Folding them over into the general shape of envelopes, she addressed one to Kevin, one to Jill at her house, and one to Paul, the only three addresses she knew by heart. On the inside of the makeshift envelopes, she wrote brief messages of the "Having a great time, wish you were here" variety in case the Lab Rats used their influence over the post office to open and read them. Tampering with the mail was a federal offense, of course, but the Lab Rats *were* the Feds. Who know what lengths they'd go to in order to find what they wanted? The "envelopes" weren't taped shut, but didn't the postal service have to deliver anything that had an address on it with postage? She thought she'd heard once of someone mailing a coconut from Hawaii to Spokane, simply by writing the address on the outer shell of the coconut and stapling the postage to it.

She felt a bit foolish creating fake mail so she'd have a legitimate reason for going into the Ione Post Office, in case someone was watching her. But you're not paranoid if they really *are* out to get you, right? However, she entered the post office, stamped and mailed her letters, and retrieved her package with no difficulty, and when she returned to the empty parking lot there was still no sign that anyone was watching. Maybe she and Jill were both paranoid. Perhaps that dark vehicle they'd seen yesterday heading up the hill toward the cabin was nothing but an ordinary car, an old grandpa taking his grandkids camping or something.

But when she emerged from Ione's quick stop grocery store with a package of toilet paper under her arm, two men stood beside her Jetta. They weren't wearing dark suits, but they still had all the earmarks of federal agents. Especially the younger one, with his sharp chiseled and clean shaven features and his short conservative haircut. He saw Kendra advancing toward the car and brazenly examined her, a cold, challenging stare. The other guy was older and paunchier, with dark bags underneath his eyes. He was examining the car, but when he saw Kendra and noted the toilet paper under her arm, he said something to the other man. They retreated across the miniature parking lot to their car. Kendra laughed uneasily when she saw it was a black Hummer. Were they afraid to face her in anything smaller, after what had happened to the Dodge Ram? But she was afraid, too. She was not paranoid. This was real.

She wasn't terribly concerned about being followed, though. She wasn't going to lead them to Jill or RIP. She was heading south, away from their campsite. She'd called Kevin on her way into Ione and asked him to gather his camping equipment and meet her at the Ram Drive-In in Riverside. They could follow her there, if they wished. They already knew about Kevin, since they'd questioned him, so they'd learn nothing by seeing them meet up for lunch. She would prefer they not know about the camping gear, but she would worry later about how to transfer it from Kevin's car to hers.

Oddly enough, though, no one seemed to be following her as she drove south. The Hummer would have been unmistakable, and there was no sign of it anywhere. Kendra was well versed in action adventure movies. She knew they could have switched cars, or had people tag teaming her, but for long stretches of highway there were no other cars at all, and when she did see one, it was generally a family with kids, or gangs of teenagers. Unlikely spies.

She tried calling Jill, but was forced to leave a message. Though there was no signal available at their campsite, she hoped Jill might search one out. "Hi honey. I got the package. You were right, the Lab Rats were in Ione. I don't think they saw me pick up the package, but they know I bought toilet paper. I'm going to meet Kevin now. I don't think they're following me, but who knows? I think they're afraid of me. They're driving a Hummer now. If anything comes up, I'll give you a call. Check your messages now and then, okay? And feel free to leave me one, even if it's just to say you love me. I love you. Kiss kiss." She hung up and continued driving toward Riverside, still unable to spot anyone following her.

The hamburger she ate with Kevin and the baby at the Ram Drive Inn was the best hamburger she'd ever eaten in her life. "Oh my God, this is so good. I haven't had meat in a week. I didn't know how much I missed it."

"Why haven't you had meat?" Kevin asked, blowing on a hot, crisp French fry to cool it before placing it on Bridgette's high chair tray.

"Jill's a vegetarian. We've had nothing but beans and rice and nuts. Thank God there's no tofu in Ione, or I'd have had to eat that too."

"Ione? So you're staying up at the cabin?"

"Not anymore." Kendra squirted a giant puddle of ketchup on her plate. "We had to move on. Oh, will you check to see if a GPS tracking device is hidden on my car somewhere?"

"A tracking device? Mom, what are you up to?"

"Don't use that tone with me. God, you sound just like your father."

Kevin spread his hands helplessly. "Sorry, Mom, but you have to admit this is all pretty strange. You disappear for a week, guys with badges come around asking about you, and now you're on the run, possibly being tracked by GPS. I don't want to have to come visit you in prison, okay?"

"Yeah, it's all about you, isn't it?" At Kevin's look, she shrugged. "Okay, sorry. I can't tell you much. I'm helping Jill with a project."

"Jill? She's usually so sensible."

"She *is* sensible, and she has a very good reason for what she's doing."

Kevin regarded his mother closely. "Is something going on between you and Jill? You seem pretty cheerful for someone who may be headed to prison."

Kendra blushed. She was sorry she'd accused Kevin of sounding like his father. He was *nothing* like Paul, who would never have noticed the subtle indications that someone was in love. Kevin still had the round freckled face he'd had as a boy, but he was a man, and a good one.

"Do you think they'd let Jill and me be cell mates?"

One eyebrow shot up, a trick he'd mastered as a young child.

"I'm in love, Kevin."

"With Jill? Good." Without taking his attention completely away from Kendra, he gently wiped Bridgette's face with a napkin dampened with his soda. "I always wondered why you two never got together."

"Really? Me too. But we were friends, and, you know, it was complicated."

"And now you're going camping with her? You must really be in love, Mom. You're not exactly the camping type."

"Tell me about it. I'm camping and I'm hiding from the bad guys and I'm eating vegetarian food. And I've never been happier in my life."

Kevin chuckled. "Then I'm happy for you."

"So will you check for a tracking device on my car?"

"This is crazy. But I'll try."

"Thanks, Kevin. Bridgette, want to come to Grammy?"

Kendra devoted herself for the rest of the meal to enjoying the company of Kevin and Bridgette. If Jill managed to send Van back to 1988, Kevin might be only nine years old the next time she saw him, and Bridgette wouldn't exist yet at all. It was possible that if Van never disappeared in 1988, Kevin's future would change. Van's vanishing hadn't had any direct impact on Kevin's young life, but it had impacted Kendra's. He was still so little, any change in Kendra's life must have affected him somehow. She liked the man he'd grown into so much, and Kendra couldn't imagine Bridgette not existing. What if, by sending Van back, Kevin never met Leslie, and they never had Bridgette? For a moment she wondered if she and Jill were doing the right thing. Was it fair to sacrifice Bridgette in order to send Van back?

She kissed the top of Bridgette's curly head and gave herself a mental shake. If there was a method to the universe, a plan, whatever, Jill was the one who had altered it up by sending Van forward in time. She had to fix it, if she could. If Bridgette was meant to exist, she would, regardless of whether Jill sent Van back or not.

They went out to the car. Kendra held Bridgette while Kevin crawled on the ground, peeking underneath the car for anything unusual. She was letting Bridgette examine herself in the side view mirror when she saw it, lying on the dash, right where the older Lab Rat had been looking.

Her day pass to the Rocky Falls Campground, dated July 3, 2008.

"Fuck!"

"Hey, Mom, not in front of Bridgette."

"Sorry. Oh, fuck!" She fumbled with one hand for her phone in her purse, Bridgette propped on her hip, watching her curiously. She had to warn Jill. No wonder they hadn't followed her. They didn't need to — *she* wasn't what they wanted. They wanted Jill and RIP, and she'd shown them exactly where to find her. How much time had passed? Too much. They could be there by now. "Fuck!"

Kendra hardly noticed when Kevin stood and pulled Bridgette from her arms, his expression reproachful. Kendra punched in Jill's speed dial number and got a recording.

She must still be out of range. She waited for the beep and said, "Jill, they know where you are. You've got to get out of there. They could be there any minute. I'm sorry, I didn't realize. Oh, honey, please, be safe. I love you. Call me."

She hung up to find Kevin and Bridgette both watching her somberly. "Did you find anything?" she asked, and Kevin shook his head.

She leaned over and kissed them both, memorizing the feel of Bridgette's soft baby cheek, in case she never felt it again. "Let's load the camping equipment," she said briskly. "I have to go."

Chapter Twenty-eight

Bennie — 2008

DINNER WAS SPARERIBS barbecued on a shiny chrome outdoor grill as large as a mini van. Every flat surface in sight was covered with pasta salads and green salads and Asian salads, baked beans, green beans, pork and beans, French bread, homemade organic nut bread, and bread pudding. There were veggie trays and fruit trays and shrimp trays, corn on the cob, cheese platters, and bowls of candy and nuts. Chocolate cake, ice cream cake, tiramisu, cherry pie, and marionberry cobbler covered the dessert table.

But Bennie could not eat. Her stomach was full of butterflies with the promise of Van. After dinner. After the fireworks.

There was also plenty to drink. Strawberry margaritas, Bahama Mamas, coconut daiquiris, four kinds of wine, seven kinds of beer, including Stacy and Sue's own home brew. Non-drinkers could pick Coke and Pepsi and Mountain Dew, both diet and regular, bottled water, fizzy water, water with flavors added, cranberry juice and orange juice and carrot juice, iced tea, iced coffee, and hot coffee with or without caffeine.

Bennie nursed a single bottle of Stella Artois and watched Van, who was thoroughly enjoying herself. She'd said she wasn't toying with Bennie, but that's exactly what she was doing, playing with Bennie like cat with a mouse, taunting her. That strip tease show she'd put on in the bedroom was only the start.

At that moment, Van bit into a huge red strawberry, stuck her tongue out to lap up the juice dribbling from the corners of her mouth, made a pout with her wet red lips as she sucked what was left of the berry, and peeked a gleeful glance at Bennie. Van was deliberately playing with her, and they both knew it, but Bennie was helpless, so full of longing for Van that she would have let her do anything with her. Van could tie a string to the back of Bennie's head, her hands, and feet, and dance her around like a marionette, and Bennie would have let her, grinning stupidly all the while, if Van looked at her like that while she did it.

"You've got it bad," Dionne said, sliding into the lawn chair next to Bennie. "I haven't seen you this whipped in, like, ever."

Bennie tore her eyes away from Van long enough to glower at Dionne, who was also watching Van. "Yeah." Bennie turned her attention back to Van.

"Where'd you find her? She's cute. A fucking tease, of course, but cute."

"I knew her years ago. Ran into her again last week."

"Have you done her yet?"

"Shut up."

"No?" Dionne laughed. "Well, from the looks of it, you might get lucky tonight. You should eat something, you may need your strength."

Bennie ignored her and kept her eyes focused on Van, who was now standing underneath the water mister installed at one end of the deck. She held her hair back with one hand and tilted her face up, eyes closed, as glistening droplets misted all over her sun-pinked face, neck, shoulders, and chest, and dampened the material of the sundress that stretched across her breasts.

"Then again," Dionne said, "maybe you're planning to eat something else. Saving your appetite. Good plan."

"Shut *up*," Bennie said, a bit more forcefully, and Dionne laughed and got up to go taunt someone else. Bennie wanted to go to Van, but she was afraid to stand up, afraid her khaki shorts would be stained from the squishy wetness between her legs. She throbbed.

She took another sip of beer and prayed for dark.

It did get dark, eventually, as it always does, and finally it was dark enough for the spectacular fireworks show over Lake Coeur d'Alene. Van abandoned her "Fuck Me" game in her childish excitement about the fireworks. Bennie enjoyed simply standing behind Van, her arms wrapped around her, while Van leaned back against her and watched the show. She was relieved that the sexual tension of the last couple of hours had eased. She'd been stretched so tight, she was afraid she might break.

Van twisted her head around to Bennie and said, "Isn't it the most beautiful thing you've ever seen?"

Bennie gazed down into Van's shining eyes, her happy smile, her curls making a dusky cloud around her head. "Yes. It's the most beautiful thing I've ever seen." Van may have blushed, it was too dark to see, but she must have been aware of Bennie's meaning. She stood on tiptoe, gave Bennie a quick, open-mouthed kiss, and whipped back toward the lake.

So much for easing the sexual tension. Encouraged, Bennie allowed her hands to stray from Van's waist. Subtly, so as not to draw the attention of anyone else on the deck, she let her right hand slide upwards to touch the swell of Van's breast. Her thumb forayed further, stroking in gentle circles upward until it reached the nipple, which already stood firm and erect, even before Bennie flicked it softly with her thumb through the thin material. Van gasped.

Meanwhile, her left hand moved lower, down over Van's belly, with her pinky twitching as it felt the outline of the top of Van's panties through the bunched fabric of the sundress, hinting at where Bennie had wanted to go, and had nearly gone, earlier in the day.

Van sagged back against her as if she could no longer stand on her own, and Bennie knew Van was as aroused as she was. Please, God, let the fireworks end soon.

They did, finally. Bennie and Van said their goodbyes and thank yous as rapidly as was decent and climbed into the Jag. They said nothing as Bennie navigated her way out of the awkward driveway, but when they reached the juncture of Stacy and Sue's lane with the paved road above, Bennie put the Jag in park and grabbed Van. Van was ready, her mouth open and inviting. She pressed her breasts against Bennie's roaming hands, and her hand ventured on to Bennie's thigh and inched underneath the cuff of the shorts. Just before she would have discovered Bennie wore no underwear, a honking and hooting from behind broke them apart. Bennie lowered her window and stuck her hand out, good naturedly flipping off her friends, before she put the Jag in drive and roared off.

They spoke little on the drive home. Bennie was afraid of saying the wrong thing and screwing things up. She'd wanted Van for over twenty years, and now to be so close. If she didn't get to touch her, *really* touch her, tonight, Bennie thought she just might die.

But, miraculously, she didn't screw things up. When they entered the house, Van slipped immediately into Bennie's arms, wrapped her own arms around Bennie's neck, and kissed her with a fervor that shook Bennie to her core. She put her hands on Van's ass, Van's beautiful, sexy ass, and rucked the fabric of the dress up so that she touched the filmy silk of Van's underpants. Mindful of the fresh tattoo, Bennie cupped Van's cheeks and lifted her up so that they matched pelvis to pelvis. Van whimpered through the kiss, and Bennie felt a fresh spurt of juice from her own throbbing vulva.

Bennie broke the kiss, set Van on her feet, took her hand, and led her to the main floor bedroom. The bed was massive, and high off the floor. Bennie spun Van toward her so Van's back was to the bed, placed her hands on Van's waist, and boosted her up onto the bed. Stepping between Van's spread legs, she ran her hands up Van's thighs and pushed the dress up until she saw the thin film of Van's panties stretched taut across her crotch. They were sopping wet.

"My God!" Bennie slid the side of her hand up the center of Van's crotch, loving the feel of Van's dripping juices through the wet silk. Van's pelvis gave a reflexive thrust and Bennie pulled her hand away. "Not yet, my darling. Not yet."

She climbed up onto the bed herself and rolled to the center. "C'mere." She held her arm out to Van, who still perched on the edge of the bed. Van rolled over and crawled toward Bennie on all fours, keeping her dress bunched at her waist. But instead of crawling to Bennie's side, Van stopped at Bennie's legs, used her hands spread them wide, and slid between them. Bennie watched, mesmerized, as Van drew closer, her breasts nearly falling out of the loose sundress.

She made a false motion as if to lower her mouth to Bennie's crotch, but instead she crept forward until her breasts hovered above it. Deliberately, keeping her eyes fastened upon Bennie's, Van lowered her breasts to Bennie's crotch, grazing first the left, then the right against the damp cloth of Bennie's shorts. Still teasing Bennie with her breasts, Van slipped her hand along Bennie's thigh underneath the loose khaki. Her eyes widened when she encountered no underwear, and she quickly tucked her thumb inside Bennie.

Bennie throbbed from the touch, and she felt another rush of juice, but she pushed Van's hand away. "Not yet," she gasped. "Not yet." She pulled Van up to her side, whipped the sundress over Van's head, and tossed it aside. She propped herself up onto her elbow and drank in the sight of Van's beautiful body, now clad only in two pieces of silk. She ran her hand across Van's breasts, gently tweaked her nipples, which were already hard, and ran her hand over Van's belly to the moist center of her panties. Bennie dipped her head to Van's left breast and nuzzled it through the thin fabric of her bra and simultaneously ran her fingers up again through the wet silk of the panties. Impatient now, she sat up and slid her fingers over the sides of the panties and drew them down.

Finally. Finally. Van's soft pink petals spread open before her, waiting, willing, darker pink on the outside, lighter pink toward the center, and all of them glistening with Van's own precious juice. She wanted to kiss it, but not yet, not yet.

She knelt on the bed and quickly undressed. She was so wet, liquid dripped down the side of her leg. Van took the opportunity to sit up and pull her bra off, and they faced each other, naked at last, Van sitting up, legs spread wide, and Bennie on her knees before her, crouched and ready.

This time Bennie was the one who crawled forward. She pressed Van back against the pillows and took a nipple in her mouth. Van's breasts were soft and full and perfect, and the nipple hard and round. Bennie wanted to linger there, but she couldn't. She couldn't. Her crotch throbbed and ached and wanted to be in only one place. She set her knees between Van's open legs. Bennie's swollen clit was long and throbbing and engorged. Forcing herself to move slowly, she lowered herself until her crotch was poised directly over Van's. She brought Van's legs up around her waist and deliberately pressed her crotch onto Van's welcoming, inviting opening. Bennie paused a moment to enjoy the luxurious feel of hot wet flesh against hot wet flesh. The ultimate kiss. The intensity of the feelings it generated was so strong, she had to close her eyes with weakness. She didn't want it to end, but her body had other ideas. Her pelvis arched, and she stroked upward with her swollen clit, right through the center of Van's vulva. She saw Van's eyes widen in surprise at the feel of Bennie's engorged clit. Bennie reared back and stroked upward again and again and again.

Oh, dear God in heaven! There was no sweeter feeling in the world than that of her clit stroking the inside of a woman's wet hot vulva, and when that woman was Van, oh, dear Lord, dear Lord, it felt so good! She peered down at Van's face and nearly wept to see the perfection of it. Van's head was thrown back, her mouth wide open, her pink tongue trembling, as tiny helpless moans issued from her throat. Her eyes were glazed, half closed. Bennie stroked again and exquisite ripples radiated from her groin outward throughout her body, down her legs to the tips of her toes, through her torso to the top of her head. Van's eyes flew open wide as the rhythm captured her and she rocked her pelvis to meet Bennie thrust for thrust. Bennie cupped Van's ass in her hands and held her pressed tightly against her crotch as the ripples pulsed and grew into waves that surged through her, one after the other after the other.

"Oh, oh, oh, sweet Jesus!" Never had anything felt so good. It was as if her entire life had been engineered for this one moment, this one perfect sweet moment. "Oh God, *Van!*" A giant wave crashed within her, rocking her body in long, deep, sweet, convulsive shudders, and she fell on top of Van.

But she couldn't rest there. Quickly, before Van lost the rhythm, Bennie inserted two fingers into Van's opening. The walls of Van's vagina closed in immediately, pulsing and caressing Bennie's fingers as Bennie stroked and pushed inside her. Bennie showered kisses on Van's neck, her chest, her breasts, her nipples, working her way down to tongue Van's belly button. She moved lower, all the while stroking her fingers inside as Van moaned helplessly. Finally, Bennie's mouth hovered over Van's pink slick shell. Without removing her fingers, she bent and captured the swollen nub of Van's clit with her mouth, rolled it with her tongue, and sucked.

Van's hips jerked. "Oh, Bennie! Oh, my God."

Bennie eased her left arm underneath Van. With an arm around her, fingers inside her, and mouth upon her, Bennie possessed Van completely. The smell, the taste, the feel of Van undulating beneath Bennie's mouth, as she called out Bennie's name, was better than anything Bennie had imagined in twenty years of dreams. The walls of Van's vagina sucked so deliciously that Bennie thought her fingers might come. Bennie licked and sucked and coaxed the most glorious sounds from Van's throat.

Finally, with a last long moaning shudder, Van clenched and rocked against Bennie's hand and mouth. Her walls tightened one last long time on Bennie's fingers, clenching, clenching, clenching, as she screamed out, "Bennie!" She collapsed, gasping, splayed, and exhausted.

Bennie slipped her fingers out, released her suction hold on Van's clit, and crawled up to lie on top of her, pressing her groin once more against Van's, but gently this time. They lay in silence a moment as they caught their breath. Occasionally one or the other made a small thrust with her pelvis, rocked by aftershocks. Afraid of squishing Van, Bennie finally rolled off, bringing Van with her, so they were both on their sides, facing each other, both heads on one pillow, mouths two inches apart.

Van's eyes glistened with unshed tears, and Bennie raised her head, concerned. Then Van smiled, tremulous, but happy, and Bennie let her head drop.

"I'm alive, Bennie," Van whispered. "I'm alive."

Bennie chuckled and cupped Van's face with her hand. "Yes, darling Van. You are very much alive."

Chapter Twenty-nine

Jill — 2008

THERE ARE ONLY so many times you can check the viscosity in a mercromometer, Jill concluded, before the air seeping into the gauge would alter the readings. She forced herself to leave RIP alone. Until she got the new supplies, she only risked making things worse with her constant manipulations. She moved on to the truck itself, checked the oil, checked the air pressure in the tires, checked the battery, checked the fan belt. But there was nothing to do there either. Grover had kept everything in tiptop shape, spotless even, in the event they needed an urgent escape. Which, as it turned out, they did. Not so paranoid after all, old Grover. She hoped he was all right.

She hoped his package had arrived all right too. Where was Kendra? Jill pulled her phone out of her pocket and checked the time for about the twentieth time since Kendra left. One fifteen. She'd have the package by now, surely, unless there'd been a problem. She should have called. Jill was about to climb to the top of the hill again, to check for messages, when she heard a car engine coming, and tires popping on gravel. Her first thought was Kendra, but no, it couldn't be. It was too soon for Kendra to be back. Jill stood silently beside RIP, listening.

The tire popping stopped, but the engine continued. She couldn't see it through the trees, but she knew the car had left the gravel road and was driving along the same narrow dirt road they had taken to reach the isolated clearing last night. Jill whipped around and checked to make sure the back of RIP was locked. It was, of course. She'd locked it automatically, as she did every time she exited the chamber. Reassured, she moved to the front of the truck right before a dark green Jeep Cherokee crept into the clearing and stopped, its nose no more than two feet from where Jill stood watching. The door to the Jeep Cherokee opened and a tall, thick man no more than thirty years old unfolded himself from it. He wore a park ranger uniform and a stern expression.

"May I see your camping pass, Ma'am?" he asked, his eyes scouring the area. There was very little for him to see, no camping equipment, no fire pit, no evidence of sleeping or cooking. The only sign that she'd been there any time at all was a plastic grocery bag looped over a nearby tree limb half filled with empty water bottles and a few food wrappers.

"Yes, of course," Jill said vaguely. She shuffled, slightly hunched over and with a faint limp, toward the front of RIP, where she fumbled with the door and finally pulled out her pass.

"This is a day pass, Ma'am. Dated yesterday. Did you spend the night here?"

"Yes," Jill said, her voice trembling ever so slightly. "I didn't mean to. I got so tired all of a sudden. I was turned around." She let her eyes rove around the clearing as if she were searching for something she'd lost.

"Are you alone, Ma'am?" he asked sharply.

"Yes," she said meekly, as if she'd been chastised. "We've always gone camping on the Fourth. It always seemed so easy with Ken. I thought I could do it myself, now that Ken's gone." She blinked rapidly, fighting real tears at worry over Kendra, and heaved a hefty, defeated sigh. "The kids will be so mad at me. They told me not to go."

"Is there someone I can call?" he asked, the sternness in his eyes giving way to concern. "One of your kids, maybe, to come get you?"

"No, no," Jill said, quickly. "They'd get mad. I know I can make my way back home, if you'll point me in the right direction out of the park. I'm all packed up and ready to go, as you can see. I was just trying to work up my courage to go back home and face them."

"You live with them?"

She heaved another defeated sigh. "Not yet."

"They can't prevent you from camping, Ma'am," he said, coming to her defense. "Just try to stay at the more populated camping grounds, where you won't get lost. Okay?"

She smiled. "I will. Thank you. Can you show me the way out of here?"

"I'll lead the way," the ranger said, heading for the Jeep. "You can follow me."

Jill pulled the plastic sack from the tree, got into RIP and started the engine, praying now that Kendra *wouldn't* show up. She followed the ranger to the gravel road, her heart thumping, but grateful for once that she was old. It was hard to be harsh with someone who could be your grandma. She continued behind him on the gravel road, but where the gravel finally met pavement, he pulled over and flagged her down.

"Where do you live, Ma'am?"

"Metaline Falls," she said randomly.

He pointed north. "Head that way. It'll take you to Highway 31. You can find your way from there?"

"I sure can. Thank you."

"I'll stay behind you for a little bit. But I'll be pulling off after a few miles. You keep going north. Good luck to you. Don't let your kids boss you around too much."

"I won't. Thank you."

She headed north, glancing periodically in her rear view mirror at the ranger behind her. Right before he pulled off onto another gravel drive, she saw another car, far, far behind them. A dark car. A large car. A Hummer. A moment later, the Hummer had disappeared. The only place it could have gone was the road she and the ranger had just pulled out of.

As soon as he was out of sight, Jill pressed the accelerator hard against the floor and grabbed her phone. The messages waiting for her from Kendra only confirmed her fears.

Chapter Thirty

Van — 2008

"WHAT DO YOU get when you cross an elephant with a rhinoceros?" Bennie asked, scraping zoo print wallpaper off the old plaster wall.

"I dunno. What?" Van splashed liquid wallpaper stripper onto the wall with a broad brush. Fresh morning air blew in through the open windows. It would be too hot to work in the attic later, but it was still early enough to cool the room with nothing but open windows.

"Eleph-Ino." Bennie chuckled at her own joke. Van rolled her eyes, but Bennie didn't give up. "What do you get when you cross an elephant with a kangaroo?"

"I dunno. What?"

"Big holes all over Australia." Bennie laughed out loud and asked, "What?" when Van shook her head. "You don't like that one? How about this? What do you get when you cross a ghost and two bees?"

"I dunno, Bennie," Van said in a long-suffering voice. "What?"

"Boo bees. Hey, you liked that one. I saw you smile."

Van laughed, finally, though she'd been trying not to encourage Bennie's string of stupid jokes.

They were in the long, narrow attic room of Bennie's 1910 home, a room that the previous owners had apparently used as a children's playroom. Bennie was preparing it for redecoration, though she hadn't yet decided what the room would be. "Maybe a billiard room," she'd said. "Or a bowling alley, or a little movie theater. It's got such great light, though. Too bad I'm not an artist. It would make a great art studio. Are you artistic, Van?"

Van had denied any artistic ability, but she'd willingly entered into Bennie's plans for renovation. Most of the restoration that had been done on the old house, Bennie had done herself. Only the attic room and some space in the basement remained untouched, and Van was eager to help with those projects.

"So you like boob jokes, do you?" Bennie asked. "Now I see how your filthy mind works. Here's one. What did one saggy boob say to the other?"

"No more jokes," Van pleaded.

"No, silly. It said, 'Don't hang so low, they'll think we're nuts.'"

Van groaned, and Bennie laughed even harder. "Hey, you love my jokes, admit it." Bennie tossed her scraper down and lunged for

Van. She wrapped her arms around Van from behind. She slipped her hands inside Van's short pink bib overalls—overalls that Bennie had insisted on buying—and ran her fingers up and down underneath Van's tank top, tickling as she went. She buried her face in Van's hair. "Admit it, Van," she said, her voice muffled as she nuzzled Van's neck. "You love my jokes, you think I'm funny. Admit it."

Van shrieked and laughed and squirmed to get away, but she would *not* tell Bennie her jokes were funny. "Oh *you're* funny, all right," she finally gasped, trying to pull Bennie's hands from her shorts. "It's your *jokes* that stink."

"Hey, what do you mean by that?"

They were interrupted by the peal of the doorbell from down below. Bennie released Van and stepped to the window to peer down at the street. "I don't see anyone. No car."

"I'll see who it is." Van stooped to gather empty glasses from the floor. "We need fresh drinks, anyway." She blew Bennie a kiss and ran down the stairs. She swung by the kitchen first to drop off the dirty glasses, then moved to the front door. She pulled the elastic band from her ponytail, quickly rewrapped it, and opened the door.

Patsy stood on the front porch.

Their eyes met, and Van felt as if she'd been socked in the stomach, as if all the air had been slammed out of her lungs. She stood, her eyes fixed on Patsy's, long enough for her to get dizzy before she remembered to breathe.

"Patsy," she said finally.

Patsy smiled tightly. "Hello, Van."

A little over three weeks had passed since the night Van had left Patsy's trailer, over three weeks since she'd gone out into the storm and ended up in Bennie's car, in Bennie's house, in Bennie's life. She knew Patsy had gone to the hospital later that day. Inez had told her. She hadn't realized Patsy had been released. But here she was, standing on Bennie's doorstep. Completely sober.

Van had tried so hard to push thoughts of Patsy away, to keep her mind and heart focused on other things. For the most part, she'd been successful. Ever since the Fourth of July, when she and Bennie had first made love, she'd slept in Bennie's bed, and when thoughts of Patsy and 1988 and her old life intruded, all she had to do was roll over and hold on to Bennie, and her terrifying thoughts receded. Bennie had done everything she could to keep Van busy, entertained, amused, even to the point of looking up stupid jokes on the Internet that she knew would make Van groan.

But now here was Patsy, her eyes clear and aware and as full of love as they always had been, and Van knew all her attempts to forget Patsy were nothing more than a futile act of burying her head in the sand.

"Can we talk?" Patsy asked. A simple question, a simple request, but she held herself rigid and solemn, as if braced for brutal rejection.

Van roused herself to glance around, surprised, almost, to find herself standing in Bennie's house, answering Bennie's door as if she lived there. A sound behind her made her look up. Bennie slowly descended the stairs in bare feet and crumpled khaki shorts, her eyes fixed on Patsy, wide and wary, as if Patsy were a dragon or a dinosaur or death.

"Hello Bennie," Patsy said. "I only want to talk to Van." Patsy shifted her gaze to Van. "Do you have a few minutes?"

Van looked from Patsy to Bennie, reminded of the fight on the deck back in 1988. Then, as now, Van stood between them, the bone of contention, but this time both women remained calm, at least outwardly, both too chastened by the mistakes of the past to repeat them now.

"You can talk here," Bennie offered quickly, but stiffly. "I'll go. I have some errands to run."

Patsy started to step through the door, but Van put her hand out to stop her, reluctant to invite Patsy into the home she'd become so comfortable sharing with Bennie. "No, let's go to the park, Patsy. It's just down the block."

She whipped through the door and closed it, pretending she didn't see Bennie trying to catch her eye as she shut the door behind her.

"Are you all right to walk to the park?" Van asked. "I know you've been in the hospital."

"There's nothing wrong with my legs." Patsy headed down the steps. "In fact, I've been riding my bike nearly everywhere for the last five years." Van joined her on the sidewalk and they strolled toward Manito Park. "I lost my driver's license," Patsy admitted, with the air of someone new to making such admissions. "Too many DUI's."

"I guessed that," Van said quietly.

"I heard you laughing up there." Patsy inclined her head toward Bennie's open attic windows. "It's good to hear you so happy."

Van felt her cheeks burn. Guilt, shame, embarrassment. She wasn't sure what she felt, but it wasn't nice. "Really?"

"Yes, really." With the air of making a clean breast of it, she added, "I'm not thrilled that you're happy with *Bennie*, of all people, but I am glad you're happy."

They continued in silence. After a moment Van said in a small voice, "I'm not that happy."

Patsy gave her a curious look, but said nothing.

"How was it, in the hospital?"

"It was the second worst three weeks of my life," Patsy said. She took a deep breath and spoke quickly. There was something she had come to say, and she was intent on saying it. "Van, I'm sorry from the bottom of my heart about what happened at my trailer that night. I'm sorry I yelled at you, and I'm sorry I threw the bottle at the wall, and I'm sorry I scared you. I'm sorry I, you know, came on to you that way. And most of all," she took a long shaky breath before continuing, "most of all, I'm sorry that I got drunk. I'm sorry I drank. I'm an alcoholic."

Van tucked her hand into Patsy's arm and gave it a squeeze. "Patsy, you are the bravest person I've ever known."

Patsy gaped. Whatever she'd expected Van to say, it wasn't that. "Me? Brave?"

"Yeah." Van was surprised that Patsy was surprised. "I've always thought that. You were the first woman to go be a guard in the men's prison, when no one thought a woman could do it. And you came out as a lesbian before anyone else was brave enough to, and you've never been afraid to speak your mind. Your courage makes everyone around you braver."

Patsy tried not to smile, but it was clear she was pleased.

"So I'm not surprised that you're being brave now," Van said carefully, "admitting you're an alcoholic, and getting help. I'm just surprised that..." She hesitated, glanced up at Patsy, and saw she was already clenching her lips, bracing herself for Van's words. "I'm surprised that it took so long for you to get the courage to do it." There was a question in Van's voice.

Patsy shook her head. "You don't know what—" She broke off midsentence. "Excuses don't help." She stopped and faced Van, putting her hands on Van's shoulders. "It was not your fault that I became an alcoholic. It was *not* your fault. But, Van, when you disappeared, I had no courage left. None. You think I was brave?" Patsy smiled sadly. "My courage didn't come from me. It came from you."

They had reached the park and entered the Japanese Gardens, and their steps took them to the elegant stone bridge that arced over the pond. They stopped at the top of the arch and leaned their elbows on the bridge railing, wavy images of themselves reflected in the water.

"That's not true," Van said.

"What's not?" They hadn't spoken in several minutes, and Patsy's thoughts had clearly moved on from her last words.

"You didn't get your courage from me. You worked at the prison long before I met you, and you were out, too. Your courage was one of the things that attracted me to you in the first place. You didn't get it from me."

Patsy absorbed that for a moment and seemed to accept it. When she spoke again, it was to change the subject once more. "Back in

1988, before you disappeared, were you going to leave me?"

"What?" Van stood straight and faced Patsy, shocked. "No, I wasn't going to leave you." Patsy looked doubtful, and Van felt herself blush. "That whole thing with Bennie, it didn't mean anything, I swear. She had a crush on me, and I didn't handle it well. I kind of led her on. I was flattered. And she didn't understand. It wasn't her fault, it was mine, but it didn't mean anything. Please believe that."

An uneasy grimace crossed Patsy's face. "And now?"

Van hesitated. "Now, I—"

"Never mind," Patsy said quickly. "I was drinking a lot, even back then. It *was* a problem, wasn't it?"

Van couldn't deny it. "It was becoming a problem. But I wasn't going to *leave* you because of it. I was going to *talk* to you about it. I was just waiting until after your birthday."

Patsy gave her old, crooked smile. "Really?"

"Yes, really." They strolled past Rose Hill on the path to Duncan Gardens. Van decided to be completely honest. "I can't promise that I would *never* have left you over it, though. If you kept drinking, I mean. If you became like, you know, like..."

"Like I am now?"

"Like you were before you went into the hospital."

"Like I am now, then. I'm still an alcoholic. I've only been dried out for three weeks and two days. That's a hell of a lot longer than I've gone without a drink in over twenty years—no, make that forty—but still. I don't expect you to believe this, but I was going to stop drinking right after my birthday. In fact, I *had* stopped drinking, when you went into RIP that night. I'd had my last drink. I'd switched to soda, I swear. It tasted like piss, but I was kind of enjoying it. Energized by the challenge, you know? I was excited to tell you. I was feeling *brave*. And then you disappeared and poof! All my courage disappeared too. Not that it was your fault. It was *not* your fault. Nobody made me drink my pain away. I did that all on my own." She laughed, a short bitter laugh. "Not that it worked. It never worked."

They maneuvered the intricate lanes in the beautifully manicured gardens before finally settling on a bench in front of the shimmering spray of a stone fountain nearly as big as Jill's house.

"Why didn't you ever tell me that before," Patsy asked, "about thinking I was so brave?"

Van shrugged. "I don't know. I guess I assumed you already knew, or that you didn't care."

Patsy kicked off her flip flops and rubbed her bare feet across the ground, as if the bottoms of her feet itched. "I wish you would have told me."

Van was taken aback. "I'm sorry. I didn't think. You were always so strong, I never thought you needed me to tell you."

Patsy watched her feet, kicking back and forth. "You never complimented me," she said thoughtfully, as if she'd never thought of it before. "I complimented you all the time, whatever you did, whatever you wore, whatever you did to your hair." With a slight smile, Patsy gave Van's ponytail a tug. "But you never complimented me."

"I'm sorry," Van said, abashed. "I didn't know you wanted them. You never seemed to like compliments."

"Once when I was a little girl, no more than eight or nine, my dad came home with a couple of his buddies. He didn't do that very often, he usually worked double shifts, didn't spend a lot time socializing, so when he brought his friends home, we all thought it was kind of exciting, and we'd hang around listening to them talk."

Van watched Patsy's face as she spoke, mesmerized. Patsy wasn't meeting Van's eyes, she was gazing at the fountain, perhaps gazing back in time.

"And both of the guys said they had little girls at home about my age, and they told us all about them, bragging about their daughters, about how clever they were and how cute they were and how smart and helpful and funny. And I sat there waiting for my dad to say something about me, about how smart or funny or strong I was, but he didn't. He just sat there smoking his cigarette, drinking his beer, and he didn't even look at me. So finally I spoke up, and I said something stupid like, 'I'm not funny, am I Dad?' And that's when he finally looked at me. He made a face that made me wonder if he hated me and he said in this real sneering voice, 'Are you fishing for a compliment, girl?' Everybody got real quiet and looked at me, and I wanted to curl up and die right there and then. I'd never heard that phrase before, but I knew right away what it meant. I was so embarrassed and ashamed of myself. I never asked for another compliment." She tilted her head and finally met Van's eyes. "But that doesn't mean I don't want to hear one once in a while."

Van felt her eyes sting, and she blinked back tears. "I'm sorry. I didn't know. I wish I could go back. If I could go back, I'd compliment you every day. You'd get sick of it. If I could go back..." She swallowed hard, choked up and feeling such deep regret that she felt sick to her stomach.

"That would be nice, wouldn't it?" Patsy took Van's hand and held it in both of her own. "But it's not likely to happen. Jill's doing her best, but her best is, well." Patsy shrugged. "Jill's best is not so great, I'm afraid. We have to assume you're here to stay. So..."

If Van had ever doubted Patsy's courage, the look on Patsy's face at that moment would have resolved all doubts. She was clearly terrified and miserable about what she was going to say, but she was determined to say it.

"I hope you're happy with Bennie. And I do mean that. But if you're not, you need to go out and find yourself a woman who will love you, really love you, like I d-d-did. I'm too old for you, Van, I know that, and there's nothing either one of us can do about it. And even if I weren't too old for you, I'm not the same woman you knew then. I've done a lot of damage and I've hurt a lot of people in the last twenty years. But the one person I never hurt, thank God, was you, because you weren't here. I never thought I'd be grateful for that, but I am. And the last thing in the world I want to do is stand in the way of your happiness. So if Bennie is what makes you happy, please know that you have my blessing. I just hope you'll let me be a part of your life, let me be someone who loves you. Think of me as...as...as an aunt, or an old friend of the family. But please, please don't cut me out of your life completely."

Van sat like stone as she listened. No, not like stone, more like glass, because suddenly she shattered into thousands of tiny fragments. All the unhappiness, all the despair, all the misery and sorrow and grief she'd been trying to deny every since she'd arrived in 2008 unleashed itself. Van let out a wail of grief, tears gushed forth, and huge bone-wracking sobs shook her body.

Patsy gathered her up into her arms and held her tightly, as Van's sobs shook them both. Van buried her face in Patsy's chest, her hands clenched in Patsy's shirt, and she wept and moaned and blubbered like a baby. She mourned for herself and she mourned for her old life and she mourned for Bennie, but most of all she mourned for Patsy, her old Patsy, the Patsy who was not here.

"I m-miss you s-s-so much."

"Shh, oh hush, baby, hush," Patsy said softly, rocking her gently. "You're breaking my heart, kid."

At the sound of Patsy's voice cracking, Van glanced up. "Don't you cry too," she said, her voice choked with tears.

Patsy shook her head, tears rolling down her own face. "How can I not, Van? How can I not?"

"Oh, Patsy." Van wiped Patsy's tears with her thumbs, put her arms around her, and they rocked together and wept.

Chapter Thirty-one

Kendra — 2008

"I NEED A critter," Jill said, poking her head out of the back of RIP.

"A critter?" Kendra paused in the act of draping a sleeping bag over the rope she'd strung between two trees. She aired them out every day, hating the musty feel of crawling into sleeping bags that lay on the ground all day. "What do you need a critter for, Granny Clampett?"

"I need to do a test. I think I might have it, Kendra!" Jill followed her head out of RIP and joined Kendra on the ground. She grabbed one end of the sleeping bag and helped Kendra drape it on the rope. "But I need to test it out, first. In case."

"In case of what?" Kendra removed the other sleeping bag from the tent and handed an end to Jill. They zipped the two bags together each night, sleeping on one and pulling the other over them, so they could snuggle. Jill complained that she couldn't sleep all cuddled up next to someone, but she was wrong. Once she fell asleep, she slept like a baby, and Kendra got to snuggle all she wanted. "What do you think could go wrong?"

Jill shrugged. "Going back in time is a lot more complicated than going forward. I don't know what to expect. If I did, I could prepare for it. What if it kills Van, or turns her into a mutant? What if she comes back in pieces?"

"Eeuw."

"Yeah." They were both silent for a moment, contemplating the seriousness of their endeavor. "So I need a monkey or something," Jill said. "I can send it forward in time first, wait a couple of hours, and then send it back and see if it works."

"How will you know if it worked? You can't go back in time to check to see if it came out okay, in the past."

"I'll record it. After the transmission is complete, we can watch the recording to see if the critter got through okay."

"Why a monkey? Why don't you use a spider or an icky bug?"

"It needs to be more humanlike than that. A dog might do, or a cat."

"No, I'm not going to let a dog or cat *or* a monkey be chopped into pieces for your experiment."

"Would you rather have Van chopped up in pieces?"

Kendra didn't bother to answer. She took the whisk broom and entered the tent to sweep out the grit that had accumulated on the nylon floor. Just because they were tent camping didn't mean they had to be uncivilized. While Jill worked on RIP, Kendra spent a great part of every day making their campsite into a cozy home, a task made considerably more difficult by the fact that they moved around every couple of days to a new campsite, in case the Lab Rats learned where they were. But there'd been no sign of anyone since Jill's last sighting at Rocky Falls. They were camped in Idaho now, at Farragut State Park.

"How about a bunny?" Jill asked, following Kendra into the tent.

"Get out. You're tracking in dirt. Shoes stay outside the tent."

Jill sighed and stepped out, but poked her head inside to repeat, "How about a bunny? We could buy one at a pet store in Coeur d'Alene."

"Not a bunny!" She thought a moment. "How about a rabbit? I'll bet we could catch one right out here."

"What's the difference between a bunny and a rabbit?"

"It's the difference," Kendra said slowly, as if explaining the obvious to an idiot, "between hunting for a wild animal and slaughtering a pet. What—you've never had a bunny?"

Jill shrugged. "How are we going to catch a bunny? I mean a rabbit?"

"It's simple. I've seen it on TV. You put a carrot under a box, and you prop the box up with a stick, and tie a string to the stick, and when the rabbit comes to get the carrot, you pull the stick away and voilá. You've caught the rabbit in the box."

Jill looked skeptical. "That might have been a cartoon you were watching."

"What do you suggest, smarty pants?"

Jill surveyed the campsite. "We could use a raccoon. We know there've been raccoons in camp at night. We may be able to catch one of them."

"Or a bear," Kendra said, inspired. "We could catch us a little grizzly cub." She laughed at Jill's troubled how-do-I-tell-the-woman-I-love-she's-completely-insane expression, and leaned over and kissed her on the lips. "Kidding, darling."

In the end, Kendra drove into Coeur d'Alene and rented a trap from the local humane society, after explaining that they had a raccoon in the attic. They set it up on the campsite's picnic table, baited it with dinner scraps, and caught a raccoon the very first night.

"Now what?" Kendra asked the next morning, as they both stood watching the angry raccoon scolding them from behind the mesh wires of the trap. His finger-like paws clung to the wires and shook the walls of the cage like a trapped man. If he'd had a tin cup, Kendra suspected he'd have run it along the bars in protest. "He needs water."

"Don't touch it," Jill warned. She switched on the miniature flip video camera Kendra had bought in Coeur d'Alene for eighty bucks. It only held 30 minutes worth of video, but that would be more than enough. They had both practiced using it the night before. "It could have rabies."

"Around here?"

"You never know. Even if it doesn't, you still don't want it to bite you, do you?"

No, she didn't want it to bite her, but Kendra did feel sorry for the creature. While Jill fiddled with setting up the camera, Kendra took one of their empty water bottles, filled it from the spigot, and put the cap back on. It was a cap with a pull-up nozzle so you could drink right from the cap. She cautiously approached the cage and propped the bottle upside down on top. She had envisioned the raccoon sucking from the bottle like the boys' hamsters had drunk from their inverted water bottles years ago. Instead, the raccoon grabbed the cap in its hands, wrestled with it for moment, bit it sharply, and the entire top came off. Water cascaded over the raccoon, infuriating him even more.

"What are you doing?" Jill asked, coming up behind her.

"He was thirsty."

"He can get water when he's sent back to the past," Jill said. "It'll take a couple of hours for us, but it'll only be a minute to him."

"If it works," Kendra said, and wished she hadn't when she saw doubt cross Jill's face.

But all Jill said was, "Yeah, if it works."

Jill took two towels and wrapped her hands up in them, and lifted the wire trap. The back door of RIP was standing wide open, and Jill carefully slid the cage inside, climbed up after it, and positioned the cage exactly where she wanted it. She climbed out, and closed the door behind her. She strode several feet to a flat rock where she had set up the video camera.

"This is where we're going to send him. We'll start the recording at 8:00 o'clock, just to be safe, but I'm going to send him back to 8:02."

"Why?"

"To give him a two minute cushion. I'm sending him to the future at 8:00. I can't send him back before that, or there would be two of him at once."

"I mean why are you sending him here? Why don't we just stick the recorder in RIP with the raccoon and turn it on? We can watch him going and coming."

"That wouldn't help me figure out how to send Van back," Jill said. "I'll never be able to figure out *exactly* where RIP was when I sent her forward. What if I position RIP a couple of feet off, and instead of landing inside on the stool, she lands half way in RIP and half way out?"

Kendra visualized Van landing in 1988, sliced neatly in two by the wall of RIP. "Gross."

"Yeah, there are too many variables that way. So I'm going to send her to a bare spot of earth where she can land free and clear, so I want to do the same thing with the raccoon. I'll send him forward two hours. When he arrives at 10:00, I'll send him back one hour and fifty-eight minutes, to this spot. If it works, we should be able to see him on the recording landing right here in the dirt at 8:02."

They both stood a moment staring at the dusty spot of earth, marked only by tire tracks from where Jill had pulled RIP into the campsite the day before. Even though Kendra knew for a fact that RIP had transported Van twenty years into the future, she still found it incredible and not very believable that Jill would be able to send that little raccoon back and forth through time, right before her very eyes.

"Before we start recording, let me get RIP fired up." Jill went to the cab of RIP and started the engine. Moments later the antennae emerged from the top and slid several feet up, a portion of the camper roof opened, and the dish folded out and began rotating. Moments later, Jill climbed out and went back to the camper. She opened the door again, climbed up, reached in, made some adjustments, and climbed down and back into the cab. "Okay, turn on the camera."

Kendra slid the switch, checked to make sure the camera was recording, and hurried to watch Jill in RIP's cab. Jill was concentrating intensely, watching gauges and dials, occasionally making adjustments or pushing buttons. Kendra watched, still as fascinated by Jill when she worked on RIP as she had been twenty years ago.

Less than ten minutes after she'd started the process, Jill shut off the engine and climbed out. She met Kendra's eyes and shrugged. "I think it's done." She moved to the back of RIP, Kendra following closely behind, and opened the door. The cage was empty. Their eyes met again, and Kendra wondered if she looked as scared as Jill did. "Now we wait. Two hours." Jill glanced at her watch.

Kendra looked from the empty cage to the empty spot in the dirt where the raccoon was supposed to arrive in the past and wanted to ask where the little guy was now. And why couldn't they just watch the dirt and see if he arrived as scheduled at 8:02? She peeked at Jill's watch. Too late. It was already 8:05. So he should have returned by now. Except he couldn't have because they hadn't sent him back yet. She shook her head. It was too mind boggling. "Do you want some coffee?" she asked.

Time crawled.

Kendra finished sweeping the tent, fixed coffee and breakfast, and heated water over the camp stove to wash the dishes and herself. Jill paced. She took the coffee Kendra held out to her and ate when Kendra told her to, but it was clear her mind was elsewhere. Several times Kendra asked her a simple question, and Jill didn't answer, as if she hadn't heard at all. And there was nothing wrong with Jill's hearing. Both avoided looking at the spot where the raccoon would return. Or had returned. *If* it returned.

Finally, it was 9:59. They had peeked in RIP at 9:55 and saw the cage was still empty. They'd closed the door, then, as if the raccoon could only return if it had complete privacy.

"I don't know why I'm so nervous about this part," Jill said with a laugh. "It's not like I've never sent anyone into the future before."

Kendra smiled and was about to answer when they heard a rustling from inside RIP. Jill opened the door. The raccoon hissed angrily.

"There he is." Jill smiled, triumphant with scientific success. She heaved a huge sigh of relief. "I really didn't know if it would work. Just because it worked with Van, didn't mean..." She shook her head. "Okay, the easy part's done. Now for the hard part."

Jill shut the door and returned to the cab of the truck. She started the engine, and backed RIP up in the dirt to the spot they had selected. Kendra checked the camera and saw it had turned itself off. In fact, it probably had been off for an hour and a half, after its 30 minutes of recording time was done. She was tempted to pick it up and see what it had recorded. After all, if they sent the raccoon to the past, that means it had already returned, right? And it should show up on the video camera. But she didn't touch it. Jill hadn't sent the raccoon back *yet*, and though Kendra didn't understand why that mattered, she didn't want to fuck everything up because she was too impatient to wait.

Jill got out of RIP and checked to make sure it was where she wanted it, and that the video camera would have captured the exact spot where the raccoon would land—had landed—whatever. She headed toward the cab, but Kendra stopped her.

"Wait!" Kendra marched up to her, put her arms around Jill's neck, and kissed her, deeply and roughly. "For luck," she said.

Jill smiled, her heart racing, but Kendra knew it wasn't because of the kiss. Jill was terrified. If this didn't work, the chance of being able to send Van back to 1988 was practically non-existent. Even worse, in Kendra's mind, was that Jill would never get to redeem herself. Van would be all right, somehow, regardless of whether she got to return to 1988 or not. But Jill wouldn't. Jill needed to correct the terrible mistake of twenty years before. It was the only way she'd ever trust herself again, the only way she'd ever be completely whole. A lot was riding on this experiment.

Jill climbed into the cab and revved up the machine. After a moment of watching Jill's intent face as she worked, Kendra turned away and wiped the top of the Coleman stove. This time it was too hard to watch.

A few minutes later, the engine stopped and Jill climbed out of the cab. Jill went to the back of RIP and opened the door. Her eyes met Kendra's. "It's gone." She bit her lip and glanced toward the video camera. That the raccoon was gone only meant Jill had transported it somewhere, sometime. If she wasn't able to transport it where and when she intended, it would be meaningless.

Kendra bent down, picked up the recorder, and hit rewind. Jill came over and stood behind her, peering over her shoulder. After rewinding it completely, she hit play. They studied the miniature screen. There was the spot in the dirt. The spot where RIP stood now. It was empty in the recording. They continued watching. Any second now, the raccoon should appear. Any second now. The recorder picked up sounds. They could hear Kendra ask Jill if she wanted coffee. They heard dishes and rustling. Now and then a gentle wind blew and a leaf fragment or a puff of dirt blew across the camera's lens. But the raccoon did not appear.

After about five minutes, Jill gave up. She sighed heavily and turned toward RIP. She faced the blank wall of the camper, braced both hands against it, arms straight, and dropped her head between them in an attitude of defeat. Kendra longed to go to her and comfort her, but what could she say? She watched the video a bit longer instead, hoping the raccoon would still show up, but it did not.

Jill climbed into the cab and pulled RIP forward, back into its parking spot. Kendra looked at the spot of dirt where the raccoon should have appeared.

Her heart lurched at what she saw. "Jill! Jill, c'mere."

Jill rushed over. "What is it?" She glanced hopefully at the video camera in Kendra's hand.

"No, not on here, look there." Kendra pointed to the dirt where, unmistakably, damp raccoon paw prints tracked through the dirt where no raccoon paw prints had been before. They started from nowhere, as if the raccoon had simply landed from the sky, then they scrambled toward the tree line and into the forest.

They stared at each other, slack jawed. Kendra spoke first. "Why didn't the video camera...?"

Jill shook her head. "I don't know. But it worked, Kendra." Her face split into a wide grin. "Kendra, it worked. Whoo whoo!"

Jill laughed out loud, and Kendra laughed with her. They threw their arms around each other and danced in the dirt, kissed, and laughed, and kissed some more.

"Maybe there's a time lag," Jill said finally. "In fact, there'd have to be, wouldn't there? I should have realized..." Her eyes shifted inward, and Kendra knew Jill was back at work. She'd figure it out.

They would be able to send Van home. They *would*. And everything that was *now* wouldn't be any more, at least not in the same way. Kendra watched Jill climb into RIP. Jill was striving with everything she had to undo the present, to send them back to the past where they'd create an alternate future, one where Kendra and Jill might never find each other. And Kendra was helping her.

Kendra shook her head, happy and sad at the same time.

Love bites.

Chapter Thirty-two

Bennie — 2008

BENNIE SCRAPED SO hard at a wallpaper hippopotamus that she gouged a hole in the old plaster wall. The attic was sweltering. The previous owner had installed central air conditioning in most of the house, but neither central air nor heat reached the attic room. Odd, for a children's playroom. Perhaps they thought children didn't need regulated temperatures. Whether the windows were open or closed made no difference. There was no breeze to move the air anyway.

Moisture dripped and made tributaries down Bennie's face and dropped onto her chest, into the cleavage made by her sports bra. She couldn't tell if they were drips of sweat or tears, except they couldn't possibly be tears, because Bennie never cried.

She'd shed her shirt long ago. She could have stripped naked if she'd wanted to. She was working alone. Van had lost interest in the project after her talk with Patsy two days before. She'd returned, red eyed and drooping, and immediately moved her things back into the guest bedroom. *It's not you*, she'd said, *it's me. I just need some time.* Fuck that. It was *Patsy*. Everything was going great until Patsy showed up and in one short hour undid everything Bennie had worked so hard to accomplish ever since Van's return.

Van was *happy*, damn it, until Patsy'd shown up. For the most part, anyway. Yes, she still had moments when her gaze drifted off to something Bennie couldn't see, and she knew then that Van was thinking about the past, seeing things that made her sad. But Bennie could coax her out of it, make her smile, make her laugh, make her happy. Even when she woke crying in the middle of the night, Bennie was there to hold her, comfort her, and love her, until she was soothed and fell asleep again in Bennie's arms.

Not any more. Bennie was so angry, she could hardly keep from jumping into her Jag, driving over to Patsy's trailer, and shoving *her* off a deck, like she'd done to Bennie twenty years before.

She jabbed at the stubborn hippopotamus. What had they glued this stuff down with, cement? She was so intent on her thoughts and on removing the recalcitrant zoo animals that she didn't hear Van's bare feet until she was in the doorway, two bottles of Stella Artois in one hand and an electric fan in the other.

"If you're going to insist on working up here in the hottest part of the day, you can at least use a fan."

Bennie eyed Van reproachfully and thought briefly of saying she didn't *want* a fan, that she *liked* working in the heat of the day, that she *loved* sweating like a pig, but she read the gentle humor in Van's eyes and saw that Van knew exactly what she was thinking. Bennie drew her lower lip back in, dropped the scraper, and pulled her shirt up off the floor. She didn't put it on, though, but instead used it to wipe the sweat, and any other moisture that might be there, from her face and neck and hair. Van had seen her naked, after all, and Bennie knew she had damned good abs for forty-eight. Let her look. Bennie accepted a bottle of beer and took a long drink while Van plugged in the fan.

"Where'd you get that?" Bennie, settled on the floor, her back against the wall with one leg stretched out before her and the other bent up at an angle.

"I borrowed it from next door." Van sat cross-legged on the floor facing Bennie, her elbows propped on her knees. "You've been up here a long time."

"Yeah, it would go a lot faster if there were two of us working on it."

Van sent Bennie a chiding glance. "I told you I'll help you in the morning when it's cool. What's your hurry? You don't even know what you want to do with this room yet."

Bennie shrugged. She knew she was being unreasonable, but she couldn't seem to help it. She felt very *pouty* and she wanted Van to know it. She tilted her head back and took another long swig of beer, thrusting her chest out slightly to give Van a good opportunity to admire her body. Remind Van of what she was missing by leaving her bed. Eat her heart out. But when she lowered her head and met Van's eyes, she saw Van was again watching her with that gentle, humorous gaze that said she knew exactly what Bennie was doing. Bennie's cheeks got hot.

"Jill called." Van picked at the corner of the label on her bottle.

Despite the heat, a chill of dread crept up Bennie's spine. "Why?"

"She's invited us to a picnic. Tomorrow."

"Tomorrow?" The first time Bennie said it, no sound came out. She cleared her throat and said again, "Tomorrow? What for?"

"She didn't say. Just a picnic." But Van raised her eyes from her bottle and solemnly met Bennie's gaze, and Bennie knew they were both thinking the same thing.

"Is this about her time machine?"

"Probably. She wouldn't say much. She wants us to meet her tomorrow at Riverside State Park. Patsy and Inez and Kendra will be there too."

Oh boy, a picnic with Patsy. "She's going to try to send you back."

"Maybe." Van ripped a good swath of label off her bottle and glanced up. "I don't know if she can do it. Inez and Patsy are both pretty skeptical. Patsy thinks it's too dangerous for me to even try."

Bennie raised her head. "Patsy thinks that?" Would Patsy become her ally in this? Bennie wasn't at all pleased that Patsy had made Van so unhappy with her visit, but as long as Van stayed in the present, Bennie wasn't worried about the threat Patsy posed. A seventy-year-old alcoholic was not going to lure Van away from Bennie. But if she could use Patsy to convince Van to stay in the present, she damned well would.

Bennie quickly got to her knees. "You can't do it, Van," she said urgently, hope giving strength to her voice. "Patsy's right, it's too dangerous. Jill already screwed up once when she sent you here. It could be worse this time. You could get sent to some other time, some other place, someplace where none of us are around to help you. Or you could *die*." Bennie felt the chill in her spine again at the thought of the grim possibilities. "Please, Van, stay here in 2008. You're safe here. I can take care of you."

Van had been staring intensely at Bennie as she spoke, seeming to absorb everything Bennie said, but at this last she shook her head. "Even if I stay in 2008, I can't stay here."

Bennie sat back abruptly on her heels. "Why not?"

"I need some space."

"Space?" Bennie shook her head in befuddlement. How had a conversation of life and death so quickly devolved into the most clichéd break-up line of all time? "I've got space." She spread her arms wide, pretending she didn't understand.

"Not that kind of space. I need some time to figure things out."

"Like what?"

Van didn't answer, focusing her attention on her fingers, which were playing with the gummy residue on her bottle.

"Is it Patsy?" Bennie asked, wondering if she had underestimated Patsy as a rival.

"Not exactly." Van raised her head. "Bennie, you've been so wonderful to me since I got here."

"Oh fuck." Bennie sat back on her butt, scooted toward the wall, and put up a hand. "Stop right there. I know how this speech goes. I've given it a few dozen times myself. 'It's not you, it's me. You're wonderful, *but, but, but, but*." There's always a *but*."

"Will you shut up and listen to me? It may be a *but*, but it's *my* but and I want you to—" Van broke off and bit her lip when she heard what she'd said, and Bennie had to smile.

"Fine, Van, let me have your butt."

Van had to smile too. "Bennie, I've *needed* you so much these last few weeks, I don't know if I would have survived without you. And you've taken such good care of me. I didn't just survive, but we've had fun, we've played and laughed and made love."

Bennie felt her heart squeeze at the thought of the love they'd made.

"But I don't know if what I feel for you is gratitude—"

"I don't want your fucking gratitude, Van."

"Well, that's my point. How can I know *what* I feel for you as long as I'm dependent on you for every stitch of clothing on my back and every bite of food that goes into my mouth? If you want more than gratitude, you should be *glad* to have me leave."

Bennie slumped against the wall and finished her bottle of Stella while Van sat in silence, watching. Finally, Bennie said, "Where will you go?"

"I don't know," Van said. Softly she added, "Maybe 1988."

"No," Bennie whispered hoarsely. "No, Van, anything but that. I'll help you get set up with your own life, here in 2008. We can resurrect your old life. You can take the bar exam and practice law. Or maybe you don't want to be a lawyer any more. You can start over and be anything you want. I'll help you." But Van was shaking her head. "Or I *won't* help you. Whatever you want. But, please, Van, stay here." *With me*, she thought, but had the wisdom not to say out loud.

"I think I have to go back, if I can. It's not fair otherwise."

"Not *fair?* What's fair about going back? It's not fair to *me*, that's for sure."

"Why?"

"It's not fair because I'll never get *you*. You're the only woman I ever wanted, Van, the only woman I've ever loved. What chance will I have with you in 1988? I was an arrogant little prick, you know I was. At least now I have a chance. At least now I've had the best three and half weeks of my life." Bennie, who never cried, had to blink away tears at the thought of those three and a half weeks never happening. "If you go back, I'll never get this. I'll never get you."

"You'll still be there," Van said gently, as if explaining to a child. "You'll still be *you*. It's not like you're going anywhere. You'll have as much a chance as ever."

Bennie gave Van an assessing look. "You never would have given me a chance back then. Would you?"

Van shrugged. "I don't know. Maybe, if things didn't work out with Patsy. Who knows? Don't sell yourself short. You are—and were—a very attractive woman."

"You know," Bennie said, thinking to plant a seed, "Patsy already had a drinking problem, even then. You didn't know it, but everyone else did."

"I knew it," Van said coldly.

"I'm sorry," Bennie said quickly, not wanting to alienate Van now. She got on her knees, crawled over to Van, and sat beside her, hip to hip. "All I'm trying to say is that *if* you go back to 1988, and *if* you survive the trip, and *if* things don't work out with Patsy, will you give me a chance? Please? It wasn't just a crush, you know. It never was. It was real, always. Will you give me a chance?" Van hesitated, and Bennie nudged her suggestively with her hip. "Don't forget how well we fit," she whispered and felt a surge of hope when she saw Van smile and blush. "If you think I'm good now, you should try me at twenty-eight."

Van laughed softly. "All right, *if* I go back, and *if* I survive the trip, and *if* for some reason things don't work out with Patsy, I'll give you a chance."

With that, Bennie had to be content. It was the best she could hope for. *If* Van returned to 1988. But Bennie knew her very best chance with Van was right in front of her, in 2008. Van was already half in love with her. If she could keep her here, she could make her fall the rest of the way in.

"What time is the picnic tomorrow?"

"Five o'clock. Will you come with me?"

"At Riverside State Park?'

"Yes. Will you come with me?"

Bennie wrapped her arms around Van and rested her lips in her hair. "Of course I will. I'll be with you right up 'til the very last minute."

Chapter Thirty-three

Van—2008

VAN EXAMINED HER knees while Bennie drove them toward Riverside State Park. She liked the way her knees looked in the long baggy shorts. They made her legs appear thinner, stronger, more athletic, than they did in the skimpy tight shorts they wore in 1988, shorts that exposed her thighs and made them feel huge and flabby. These shorts made her feel like a kid, like she could hop up and go play a game of sandlot baseball or a pickup game of basketball down at the local school ground, maybe even swing on the monkey bars over and over and over, like she had when she was little.

She was nervous. She wasn't worried about Jill or RIP or even about getting back to 1988. What happened would happen, a lá Doris Day and "Que Sera Sera." There was no point in worrying about that. She was nervous about Bennie and Patsy, the two of them together at this picnic. Aside from that brief moment at Bennie's front door three days before, Patsy and Bennie hadn't seen each other since Van and Bennie had become lovers. Temporary lovers, she amended.

Van hadn't felt any guilt at first about sleeping with Bennie. The 1988 Van might have, but that Van was dead, right? May she Rest In Peace. But Van had only been playing tricks with her mind, trying to use a tattoo to convince herself she was no longer the person who loved Patsy, who had sworn to be faithful and true to her forever. She used a trick of the mind to convince herself it was all right for her to fall into Bennie's arms for comfort and security and love. But when Patsy had shown up at Bennie's door that day, clean and sober and genuinely Patsy, just older, the tricks had stopped working. While Patsy had changed a great deal from the woman Van had loved in 1988, she was still Patsy, enough so anyway to make Van realize how much she loved her and missed her. That's when the guilt had hit her. How could she be sleeping with another woman? Twenty years may have passed for Patsy, but it was less than a month for Van. What was she thinking?

She knew Bennie was hurt when she moved back to the guest suite, and she was sorry for that. It wasn't Bennie's fault, none of it was. Bennie had been truly wonderful, and Van *was* grateful, no matter how despicable that word was to Bennie. Van didn't only feel gratitude for Bennie, though. In such a short time, Bennie had become her friend, her companion, and her lover. Bennie had not only given her shelter and comfort, she'd made Van laugh, convinced her to play, and made passionate love to her in new and exiting ways. She loved Bennie. And she loved Patsy. It was no wonder she was nervous about being with them both at Jill's picnic.

Glancing at Bennie now, Van knew she wasn't the only one nervous about the upcoming meeting. As she drove, Bennie tapped rhythmically on the steering wheel, quietly whistling bits of an unrecognizable song under her breath. There were no smiles, no spontaneous touches, none of the quick playful winks Van had grown accustomed to as Bennie squinted into the rear view mirror. Her thoughts were clearly elsewhere.

Bennie noticed Van watching her. She shot her a quick, distracted smile and patted Van's leg. "It'll be all right, Van," she said vaguely.

Van picked up Bennie's hand and pressed it to her lips, feeling tender. "I know."

They entered Riverside State Park, and Van read Jill's directions aloud to Bennie from the notes she'd written when Jill had called the day before. They veered left onto a dirt road that led to a string of campsites along the Spokane River. They pulled into the campsite on the far left end. Kendra stood beside a picnic table in the center of the campsite, stirring something in a pot over a camp stove, while Jill tended a brisk little fire nearby. They looked up as the Jag nosed between two trees and parked on a bare spot intended for a camper. Kendra's car was pulled to the side of the site next to a tent at the far end. There was no sign of RIP. Van felt a twinge of disappointment. She hadn't really expected to be sent back to 1988 today, and wasn't even sure she was willing to risk the attempt if it were offered, but she'd hoped there would at least be a chance.

They got out of the car, and Kendra danced forward with iPod cords dangling from her ears. "Hi Van." She tugged Van into a wrap-around hug. "Love the nose stud." She danced around the car and hugged Bennie as well, hips shimmying as she did so.

Bennie laughed. "What are you listening to?"

"Pink. Have you heard this?" She held her earpiece out to Bennie's ear.

Bennie listed her head a moment listening, then nodded. "Yeah, she's pretty good."

Jill set down her fire-poking stick, advanced toward Van, and pulled her in for a strong hug. "Thanks for coming."

"Of course." Van took in the cozy campsite, the single tent, the clothing draped over a clothesline, and most of all at Jill's tender look as she watched Kendra dance around Bennie, and came to a conclusion. "Are you and Kendra camping here? I mean, together?"

Amazingly, Jill blushed. "Yeah. It just happened..." Her voice trailed off as she gazed in awe at Kendra, shimmying back to the stove. "I don't know what took me so long. Isn't she something?"

Van grinned. "Congratulations."

Jill ducked her head. "Thanks."

"Are Inez and Patsy still coming?" Van surveyed the camp as if they might be hiding.

"Yes." Jill hesitated a moment and said, "You know Patsy stopped drinking?"

"Yes. I saw her a couple of days ago."

"It's incredible. You don't know." Jill shook her head. "She's been drinking steadily for twenty years. It's hard to believe she's stopped."

The sound of another car approaching made them all watch the road. The car pulled in and parked beside Bennie's. Inez got out of the driver's side and Patsy climbed out of the passenger side.

Patsy looked drawn and tired. She glanced around the campsite, her gaze stopping briefly on Van before moving on and settling on Bennie. Purposefully, with everyone watching, she trooped up to Bennie and stopped in front of her. Bennie stood stock still and met her gaze solidly, her jaw chiseled with tension. But Patsy only smiled and said, "I'm glad you're here, Bennie." She held out her hand. After a long moment, without altering her expression, Bennie held out her hand as well. They shook, and the group breathed a collective sigh of relief.

Inez came over to Van and hugged her. "You're looking good."

"Thanks. So are you." But Van's attention was on Patsy, who was making her way toward her.

"She's having a hard time of it," Inez said quietly. "But she still hasn't taken a drink."

"I'm glad."

"Hello, Van," Patsy said.

"Hi." After a brief moment, they exchanged a quick awkward hug. "How are you?"

Patsy shrugged. "I've seen better days."

"They say it gets easier, after a while."

"Yeah," Patsy said, her voice surly. "That's what they fucking say."

"C'mon, Jill, can't you just pick the meat out?" Kendra asked plaintively from the camp stove, where she was poised to add chunks of kielbasa to the pot.

"No." Jill elbowed Kendra aside to spoon out a portion of the camp stew from the pot into a smaller pan. "I'd still be eating meat juice. And you know what meat juice is, don't you? It's *blood*."

"Blood is good." Kendra assumed an impish smile and advanced on Jill. "I vant to drink your blood."

"You are a disgusting woman," Jill said, as Kendra wrapped her arms around her and bit at her neck.

"Can you believe those two?" Patsy asked, watching them with a tiny smile. "For twenty years they've been buddies, and now all of the sudden they're like randy teenagers."

"Yeah." Van hesitated. "I like your hair like that." She blushed at the awkward compliment.

Patsy touched her short gray hair, shot Van a quizzical look, and gave a low chuckle. "Thanks for trying, kid."

They stood in silence a moment, watching the camp activity. Inez laid out a table cloth on the picnic table, and Bennie took over tending the fire from Jill. Van helped Inez set the table with paper plates and plastic utensils, and Patsy went to the back of Inez's car to pull out an ice chest, which was filled with ice, soda, and water. There was no beer.

"Remember that cute nun I told you about?" Inez asked as they set the table.

"Yes, I remember," Van said.

"I asked her out," Inez said, self-consciously pleased.

"No kidding? Good for you? And she said yes?"

"She did. I was afraid at first that she didn't know it was a *date*, you know? But she told that other nun we had a date, so she does know."

"Where are you going to take her?"

"I thought maybe out for ice cream. Innocent, but potentially romantic, you know?"

"Good idea."

Inez eyed Van curiously. "You know, things seem a lot better around here since you showed up."

"What do you mean?"

"Look around you. Jill and Kendra finally get together. I've never seen Jill so happy. Patsy stopped drinking. And I've got a date!"

Van was surprised. "I didn't have anything to do with any of those things."

"Maybe not directly, but you did. Your disappearance made Patsy fall apart, but your reappearance has made her pull herself together. And your disappearance threw Jill and Kendra together as friends, but your reappearance drew them together even closer. And as for Sister Alice, well, I don't know if I'd have had the courage to ask her out if you hadn't returned. Seeing you take hold of life after it threw you such a curve ball, even getting your nose pierced. You inspired me. Thanks for coming back."

Van smiled, but said for what felt like the thousandth time, "I didn't *come back*. I didn't go anywhere."

Inez grew serious. "I don't know what Jill has in mind here today. But don't let her talk you into trying to go back in time. You do get more than one chance at happiness in this life. Grace was the love of my life, and I wish to God she hadn't died. But she did, and life goes on. Maybe I'll get another chance at love with Alice, and maybe I won't. But either way, I'm happy. You don't need to go back to 1988 to be happy." She inclined her head toward the fire, and Bennie. "You can start over now."

Bennie seemed to sense their attention. She looked up, met Van's gaze, and winked, a slow, intimate wink. Van smiled, ducked her head, and hoped Patsy hadn't seen.

"I forgot the napkins," Inez said, and moved to the car to retrieve them. She passed Patsy, who dragged the ice chest next to the table.

"Jill's up to no good," Patsy said abruptly. "Look at her." Van glanced over at Jill. She was standing beside the fire, but she was doing nothing but staring off into space, with a secretive smile on her face.

"She does look like she's up to something," Van said.

"It's got to be about RIP." Patsy peered around the campsite as if the camper were hidden behind a bush. "She must have it stowed around here somewhere. Where is it?"

Van had wondered the same thing herself.

"Listen, kid." Patsy touched Van's hand. "I may not be any wiser than you are, but I'm a helluva lot older all of a sudden, so let me give you some advice based on my vast years of experience, okay?" She waited until Van nodded. "First of all, don't trust Jill. She doesn't know what the hell she's doing, and you're Exhibit A. You wouldn't be here if she had a clue. Or if you were, you'd be an old lady like the rest of us. And second, you don't need to go back in time in order to be happy."

Patsy's words made Van wonder if she and Inez had discussed this on the ride over.

"You're not going to make anybody's life all rainbows and roses by going back, even if you could."

"What about you?" Van asked. "Wouldn't you like to do the last twenty years over?"

Patsy winced.

"Everyone says you fell apart when I disappeared," Van said. "Wouldn't my return to the past be better for you? Wouldn't you like another chance?"

Patsy shook her head roughly. "I only know two things: You disappeared in 1988 and I become an alcoholic. I don't know if that's *why* I became an alcoholic. I know that's the excuse I've been giving myself for the last twenty years, but I don't know if it's true. I can't guarantee that I wouldn't have become an alcoholic anyway. For all I know, even if you'd stayed I might have become exactly like I was when you found me, four weeks ago."

It was Van's turn to wince.

"Besides," Patsy said, "Look at all these women. Look at them, Van. Every single one of them is happy right now. Kendra and Jill are in love. Inez has a date. Even Bennie's only sad because she thinks she might lose you. If you stay, she'll be ecstatic. But if Jill sends you back, assuming for purposes of argument that she even *can*, all this will disappear. All these happy women will vanish. Do you want to do that to them?"

Van hadn't thought of it quite like that before. Who was she to decide her friends should all do the last twenty years over, just so she could go back to 1988? "What about you, Patsy? Are you happy?"

Patsy blinked twice and said, "I'm only one person. And like I said, I might have turned out this way anyway." She took a long, wavering breath. "If you want to know the truth, I'm scared. I'm afraid Jill will fuck it up again. Who knows where she'll send you this time, or what shape you'll be in when you get there? She's never done this before. We're talking about it like we all get Do-Overs. We don't know that's what's going to happen. What if she sends you off, and you're *gone*, and we're all left standing here, wondering for the rest of our lives where you are and if you're all right. For God's sake, Van." Patsy's voice became a harsh whisper and tears welled in her eyes. "I can't do it again!"

They were interrupted by Kendra, calling from the camp stove. "Soup's on! Camp stew and French bread fresh from Albertsons. Dish up your own."

Patsy surreptitiously wiped her eyes and turned away. Van, quiet and thoughtful, followed the crowd to the pot of stew.

Each woman filled a plate, grabbed a soda or a bottle of water, and sat around the picnic table. Van settled with Bennie on her right and Inez on her left. Patsy sat across from Inez, Jill across from Van, and Kendra across from Bennie. If Van peeked only to her left, excluding Bennie and Kendra from her sight, it seemed hardly any different from the dozen other times she had sat at a picnic table with these women. Patsy sat at her side all those other times, and Inez sometimes brought a date, but the four of them were always there: Patsy, Inez, Jill, and Van. And before Van had joined Patsy, all the way back to their freshman year in college, it had been Patsy, Inez, and Jill. These three seventy-year-old women had been through more than fifty years together. They'd never dated each other, except for that brief period their senior year when Patsy and Inez thought they were in love, but they had all remained steadfast friends through some very difficult years.

The mood at the picnic table was jovial. They quizzed Van on the biggest changes she'd noticed between 1988 and 2008 and were surprised by her answers.

"Coffee," she said. "Whatever happened to a plain old cup of coffee? There are coffee shops everywhere, but I don't know how to order a simple cup of coffee. And since when do kids get to drink it? There are laws that you can't smoke around kids, but *they* get to drink triple shots of espresso? Don't they know it'll stunt their growth?"

"Not computers?" Jill asked, surprised.

"That Wii game is pretty amazing," Van said, with only a hazy idea of what ordinary computers did. "You can bowl without a bowling alley or pins, or even a ball. How does it know where you're throwing the ball? I don't get it."

"We have one of those at our community center," Inez said eagerly. "I've been playing with my nun."

There was a sudden silence, broken when Patsy said, "Jesus, Inez," and made a quick sign of the cross, causing the table to erupt in laughter.

"Patsy, it is so good to have you back," Inez said impulsively.

"I didn't go anywhere," Patsy said, unconsciously mimicking Van.

"Your soul is back," Jill explained. "We've missed you."

Patsy grimaced, but appeared pleased nonetheless.

Bennie was silent throughout most of the dinner, but she kept her thigh pressed firmly against Van's, as if to remind her she was still there.

Finally, dinner was finished and Kendra passed around a store bakery box of cookies for dessert.

Jill took that moment to make her announcement. She rose. "You're probably all wondering why I asked you to meet me here for dinner tonight." Movement around the table stilled. Patsy, Bennie, and Inez all looked at Van, while Kendra fixed her eyes on Jill. Jill addressed herself directly to Van. "I have some good news. I've fixed RIP and I can send you back to 1988."

The news was not entirely unexpected, but a shock still rippled around the table. Bennie and Inez both put their arms around Van as if to hold her in place. Patsy's eyes blazed at Van from across the table before she turned them on Jill.

"The hell you can," Patsy said harshly. "You don't know what the fuck you're doing, Jill. You could send her off to God knows where this time, or worse. You leave her alone!"

"Patsy's right," Bennie said quickly. "It's too dangerous. There's no reason she can't stay here in 2008."

Jill blinked with surprise. "This is what Van wants. She *asked* me to send her back. And I've figured it out. I've tried it on animals, and it works."

Kendra rose from the bench to stand protectively beside Jill. "We have just spent the last four weeks on the run from Lab Rats, sleeping on the ground, dirty and cold and hungry, with Jill working practically nonstop on RIP, so she could send Van back. Like Van *asked* her to do. Don't tell her she can't do it now."

"You've wasted your time," Patsy said. "She's not going."

"It's not your choice," Jill pointed out, her jaw set at a stubborn angle. "Van, don't you want to return to 1988?"

Van hesitated. "I think—"

Inez interrupted. "She doesn't need to. There's no reason to take such a dangerous risk. She can start her life over again here and be perfectly happy."

"No, she can't," Jill said, still befuddled by the unexpected opposition to the plan she had worked so hard to arrange. She looked back at Van. "Not as yourself, anyway. If the Feds find out you're here, your life might as well *be* over."

"So she gets a new identity, then," Patsy said. "What's wrong with that? It's better than risking another ride on RIP. You could kill her."

"It's not going to—"

"Wait!" Bennie stopped Jill sharply. "What do you mean, 'If the Feds find out she's here?'"

"If they find out Van's back," Jill said, "they'll know RIP works. They'll do anything to get their hands on it. And on her. She'll belong to them for the rest of her life."

Bennie rose abruptly from the table, clearly agitated. "What do you mean? Wh-what will they do? They won't—I mean, they can't—" She broke off and gaped wildly from Jill to Van, her fingers trembling on the top of the table.

They all stared at Bennie.

"Oh my God," Patsy said softly. "What have you done?"

Chapter Thirty-four

Patsy — 2008

BENNIE IGNORED THE question and instead stared Van in horror. "Oh God, Van, I didn't know. I didn't know!"

"What have you done?" Patsy asked again, pushing herself up from the picnic table, wishing she were hale enough to leap over the table and choke the answer out of Bennie. Van's stricken face, pale as paper, made Patsy's heart lurch.

"I just didn't want you to go!" Bennie said, still ignoring Patsy, imploring forgiveness from Van. "I thought if they got RIP, Jill couldn't send you back. You could stay. I didn't mean to—" She gazed helplessly at the rest of the women, who sat watching her, stunned. "I called them," she confessed hoarsely. "I called the lab. I told them you'd be here. Today. With RIP. I told them about Van."

Kendra, less hampered by the table than Patsy, leaped up and lunged toward Bennie. "You did *what?*" She slapped Bennie hard on the shoulder, once, twice, three times. "After all we've done for the last four weeks? Jill risked her *life* for this. We both did!" She raised her hand to strike Bennie again, but Jill grabbed both Kendra's hands and wrapped her arms hard around her from behind.

"Hush, Kendra, don't."

"Are you kidding? After what she did? Did you hear—?"

"I know, I know. She didn't mean any harm."

Bennie didn't seem to have noticed Kendra's blows or her exchange with Jill. She stood staring helplessly at Van. Patsy almost felt sorry for her. Who knew better than Patsy what it was to love Van more than life itself? Then to find out she'd put her in harm's way? Yes, she felt sorry for Bennie. Almost.

Van sat frozen, staring in horror at Bennie. Slowly her gaze shifted to Patsy, and Patsy's heart gave another lurch. She quickly circled the table. "No, baby, don't be scared." She stood behind Van, and placed her hands reassuringly on her shoulders. Van gripped Patsy's hands tightly. "We won't let them get you. Will we, Jill?"

The women stared at Jill. She still held Kendra tightly in her arms, but her gaze was already turned inward, her eyes darting from nothing to nothing, thinking rapidly, searching for a way out. Even Kendra broke off from glaring at Bennie to crane her neck to watch Jill.

After a moment, Jill focused on Bennie. "Where are they?"

"I don't know. I think they must be around here somewhere. I gave them the same directions you gave us."

"Watching us?" Inez asked softly, peeking surreptitiously around camp as if trying to spot someone hiding behind a tree.

Bennie scrutinized the camp as well. "But they were expecting to find RIP."

"RIP's not here," Jill said unnecessarily. "I wasn't about to let Van and RIP be in the same place, not until it's necessary."

"She's not stupid," Kendra said angrily at Bennie, as if Bennie was accusing Jill of being exactly that.

Jill said, "They've been following us for weeks. We've been careful, but there was always a chance they'd find us. The only difference is, now they know about Van." Her eyes searched inward, and five pairs of eyes watched her anxiously. Abruptly she turned to Bennie. "How fast does your car go?"

"Very." Bennie perked up at the suggestion that she might be able to help. "Why?"

Patsy jumped on the idea. "Yeah, we can sneak her out. Kendra, you're closest in size. You and Van, go in the tent and trade clothes. We'll sneak Van out and they'll think it's you."

Jill was shaking her head. "It's too late for that. We'll only be delaying the inevitable. We have to get her into RIP. Right away, before they have a chance to know we're doing it."

"No!" Patsy cried out, tightening her grip on Van's shoulders until Van had to pry her fingers loose. "Van, no." Patsy leaned over to peer in Van's eyes, compelling her to understand. "It's too dangerous. You could get sent somewhere strange. You could get hurt. You could *die*. It's just too damned dangerous."

Van lifted her legs over the bench and swung around to face Patsy, taking Patsy's hands gently in her own. "It's too dangerous for me to stay. I'd have to go into hiding. I'd never get to be myself, ever again."

Patsy sat down hard on the bench next to Van, where Bennie had been sitting earlier. "You'd still be you, Van. No one can take that away from you."

"We need to get moving," Jill announced. "Van, you and I will go in Bennie's car."

Van rose.

"No!" Patsy felt like crying. She couldn't let Van disappear on her again, never knowing where she was, if she was safe, if she was happy. It would kill her. In desperation, she turned to Bennie. "Here, you take her." She held Van's hands out toward Bennie. "Help her start over. Get her a new identity. Keep her safe."

Van pulled her hands free and instead cupped them around Patsy's face. "Honey, no. That isn't the life I want. Not when I have a chance to go back. I can give us another chance."

"Kendra, your car's fast too," Jill said. "Feel like playing a game of chicken?"

"You bet."

Jill said, "Van, you go down that trail toward the outhouse. If anyone's watching, they'll think you're using the loo. But instead of going inside, go around and climb the hill behind it. It's not steep. Bennie, you and I'll pick Van up on the road back there when she gets to the top. Kendra, you follow a couple of minutes after us. You know what to do, love. Inez, you and Patsy put out the fire and bring up the rear. If you see anyone follow us, slow them down if you can. Ready?"

They all nodded, except Patsy, who sat in defeat, unable to think of how she could convince these women, her dearest friends, to give up their foolish, dangerous plan.

Van took a step toward the outhouse, then stopped and looked back at the five women, doubt on her face. "I don't want anyone to get hurt."

"Once you get back there," Kendra said, "none of this will even have happened."

Van appeared stricken, as if she'd only just realized that the women's present existence would vanish if she returned to 1988.

Van strode back to the table, stopped in front of Patsy, and put her hand to Patsy's cheek. Patsy leaned into the palm of Van's hand, savoring the touch, wondering if she would ever feel Van, ever see her, again.

Van's green eyes, darkened with intensity, stared into Patsy's. "If I disappear again, and you're left here, will you promise me that you won't go back to drinking?"

Patsy blinked, momentarily stunned, and a bubble of laughter erupted from her. She reached up, took Van's hand from her face, and kissed the palm. "No, baby," she said gently, thinking of the struggle she had each day already just to stay sober, and of how her life would crash into a thousand kinds of hell if Van disappeared again. "You're asking too much."

Patsy watched those eyes she knew so well and saw the instant Van understood.

"She won't vanish on you," Jill said impatiently. "We'll *all* vanish, because *this* present will no longer exist."

Van ignored her and continued staring into Patsy's eyes, then leaned down and put her mouth full on Patsy's. The feel of Van's mouth on hers was an instant balm on Patsy's wounded heart. The kiss was long and deep and sweet, the tongue sweeping against hers instantly familiar, yet reminiscent of kisses that were twenty years old, or more. The kiss would have to make up for the last twenty years, and be a kiss to last her through the next twenty years, if she were cursed to live that long without Van.

Finally, Van lifted her head and whispered, "I love you, Patsy." She whipped around and headed down the path toward the outhouse. This time, she didn't look back.

Chapter Thirty-five

Bennie — 2008

BENNIE PUT THE cooler in the trunk of her car, to suggest to any watchers that she might be going after some ice, pulled the Jag around the loop, and headed out of the camp site. At the last moment, as if in afterthought, Jill climbed into the passenger seat, though not before getting a sound kiss from Kendra, along with a tearful but airy, "See you in the last century, darling!"

Bennie drove away from the campsite at a leisurely pace, stopping only briefly when she saw Van pull herself up the last of the slope behind the outhouse. The door opened, Jill hopped out, and Van dove inside, keeping herself flat on the rear seats. Jill climbed back in, and Bennie continued on at the same pace.

"Do you think they saw me?" Van asked.

"I haven't seen a sign of anyone." Jill peered anxiously out the windows. "But keep down, in case."

"And put your seatbelt on," Bennie said.

"How can I do both?" Van asked, trying to sit upright enough to put on a seatbelt while keeping her head out of sight.

"Keep down," Jill said. "Nothing else matters, as long as we get to RIP before they do."

"You can't return her if she's dead." Bennie said.

Jill opened her mouth to object, but closed it again, as if struck by Bennie's logic.

Van clipped her shoulder belt in place and tried to pull her head in, like a turtle.

"Your hair," Jill said, glancing back at Van's red curls, clearly visible in the window.

"Put this on." Bennie tossed a baseball cap into the back seat.

In the rear view mirror, Bennie watched Van put the cap on. It was too big for her, so she tugged her loose hair out the back to hold it in place. As long as she slouched down, she was nothing but an anonymous white cap in the back seat. Then Van glanced up, met Bennie's eyes, and smiled. Bennie's stomach dropped. Anonymous white cap, my ass, she thought. Van was adorable with those wispy red tendrils of hair curling around the edges of the cap and the dark green piping making her eyes glow like emeralds. How could she possibly let this woman out of her life? She was tempted to stop the car, kick Jill out, and keep on driving, do as Patsy suggested and take Van somewhere far away, create a new identity, a new life together. She could keep Van safe.

Then she recalled the horror in Van's face when she realized Bennie had called the lab about her, and she could see the excitement in Van's face even now at the thought of returning to 1988, and Bennie knew she couldn't do it. Van didn't *want* to run off for a new life with Bennie. She wanted to go back to her old life in 1988. And even though watching Van kiss Patsy moments ago had made Bennie feel as though a thousand razor blades were slicing her heart, she knew she had to let Van go. To Patsy. It was what Van wanted. Bennie sighed. Forty-eight years old, she thought, and here I am still learning what love is all about.

A moment later she pulled out of the park entrance onto the paved road, and what she wanted didn't matter anymore. A black Hummer idled on the side of the road, doors open, and two men standing nearby, one sending a yellow arc of urine from a fat white penis to a nearby tree. They looked up curiously at the Jag. Van slumped even farther down in the seat, and Jill turned sharply away, in case they recognized her. Bennie couldn't hide, so she smiled and drove the Jag smoothly past them. The men weren't fooled. After a moment's consultation, the urinating man zipped up quickly, while the other whipped out a cell phone. They hurried to the Hummer's open doors. They'd be following in seconds.

Bennie kept a steady pace long enough to create the illusion that she was not fleeing. As soon as the Hummer was out of sight, she hit the gas and the Jag erupted with speed. Jill opened her cell phone and punched one button.

"Hi love. Guys in a black Hummer at the end of the road spotted us. I don't know if they saw Van, but they'll catch on soon. There's probably more of them. These guys were calling someone. Okay. And Kendra, be careful. I love you. Yeah. Oh? Okay." She handed the phone over the seat to Van. "She wants to talk to you."

Van took the phone. "Hello? Sure." She listened a moment, glanced up, and met Jill's anxious eyes. Van smiled reassuringly. "I will. You're sure? Absolutely sure? Okay, I will. What you do with it is up to you. Okay. I promise. Bye." She clapped the phone shut and handed it silently to Jill.

Jill chewed her lip a moment. "Well? What did she want?"

"I can't tell you," Van said, trying not to smile. "I promised."

Jill narrowed her eyes, but allowed the subject to drop.

"Where are we going?" Bennie asked. "There's a Y coming up."

"Take the right," Jill said.

As she did so, Bennie peeked in her side mirror and saw a black speck behind her, rapidly gaining on them. "They're moving up fast behind us."

Jill and Van spun around to peer out the rear window.

"Can you go faster?" Jill asked. They were already going eighty-five.

"Sure." Bennie pressed the gas, and the Jag zipped smoothly forward. Eighty-eight. Ninety. Ninety-three. She desperately wanted to peek at Van again in the rear view mirror, but she couldn't risk it. She couldn't even spare a glance to see if the car was still behind them. Keeping the Jag on the road took all her attention. Ninety-six. Ninety-eight.

"Wait," Van said. "There's another car passing the Hummer."

"It's Kendra," Jill said. "She's playing chicken with them."

Bennie laughed, adrenaline pulsing through her veins. "How fast can a Hummer really go?" She pushed the Jag harder. One hundred. One-oh-one.

"I can't see them any more," Van said a moment later. "We've lost them."

There was tense silence in the car, the only noise the smooth sound of the Jag's engine, as they thought of Kendra, all alone in her little bitty Jetta, playing chicken with the giant Hummer. Jill heaved a long shaky sigh.

Soon they approached another Y, and Bennie had to slow down to navigate it. "Which way now?" Jill gave her directions, but would not tell Bennie where they were going. Maybe Jill had asked Bennie to drive because she had a fast car, or maybe it was because she wanted to keep an eye on her, but it wasn't because she trusted her.

More traffic appeared as they reached more highly-traveled roads. Bennie paced the Jag slightly faster than the flow of traffic, careful not to go so fast as to call attention to themselves. They were heading north, and Bennie suspected she knew where. Now that she wasn't driving so fast, she could spare a moment for the mirror. Van sat, still slumped in her seat, staring out the window, apparently lost in thought. What was she thinking about? What she was leaving in 2008? Or what she was heading toward in 1988?

Finally, right before the exit for Van's old house, where Bennie thought they were going, Jill directed her off the highway to a brand new storage rental facility.

"Here," Jill said. "Let me out."

Bennie stopped the car. Jill jumped out and leaned in to give her final directions. "Take Van to her old house. Hide the car, if you can, and keep out of sight. Be ready for me. I'll be right behind you. Van, you know the spot. Go to the same place you landed when you got here. I'll be there as soon as I can." She slammed the door and hurried toward a security gate.

Van climbed out of the back seat and slipped in the front. Bennie slid the car out of the parking lot and onto the highway. There was only one more exit before Van's. Bennie picked up Van's hand. The temptation to drive right past that exit and keep going, head on up to Canada, was overwhelming.

Van lifted Bennie's hand to her lips and smiled trustingly at her.

"Thank you for helping me."

Bennie quirked an eyebrow at Van. "Even though I'm the one who sicced the Feds on you?"

"You didn't know. Anyway, it's better for me this way, because now I get to go home right away."

Bennie sighed and signaled for the exit.

Chapter Thirty-six

Van — 2008

THEY HID THE Jag behind Jill's house and slinked through the pristine neighborhood to the white rock road where Van had landed on her butt four weeks before. There weren't many hiding places. The forested hills surrounding Van's old home had been replaced by long sleek ranch houses, sloping green lawns, low fences, and immaculate flower beds. They slunk behind a tool shed designed to resemble a miniature cottage that was placed next to Van's house. Van hoped the kids who lived there now wouldn't report them as prowlers.

Van peeked out and saw the old faded board that contained her photo and the "Missing Woman" language. Twenty years ago that sign had been placed there, the photo replaced now and then, the painted lettering updated and refreshed when necessary. Jill had done that, confident Van would show up one day. Jill knew what RIP had done, and what RIP was capable of doing. Patsy was wrong this time, Van decided. There was no danger in trusting Jill. She said she had fixed RIP and could send Van safely back to 1988, and Van believed her. She had to.

The sun was setting, its red rays reflecting in the water on the river. From where Van and Bennie stood, the river hadn't been visible in 1988, the view was blocked by trees. You had to go down the dirt path to the water, where the banks were shaded and damp. You could find beaver dams there, and the occasional black bear, foraging in the huckleberry bushes, and you had to go out to the very end of Van's wooden dock to catch the sun. Not now. The trees were gone, as was the shade, and instead of Van's wooden dock, there was a row of docks, sticking out into the water one after another like black piano keys. The river bank consisted of imported sand and multi-colored miniature gravel. Van felt sad, wondering where the beavers and the bear had gone.

The distant popping sound of a heavy vehicle on gravel caught Van's ear. RIP. She looked at Bennie and saw she was watching Van as solemnly as Van had stared at the river. Dear Bennie. Her savior. Van knew she was causing Bennie pain by leaving, but she had no choice. She *had* to go back. If nothing else, she had to protect the land from this God-awful development, save the beavers and the bear. Besides, if she returned to 1988, Bennie would never feel this pain.

Bennie peered sharply at the road, concerned. RIP was coming fast.

The camper careened down the road, too fast for gravel, lurching back and forth, before grinding to a halt, white rocks spitting from beneath the wheels. Jill flung herself out.

Van and Bennie stepped out from behind the tool shed.

"Hurry," Jill said, waving them forward. "They're coming. Kendra called. They got away from her, and they're headed this way. They know where we are."

Van rushed toward RIP, Bennie right behind her, but Jill stopped them. "No, not yet. I have to get it placed right. Do you remember where RIP was when you left in 1988?"

Van felt Bennie's hands clutch her shoulders protectively, as if she would hold her back, but Van shrugged them off. "I can tell from there." She ran up the stairs onto the deck of her old house, matching her feet up with where the old part of the deck ended. She faced the direction where RIP had been parked, and closed her eyes to visualize the land as it had been at Patsy's birthday party. In her mind's eye, she saw the trees, the dirt road, RIP pulled off to the side ready for Jill to begin her experiments. She opened her eyes. "There." She pointed. "It was right there, about three feet back from where it is now, but pointing in the other direction."

"I'm going to send you a little further down the road," Jill said. "I don't want to try to land you *in* RIP. It would be too hard to find the exact spot, and you could get hurt."

Jill started the engine again and backed RIP down the road.

Van heard a sound behind her and spun around. Maddie had opened the door and stood watching Van.

"Get off our deck," the girl said.

Van grinned. "It's my deck."

Maddie's eyes widened in shock. "It's not your deck. It's our deck."

"Uh uh. You'll have to grow up somewhere else."

"Van, hurry!" Jill called from the cab of RIP, as she backed into position.

Van whipped around and leaped to the ground, abandoning her argument with the child. When she got back to 1988, she'd keep the house. That child would never set foot in Van's home, and the walls would *never* be painted brown. Jill climbed down and unlocked the back door of RIP. She returned to the cab to raise the dish and antennae. Bennie stood at the side of the road watching, her hands dangling helplessly at her sides, a forlorn look on her face. Van stopped abruptly in front of Bennie, put her arms around her neck, and pulled her down for a kiss. Bennie's arms wrapped around her tightly, and the kiss deepened, but the sound of more tires on gravel broke them apart.

"Van!" Jill poked her head out the window. "Get in, *now*. Bennie, shut the door and get out of the way."

Van leaped for the doors and climbed into the belly of RIP, but stuck her hand out to prevent Bennie from closing the door.

"I love you, Bennie," Van said quickly, breathlessly.

Bennie blinked in surprise, then broke into a smile, albeit a smile marred by the tears that coursed down her cheeks. "I love you too, Van."

The black Hummer loomed over Bennie's shoulder, heading straight toward them. "Go," Bennie said hoarsely. She pushed Van's hand inside and slammed the door. Van was alone in the blackness of RIP, lit only by tiny amber lights flickering on the walls like lightning bugs. She perched on the stool bolted to the floor and held on.

The next instant a violent crash shook RIP, the force of it knocking Van from her perch on the stool to the hard ground, and the tiny amber lights flickered out.

Chapter Thirty-seven

Jill — 1988

JILL FOUND IT unnerving to have Inez's date watch her so attentively as she prepared RIP for its run-through. It wasn't uncommon for a date of Jill's to fall for Inez or Patsy. She was used to that. But it never happened the other way around. *Nobody's* date ever fell for Jill. And this woman was a bombshell. She clearly had a scientific mind. It had to be RIP that fascinated her. Still, the fact that the woman watched her so closely made her nervous. Jill tried to ignore her. Then the woman, Kendra, arched upward awkwardly to peek through the window at the modified dashboard, pulling her blouse taut across her breasts. Jill glimpsed the distinct outline of an erect nipple thrusting against the flimsy silk, and all of a sudden she couldn't remember if she'd pushed the Sim button.

Oh damn. The Sim button had to be pushed, or the run-though wouldn't be a run-through at all. RIP would think this was the real deal. But if she pushed the Sim button now, and she'd already pushed it once, it would be like not pushing it in at all. Which would also make the run-through real. Why couldn't she remember? She peeked out at Kendra again and saw a sliver of black lace at the top of her blouse. She forced her eyes back to the Sim button. It wasn't Kendra's fault. Jill should never have let her attention drift, not in the middle of an experiment. Her finger hovered over the button. Oh, what difference could it make? It's not like RIP really *worked*. She pushed the button.

Moments later, she climbed out of the cab. She glanced at the women sitting on the deck, watching her. Patsy had returned from the garage and was sitting peacefully next to Inez, who rocked Michael. She was not surprised that Patsy had calmed down. Patsy had a quick temper, but it usually burned itself out as quickly as it rose. But what kind of date was Inez, Jill thought indignantly, letting her date roam all over the place, showing off her sexy underwear to other women, while Inez sat there rocking a baby. Kendra even followed Jill to the back of RIP and watched as Jill unlatched the door and swung it open.

RIP was empty.

Jill felt all the blood drain from her face. She gripped the edge of the door to hold herself up.

"Where is she?" Kendra asked, but Jill couldn't answer. Kendra's voice grew concerned. "Jill? What's wrong?"

Jill shook her head, speechless, and peered again inside RIP.

There was nowhere to hide in RIP. It was too small. With all the equipment, there was barely room for one person to sit. And there was no way out. She looked uneasily at the women on the deck and saw them grow puzzled too. Patsy stood and descended the deck stairs.

"Help me up," Jill said hoarsely, her normally strong legs suddenly limp. Kendra boosted Jill into RIP. Jill sat on the stool and swiveled around. Nothing. No sign of Van anywhere, nowhere she could have gone. Nothing at all.

"Jill?" Patsy stood in RIP's doorway, confusion on her face as she took in the empty lab. "Where's Van?"

Jill simply stared, her heart hammering in her chest, as she watch Patsy's confusion grow from unease to alarm when Jill didn't move.

"Where's Van?" Patsy demanded, bracing both hands on the door frame and thrusting her head in to confirm what was already obvious. Van was not in RIP.

"I think I sent her," Jill said finally, her voice weak.

"Sent her? Where?"

"To the future."

"Not funny." Patsy pushed away from the door, her face hard as granite. "Where the fuck is she?"

Jill followed her out the door, ignoring Kendra's outstretched hand, and watched helplessly as Patsy prowled RIP's exterior, ran her hands along the smooth walls, climbed up into the cab and through to the other side to stand, hands on her hips, glaring at Jill. "Where the fuck is she?"

Jill shook her head in despair, but forced herself to speak clearly. "I think she's in the future, Patsy."

"Don't be stupid." Patsy knelt on the ground and peered underneath RIP. She struck the side of it with the flat of her hand. She stood and kicked it.

"I...I think I made a mistake. I pushed a button. It was an accident."

Patsy stared at Jill in disbelief. "No."

"I'm sorry. I didn't mean to."

The disbelief in Patsy's eyes changed to horror. "How far in the future?"

"I don't know." She shook her head. "I don't know."

"Get her back!"

"I don't—" Jill broke off. How could she tell Patsy she didn't know how? Van was gone. If Jill couldn't bring her back, no one could. She had to do *something*. "Yes." She veered back and climbed into the cab. But what could she do? RIP wasn't designed to bring someone *back*.

RIP started rocking, gently at first, then with greater force. Jill scrambled out and saw Patsy, her hands braced against the side of RIP, pushing it back and forth, rocking it, as though she could push it over, as though she could shake Van out of it. Her face was red with fury and effort. But a moment later her strength gave out. She stood panting. She raised her face to the sky and let out a roar loud enough to startle birds out of the trees, to send deer crashing through the woods, to wake Michael up and make him cry.

"*Va-a-a-a-a-a-an!*"

Chapter Thirty-eight

Van—1988

VAN LANDED HARD on her side. It was dusk, her hands were in dirt, and she faced a wall of dark trees. There was no sign of RIP, no sign of Bennie or Jill or a black Hummer. Somewhere nearby a baby cried.

She heard her name being called. "Van! *Va-a-an!*" Was that *Patsy?*

"I'm here!" she yelled, or tried to. Her voice came out in a squeak. "Here!" she yelled again, slightly louder. She scrambled to her feet, prepared to call out more, when a shape barreled through the trees, barking a welcome. "Sadie!" Van leaned down and let Sadie lick her face, something she rarely did. Sadie was alive!

She must be in 1988. This was her dog, her road, these were her trees, growing tall and unmolested by developers.

"Van!"

"I'm here." Van ran around the bend of the road and stopped. There they all were. RIP, Jill, Kendra, Inez with Michael wailing in her arms, the house. And there stood Patsy, in the middle of the road, her fists clenched, her face raised to the sky, yelling for Van.

"I'm here, Patsy."

Patsy turned, saw her, and slumped in relief. "There you are. You'll never guess what Jill—" She broke off as she took in Van's appearance. Her eyes widened and her brows rose. "Van?"

Van drew closer, staring in wonder at Patsy's strong, beautiful face. She stopped in front of her and put her hand up to stroke Patsy's smooth cheek. She was so young. Overwhelmed with relief, Van leaned against Patsy's strong body. She wrapped her arms around Patsy's waist and rested her head on her shoulder, closed her eyes, and heaved a deep sigh. "It's good to be home," she whispered.

Patsy held her tightly for a moment, then put her hands on Van's shoulders and held her away so she could see her better. Her eyes were wide with shock. "Van, what the hell happened to you?" Jill, Kendra, and Inez had all moved closer and eyed her curiously. Patsy ducked her head down to peer directly into Van's eyes. "Baby, what's happened?"

"Where did you go?" Jill asked.

"What's that you're wearing?" Kendra asked.

How could she explain? Where to start, and how much to tell? "I've been in the future," Van said finally, glancing from face to face, unsurprised at the disbelief and amazement she saw reflected there.

Except for Jill, who seemed mostly curious and a bit ashamed.

"The future?" Patsy fingers bit sharply into Van's shoulders. Van removed Patsy's hands, but kept hold of them in her own.

"How far?" Jill asked, much quicker than the others to accept Van's words as true. "What year?"

"Two thousand eight."

They stared.

"Two thousand eight?" Inez asked, as if puzzled by the number. "You mean the year twenty-oh-eight? The twenty-first century?"

"Twenty years from now?" Jill asked.

"Yes," Van said. "And you were there, and you. You were all there." She felt like Dorothy after her return from Oz. "But you were older. You were all twenty years older than you are now."

"Is that where you got those clothes?" Kendra asked.

Van looked down at herself. Her layered spaghetti-strap tank tops, long baggy cargo shorts with the droopy pockets adorned with strings and buttons and zippers, and her bright blue and yellow Croc flip flops appeared strange in the 1988 twilight. She shivered. The June evening was considerably cooler than the hot July she had left only moments before.

"Let's go inside, where it's warm," Inez said.

"And we can see you better," Kendra added.

Patsy let go of Van's hands and wrapped an arm around her shoulders instead, and they headed toward the house.

"How long were you there?" Jill asked. "In 2008?"

"A month."

There was silence as they absorbed her answer. Then Patsy said quietly, "You've only been gone about thirty minutes."

Jill asked, "How did you get back, Van?"

"You did it. You sent me back. You and Kendra."

"Me?" Kendra stopped in midstride, astonished.

"Yes, you helped." They reached the deck. "Oh, my beautiful house." She spun around to drink in the view, wrapping her arms around herself for warmth. "And the trees. They smell so good! They cut them all down. They built houses along the river. They painted the walls brown. And Jill, you lived in the garage."

They all stared again, until Inez ushered them inside with her one free arm. "Let's go in," she said. "We can build a fire, and I can put Michael down, and you can tell us all about it."

They went inside, and Van was immediately overwhelmed by the comfort of the house. Her own house, her own things. The pineapple upside down cake she had made for Patsy's birthday still sat on the dining room table, mostly untouched.

"Let's have cake," she suggested. "I'm starved."

"We just ate," Kendra said.

"Not me," Van said. "All I had was your camp stew about an

hour ago, and, well, it really wasn't very good."

"*My* camp stew?"

"Yes. You made it."

"I made you camp stew?" Kendra asked, eyes wide with astonishment. "An hour ago?"

"In 2008."

Silence dropped over the room, finally broken by Kendra's whispered, "That's crazy."

Van felt a bubble of panic. She searched each beloved face, seeking reassurance. It hadn't occurred to her they wouldn't believe her. Jill watched her with a clinical frown, Kendra with wide-eyed wonder, and Inez with what might have been fear. Patsy, the woman she knew better than any other, simply stared at her somberly, with an expression Van could not read.

Finally, Patsy spoke. "You've been out in the sun. Your freckles have come out."

Van breathed a sigh of relief.

"Everyone sit," Inez said, settling Michael into the playpen and popping a binky into his mouth. "Kendra, you get the cake. Patsy, make up the fire." They did as directed, but kept their eyes on Van. She sat on the love seat, and Patsy knelt with a box of wooden matches in front of the wood stove, which she had prepared earlier in the day for lighting.

"You're so tanned," Kendra said, handing Van a plate with a slice of cake on it. "What's that on your nose?"

"It's a nose stud," Van touched it with a finger. "I meant to take it out, but we were a bit rushed there at the end."

"Cool." Kendra leaned forward to examine it more closely.

"Why did I live in your garage?" Jill asked.

"So you could help me." Van shoveled in a forkful of fresh, delicious cake. Hard to believe she'd baked it a month ago. "You always knew I'd show up someday, and you knew it would be here. So you wanted to be on hand when it happened."

Patsy swiveled on one knee from her position in front of the stove to peer somewhat warily at Van. "Where was I?"

Van stared into Patsy's beautiful brave blue eyes, eyes that showed she was afraid of the answer to her question, but brave enough to ask it anyway. "You were there," she said carefully. "But only Jill could help me." Patsy stared hard at Van, seeming to sense there was more to the story, but she returned her attention to the fire, closed the stove door, and sat next to Van on the love seat. She reached for the cigarettes on the table, pulled out two, lit them both, and offered one to Van.

"No thanks," Van said. "I quit." There were gasps.

"You quit smoking?" Patsy asked, dumfounded.

"So did you." Van gazed around the room. "You all did. It's

practically illegal in 2008. And very expensive."

Patsy scowled at the two burning cigarettes in her hand as if puzzled about what to do with them.

Kendra solved the problem by plucking one from Patsy's fingers. "Don't want to waste it," she said, lifting it to her lips. "What's 2008 like? Do cars fly and all that? I'll be 59 years old. What do I look like?"

Kendra was the one who had asked, but Van could see the questions reflected on all their faces. She longed to tell them. Who wouldn't want to know what a glimpse into the future would reveal? These were the women who had risked everything, sacrificed their very existence to send Van back to this moment, and they didn't even know it. She wanted to share everything that had happened to them and to her, but she held back. The future Van had experienced was not what was going to happen to these women after all. Everything had changed. The future Van had visited no longer existed. Whatever unfolded ahead of them now was influenced only by Van's mysterious half-hour disappearance. She had to take care not to divulge too much.

"Cars don't fly," Van said. "And you're beautiful then, too, of course. But I can't tell you what the future holds for you, for any of you. The future I was in, the one where we lost this house and where Jill moved into the garage, that only happened after I went missing for twenty years. But that's not what happened after all. I came back. It's not the future that's going to exist now."

"Of course," Jill said. "That's the purpose of RIP, to show what will happen only if certain precedents occur."

Patsy put her arm across Van's back and pressed her tightly to her side. "Do you mean to tell me that you went missing for twenty *years*? And I lived through it?"

"It...was hard on you. I can tell you all a few things, though. For one thing, Jill, you've got a lot of work to do on RIP before you do any more experimenting with people."

Jill bit her lip and nodded, chastened.

"And Inez, you need to make sure Grace gets regular breast exams."

"Grace? Why are you telling me?"

Van gave her a significant look. Inez gasped, then smiled as she grasped Van's meaning. "Oh." No one, not even Kendra, found it strange that Inez was so delighted at the suggestion of a future with Grace, while her own date sat right next to her.

"And Kendra," Van said, "I have a message for you, but it's private."

"A message for me? Who from?"

"From you," Van said. "You asked me to tell you something. But it's private."

"You have a message *for* me, *from* me?" Kendra asked, her mouth agape. "You mean, from the *old* me to the *young* me?"

"Yes. I'll tell you later."

Kendra sat back, stunned.

"And you." Van leaned in to Patsy, who sat watching Van with a troubled frown. Van was struck anew by how young and strong Patsy was. She gripped Patsy's hand in both of hers and put her lips up to Patsy's ear. "I know you stopped drinking tonight," she whispered.

Patsy froze, but her eyes widened.

"You told me. In 2008."

Patsy stared in disbelief. "I told you in 2008 that I stopped drinking? Tonight?"

"But when I vanished, you started again."

"Well, no shit."

Van bit her lip, worried about saying too much, or not enough. "I've seen the future. Please believe me, sweetheart, you don't want to drink anymore."

A crease appeared between Patsy's brows. She wrapped her arm tightly around Van's shoulder and rubbed her cheek against her hair. "Don't worry, baby. It's going to be all right."

Chapter Thirty-nine

Patsy—1988

LATE THAT NIGHT, after Ellen and Terri came by to pick up Michael, and everyone else had gone home, Van lay sleeping soundly in her own bed, her hair splayed over the white pillow case, her hands thrown up beside her head, palms upward, like a little doll. Patsy sat in the bedroom chair, silently smoking a cigarette and sipping a ginger ale. Watching Van. Now that Van had quit smoking, Patsy supposed it was only a matter of time before she had to quit as well. But not yet. Giving up booze was going to be hard enough without giving up smokes at the same time.

Patsy had dodged a bullet. She was still fuzzy about the details, and maybe always would be, but she understood that one fact clearly enough. Van nearly hadn't come back. And Patsy didn't need Van's sneak peek into the future to know what a sewer her life would have been if that had happened. Van's eyes were still haunted by whatever horror Patsy had become by 2008. *"Please believe me, sweetheart, you don't want to drink any more."*

Well, she did *want* to, c'mon, she couldn't kid herself about that. But she wouldn't do it. She'd do whatever she had to do to remove that awful haunted look from Van's eyes.

Patsy wondered if she'd ever know what really happened to Van in the last four weeks. She'd gone to a world Patsy would never know. Even twenty years from now, if Patsy lived that long, it wouldn't be the *same* 2008 that Van had visited.

When Van was undressing, she'd shown Patsy a tattoo on her left butt cheek. A tombstone, with 'RIP 1988' etched inside, a tiny red rose trellising over it. Van didn't tell her what it was about, she'd simply been a bit sad and said she got it when she thought she'd never get to come home.

Patsy breathed a silent chuckle. Her conservative little Van, always so neat in her go-to-court black suit and matching pumps, sporting a tattoo and a nose stud. She'd love to have been there for that.

But no. No. Patsy picked up the white softball cap Van had worn back from the future, twirled it in her hands, and read for perhaps the hundredth time the neat signature in indelible ink on the lining, *Bennie Sanchez.* No, it was probably better that Patsy hadn't been there for that. It might be better if she never knew exactly what happened in 2008. Van came back, and Patsy had another chance. That was all that mattered.

Van stirred in the bed and sat up. "Patsy?"

"Right here, baby." She stubbed out her cigarette, moved to the bed, and sat beside Van. Van clung to her, something she'd done almost continually since her return.

"I'm worried about you," Van said.

"Me? I'm fine."

"Not *you* you. The *old* you, in 2008. You were so sad when I left. You didn't want me to come back."

Patsy was thunderstruck. "*I* didn't want you to come back? That's a crock of shit."

"You said you couldn't take it if I disappeared again."

"You didn't really disappear the first time, so you couldn't disappear *again*."

"Yeah, but you didn't know that. Patsy, what if we live more than one life? At a time, I mean? What if there are parallel lives going on? What if *that* Patsy is still stuck in that life, wondering where I am, thinking I did disappear again?"

Patsy put her hands on both sides of Van's face and gazed deeply into her eyes. "I'm right here, aren't I? How can I be somewhere else? If there's another Patsy out there, she's not *me*. I'm *it*, kid. Okay?" She kissed Van soundly, first on the lips, then on the forehead. "Now stop thinking. You'll make yourself crazy."

Van sighed deeply and nestled further into Patsy's arms. "Thanks, Patsy. You're so smart and strong and wise and beautiful."

"Hey, c'mon." Patsy gave Van a gentle shake. "Knock it off."

Van chuckled. "No, I won't knock it off. Your secret's out. I know you love compliments."

"*Wha-a-at?*" She held Van away from her. "What secret?"

"I know about the time your dad hurt your feelings when you were little, when he accused you of fishing for compliments."

Patsy mind was momentarily blank, but then she remembered that day in front of her dad's friends. How hurtful that had been. "How do you know—"

"You told me. In two—"

"I know, I know. In 2008." She was stunned all over by the enormity of what Van had gone through, what they *all* must have gone through in some unfathomable way. She *had* to have been the one who told Van that story in 2008. No one else knew it. But how had this time travel happened? She shook her head, determined not to think about it. If she did, she'd go crazy.

Patsy rubbed her cheek against the top of Van's head. "So what message did Kendra send herself?"

Van laughed softly. "To take a chance on Jill. That she's worth the risk."

"Jill and *Kendra*? I'll be damned."

"Yeah. They were best friends for twenty years, and they finally fell in love. Kendra figured, since she was getting a chance for a Do-Over, she'd like to take the risk."

"Is that what this is? A Do-Over?"

"Maybe," Van said thoughtfully. "Yes. Yes, I think that's exactly what it is. And now," she stirred, "I have to pee."

Patsy stood and let Van fling the covers back. Van went into the bathroom and flipped on the light switch. A moment later she said, "Fuck."

"What's the matter?"

"I need a tampon."

THE END

Other Quest Titles You Might Enjoy:

The Ties That Bind
by Andi Marquette

When the Albuquerque paper reports that an unidentified white man was found dead along a remote stretch of road on the Navajo Reservation in northwestern New Mexico, UNM sociology professor K.C. Fontero thinks she might be able to use the case as an example of culture and jurisdiction in one of her classes. But it's soon apparent that this dead man might have something to do with a mysterious letter that River Crandall, brother of K.C.'s partner Sage, recently received from the siblings' estranged father, Bill. What does the letter and Bill's link to a natural gas drilling company have to do with the dead man? And why would Bill try to contact his son and daughter now, after a decade of silence?

From the streets of Albuquerque to the vast expanse of the Navajo Reservation, K.C. and Sage try to unravel the secrets of a dead man while Sage confronts a past she thought she'd left behind. But someone or something wants to keep those secrets buried, and as K.C. soon discovers, sometimes beliefs of one culture jump the boundaries of another, threatening to drive a wedge into the relationship she's building with Sage.

ISBN 978-1-935053-23-1

Tunnel Vision
by Brenda Adcock

Royce Brodie, a 50-year-old homicide detective in the quiet town of Cedar Springs, a bedroom community 30 miles from Austin, Texas, has spent the last seven years coming to grips with the incident that took the life of her partner and narrowly missed taking her own. The peace and quiet she had been enjoying is shattered by two seemingly unrelated murders in the same week: the first, a John Doe, and the second, a janitor at the local university.

While Brodie and her partner, Curtis Nicholls, begin their investigation, the assignment of a new trainee disrupts Brodie's life. Not only is Maggie Weston Brodie's former lover, but her father had been Brodie's commander at the Austin Police Department and nearly destroyed her career.

As the three detectives try to piece together the scattered evidence to solve the two murders, they become convinced the two murders are related. The discovery of a similar murder committed five years earlier at a small university in upstate New York creates a sense of urgency as they realize they are possibly chasing a serial killer.

The already difficult case becomes even more so when a third victim is found. But the case becomes personal for Brodie when Maggie becomes the killer's next target. Unless Brodie finds a way to save Maggie, she could face losing everything a second time.

ISBN 978-1-935053-19-4

OTHER QUEST PUBLICATIONS

About the Author

Kate McLachlan lives in Eastern Washington with her wife, two dogs, and two cats. After teaching in the public schools for fourteen years, Kate developed a case of temporary insanity and entered law school. All she really wanted to do was write stories but, despite the common misperception, legal briefs are not fiction, and Kate's creative urge was not satisfied by her day job. She writes novels for the joy it brings to her and for the joy she hopes it will bring to others.

VISIT US ONLINE AT
www.regalcrest.biz

At the Regal Crest Website You'll Find

- The latest news about forthcoming titles and new releases

- Our complete backlist of romance, mystery, thriller and adventure titles

- Information about your favorite authors

- Current bestsellers

- Media tearsheets to print and take with you when you shop

Regal Crest titles are available directly from our web store, Allied Crest Editions at www.rcedirect.com, and from all progressive booksellers including numerous sources online. Our distributors are Bella Distribution and Ingram.

Breinigsville, PA USA
08 December 2010
250909BV00003B/41/P